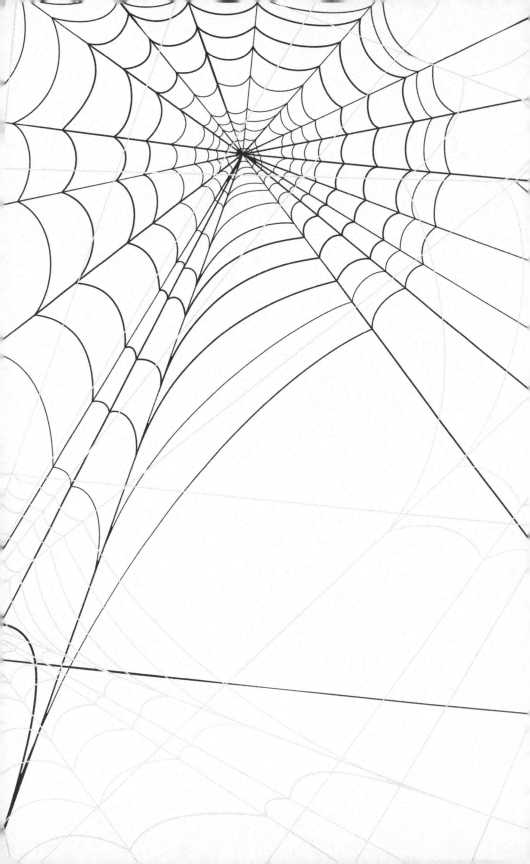

SCREAMS
OF THE JUNGLE

ZACH CUTLER-ORREY

Zach Cutler-Orrey www.facebook.com/ZachCutlerOrreyAuthor

©Zach Cutler-Orrey 2021

Print ISBN: 978-1-66780-980-9 eBook ISBN: 978-1-66780-981-6

Printed in the United States of America on FSC and SFI Certified eco-friendly paper.

This is a work of fiction. Any resemblance to actual events or persons, living or dead, is entirely coincidental.

The countries of equatorial Africa are some of the most beautiful in the world, with amazing and loving human beings. The events in this book exist solely within the author's imagination and are not meant to represent any person, or group, or any sovereign nation.

First Edition

ACKNOWLEDGMENTS

FOR MY WIFE, THE MOST IMPORTANT PERSON IN MY LIFE AND the most supportive person I know. This would not have happened without you.

For my son, who I cannot expect to believe in himself unless I lead by example.

For my parents, who I lucked out on big time, and who do so much for me.

And, finally, for my friends and all my cheerleaders.

PROLOGUE

IN THE THICK JUNGLE, A CRITICALLY ENDANGERED AFRICAN Forest Elephant wades her way through the swamp. This adult female forgets her hunger momentarily, plunges her trunk into the murky water, and sprays herself to cool off. Should the occasion call for it, she is big enough to kill just about anything in this forest, and she instinctively knows this through years of experience.

Aside from a pride of lions, there is only one creature in this forest that can single-handedly bring her down, and it's the most lethal killing machine on the planet.

She and the rest of her herd, twenty elephants total, do whatever they can to thrive in this harsh, hot, humid environment.

Today will not be their lucky day.

Several hundred yards away, such a killing machine lies in wait—waiting for his moment to strike. This two-legged creature only evolved approximately 200,000 years ago, but has already set into motion another mass extinction and pushed countless species to the point of no return. Sweat pours off his forehead as if he's in a sauna. The temperature stands at 103 degrees Fahrenheit with 98% humidity, soaring to some of the highest levels that this already unforgiving region has ever seen. It's the dry season.

Ntumba Boku, a Congolese ivory poacher, has been cautious to avoid other people who may have the guts to report—or worse—kill him outright to protect these majestic creatures. Ntumba hasn't seen any trace of an anti-poaching unit for days. Almost as if in sync, the teeming wildlife of the jungle goes eerily quiet as Ntumba readies his Winchester Model 70 bolt-action rifle. But he's not quite ready to shoot yet. He pulls the bolt of his rifle into the first of four clicks to chamber the round.

First click. She and the other elephants do not notice. He keeps his eyes locked on her like a hawk.

Second click. He can see his bullet clear as day. The afternoon sun reflects a glare off of it right into his eyes like an expensive Rolex watch.

Third click. He hears something skittering through the brush near him. It startles him momentarily. There's no way it could be another elephant. No adult elephant would have slipped through the brush near him unnoticed, especially not a bull or a matriarch serving as a watchdog for the herd. And no adult elephant would ever allow a calf to wander so far away from the herd. Nor did this match the cadence of an elephant's footsteps. This split second of caution, with a hint of curiosity, on Ntumba's part is quickly ended by a much louder thought in his head.

Focus! He has come too far not to secure the prize. Even one tusk will go a long way. Even one measly tusk will run his show for at least a few weeks, maybe even a few months! He shakes the thought away, knowing it's probably just a bird or something moving through the undergrowth nearby.

Finally, the fourth click, the final step in chambering the round. He raises his rifle to put the crosshair of his scope right up to the adult female elephant wading in the water. But just as he's about to pull the trigger, a splashing in the water behind her catches his attention.

It's a calf. It's *her* calf. The baby is barely old enough to walk along the floor of the murky swamp water, his head, ears, and trunk staying just above the water line. He splashes through the water and affectionately rubs his trunk against his mother. The cow looks at her baby, with more love filling her body than she is capable of expressing. She lets out a faint trumpet.

Ntumba hesitates. If the mother dies, what if the herd is unable to raise the calf? What if he'd be killing him as well? Ntumba hates these feelings. He usually scoffs at pity. Pity is for the weak. He considers just pulling the damn trigger and getting it over with, but the sound of the mama and the baby trumpeting to each other stays his hand. He exhales quietly, not realizing how long he had been holding his breath, and lowers the barrel of his rifle. He rolls his eyes and uses his tattered shirt to wipe the sweat off of his forehead and around his eyes, which are stinging from his own perspiration. Then she wanders into view.

"Perfect," Ntumba whispers quietly to himself after quickly studying this other cow. It's not the mother. It's the matriarch. She's slightly bigger than the others. She lumbers through the swamp water, sprays herself with the water in her trunk like a hose, and then lumbers slowly and awkwardly onto dry land. She must be in her sixties, at least. The two-legged predator, squatting in the nearby vegetation overgrowth, raises his rifle to center the matriarch in his sights. She is old, and slow, and looks rather weak, too. He can almost see the outline of her ribs and hip bones. He hopes that a single, well-aimed shot will bring her down and assure him his much-needed keep. He puts the crosshair right up to her eye and squeezes the trigger.

The matriarch keels over, dead. The peaceful afternoon for the herd is shattered as they erupt into a chorus of distraught trumpeting sounds and flee the area. Ntumba pays no mind to the fact that there are only about 30,000 of them left on earth, or that their highly developed brains will allow them to feel sorrow for the loss of their beloved leader. All he can think about at this moment is the ear piercing sound of his own gunshot, and how the rifle's harsh recoil catches him off guard every time. Ntumba chambers the next round with the bolt of his Winchester and stands up, making his way over to the slain matriarch.

He begins picking up speed. His steps become more rapid and purposeful. He closes in on his kill just as the haunting sound of a woman *screaming* sounds out from the canopy to his left. A human woman.

There's somebody else out here with him.

The scream catches him completely off guard, scaring him half to death. He freezes in place. "What the . . . " Ntumba says to himself, worried that he may have just been caught. He stares toward the direction of where the woman's scream just came from.

Nothing.

Only now does he realize that the jungle, teeming with the sounds of insects and other wildlife just a few seconds ago, has gone dead quiet. Even the shot of his high-powered hunting rifle didn't have this effect.

"Hello," Ntumba says out loud like a scared schoolboy. He then remembers who's carrying a Winchester rifle.

"Hello!" he says much louder and more confidently this time. Nothing.

Ntumba cannot fight his curiosity. He readies his rifle and wanders into the jungle from where the scream came. It's too quiet. What if a woman is in trouble? What if a predator got her? Would that predator still be nearby? All of this and more race through Ntumba's mind as he wanders into the brush, occasionally looking over his shoulder back at the clearing, at his kill, to make sure that he can retrace his steps back to his beloved tusks.

There's nobody around. *Where is she?* he thinks to himself in his loudest thought yet.

Ntumba calls out again, "Hello!"

Nothing.

He takes a deep breath and composes himself, looking around for a final time before heading back to the kill to get his ivory and get out of there. He keeps his hand firmly at the trigger and the butt of his rifle firmly tucked into his right shoulder. Shaking his head, slowly, dumbfounded, Ntumba whispers to himself.

"Nah, I don't believe in ghosts," unsure he has himself convinced.

The soreness from the rifle's recoil catches his attention again and he shakes it out of his right arm and shoulder. Ntumba makes his way back to the clearing where his African Forest Elephant lies slain, trudging his way over thick vines and an overturned log.

Off to his left, in the shadows, he hears it: *hisssss*.

The hissing sound startles him and he swings his rifle up towards the overgrowth from where it just came. It almost sounded like it came from above him, but he can't be sure. Ntumba looks frantically, not sure if he really heard the hissing sound or if the heat is just getting to him. But the woman's scream was *unmistakable*. Fearing that there may be a venomous snake near him, he hurriedly leaves the area and gets back to his kill. Pulling out a rusty old saw, he begins at once to saw off the tusks from the matriarch's dead body to put in his pack.

What the hell was that? he wonders to himself, sawing harder and harder as his desire to leave grows ever stronger. The hissing sound almost doesn't make sense. It sounded, at first, kind of like a snake, but then the sound morphed into that of a woodpecker pecking away at a tree. *Maybe it is just a woodpecker. A common African grey. Maybe you're just losing it,* Ntumba tries to reassure himself. He pauses briefly to check his surroundings and, especially, the foliage from where the noises had come.

Nothing.

He quickly resumes sawing. Squatting down, he gets the second tusk free from the carcass and opens his pack to stuff them inside.

Out of his right-side peripheral vision, he sees a brown object on a boulder about a couple hundred yards away from him. He stands up to leave. *Wait a minute,* he thinks to himself, turning back around to get a better look at what's on the boulder.

It looks like a baboon. Olive Baboons are common in this region, so Ntumba doesn't think much of it. He studies the small, brown primate for a second. This one sits perched on the boulder as if sunning itself. Ntumba realizes how much sweat is running down his face, affecting his vision, and wipes his eyes again in order to see better. Squinting, he notices something that he didn't before. *Something's not right.*

Ntumba raises the scope of his rifle.

His heartbeat accelerates. That thing is *not* a baboon. Ntumba is horrified to see that it's a gigantic, brown, hairy, tarantula-like *spider* with the slightest hint of a purple color streak on its abdomen. He doubts his own eyes for just the slightest moment, until he sees it move …

Crawling over the boulder, there's no question about it. Ntumba is astonished by the sight. He has grown up in the Republic of the Congo all his life, and has seen arachnids that would give your average squeamish Westerner nightmares, but he has *never* seen anything like this before.

This spider has a leg span at least two feet wide.

"Mother of God," Ntumba says out loud. He raises his Winchester and centers his crosshairs right on the freakishly large spider, about to squeeze the trigger, when another *scream* is heard coming from the tall grass *right behind him.*

The sound of the ivory poacher's horrified yell is drowned out by the subsequent sounds of his rifle firing as he chambers each shot with the bolt-action mechanism as fast as humanly possible.

One shot …

Two shots …

Three shots …

Ntumba Boku was never seen or heard from again.

1

FEW THINGS COULD PREPARE DR. DAVID HALE FOR THIS RIDE. He had only reluctantly agreed to do this documentary with the Curiosity Channel, knowing full well that he'd barely be back in time for his son's eighth birthday. Never before has he missed a birthday, or any occasion for his son, Alex, and *goddammit he was not about to break that record now,* he swears to himself as he feels the bile rising up in his stomach from the bumpy ride that they're on.

He tries to remember how monumental this will be for his and the others' careers, should they find what they're here looking for. David is a great dad and a sought-after marine biologist specializing in the study of cetaceans. But he is a terrible passenger. He hates road trips and always opts to fly. Like Austin Powers—one of his favorite movie characters of all time—once said, "That's not my bag, baby!"

Every few minutes he feels like he just might have to blow chunks right then and there. Plus, forgetting to eat breakfast before they left Cameroon's capital, Yaoundé, doesn't help either.

"Hey," his colleague Dr. Molly Hendricks looks at him with concern.

"You okay?"

She doesn't know him all that well outside of this trip, despite being a renowned cetologist herself, but it doesn't take a rocket scientist to recognize when someone is miserable. David looks at her, trying to hide his discomfort.

"Outstanding," he says, monotonously.

She chuckles a bit. "Sure isn't Southern California. I guess none of the roads here are paved."

"It's all right; there's worse problems in the world," David says, trying to brush away the attention while taking a couple deep breaths to center himself.

"You're absolutely right," she smiles. "Here," Molly hands him a paper bag and some Pepto Bismol from her knapsack. "Please, I insist."

"Why thank you!" he shoots back. David holds up the pink bottle as if it was an ice cold Corona. "Cheers. Here's to a new discovery ... maybe? Hopefully?"

"Hopefully! Cheers," Molly says.

It's been a few weeks since the members of this team have gotten the call from the Curiosity Channel. For decades, people in this extremely remote region of Africa have reported run-ins with what can only be described as a small, skittish river dolphin. Should this creature be real, it would be a major discovery at a time when, here in the twenty-first century, marine biologists had thought that they had identified all cetaceans. The network sought them out personally for the job, and hired a few others in order to go in with them and film a documentary. Molly had only agreed after realizing that she could donate her payment from the network to her university's aquatic research program. David had only agreed to it for two reasons: One, he'd be able to put the money towards a nicer apartment for him and his son, and, two, because he knew his son would be proud of him.

"There are worse things," David whispers solemnly to himself, feeling the Pepto Bismol kicking in thus—ironically—allowing his mind to drift to an entirely different, even more unpleasant topic. David's wife, Angie, had left him and their son almost nine months ago. It was a devastating blow both to David and, especially, to his seven-year-old son, Alex. David, a full grown man in his thirties, could not for the life of him understand why she had left them. So he couldn't even begin to imagine how confusing and unsettling it must have been for his son, who can barely ride a bicycle. *I don't have the balls to tell him the truth,* David thinks to himself.

He wouldn't dare tell his son that his mommy had left him willingly. Even after nine months, David still hasn't blatantly revealed this truth, for fear that it would permanently ruin his son's self-esteem, even if at a sub-conscious level, for the rest of his life. He could never tell Alex that his own mother had left him.

Dr. Hale feels his anger towards his now ex-wife rising up inside of him. *How* dare *she. Shameless fucking bitch.* His anger towards her quickly evolves into anger towards himself for not being home right now with Alex, even though he knows that his sister is spoiling the crap out of the boy while he stays with her. He hates himself for being on the other side of the world, away from his boy, on this wild goose chase. He swallows the sob rising up in his throat, as the feelings come out of his mouth way harsher than he intended: "We almost there or what?"

Hale catches himself, immediately regretting his tone. The Cameroonian driver of their primitive van—bouncing and banging back and forth on the dirt road—looks at him with a blank gaze through the rear-view mirror and David secretly hopes that the driver didn't under-stand him. Even though he is a Black man himself, David feels just as much of a foreigner here, if not more than, he suspects, his fellow researchers feel.

A blonde woman, a few years his junior, leans over to him, "You said your name was Dr. Hale, right?" She reaches out and he shakes his hand.

"Yes, but please, call me David. I don't make *that* much," he says. The woman laughs out loud.

"Sorry, I'm terrible with names. Anne Matthews. We met at the airport," she says with a smile.

"Indeed! You're our equipment expert, right?" says David.

"Yeah, but they don't pay me much either. I'm mainly just along for the adventure," she retorts while David laughs. His laughter is interrupted by the worry that Anne is only doing and saying these things because she heard the tone in his voice and wants to diffuse any possible awkwardness. He shoos away the thought.

"We are almost there, my friend, not to worry," says another voice.

Sitting up in the front passenger seat is Paul Lumumba, their hired guide. At only five feet and five inches tall, the multilingual local man achieves a rare feat: he commands respect everywhere he goes, and simultaneously knows how to light up any room with his friendly personality.

"Are you hungry, my friend?" Paul bellows out, needing to speak up over the sound of their van's old motor.

"I'm so sorry, there is noooooo MacDonald's in Cameroon!" he jokes, receiving laughter from everyone, including their driver.

David's laughter immediately ceases. *Shit,* he thinks to himself, realizing that the driver did in fact understand him a moment earlier. David turns back to Anne.

"I assume you have some gadgets that can help us along the way?"

Anne points to the storm clouds above them.

"Sticking a regular camera underwater won't be enough if the storm has stirred up the river bottom. I'm sure you're familiar with the technology."

David nods.

"I have a device that can register shapes under the water that we otherwise wouldn't be able to see," Anne continues. "Kind of like echolocation. So if our dolphin is there, and within range of my equipment, then we should be able to see it!"

Paul turns his head around to look at Anne and David and the others. "The D'ja river is teeming with life, my friends. Will you be able to tell the difference between this new friend and, say, a crocodile?"

"Depending on if the signature is moving underwater," Anne says. "And how rapidly, yes."

Henry Doyle, their camera man, chimes in, "Hey, don't quote me on the amount guys, but my employer from the network said that, if we capture this new river dolphin species of yours on tape, then the documentary's ratings are gonna shoot up... and... we'll all get paid more. All of us. A lot more."

The expedition's assistant, Avery Chambers, blurts out, "Fine by me. I like money. Woo!" He adds on, "Wait, does that include us little people or just the PhD's?"

"Everyone, numb nuts," Henry responds smugly, turning into a grin.

He and Avery exchange a well-timed fist bump. It's unclear to David how long they've known each other prior to this trip, if they are coworkers, or if Henry is technically Avery's boss, but it's clear that they're buddies. Ever since the airport they've been chatting up a storm.

Finally, after hours and hours in the car going no more than 15 miles per hour on the bumpy, muddy roads, they reach the small riverside village of Mutengoua, where they will charter their boat. Add on the fact that their van had gotten stuck in the mud along the way, forcing them all to break their backs to get it rolling again, and their little road trip has gone easily into the double-digit hours.

Arising the next morning after their long road trip, they board their boat and set sail down the infamous D'ja River, where very few Westerners have explored before. David ponders this, half honored to be here but also still feeling a little guilty about not being home with Alex. Molly steals the thought right out of his mind.

"It's so peaceful here. Much better than the ride out," she smiles and snaps some photos with her personal camera. "Paul," she asks, looking to the rear of the boat. "Why do you think this region of the continent sees so few visitors?"

"That's easy, movie star," Paul says.

This makes Dr. Hendricks blush, even though Paul refers to many of his American clients by the nickname "movie star."

Earlier on the drive, David recounts, Paul warmly explained that "all Americans want to be movie stars, yes?"

Paul looks at the others while he steers, kneeling at the stern of the vessel. "It's dangerous. Cameroon has enough predators as it is. I don't just mean crocodiles, but other large game too, like hippopotamus. Be happy, movie stars, that this boat is bigger than your standard hollowed-out canoe," he goes on.

"And don't forget what the representative from the US embassy warned you about. The neighboring country here next to us, the Congo? Strife with crime and armed militias."

Paul mutters something under his breath in French that none of them, being English speakers, can recognize.

"If your dolphin friend is out here, that may be why she's never been seen by, how do you in the West consider it, a 'real' scientist?"

Henry leans back into a comfortable position and looks at their guide, "Then what brings you here, my friend?"

Even under the sunglasses that he's wearing, Paul's expression shifts noticeably. The spunk and humor and optimism leave his face in a fraction of a second after hearing the question. Henry catches on and looks over to Dr. Hendricks seated across from him, who flashes him an almost imperceptible shake of the head, warning him not to touch the subject.

David, curious if she knows something that they don't, catches Paul Lumumba's gaze and anticipates his response.

"It's okay, my friends," Paul says, looking both to Henry and to Molly.

Dr. Hendricks interrupts the awkward pause that follows.

"Let's get to work," she says.

All traces of the village or any sign of civilization has long left the team's sight, as they've been on the misty river for hours now. On both sides, the thick, seemingly impenetrable jungle's greenery envelops the D'ja River. Henry gets his camera equipment ready while Anne looks over hers. Avery has his phone out, supposedly recording a TikTok or doing a story reel for his Instagram page. How he has any service out here at all is beyond David's comprehension, though he suspects that Avery may be simply recording a video to post later on his page to promote the documentary before it comes out.

"All right, y'all. Your boy Avery Chambers here. If you're watching this, you get a sneak peek at what me and the fellas are up to," He pans the camera to look out over the river.

"We are in equatorial Africa with yet another Curiosity Channel special. We are here to hopefully find and 'document' an entirely new and exceptionally rare species of river dolphin, which apparently there's been a lot of sightings of in the area. For real, though, that'd be hella tight if we found it."

Avery is very flamboyant with his speech, using his index and middle fingers to make quotation marks in the air and talking like he's doing a theatre audition. He pans the camera around to show the others on the boat.

"Here we have our very own fancy-shmancy marine biologists, Dr. David Hale and Dr. Molly Hendricks. Don't be shy y'all, come on!" he motions to them.

"David works fine, I promise," David says, smiling at Avery's selfie.

"Same here! Molly!" she follows up with.

"This nice lady is our equipment expert, Anne Mathews. Here's my cameraman. Henry Doyle—"

"*Your* cameraman?!" Henry interrupts him. "Fool, you work for me, remember!?"

"Oh yeah, but you know I'm still your favorite, you know it!" Avery says, throwing his palm skyward.

"Yeah, yeah, don't get cocky, kid. I haven't written the will just yet." Henry says pointing his finger at him, joking even though he's only five years older than Avery at best.

Avery smirks.

"And last but definitely not least," Avery leans right up to his phone recording the selfie video and whispers loud enough for Henry to hear, "Henry's definitely least."

Henry looks up from fumbling around with his camera and shakes his head, shooting Avery a look that reads *I'm gonna get you*, their banter and teasing as buddies never ending.

"I swear to God I'm gonna send your ass to Canada or something!" Henry remarks.

"Hey," says Avery. "Sounds nice, especially in this heat!" Henry and Avery posture at each other, while the group is entertained by their antics.

Avery resumes, "Last but certainly not least, our badass Cameroonian local guide, versatile man of multiple languages, a driver, a boater... Paul Lumumba!" Paul looks at Avery from the back of the boat and waves at him.

David, feeling relaxed for the first time in days, looks over at Molly. "So ... what's your story?" he says, immediately regretting his choice of words. While his tone is friendly, he has never been very good at conversation. With anybody. Nor does he think of himself as particularly courageous.

Molly chuckles a bit, her eyes widening.

"Well, to be honest, work has been a welcome distraction ever since my wife passed away."

David feels terrible for her, like his problems suddenly are not the center of the universe. "Oh," he hesitates. "I'm... I'm so sorry."

"It's okay. She, umm, she had cancer. We had a lot of time to prepare ourselves for it."

David is at a loss for words. She goes on, "In a really fucked up way, I think it's a blessing that we knew."

The remainder of the evening, Molly, Anne, and David spend time talking together. David had forgotten what it was like to have a social life outside of his son and his career.

Molly zones out of the conversation momentarily, but then rejoins to hear David ask Anne, "Was that before or after you guys went to Sardinia?"

Anne laughs and resumes her story, but Molly zones out again, this time her attention being pulled to something in the distance, in the water. She stands up and turns to get a better look. It's getting dark now; the stunning African sunset is descending over the jungle in the distance but still lighting up the river just enough.

"Guys," she says loudly, her voice stopping the others' conversations abruptly. "What is that?"

They gather around her and Paul cranes his head in their direction. Hundreds of yards away, an object is seen moving through the water, slowly emerging and then submerging again over and over.

"Get that camera, Mr. Doyle," one of them says.

"Yep, yep, already on it!" He whips his camera up, hoping for the best that this may be exactly what they've come for.

"It's too dark! This camera's not gonna pick anything up in this light!" Henry says.

"That's my cue," Anne immediately follows up. Breaking out her equipment, she pulls out a device designed specifically to see heat signatures where the human eye cannot: FLIR, a Forward Looking Infrared thermal camera. Scanning the river for a long few minutes in the direction of where Molly first spotted the object, she finally picks it up on the FLIR. The others can see the FLIR monitor, and it submerges again. A few minutes later, it reappears, and Henry is able to record with his much smaller camcorder the screen of the FLIR.

"So loud as it gets dark, and yet so humid still," Paul says, noting their surroundings and referring to the jungle that is absolutely teeming with life on the shores on either side of the river. David, Molly, and the others are studying the image captured on the FLIR. They zoom in and use advanced software to make the image less and less blurry.

"Please be our dolphin, please be our dolphin, please be our dolphin," David says out loud with Molly by his side. The image goes through one final stage clarification. Molly continues off his words-

"Please be our dolphin, please be our..." She stops mid-sentence, upon them all realizing what it is. "...hippopotamus. Ah."

"Hippopotamus are especially dangerous," Paul says. "We must be careful."

"Hopefully we'll get lucky tonight. Or tomorrow!" David says reassuringly.

"Network's only funding us to be out here for a limited time. We better get lucky fast," chimes in Henry.

David pauses for a moment and then exhales, "We don't even know if this species exists for sure or not. There's that. Plus, if it is out here it's extremely unlikely we'd capture some quality film in just a few days of being here." The others look and begin to nod in agreement.

"He's right," Molly says, smiling,

"So let's try to remember to enjoy the trip."

2

"HERE, HERE!" SHOUTS DAVID. "GET THAT SUR!"

Molly rushes over with one of her devices, a Sonar Underwater Reader. "This may be it!" Molly says.

For days now the team has been out on the river, pushing further and further along the D'ja until finally coming up on the Boumba and Ngoko rivers. After their first official night of searching, and attempting in vain to get some sleep on the boat, they unanimously decided to pitch tents and camp out on shore, desperate to get a break from the motion and get a good night's sleep on solid land. That was a few nights ago. They are now several days' worth of boating away from the nearest Cameroon settlement with any kind of supplies. David, a dad after all and king of the horrible puns, jokes every now and then that their "*curiosity* keeps them going!" to which more than a couple members of the group will groan.

"You think that's it, movie star?" Paul asks Molly.

Anne turns on her SUR and goes to plunge it into the water.

"Wait!" David stops her. "Quietly. We don't want to scare it away before we can see what it is. Paul, do us a favor and keep the motor turned off, will you?"

"You got it, boss," whispers Paul, loudly. "We'll drift quieter than my unemployed brother Pierre. He never worked a day in his life."

"You have a brother named Pierre?" asks Henry.

"No," says Paul with a shit-eating grin. "I just made that up."

The group stifles their laughter, remaining careful not to scare away the skittish mammal. Anne hands the SUR to Molly. Molly takes it and looks at David. They nod in agreement, no words needing to be said. She slowly lowers the SUR—disguised to look like a fish—into the water on one side of the boat while David lowers the waterproof camera slowly, gently, into the water on the other side of the boat. Just then all of a sudden, a grayish colored object makes a splash at the water's surface and dives back down before it can be registered by the devices.

"Holy crap!" says Henry while holding his camera mounted on his shoulder. Everyone on the boat saw it, albeit it only appeared for a split second.

"That was no crocodile!" says Avery. "Hippopotamus? It was gray."

"Too small! Call me an optimist, but that skin looked a little too smooth to be a hippo. Maybe a fish. We'll need to rule it out until we're sure. We're going to need to do better than that to get hard proof," explains Molly.

The sun is just beginning to rise over the river. The group can feel the effect of many late nights and many early mornings with little sleep in between on the shores in the jungle. Factor in the time that it takes to pitch tents and make camp, they are running on very little sleep. Paul will sleep very well for a few nights once he has seen that his new American friends are back to the Yaoundé airport safely.

Despite this, David, Molly, Anne, Henry, Avery, and Paul spend the next several hours diligently combing the waters below to see if they can pick up whatever had made that splash on camera.

Finally, by the late afternoon, it's become clear that whatever it was has now vanished. Paul explains that this will be their last night camping out here, and that promptly tomorrow morning it will be time to head back up the river.

Henry wonders, *I didn't know he ran the network now. Who put him in charge?* Although after a brief moment of consideration, Henry realizes that Paul knows the place better than all of them combined, and that they'd be wise to heed his advice.

David, missing Alex and becoming less and less excited about finding this supposed dolphin, is happy to hear it. Molly on the other hand seems to be less enthusiastic about going back, even though they've already been on the river for several days, but David doesn't dare ask if it has to do with her late wife.

The group is talking, murmuring, amongst themselves, when Paul slowly looks up from the motor and his expression turns to the slightest hint of concern. David is the first to notice this.

Paul catches David looking at him and reassures him, "It's okay, movie star. It's just that I recognize the area. We're getting close to the border with the Congo. We'll be fine to camp out one more night on the shore, just inside of the border, and then we'll have to hit it."

"Guys ..." Avery says. "Look!"

His words catch the group off guard. Sure enough, right along the surface a mere thirty yards away from them and coming around a bend in the river, they see a tiny spurt of water into the air like a tiny theme park water fountain. David's eyes widen.

"A blowhole... a dolphin!" David exclaims.

The group comes to life. Henry swings his camera up but the river dolphin disappears underwater again, narrowly avoiding the camera.

"Damn it!" yells Henry.

"I've got an idea," says Molly. "I hope you guys will forgive me; it's for the sake of research ..."

"And money!" says Avery. Molly pulls out a firearm-looking device that's usually used to tag great white sharks in the wild.

"There's no way that we'll be able to get decent footage unless we know exactly where it is," she explains.

"She's right," says David, handing her an arrow that will serve as a GPS tracker.

"I'll make it count," she says. "These things don't grow on trees like car GPS's do."

Henry once again misses the dolphin as it reappears at the surface. But Molly fires. After a long pause with everyone staring at hers and Anne's equipment, the silence is finally interrupted.

"I got it!" says Molly. "I fucking got it!" The group comes to life, cheering so loud David thought the entire Congo river basin might be able to hear them.

"She's on the move!" says Anne. She continues, "You said the network wants hard proof, right? Will some quality footage suffice?"

"Yes." says David. "And not just the network. If we can catalogue this thing, it'll be a huge milestone in our careers." David turns to look at everybody as if ready to give a motivational speech, "*All* of our careers!"

Avery seizes the moment, "You get a career boost! And you get a career boost! And *you* get a career boost! Look under your seats ... *Everyone* gets a career boost!"

The group cheers, feeling more energized than they have in days. Paul follows their wishes and throws the boat into overdrive in order to follow the surprisingly fast dolphin further and further down river, keeping on it with Henry's camera ready. David and the other scientists know that the motor will scare it, but insist that it is "now or never." The thick jungle overgrowth seems to be getting thicker than ever on either side, with enormous trees, vines, and all kinds of foliage, which—David suspects–there could be myriads unclassified by modern botany. David cannot help but wonder just how remote and unexplored this area is, changing little or not at all since the French, Belgians, English, and Germans colonized this area in centuries past. Most of all, he marvels at how lucky he and the others are to have even gotten a glimpse at what they are here to find.

Paul brings them around to another bend in the river, at the meeting point between the Ngoko and the Sangha rivers where they merge into one. The air here seems especially humid and the fog is thick enough to be cut with a knife.

Suddenly, Paul cuts the engine, bringing the vessel to an unexpected stop.

"What's going on?" demands Molly. "Why are we stopping?"

Paul looks ahead at the bend in the river where they are now suddenly drifting, only just now having a clear view through the thick fog behind them.

"This is as far as we can go, movie stars. One hundred yards that way," Paul says pointing to the river ahead of them. "Is the border with the Republic of the Congo. This is as far south as we go."

"You gotta be kidding me!" Henry retorts. "We know *exactly* where that thing is now. Just a little bit farther and I can get us the footage that we need!"

"That *you* need," Paul says. He continues, "Your employer hired me to take you as far south as is safe to proceed. This is it."

Anne cannot contain her frustration. "Oh my God! We are *so close.* Just a little bit farther! If we don't catch this thing on camera, it will mean nothing to the rest of the world."

"Don't you remember what your American embassy said?" asserts Paul.

"We need documentation! We need proof!" exclaims Anne.

Molly follows up immediately, cutting Paul off before he can get in another word.

"Look! Look at the monitor! Every second we sit here, it's getting away! Pretty soon her equipment won't be able to pick up its exact location anymore and we'll lose it!"

David and Avery say nothing. David wonders if they realize that Paul has no financial incentive to go any further like they do. He's already been paid, and the network is offering big money to the *team* if they capture the dolphin on camera, not to their guide. David considers chiming in, when Molly says something that floors him.

"Paul, we are a group here. With all due respect, you are outnumbered. Besides, I don't expect you to understand the importance of making sacrifices for the sake of science."

Paul looks at her, and, for the first time that they've ever seen, anger registers on his face.

"Sacrifice?" Paul says. The vibe has gone from excitement to tension faster than David and the others could realize. Molly immediately regrets her words.

"You... want to talk to... *me*... about sacrifice?" Paul says, curling his lips at every syllable. A tense moment ensues. David, allergic to conflict, immediately chimes in before they exchange another word.

"Paul."

Paul looks away from Molly, Anne, and Henry towards David and Avery.

David continues, "Hey, we'll make it worth your while. This should go without saying! We will all give you a cut of what we earn once we get this thing on video. We promise. And we will make sure the network gives you a reward on top of that!" David pauses, anxiously awaiting Paul's response.

The conflict within David is screaming. *As long as we make it a fast incursion, we will be fine. We can slip in and back to Cameroon like nothing ever happened,* he tries to assure himself. *But what if we take the risk for nothing and don't get it on camera?* David's thoughts travel at a mile-a-minute pace with each passing millisecond.

Paul looks at him, the sting of Molly's words still with him. He shoots her a look, then looks at the river, then back towards David.

"Fine. But if we run into anybody, *I* do the talking."

Anne adds, exhaling, "Thank you, Paul."

Paul says nothing.

"I'll be sure to have my camera ready, okay man? We good, right?" adds Henry.

Paul reluctantly nods and throws the motor into overdrive.

"I am counting on it, movie star," he says to Henry.

Thundering down the river, the team follows the dolphin's signature. Henry's upper body begins to tremble after a while from the soreness that he begins to feel by having his camera ready to "capture" the small dolphin at a moment's notice. Approximately every ten minutes, the crew sees a spurt of water coming from the creature's blowhole, many of which are captured by Henry on film.

"No wonder the little guy is afraid. Boats here don't typically have motors, right? And think about how many natural predators it must have in these waterways!" says Molly.

The ensuing hours are an awkward string of excitement for the team's new discovery, Paul returning to his normal, upbeat—albeit uncomfortable—self, and Molly and the others who argued with him awkwardly and clumsily trying to be extra friendly towards him to make up for it. As the team keeps their eyes on the tracker, Molly finally gets Paul to come around. She goes on and on about what Paul can do with the cash when he receives it, at first receiving enthusiasm from him until finally she senses that he's had enough, and discontinues. The group brainstorms with each other during their pursuit, enthusiastically sharing with each other on what they should name this new species.

"Wait a minute," says Anne. "Where did it go?"

"The day?" jokes Avery. It is not lost on him that the day has flown by and the sun is already setting. The disappointment in Anne's voice becomes more and more obvious.

"No, I'm serious. The dolphin. It just vanished!"

"What?" Molly and David say at the exact same time.

Like a schoolyard bully popping his victim's balloon, the group's excitement vanishes in the blink of an eye.

"It's gone... we lost it," Anne says. David rubs his face. Molly inhales deeply and exhales, while Henry bows his head and rubs the soreness out of his arms and shoulder after hours of holding his camera up to the river ahead.

"That's not all that we've lost," Paul adds, disconcertingly. The group looks up at him, awaiting his next words. He continues, "We do not have enough daylight left to get back to the border of Cameroon. We will be forced to camp out here tonight, along the shore."

Paul points to a thicket of vegetation along the edge of the river. It is slightly less thick than the jungle that surrounds it.

"No more risks, movie stars. We've come way too far as it is. At first light, we head north. No negotiations." Paul's words, this time, are met with no argument. Only silence and a couple of heads nodding.

With the boat along the shore, the team rushes setting up camp just in time before the very last of the evening light vanishes. David zips up his tent and plops next to the others sitting around the fire.

"It's so goddamn hot," says Henry. "Shouldn't've even bothered to make a fire."

"Patience, my friend," Paul says as he turns on another lamp. Paul's spunk and upbeat personality by now has almost fully returned. The group's fire, lanterns, and flashlights are their only source of illumination in the loud, humid, dark jungle. All around them they can hear insects and numerous other noises of the jungle that make up the biodiversity of this little-explored area.

"You know," says David. "We know the truth. Just short of getting some HD footage, we saw it for ourselves. I honestly didn't even think that was gonna happen." David raises his hands in a content shrug, "End of the day, we made one hell of a discovery!"

Molly adds, enthusiastically, "We should be glad Henry was able to get so many shots of it coming up for air!" Henry does a sort of mock-curtsy.

"I agree. You know …" David's enthusiasm is rekindled at the thought, more so because Alex will get to see it on TV than because of the money. "…I bet we could negotiate with the network. Maybe that'll be good enough for them!"

"Yeah, yeah!" Molly exclaims. "Do you have any idea how big this is for cetology?"

Paul holds up his canteen, "Cheers to you, movie stars!"

"No, Paul," says Molly. "Cheers to *you* for getting us here!" Molly holds up her water canteen above her head. "To our hero, Paul!" she says.

The group erupts into praise for their guide.

"To Paul!" they say almost in unison.

Anne pulls out her smartphone. Ignoring the fact that she has no service, she goes into her downloads and pulls up the song "A Thousand Miles" by Vanessa Carlton and plays it out loud. Paul smiles and shakes his head. He looks at his new friends, and then at David. David looks back and shakes his head as well, with huge grins forming on both of their faces. They say no words, but if they had, it would be something to the effect of "They are crazy, aren't they?" The vibes of the group are positive. David pulls out some full-sized Hershey's milk chocolate bars. Eyes widen as David passes them out.

"Enjoy every bite. These are the last ones I've got!" he says. "With how friggin' hot it is I can't believe these aren't melted."

Sounds of the music and members of the group going "Mmmm" fill the air around their dark campsite.

"Whoa whoa, now," says Avery. "If we wanna have some bops then I got one for the moment." Henry pulls out his phone and selects play on none other than his download of "Sympathy for the Devil" by the Rolling Stones.

"I know this is before my time, but you ain't gonna tell me this place doesn't give you Viet Nam vibes," he says, putting extra emphasis on the "nam" part with a drawl. Henry shoots him a look.

"Okay, grandpa!" The group laughs. Avery sets his phone down to let it play. The group begins to sing along with the lyrics of the song, and their makeshift campsite becomes a mini makeshift party.

"*Woo! Woo!*"

In the canopy above them, something moves slowly through a tree. Attracted by the movement below, it wanders closer and closer.

"*Woo! Woo!*"

The fire reflects ever so slightly in the thing's eyes as it decides to move closer, through the tree's leaves, the movement of the group irresistible to its instincts. Above the group, a spider three inches in leg span moves slowly across the branch that it's perched on—one leg at a time—slowly making its way to the end of the branch where the leaves won't be able to hold its weight for much longer.

"*Woo! Woo!*"

The spider, bright yellow with a purple abdomen, pauses momentarily and then crawls to the edge. Running out of branch, it slowly turns its eight eyes downwards, the appendages on either side of its face "feeling" the air in front of it. Sticking its abdomen in the air, the spider attaches a string of web from its abdomen's spinnerets to the surface of the branch on which it sits.

"*Woo! Woo!*"

Twelve feet above Paul's head, the spider slowly begins its descent. The top of Paul's head gets closer, and closer, and closer, until the arachnid's "feelers" are just above him.

"*Woo! Woo!*"

Suddenly Paul leans over to set his canteen down, and the spider narrowly lands on his shoulder instead of the top of his head. In the dark jungle, nobody can see the arachnid on his shoulder as it crawls from his shoulder to his back. This object moves differently than any of the other surfaces that this spiderling has crawled on, but nonetheless it keeps itself in place on the mysterious new terrain that is the shirt on Paul's back.

"*Woo! Woo!*"

Paul starts movin' and groovin' with the others, enjoying himself despite not knowing the lyrics like his Western friends do. The spider suddenly loses its footing and falls off of Paul's back, landing on the log on which he sits right next to him. It lands for a moment on its back with its prickly eight legs grabbing at the air as it turns itself right-side-up again.

"*Woo! Woo!*"

Recovering quickly, the spider gets back up and wanders aimlessly in the direction that happens to be Paul's leg. The spider reaches the material of Paul's shorts and begins climbing up until it is past his hip and on his thigh, mere inches away from his hand.

"*Woo! Woo!*"

Paul leans forward, placing his left forearm *right* in front of the spider whose presence is completely unknown to him. The presence of Paul's left forearm scares the spider and puts it on high alert, not knowing what this massive object is right in front of it. The spider holds its position, standing guard with its instincts governing its every move.

"*Woo! Woo!*"

"Damn y'all, I'm having memories of a war I didn't even fight in!" Avery exclaims, his love for sixties music never waning and his delight at the group singing along uplifting him.

"Woo! Woo!"

Paul, completely oblivious to the eight-legged creature perched on his left thigh, leans further forward, pinning one of the spider's front legs under the weight of his forearm like a horse-mounted rider stuck beneath its fallen horse. Like two thumb tacks poking holes in butter, the spider immediately reacts and drives its small fangs into Paul's forearm, piercing the skin and upper layers of his tissue.

3

"OW!" PAUL YELLS, SHATTERING THE MOMENT. "SON OF A BITCH!"

"What happened?" shrieks Anne. Paul shoots up off the log that he was sitting on and shakes his left arm in a way that David hasn't seen since his college roommate burned himself on the stove. Avery struggles with his phone to turn off the music as if suddenly it was a hot potato in his hands.

"Something bit me!" says Paul frantically, the tone of his voice showing frustration more than fear.

Henry reacts, "What, oh my God, where?"

Paul and the others search the ground with their flashlights until they see it. The three-inch spider, bright yellow with a purple abdomen, skitters quickly along the ground. Paul angrily moves to step on it, holding the now-mildly bleeding two puncture holes in his forearm with his right hand.

"Wait, get a picture of it first in case we need to identify it for an antivenom!" asserts Molly. Henry snaps a few photos while the others use sticks to keep the arachnid from leaving their view.

"You have a goddamn picture or not!" Paul asks him.

"Yep," says Henry. Paul lunges forward and stomps on the spider with his shoe, crushing it. "Good riddance," he says.

Anne, scared out of her mind, begins to feel itchy sensations all over her body and begins going on and on about how much she hates spiders.

"No-no-no-no-no, fuck that," she says multiple times, before composing herself and helping David and Molly check on Paul's bite wound. Paul looks at it, shakes his head a bit, and then waves the others away.

"It's fine. Seriously, it just stung a bit. Took me by surprise. I'm okay," he insists.

Molly takes him by the arm and uses her flashlight to examine the bite. She wipes away an infinitesimal amount of blood from the two puncture holes and asks the group, "Do we have any alcohol?" The group has none.

"I do," says Paul. "But that's for... urgent situations."

"This is an urgent situation, movie star," Molly says using Paul's line. "We need to use it to clean the wound."

At Molly's insistence, she pours some of Paul's hard alcohol from his flask on the bite area. Paul refuses to let her pour any more than the absolute bare minimum. He takes his flask back from her and throws back a gulp as if it were electrolyte water.

"You should be fine," Molly says with a reassuring smile. She adds, "Remember, we are doctors," with a big wink.

"You are marine biologists," says Paul, half annoyed and half light-heartedly teasing them.

"Hey, now" says David. Molly grins and the researchers register no offense taken from Paul's words.

"I *am* okay. Now let's get on with it. We all need sleep, and we are heading back at first light. It's going to be at least a few days' ride up the river back to any kind of substantial Cameroonian civilization." Heeding his words, Henry and Avery begin settling down for the night.

David, Anne, and Molly ask him for his camera and they gather around to examine the photos of the spider. They require no flashlights for this; the blue light of the images from Henry's personal camera slightly illuminate their faces in the campsite. Anne gets squirmy again and frantically shines her flashlight all around them in every direction to make sure that there are no other arachnids—or any other unwanted guests—in the vicinity. The irony of a spider being an "unwanted guest," even though it is *they* who are in *its* jungle, is not lost on Anne. She feels a panic attack rising up in her as her mind spirals into a rabbit hole of wondering if, perhaps, they may be the first outsiders to explore this area *ever*. She takes several deep, long breaths, counts down slowly from five, backwards, until she reaches 'one' and gets a grip on herself. The group looks at the photos.

"To be honest, I... I've never seen a spider like that before, but with all due respect..." David says, puzzled, looking at the others. They look back at him and he continues, "...none of us here are arachnologists or entomologists, so what do we know?"

"Nothing. You're absolutely right," says Anne. "I'm a researcher along for the ride with fancy equipment."

Molly chimes in, "Don't sell yourself short, Anne. You've been instrumental for this trip." She continues, "But David's right. This isn't our arena. I think we should just watch each other's backs and keep an eye on Paul. Check in periodically."

"Yes and not let our *curiosity* get the best of us," David says, adding in his dad joke again.

"Har, har," says Molly. "The best thing he needs is sleep. We all do."

Paul, overhearing their conversation and never missing a beat, says "I'm way ahead of you, movie stars." He zips up his tent. "*You* all need sleep, too, so please get some. Seriously, I am *fine*. Good night."

"Good night, my friend," says David.

The fire has died down to just a few mild embers. The jungle is teeming with noise from its immense wildlife. Paul lays in his sleeping bag and thinks, *This is the true "city that never sleeps."* Paul has never been to the United States, instead choosing to settle down for a life of freedom in Cameroon, after fleeing Uganda.

A cold chill starts at the base of Paul's spine and slowly creeps its way up his entire body. *Jesus Christ,* Paul thinks to himself as he climbs deeper into his sleeping bag—something he has never done in the hot jungle outside of the rainy season—and zips it up as high as it can go. He feels chills, and begins to notice a slight pain coming from his right temple. A headache is brewing.

After hours of tossing and turning, Paul simply accepts the fact that he will not be falling asleep tonight. Blaming the alcohol, poor sustenance, and nights of terrible sleep, or the lack thereof, Paul at first thinks nothing of his symptoms ... until he rolls over onto his left side and feels pain shooting up his arm. He touches the area where the bite wound is and realizes that the area feels jagged and huge.

Something's not right, Paul finally admits to himself. Working up the courage, he sits up from his sleeping bag. Upon doing so, the temperature of his body feels like it suddenly plummets. *Is this Africa near the equator or is this fucking Greenland?* he thinks to himself. He slowly sits up and suddenly notices something else: aches throughout his entire body where they were not as noticeable when he was laying down. He awkwardly reaches for his flashlight, inhaling and exhaling deeply, and turns it on.

The sight of Paul's own left forearm startles him. It has swollen so big that his forearm has gained at least three to five inches in circumference, with the bite area looking puffy and jagged. The veins in his arm seem to be turning purple before his very eyes. Paul attempts another deep inhalation, before gathering his strength and approaching the zipper of his tent. He can tell by the growing light outside that dawn is breaking.

David begins to stir, checking his phone out of habit, even though they have zero service signal in the Congo. He consciously reassures himself that he will make it back in time for Alex's birthday as long as they leave promptly. David pops out of his tent like a piece of toast, excited to get on with the day. The sun is coming up and the thick vegetation of the jungle surrounding them near the shore of the river, where their boat is tethered, is becoming more and more colorful after such a dark night with little to no moonlight. With his eyes adjusting to the morning light, David steps several yards away from their campsite to relieve himself in the bushes. After zipping up his pants, David hears a rustling nearby that startles him awake. He looks over, inquisitively and cautiously. By now other members of the team are waking up as well and getting their stuff together. David squints his eyes and sees a figure step into his sight.

"P... Paul?"

Paul stands there looking at David as if something has him hypnotized. There is a confusion behind his eyes. David looks at him and repeats himself, "Paul?"

Paul looks around like a zombie, feels a trickle of sweat run down his forehead and then another one running down the calf of his leg. He looks down at himself, and he and David both realize that Paul has wet himself, unable to get somewhere to properly do so fast enough. David's eyes widen with concern.

"Molly? Guys?" The others now begin to notice as well. Suddenly, David and the others notice his swollen forearm and gasp.

Paul finally croaks, weakly, "Movie stars... I... I don't feel so good."

Paul collapses to the ground just in time for David and the others to catch him. He is huffing and puffing like a morbidly obese person trying to run track. The sweat runs right off of him, and his chills worsen.

"It's the bite!" says David, who secretly can't stand the smell of Paul having wet himself. He continues, "We need to get him help, now."

"Where? We're days away from Mutengoua! What supplies do we have?" says Henry. The others look around helplessly, in some ways still trying to shake themselves awake, even though the sight of Paul's arm seems to be jolting them awake better than an espresso.

"We used a lot of them with the ride out here. David wasn't the only one who was car sick," says Molly.

"Gee, thanks," says David.

She continues, "But I think I still have some aspirin." She rushes to get Paul the medicine while the others wrap him up in a blanket and a sweatshirt like a baby being swaddled.

"Here, Paul. It's not much but it's better than nothing." She hands him two tablets and he insists on taking three. Upon washing the pills down with water, he notices that it hurts to swallow. The aches are all over his body now, coming and going in waves. Paul explains this to the group even though he knows that they have no expertise in this matter.

Avery quickly drenches a cloth with some water from his canteen before Paul can shout, "No! Save your water. We need it for ..." David kindly interrupts and reassures Paul that they have with them a Lifestraw designed specially to drink from virtually any source, turning dirty water clean and safe to drink as it passes through the straw. Avery rings out the water from his cloth and places it on Paul's forehead.

"Thank you, friends," Paul says weakly. He struggles to stand up and the others help him. Stumbling to his feet like somebody struggling to walk after having a stroke, Paul takes a deep breath and explains, "Some villages in the area might have venom antidotes, but it's hit and miss. It's better if we just got back to Mutengoua as fast as possible. And you said yourselves, you don't know what kind of creepy crawly that thing was, so it's better just to get on with it."

Molly says, "It's probably just a common species in this area. Hopefully your symptoms don't get worse. We will look out for you."

Paul presses the wet towel to his forehead and winces, "I need to let your medicine kick in. And then I'll show one of you how to drive the boat."

Paul points to their stuff and then to the shore where their boat is about fifty yards away. The others waste no time. Breaking down their tents and gathering up their belongings, the group hastily prepares the boat for departure. Paul sits on the same log from last night, barely holding himself up. Henry and Avery work together to take care of Paul's stuff for him. The others cannot help but notice his ghostly pale complexion. He looks absolutely miserable, yet he insists that the aspirin is helping.

Henry and Avery go to retrieve the last thing that they need: Paul himself. Despite the group's haste, a considerable amount of time passes as they break down their stuff and load up the boat. Ten or so minutes feels like an eternity to Paul, who is beginning to have sensory hallucinations. A particular hallucination startles him as Henry and Avery walk towards him. For the slightest moment Paul swears that he can hear some kind of an odd hissing sound coming from the jungle nearby.

Suddenly, the earth begins to spin and the landscape turns on its side as Paul keels over. The wet towel rolls out of his hands as he hits the ground, aching and shivering.

"Paul!" one of the team members shouts. They rush over to him with the others following closely behind. Paul's eyes look as if they are going to roll backwards into his head. The group notices that the purple color of his veins have now traveled up his arm and are forming at the base of his neck above the left-side collarbone.

"Son of a bitch!" shouts David. He looks at Molly, who looks like she's trying to keep herself from bursting into tears.

"He needs a doctor! A real doctor!" shouts David.

"There is nobody out here in either direction for days!" cries Molly. The group gathers around. Molly continues, "I was so fucking stupid for sending us here. I'm so sorry. Fuck this, fuck me!"

Henry says, "We need to get back to Mutengoua *now!*"

"Look at him!" says Anne. The group looks at Paul. David tries to get him to speak, but he is delirious. Anne continues, "Look at him. We need to get him help sooner than that. We need to try our luck at one of these closer villages!"

The group erupts into argument. One side insisting that they need to board the boat and get back to Cameroon. The other side insisting that they need to try their luck and head to the nearby Congolese village of Zatoumbi since his symptoms are rapidly worsening. David interrupts their argumentative and panicked exchanges when he realizes that Paul is trying to tell them something.

"H-help," croaks Paul.

"Yes, buddy, we're here." He leans in but cannot hear Paul over the others arguing. Paul moves his lips but no sound comes out.

"HEY! Guys, SHUT UP!" shouts David. The group ceases and falls in line. Paul looks around and then locks his eyes right onto David. Mustering all of his strength, he grabs David's shirt and pulls himself closer, mustering all his energy to speak clearly.

"David … David. I did not escape the LRA to be killed by a *fucking spider. Get... me... the fuck out of here,*" Paul says, losing consciousness after his final word.

Far past delirium and now unconscious, the group checks Paul's labored breathing and finally decides that he will not make it back to Mutengoua fast enough by boat. They pick him up, with David carrying him under his arms and Avery carrying his legs. With Henry, Molly, and Anne carrying their stuff, they begin venturing straight into the jungle towards the coordinates where the map says that a small Congolese village exists.

Molly holds back tears. The guilt riddles her body and mind. She is no arachnologist, but she knows damn well that if this nearby village does not have the necessary antidote for *that* particular species of spider that they caught on camera, then Paul could die before they can reach a place that does.

Bright yellow, purple abdomen, three inches circumference, she keeps telling herself over and over again. Molly remembers her words that offended Paul, and hates herself for saying such a *preppy arrogant white girl thing.* She loathes herself with every step, every lunge, every tree and plant and vine that she must push out of their way to continue on. *And what if it's a new species altogether and there is no antidote?* The "new species" irony is not lost on her.

David feels unsettled by Paul's words before he slipped into unconsciousness. He wonders to himself: *LRA? What the heck is that? LRA? Why does that sound so familiar?*

Coming over an especially difficult piece of terrain with thick vegetation, David and Avery require help from the others to keep Paul from being dragged through the mud. David's mind races a mile a minute, not helped by the fact that he's worried about Alex back home.

LRA, he wonders to himself. *LRA?...* Then it hits him like a freight train.

Paul Lumumba escaped Joseph Kony's reign of terror, probably after being made to be a child soldier in the Lord's Resistance Army. He might've even been forced to hurt his loved ones or something even more ghastly. David does not remember the grotesque details of what the Ugandan warlord carried out, but he remembers the assembly about it in high school. Everyone who had watched the documentary in the gymnasium that day in 2012 was floored, students and faculty alike. Paul Lumumba had escaped the LRA, fled here all by himself to start a new life in this region of Africa, probably as a child. He probably had to reinvent himself after horrible trauma, and ended up being a bubbly, fun-loving man anyway ... who was unlucky enough to be hired to be *their* guide in particular. In this moment, David feels an overwhelming sense of respect for their beloved guide, eclipsed only by his guilt that this is all their fault. David stifles an outburst of frustration and loses his footing.

Paul, whimpering every once in a while, slumps to the ground on David's end for a split second until David can reorient himself and get Paul back up. The movement must have hurt, because this particular whimper was louder than the others.

"I'm so sorry," David says under his breath. Just then, Paul, drifting in and out of consciousness, mutters something inaudible. David leans over, his lower back on fire since this whole time he has been neglecting to lift with his legs. Paul struggles with his breathing. He whimpers softly, with a haunting sense of desperation. The group cannot understand what he's saying. Until finally Avery can make out one word, a word that they realize he's been saying incoherently over and over and over again.

"Home."

4

"THIS IS HORSESHIT," COMPLAINS HENRY.

"I thought you guys said this village was only a few hours' walk!" By now, every member of the team has had at least one turn carrying Paul, rotating carrying positions, with those not carrying him navigating and bush-whacking. The team exerts muscles that they didn't even know they had, pushing themselves to near exhaustion.

"We're not cartographers, genius. We are doing our best!" shoots David.

"Well, we shouldn't be here." Henry sneers. David bites his tongue. It is getting dark out, and Paul still has not regained consciousness.

"It's the heat," says Anne. "It's getting to us, and we're not consuming nearly enough water and calories." Suddenly, she and David become aware of a faint sound coming from nearby. Then Henry hears it, then Avery, then Molly.

A moment of silence ensues.

"You know what we really need? Other than for him to be back on his feet..." Henry says inconsiderately, pointing at Paul and breaking the silence. "We need to know who the *fuck* was stupid enough to send us out here without an antivenom. All fun and fuckin' games until your guide gets clapped!" Henry throws up his arms and puts them on his hips, in what David interprets as a show of self-pity. Henry's contempt irritates David more than he allows himself to show. Pouting about a tense situation and being a martyr was exactly what his now ex-wife used to do. David talks himself out of verbally ripping into him, reminding himself to "take ten," inhaling and exhaling deeply.

"Henry," says Molly, with an astonishingly calm tone that David knows he could not match. "There are more species of spider in this region than there probably are individual people. Antivenom only works if you have the *right* antivenom for the *right* spider. We would need ten times the funding from the network to have the antivenoms of all known species in this area with us. Probably ten times the boat size, too. And not just spiders too, but snakes."

Henry is visibly annoyed with her words, trying to swallow his pride but also unable to talk himself out of looking for someone or something to blame.

Molly continues, "And, there's not an antivenom for every known venomous species out there. The best we can do is get him to this village and hope to God that they ha-"

Molly ceases speaking upon hearing *that* sound again. The group turns towards it. Sweat drips off of their heads. Even as it's getting dark, the humidity level is unbearable.

Avery feels like his knees may just give out right then and there. He wonders how the others must be doing. The fact that he's the youngest of the group is not lost on him. *Damn, if I'm sore as fuck, they must be miserable,* he thinks to himself.

David is miserable. Although he would never admit it, the last thing he wants to do is carry Paul any further.

"Water. It's a stream!" says a delighted Anne.

By now, the water in their canteens run dangerously low with the rest being saved for Paul for when he regains consciousness. That strange sound getting louder and louder is the unmistakably divine sound of running water. They hurriedly carry Paul through the remaining brush until the creek with the small "waterfall" is in their sights. One by one, they fall to their hands and knees and share the Lifestraw, drinking what feels like their body weight in water.

David reaches into his bag and pulls out a hefty bag of granola. They go to town. For the first time in hours, the group feels a bit of relief, and David and Henry don't feel like squaring up with one another. Anne and Molly gently lay Paul down next to the stream, using an article of clothing to place under his head as a makeshift pillow. Even while unconscious, his shivers have not ceased. The group pitches in various clothing pieces to bundle up their likeable guide until he is practically swaddled like a baby.

David stands up and looks down at an unconscious Paul, and all he can think about is the memory of Alex contracting Covid-19 as a baby. He was scared to death for his son then, and is scared to death for their friend now. He wasn't even allowed to visit Alex in the hospital then, but if he had … he imagines he would've looked something like Paul does now … helpless and on the precipice between life and death. His image of his infant son, Alex, begins to blend with the real-life image of Paul right in front of him.

Anne kneels beside Paul and gently touches his shoulder, "Paul? You okay?" she tries to ask him, in vain.

"He will pull through. I know he will," says David.

"Home," mutters Paul, barely audible, the first time that he's said the word all day since they left with him that morning.

"Paul!" The group gathers around him. They try to wake him up but it's no use. It's as if Paul is talking in his sleep.

"Pull up the map! How far away are we from the village?" barks Henry.

Unable to use their GPS locator due to the batteries dying, David again pulls out Paul's folded up paper map of the region. It's written in French, the primary official language of the Congo after its European invaders.

"Anyone speak French?" asks David, trying in vain to lighten the mood.

"No, Mom made me take Spanish since we lived in California," says Anne. David and the group examine the map.

Molly squints her eyes, "It should be close. Wait a sec, it should be …" The group looks and notices her eyes widen. She looks down, pauses, then looks up.

"It should be... right… here."

"Fuck me, fuck me, fuck me, fuck me," says Henry over and over again.

"My dude," Avery says to him, "You gotta pull yourself together!"

Henry lets loose, "I wouldn't have to pull myself together if we were actually prepared and actually had *real* fucking doctors with us!"

David, overhearing him, stands up from the map on the ground and looks straight in Henry's face. "You got something you wanna say?" he says.

"If it weren't for you people, we wouldn't have even left the Cameroon border!" says Henry.

"*Us people?* If I remember correctly, *you* were the first one to argue with Paul that we should proceed!" snaps David. "Wanna point fingers?" he proceeds. "Wanna talk about 'real' vs. 'not real' doctors?" David's anger rises. "Maybe go back to film school so you can get a good fucking shot of the animal the *first* goddamn time we see it!"

The group erupts into explosive argument, with David and Henry nearly exchanging blows until, finally, Molly intervenes.

"Shut up, both of you! All of you! It's *my* fault."

The sound of Molly's word "my" brings the group's hostility towards one another to a screeching halt.

"Yes," Molly continues. "It *is* my fault. Henry, you are a great camera guy. And I know it's what you love doing because you told me that you've been interested in photography ever since you were a child." Henry gives her a sad, almost disarmed, look. One by one, Molly goes around giving personalized pep talks to everybody except herself.

"It's not your fault, Molly," says David.

"Yes. It is," she says.

"Then it looks like we'll be agreeing to disagree. Can people still do that?" David asks with a calmed down tone.

"Fine," says Molly, solemnly.

Finally, after a moment, Henry finally chimes in, "I'm sorry, too, I've been such a dick. This isn't about me... this is about Paul." David and Henry look at each other and nod slightly.

"So, basically... we're lost," says Anne, holding out her index finger. "No Zatoumbi," she says, adding her middle finger.

"*And* we've just carried him through the jungle all day for nothing," she concludes, adding her thumb to make a three on her hand. David bows his head. Henry and Avery rub their faces.

Anne continues, "Like, I'm sorry to ruin the moment of kumbaya and all that, but we need to focus."

"You're right," says Henry, "But it's getting to be nighttime again. We need to rest. Even just for a little bit."

"So are we bringing him back to the boat or even further to another village that also might not even be on that map?" asks Avery, sounding more serious than the group has ever heard from his otherwise flamboyant and party-centric personality.

"I don't freakin' know," Anne says with a massive, exhausted sigh. She looks around for other input. Henry again asserts that they need some rest.

"He's right," says David, siding with Henry, which takes Molly by surprise.

He continues, "We can't help Paul if we ourselves keel over. He looks as comfortable as he can be right now. We rest here by the stream for a few hours, and then we decide what we're doing next. I don't really do religion or any of that stuff, but I'm holding out faith that he will pull through. Maybe the symptoms just need to run their course."

The group doesn't even bother pitching tents. David's last words travel through Avery's head as he falls asleep. "Pull... through."

Avery and the others are out within minutes.

THE SMELL WAKES UP MOLLY. IT'S STILL DARK OUT, BUT NOT as dark as it was when they went to sleep. *We've overslept*, she thinks to herself. She wonders what that smell is. It's not overwhelming, but it's bad enough to have stirred her awake. She waves it away at first, knowing full well that she has a sensitive nose and is a light sleeper, something she thinks of as a curse "back in the world." She decides to get up and relieve herself.

THE SOUND OF DR. MOLLY HENDRICKS' SCREAM WAKES THE others.

After deciding to check on Paul, she grabbed her flashlight, flipped his blanket off and discovered the source of that subtle, unpleasant odor. The others shoot up to their feet and see her standing over their friend with a look of horror on her face, her hand covering her mouth while the other uses her flashlight to illuminate Paul.

"Oh my GOD," says Anne. David reluctantly kneels down and checks for his pulse, both at his neck and also along his wrist. David looks up.

"He's gone."

Paul Lumumba has succumbed to the spider's venom and died while the others were resting. His body is in horrendous condition. Even with his dark skin, they can see that the purple colored veins have spread to virtually every visible part of his body, including his face. He has purple boils that look eerily similar to the black boils caused by the bubonic plague of 14th century Europe. The largest of these boils sits on his forehead, which has popped like a bubble to reveal a white, frothy pus. His eyes are wide open, giving David the haunting suspicion that he woke up just before passing away. His eyes are bloodshot, and there's no white left around his corneas ... only red. His body looks like something out of a "Resident Evil" film. David covers his nose, and then proceeds to lift up more of the blanket ... making the mistake of examining the bite area. The stench hits them harder now. The swelling has gotten so bad that Paul's left forearm is almost as big as his thigh. At the bite area itself, necrosis ravages it to the point that the tissue decay makes it look like he has a fleshy crater on his arm. David feels the bile rising, and rushes off to get sick.

"Oh my god, oh my god," Molly says as she bursts into tears.

Henry runs his hands through his hair and squeezes them together. Avery looks at Paul, back up to Henry, and then the others. His eyes well up as if he, too, is about to cry, although he manages to hold it back.

"Fuck," says David, stumbling back after throwing up what little granola he had had several hours prior. "Fuck, fuck, fuck, FUCK!" he shouts, the last one coming out loud enough to wake the jungle.

"We just had to do it, huh. We just had to get our prize money and all this shit!" David shouts as he kicks at his stuff. Kicking again and again like an angry toddler, David stays at it until Avery and Henry intervene.

"*A rare, new species.*" David says with an overly dramatic scoff. "Careful what you fucking wish for, I guess." Near them, Anne comforts a distraught Molly.

"There's nothing we can do about it now," says Avery to David while he and Henry try to calm him down. Avery continues, "It's over. We need to go back."

Night turns to morning and the group finishes burying Paul just in time for it to start getting hot again. They take a moment and say a few words. With none of them being particularly religious, they opt instead to leave one of Henry's expensive camera lenses on his grave, rather than sticking a cross made from two sticks into it. The group swears that they will be dedicating the discovery of this new African River Dolphin to Paul, and naming it after him as well. Henry's camera lens serves to remind them of their friend. Because, in Henry's words, "What's a 'movie star' without a camera?"

Distraught, quiet, and slightly panicked on the inside for having lost the only member of the team who even remotely knows this area, the group nonetheless gets their stuff together and begins their journey back to the boat in the direction that they came.

Later on, in the blazing afternoon, the group of five comes across a swampy clearing where they see something that infuriates them all, but that they don't have the energy to express: a dead and decayed elephant carcass with both tusks removed.

"I've seen the work of poachers before," says Molly. "I studied up on it when I was in the Pacific trying to intercept the Japanese from killing whales. This isn't a very neat cut. Whoever did this must've been in a hurry."

"Weird," says David, who is also curious but still mentally not present. Suddenly, he and the others look up and notice that Anne has fallen behind them.

"You good, queen?" says Avery, a bit of himself returning.

Anne stands there staring at a nearby game trail, about fifty yards away from them, where a path seems to cut through the jungle.

"I... yeah, I'm good. I just–did anybody else see that?" Anne says.

"See what?" Henry asks.

Just moments ago, Anne swears that she saw a "blur" out of her right peripheral vision crossing the game trail. It only lasted a split second. "It," whatever it was, looked large and brown. *Probably just some kind of a monkey or a jungle cat*, she thinks to herself.

"I'm... I'm sorry, I don't know. Maybe I'm just trippin'," she says to them.

"You need to drink up," Henry asserts. "You're probably dehydrated." David looks around, anxious to get a move on.

"He's right," says David. "We all are. We'll take a break at the next creek or source that we find." David points to the marsh-looking swamp water near them. "Cause I ain't drinking that if you paid me ... looks too nasty even for the special straw."

Proceeding ahead, Anne abruptly turns her head back, swearing that she's just heard a rustling in the bushes nearby. Writing it off as her mind playing tricks, she quickly catches up with the others.

Pushing aside thick vines and plant matter on their way back to the boat, the team is careful to retrace their steps in order to make it to their intended destination rather than veering off course. David remembers learning that airline pilots can't even be off by a few feet of the nose of the plane, otherwise they could land miles and miles off course. All along the way, he has vivid memories of this, that, or the other hill or bush from where they carried Paul the day prior. David desperately tries to shift the course of where his thoughts are taking him.

"Anyone else need a cold shower?" he says out loud. His question triggers the group spontaneously chatting up a storm about cooling off and getting clean.

"Oh, good god, yes." Molly says.

"I haven't smelled this rancid since I came across that skunk at Lake Tahoe," says Anne.

"Skunks are nothing compared to a garter snake in heat. Don't ask," says Henry, and the group chuckles a bit for the first time since Paul was first bitten.

"I am telling you, you guys... !" says Avery with anticipation in his words and a pause in his sentence. He looks at Henry with a smirk and raises his hands as if he's going to say something mind blowing to the team, "...Canada!"

"Okay. Ice skating on me in Canada when we get back to civilization!" Henry says, looking at Avery.

"I'm holding you to it!" says Avery, pointing at him.

Moving much faster than when they were taking turns carrying Paul, the group makes up for lost time and reaches their destination, despite being held back by the climate, terrain, and their exhaustion.

By the time they get back to their boat, the team is too tired to see the figures commandeering their vessel on shore in front of them. David snaps awake at the sight and abruptly stops the others before they can be seen.

"Wait, wait, wait!" he whispers loudly. "Get back!"

Peering through the vegetation, the group from the Curiosity Channel can see four men who have pulled their ragged-looking boat to "park" it on shore right next to *their* boat, using ropes with hooks on the ends to keep their boat tied to the one used by the Westerners. All of them are Congolese, from what David and the others can tell, except for one. Tanned with wavy hair, this heavier set man alongside his African buddies looks to be white. He appears to be directing the others with his index finger and his words.

"Oh, good god," says Molly.

"Who the heck are these guys?" asks Henry, all of them trying to be cognizant of their volume in order to stay hidden. David takes another glance and notices the white man is carrying something alarming ... he sees the tip of a barrel that he recognizes from countless movies and video games. Turning slightly towards their eyesight, they can see that the tall white man is holding an AK-47 assault rifle fitted with a folded-in bayonet. One of the Congolese men has a machete on him. Although this is the only firearm the group can see on the other group, this is more than enough to make David and the others take pause. David exhales with a sigh, drooping his head down with a display communicating the words "just our luck" without actually saying them.

"River Pirates," says David.

This is exactly what Paul was worried about. The group looks around at each other, knowing full well that they *need* their boat to get home.

"Congolese river pirates. Lovely," says Anne. She continues, "Do you think they may be in a good mood?" she says sarcastically but also kind of serious. "If they take that boat then we're going to be stuck out here. We'll never be able to survive on foot all the way back to Mutengoua."

"Maybe we can reason with them! Maybe they think we just abandoned it. Maybe we can even bribe them!" says Henry.

"You have any cash on you, big money Mr. Doyle?" Avery retorts with a sassiness.

"Not Central African francs," Henry replies like a disappointed child.

"Maybe we can give them something. Oh, maybe we can do them a favor or something," says David.

"No! Absolutely not!" says Molly. Anne looks sternly and nods alongside her. David realizes what they're referring to.

"What? No, I don't mean that!" he says.

Anne looks as if the panic is rising inside of her. She says, softly, "We need Paul here. Remember how he said, If we run into anybody, you let him do the talking?"

"Well, we need to think of something fast becau—"

"HEY!" a voice shouts at them from the boats.

The team tries not to panic as they realize their cover's been blown. The lead pirate swings his AK-47 up and points it directly at them.

5

"DON'T SHOOT! DON'T SHOOT! PLEASE! WE MEAN NO HARM!" shouts David. He and the others throw their palms skyward to put the man at ease.

"How many are ya? Come out now! Right now!" the voice shouts back.

David and the others clumsily step out into view where they see the man holding his assault rifle, pointed directly at them. They hold their hands up, communicating surrender. The pirates do a double take, looking them up and down. The white man with the AK-47 notices Molly and Anne, and slowly lowers his weapon.

"I count five. Are there any more of you out there?" he demands. He continues, "Be honest with me now. Try to mind which of us has a weapon, remember."

"It's just us," says Molly. "Please," she continues, "we've been through hell and back. We don't mean any harm." The pirates look her over, then look to the others.

"You guys obviously aren't from around here," the mysterious man says. The other pirates look at the researchers like hawks zeroing in on breakfast. The mysterious man slowly shrugs his shoulder up to his neck as if slightly irritated that the opposing group hasn't started talking yet.

"So?" he says. "State your business."

He now holds the Kalashnikov pointed downwards and away from the group. The Westerners, intimidated, look at each other for a split second as if anxiously trying to decide who will speak. David reluctantly steps forward.

"We ... we're from the United States. We came here to film a documentary with the Curiosity Channel. We were here to find and document a new species of dolphin that resides in these rivers here. But ... we made a big mistake. Our guide ... our *friend* ... is dead. We've had a really rough couple of days. We don't want any trouble at all! We mean no harm to you guys. We mean no disrespect. We've been to hell and back, and ... we just wanna go home."

The man looks puzzled, ponders his words, then a large smile forms on his face, and he begins chuckling. David cannot tell if his laughter is fake or sincere.

The man replies, "Hell, huh? You all 'been to hell and back.' I am sorry to hear that. That's too bad," he says with a smile. "Then why'd you come *here*?"

He and his Congolese friends look at each other and start to snicker. One of his buddies says something to him in a language that the Americans don't understand. David can't tell if it's French or an indigenous dialect. The man smiles big and nods in agreement with whatever his acquaintance has told him. His eyes then widen and he opens his mouth wide into an O shape,

"Ohhhhhhhh!" he says. "So *this*. This must be *your* boat!" he says pointing back at the boat that the Americans chartered. David nods like a busted child.

"My name's Oskar, by the way. Oskar van Vuuren," the man says.

"I'm Dr. David Hale," says David. "These are my colleagues. Dr. Molly Hendricks." He waves his hand to each of them as he introduces the crew sheepishly.

"Ohhh-hohohoho! Doctors! So fancy," interjects Van Vuuren with a raise of his eyebrows and his bottom lip curling under. David immediately regrets using their professional titles, at first thinking it would give them some clout but now fearing that he just sounded pretentious instead.

"We're marine biologists. This is Anne Matthews, researcher. Our cameraman Henry Doyle," continues David.

"And that's Henry's friend and assistant, Avery Chambers."

Van Vuuren looks over each one as David names each of them. The American researchers nod hello sheepishly rather than exchange hand-shakes. Van Vuuren's Congolese counterparts remain quiet, but observant.

"Come on down, don't be shy. Especially you two nice ladies, come on down," Van Vuuren says, beckoning the group. Van Vuuren reaches his hand out warmly and David shakes it. David wonders who Oskar van Vuuren is and where he's from. *Could he be from the U.S., too? Europe, originally? His last name sounds kind of Dutch,* David thinks to himself. *Maybe an Afrikaner? The man has a slight accent. Must be South African. But what is he doing here?* David doesn't dare ask him.

Just then, the American group notices somebody on the pirates' boat that they hadn't before.

Peering up at them like a helpless puppy, a small Congolese child, barely ten years old, looks back at them. He is seated on the deck of the pirates' boat, with his knees up to his chest, arms wrapped around them in a fetal position. He is dead quiet and has been this whole time. The boy looks malnourished and tired. The boy catches David's eye, and for a split second David sees his own son, Alex, in the boy. Although the boy looks like he could be a couple of years older than Alex, his ghostly shy appearance and undernourished state make him look, physically, as small or smaller than almost-eight-year-old Alex. David's curiosity is noticed by Oskar, causing his warm expression to change suddenly.

"Hey, don't pay any attention to that boy. You want somethin', you talk to one of my men. More specifically, you talk to me," Van Vuuren says sharply, pointing his index and middle fingers up to his eyes to get David and the others to adjust their gaze back to him and the other adult men. David falls in line. Van Vuuren's tone then immediately shifts back to warmth and friendliness.

"These are my men. We've spent many seasons on this river together. This is Beza Kumba. His brother, Babila. That's Wanjala Killian. My second-in-command, Kumni, couldn't join us today, I'm afraid. He had some... matters... to deal with," Van Vuuren says with a smirk. "So, again, back to logistics," Van Vuuren says warmly and friendly. "Ah, yes. So this is your boat?"

"Yes. Yes," says Anne, "We're sorry. We don't mean to intrude or anything. We don't want any trouble. We just want to be able to go home."

David can hear the shakiness in her voice.

"Trouble?" says Van Vuuren. "No, no, no, no, no!"

He steps up to the others until he is right up in Anne's face. He puts his hand on her shoulder, rubbing it slightly, then continues. "Look. We get it. We get it! Shit happens, you know?" He turns back towards his Congolese acquaintances. "Right?" he asks them. He then turns back to David and continues on, "Dr. Hale, right? We definitely get it," Van Vuuren says with a smile on his face. A feeling of reassurance falls over the American researchers.

"So... you mean, we're good to go? We can just... take our boat and leave?" asks David.

Van Vuuren squares up with David, getting close enough that David thinks he might be going in for a hug. David feels the anxiety riddling his body.

"Of course, Dr. Hale. This is your boat. And yes, even though this is *our* river, and you all came here without weighing your options; still, we know what it's like to fall on hard times. We get it."

Van Vuuren puts his hands on both of David's shoulders, warmly, and says, "We know." David feels a surprising sense of relief.

Van Vuuren carries on, "And, because we know …" he says waving his hand at the riverscape behind them like a salesperson doing a presentation, "...our river is your river."

Van Vuuren smiles, "Now, go."

"Thank you," David says.

"Yes, thank you." says Henry, pleasantly surprised. Van Vuuren waves his hand and steps aside ushering the group like an usher at a fancy theatre. One by one the group passes him.

Oskar van Vuuren looks up to Wanjala and raises his eyebrows. Just then, Wanjala pulls a pistol out from his back and shoots Henry right in the leg. The sound of the gunshot rings out and Anne screams.

"AHHHHH!!" cries Henry, falling over and clutching his leg tightly. David and the others are rattled to their core.

"Henry!" Avery shouts, running to his aid. Henry lies there, panting heavily in pain.

"So," Van Vuuren says. He pulls out a flask and, casually, takes a sip of its contents. "This is what my men and I see. Some people. *You* people … have the audacity to come in through here. I guarantee that your travel agent, or whoever the fuck, told you not to come. Yet you did anyway. You hired a local to be your guide. Somehow he's dead. And you think you can just pass through our river and leave your shit here like nothing ever happened. Like little kids expecting mommy to clean up after you. You people must all be American. So typically American... no respect. Well... you spoiled, disrespectful Americans are going to see exactly what happens when you pass through our river. It's time to pony up!"

David feels the adrenaline pumping through his veins. He knows Henry will survive the gunshot wound to his leg, as long as they can get by without further molestation. But Van Vuuren's next words leave him terrified.

"So, here's what's gonna happen. Your boat belongs to us now. So does your stuff. All of it. If you try to hide any of your stuff, my men and I kill you like dogs. And…" Van Vuuren looks at Molly and Anne. David swears that he can see him *almost* lick his lips.

"Your lady friends here… they're staying with us."

Molly and Anne run to each other, holding on tightly to one another like scared siblings seeing a scary movie.

"We can barter with you!" pleads David.

"Fuck you!" shouts Van Vuuren.

David pleads, "We have money… we, we, we… we'll *get* money. We'll be getting a huge chunk of money from the network. We'll give you *everything* we have."

"Like hell you will!" shouts Beza.

"He's right. We swear, we'll give you everything we have!" cries Avery, still comforting a wounded Henry. Van Vuuren casually hands his AK-47 to Beza, who trains it on David to keep him and the other men at bay. Beza's brother, Babila, pulls out his machete and keeps it pointed at them as well. Wanjala keeps his pistol pointed directly at Henry, threatening to shoot again and again if they try anything.

Van Vuuren walks over to Avery and squats down right in front of him, "I know you will," he says matter of factly. He gets up and points at the small Congolese boy sitting in their boat. "You can ask little Deion here!" says Van Vuuren with a snarl, enjoying toying with their emotions. "Ask him what happens when people disrespect us and pass through our river!!"

Beza and Babila laugh like maniacal hyenas.

Van Vuuren continues, "But he won't tell ya, though. We beat it out of him. We got him trained." He looks down at the boy in their boat, who avoids making eye contact with him.

"We let him live... but we might not be so generous with you guys. *Unless* you do exactly as we say."

"Please!" cries Anne. "I have a family back home. I have a boyfriend, and I take care of my grandma when I'm not traveling." Her voice shakes with fear and hints of a sob ready to come up to the surface at any moment.

Molly, on the other hand, holds a gaze of sternness... almost, defiance... in her eyes.

"You should've thought about that before coming here, my dear," says Babila. He and his brother seem synchronized with each other, much more so than Wanjala and Oskar.

"LISTEN, tough guy," says Molly. Her gaze has never left Van Vuuren's.

Stunned by the boldness in her wording just as much as David, Henry, and Avery are, Van Vuuren slowly turns his head to listen to her. His fiery glance reads something to the effect of "You're lucky we haven't seen a woman in weeks, or I'd kill you right now."

"She and I aren't going *anywhere*. We'll give you guys whatever you want, but the five of us stay together. And once we've given you enough so that you feel like you have gotten your respect, then you will leave us alone. We will not be intimidated by you thugs."

Van Vuuren back hands her across the face.

David feels the adrenaline ready to pop from his veins. He thinks of his son back home. The nausea from his fear of what might happen next goes completely unnoticed by the adrenaline pumping through him. He knows, it's *now or never*.

The Kumba brothers look at each other, "She's got spunk," one of them says.

"That she does," says Van Vuuren. "We'll see how she feels tonight after we've shown her the ropes."

He motions for Wanjala to grab the women. Wanjala grabs Molly by the arm and yanks her towards them. *Now or never,* David thinks to himself.

He lunges toward Beza and grabs the AK-47, turning it skyward just in time to narrowly avoid being shot. Several rounds fire into the air in rapid, clattering succession, narrowly missing David's head. Despite being much lankier than David, Beza is impressively strong.

Babila moves to swing his machete at David and hack him to pieces, when Avery grabs a large rock and hurls it at him, hitting Babila directly in the temple of his head. Babila falls over, stunned by the rock, concussing him. Not being athletic in any way, Avery is surprised by his own luck in the throw.

Wanjala raises his pistol, but Molly turns on him just in time. Wrestling Wanjala by the arm, Molly almost immediately begins to be overpowered. A couple of shots get discharged, narrowly missing her and the others. Wanjala gets her into a choke hold and goes to shoot her in the temple just in time for Anne to smash him right in the center of his back with her FLIR camera from the boat. The two ladies tussle with Wanjala. Molly bites down *hard* on the arm that Wanjala is holding his pistol with and he lets out a yell. Bashing him over and over with the FLIR, Anne helps Molly to overwhelm him.

With Babila still knocked out, Avery neglects the opportunity to grab his machete but turns towards Oskar, who strangely has not made a move yet. Avery knows full well that Oskar van Vuuren, the husky man that he is, will certainly overpower him.

Just then, like a landmine that Van Vuuren hadn't noticed, Henry musters all his might and uses his good leg to kick Van Vuuren in the groin. Van Vuuren turns to curb-stomp Henry's head in, but a quick-thinking Avery saves his friend by grabbing the machete and brandishing it at Van Vuuren, swinging and posturing with it to get him to back off.

Van Vuuren looks around, calculating his next move, then looks back to their respective boats. He scoffs and jumps back onto his boat, fumbling with the engine as if attempting to get it started and drive it away.

Wanjala, still with the pistol in his hand, fires several shots one right after the other, emptying the magazine, trying but failing to shoot the two women. Three of his shots land directly into the gasoline-powered engine of the researchers' chartered boat, puncturing their motor three times at an unlucky angle.

David and Beza drop the Kalashnikov and begin going to town, kicking and throwing fists at each other until Beza manages to land a few good "knees" straight up into David's now-defeated and bleeding face. Beza grabs the AK-47, yanks back the charging handle on the right side of the weapon, and walks right up to David to finish him.

"No!" screams Molly.

She gets off of a now-subdued Wanjala, grabs Anne's FLIR from out of her hands, and chucks it at Beza... hitting him in the back of his neck. David sees his life flash before his eyes, his eyes wide, just before the FLIR comes out of nowhere to save him.

David shoots to his feet and charges Beza again.

By now, Babila is slowly beginning to come to.

David elbows Beza over and over again. The two fight with all their might to keep the barrel of the AK-47 pointed away from themselves and towards the other. Beza makes a move to flip open the bayonet at the barrel, but he cuts his hand in the process. Seizing the opportunity, David lunges forward and Beza trips on a rock behind him. The two go tumbling to the ground and their tussle resumes.

Like an angry stepfather trying over and over again to get the lawn-mower going, Van Vuuren finally gets his boat's engine started. The motor comes to life. Seeing his men in distress, and seeing that Avery is closing in on Beza to help a struggling David, Van Vuuren leaps out of the boat and charges at Avery, intercepting him while Henry watches it all helplessly... the bullet wound in his leg preventing him from even standing on his own. Van Vuuren grabs Avery by the shirt and rag dolls him into the dirt. Van Vuuren kicks Avery right in the stomach while he's down, and then bends down to grab him. Yanking him back up, Van Vuuren shoves him into the dirt, then again against a nearby tree, then again, and again.

Molly and Anne are unable to assist, as they must contend with Wanjala, who regained a bit of control when Molly had gotten distracted and saved David.

Babila squints his eyes and, holding his temple, tries to stumble to his hands and knees and reorient himself.

Using all of his strength, Beza pushes with all his might until the barrel of the Kalashnikov is hovering right by David's ear, but he fails to pull the trigger. David feels a drip of sweat trickle down into his eye, and he grunts. Clenching his teeth and giving it everything he has left after two full days of hiking through the jungle, David pushes the AK-47 barrel back towards Beza, slowly, inch-by-inch until it's right beneath his jawline. Squeezing the trigger, a five-round burst lets loose, spraying bits of Beza's brain into the air.

"NOOOOOOO!!" wails Babila, watching in horror and then bursting into tears.

Everybody in both groups gets a glimpse.

Beza's body immediately goes limp and slumps over. David takes the AK-47 and swings it up, pointing it directly at Van Vuuren and Wanjala, before either of them can cause any more injury to Avery, Molly, or Anne.

"I'M GONNA KILL YOU!!" shouts Babila, who gets up to sprint towards David. David points the rifle right at his face, keeping him at bay. Babila looks like he might erupt right then and there. Realizing that there's nothing he can do, Babila halts in his tracks and then looks at Beza's body. Van Vuuren and Wanjala usher him away by the arms.

"Brother! BROTHER!!" Babila cries in vain. He clutches the back of his head with his hands, elbows in the air on either side; his bottom lip trembling as it forms an upside-down U shape.

"Beza … Beza …" he cries, as the two other pirates pull him away.

Wanjala manages to get his pistol back, but it's either out of ammo or he's smart enough not to challenge an automatic assault rifle with a semi-automatic pistol. In the chaos, Avery loses Babila's bushwhacking machete.

Paying no attention to the gas leak on the researchers' boat caused by the stray bullets, both groups are taken by complete surprise when a large explosion engulfs the Americans' boat in flames, destroying it.

"GO! Go now! Leave us alone and GO!" shouts David, realizing that he is the only one now wielding an assault rifle. Not thinking straight, David keeps the rifle trained on the stunned pirates as they board their boat, the *only* boat left, and motor away from the scene with haste. Van Vuuren turns back and gives David a venomous look … the savage-looking anger on his face causing his underbite to jut out slightly as he bares his teeth.

Huffing and puffing in a daze after what has just unfolded, David slumps to the ground with one hand touching the muddy shore while the other clutches the AK. The taste of his own blood in his mouth prompts him to wipe it away. The group, rattled, tries to compose themselves and tend to Henry's leg injury.

"We're fucked," says Avery, feeling the abdominal pain from getting kicked in the stomach. "We... are so... so... fucked."

Anne begins to cry, both from the realization of their circumstance and also from relief that she and Molly weren't taken.

"We're stuck out here," winces Henry, trying to ignore his leg. "We're stranded out here for real now."

"It could be worse," says Molly.

"HOW?" barks Henry.

"We could've been killed. Her and I too, maybe, once they got bored with us." she says.

Thoughts suddenly race through Anne's head of what her and Molly's fate could've been. *What if they raped us over and over again and then still didn't let us go? What if they sold us into human trafficking or something?* Her mind spirals down a rabbit hole of what-if's.

"Guys!" says David. "You heard what he said. His 'second in command not being here?' They could very well come back for us. They could come back with more guns... with more of *them*! We need to move, *now*!"

The group hastily moves to get Henry to his feet and to get moving. Avery and Molly help him along, one under each arm. Suddenly the group hears a loud rustling in the bushes next to them near the shore ... David swings the rifle and points it directly at the source of the noise.

"Holy shit," says David, lowering his weapon. "It's the kid. It's the little kid!"

Quiet as a mouse, the Congolese boy from the pirates' boat hides in the bushes with a bag full of stuff.

"He must've gotten off their boat during the scuffle. Grabbed some belongings, too." continues David.

"What's in the bag do you think, lotto scratchers?" says Avery. The kid looks eager, but is visibly scared. He hides in the bush like a stray animal that is both desperate for help but also afraid of humans. David kneels nearby.

"What's your name, young man?" The child does not respond.

"What if he rats us out or something, man?" says Henry.

"You can't be serious!" says David. "Look at him. He's no friend of theirs. Don't you remember what that asshole said? 'Ask the boy what happens ... we let him live ...' yada, yada."

Molly kneels down beside David, near the child. "Did they hurt you, young one?" Again, he does not respond.

"Come on, young man, you can stick with us for a bit," says David, summoning him.

"Deion," croaks the boy, timidly, uttering the first word that they've heard from him yet. He says, cautiously, "My name is Deion. But, my friends called me Dee."

The group is surprised by how well he speaks English. Anne looks around rather frantically, "You said it yourselves. We need to go! Now! Come on!" she demands.

The kid springs forward and urgently taps David on the arm as he and the group start to leave. David stops, as do the others, albeit in frustration.

Dee motions to the bag that he must've stolen from the boat during the fiasco. He opens it and shows David something. He peers inside and sees what may be the group's first and only stroke of good luck yet: A satellite phone.

6

"IT'S A SAT PHONE!" SAYS A REINVIGORATED DAVID. THE BAT-tered group seems to regain a substantial amount of energy at hearing these words. His eyes widen and he takes the phone out of the bag. He fumbles with it.

"Dang, little man. You may be our little superhero!" says Molly. Her words elicit an ever-so-slight perk up on the boy's face, albeit not quite a smile.

"Somebody get that GPS up and running, I found some batteries. I'm making the call right now. I'll need our coordinates," says David.

"No! Not here. Again, we need to put some distance between us and here in case they come back!" says Anne. The others look at her and agree. They urgently begin heading into the jungle, paying no mind to which direction they're going other than that they need to get away from the river for the time being. David fumbles with the satellite phone but notices little Deion lagging behind.

"Hey kid," says Henry, wincing as he looks back, "If you're sticking with us, it's now or never!"

David uses the strap on the Kalashnikov to swing it onto his back. He kneels down to the boy, thinking that they can easily catch up to the others on account of Henry's leg slowing them down. Behind him, Henry limps off with Avery and Molly on each side of him acting as crutches.

"Come on, bud. It's okay, I promise. We need to go. You can stick with us for a bit--" David says out loud. His sentence trails off into the rest which he just thinks quietly to himself: *Until we figure out what we're doing with you.*

David feels bad for this mysterious child, but feels he does not have the energy or bandwidth to worry about yet another problem. Though he would never tell the boy this. Dee begins walking, never fully walking alongside the adults but rather choosing to remain behind them. Every so often, David or another member of the group looks back to make sure that he is still with them. Without fail he is, making almost no noise and never missing a beat.

How or why the person at the network in charge of planning their expedition neglected to send them with a satellite phone is something that Henry repeatedly insists that "they'll be hearing from me about!" over and over again.

"Hey," Henry continues. His rambling almost begins to seem like a purposeful distraction from the pain in his leg. "Maybe a different network needs a camera guy, ya know? I've seen enough action for three lifetimes. Maybe the Cooking Channel will take me. Or, shit, even Gordan Ramsay!" The group comes across a particularly thick set of vines, and Henry needs extra help maneuvering through them. He winces loudly with each movement at varying intensities, depending on how much he needs to move his wounded leg.

David feels something caress his face: a light strand of web. He shoos it away like a bug and continues on.

Henry takes a breath and continues, "Hey, maybe this whole mess *is* on that bozo. Paul, my leg, all of it. You'd think, if a couple of random

African river pirates from the middle of nowhere would think to have a sat phone, then the salaried guy or gal at Curiosity would have the sense to—"

"Nothing stopped any of us from bringing one ourselves," David interjects somberly, ever-so-slightly irritated. He pauses, taking a deep breath and wiping the sweat off his face, placing his hands on his waist for a moment before continuing,

"We were stupid. And there's only so much we can blame on others. We're here and what's done is done. It's a waste of energy."

Henry is floored by David's words, but he ceases talking for the time being.

For the first time since the prior incident, it dawns on David that he just murdered another human being. His posture slowly worsens... his chin down and his shoulders forward. Feelings of guilt rise up in him, though he keeps reminding himself that it was in self-defense. *If I can't tell Alex that his mom left, how can I ever possibly tell him that I've killed somebody? Will I end up taking it to my grave?* Repeatedly, David tries to convince himself that he did the right thing.

Just then Molly starts jumping and flopping around like a nervous, frantic energizer bunny. She swipes at herself and at her surroundings. A long strand of thick spider web from a nearby tree clings to her hand despite her violently trying to shake it off.

"A web! A web! A fucking web!" she says.

"You're good, you're good," says David. "I don't see anything on or near you."

"God, I hate spiders," Molly continues as she tries to calm herself down. "Fuck! You're not the only one who hates spiders, Anne. That's why I chose to study fucking dolphins!"

Anne chuckles, "Just make sure it's not … like that other one?"

"Don't remind me! Ugly little bastard. But please check me!" says Molly, twirling a bit to let the group examine her.

"You're good," David says as the others decide to "check" themselves and their surroundings as well. David motions to check Dee, but he flinches with timidity, opting to stay at least five or ten feet away.

Further along, Anne pauses the group and helps lower Henry to sit down, insisting on creating a makeshift bandage for his leg. Anne agrees to let Molly take a turn helping to support Henry on his left side for a while. Avery, on the other hand, declines David's offer to take his place.

Henry winces and looks up at Avery while Anne tightens the bandage, "You've always been a stubborn one, kid."

"You know it," says Avery. "Just *your* sorry ass had to be the one that we gotta babysit."

"You know I like to be pampered," says Henry with a grin.

Avery snickers, "Age before beauty!"

Henry gives him a look, "Ay, you keep it up. Soon as my leg heals I'll kick your ass."

"In that case I'll just drop your ass while we're helpin' you along," Avery retorts.

Molly interjects into their banter, "You two are adorable; now let's go. I say just a little farther and then we pull up that phone and get the fuck outta here."

They help him back up. Henry looks to David, who struggles to push more vegetation out of their way.

"Maybe use the bayonet on that thing to whack your way through," suggests Henry.

"Maybe he don't wanna blow his hand off, dude. Geesh," says Avery.

"Shh!" says David, holding up his hand. A long silence befalls the group, and the jungle seems to go quiet.

Finally, Molly whispers, "What is it?"

"I... I swear I could hear this... I don't hear it anymore, but..." David looks back at them, confused. He hesitates and then continues, "I thought I heard some kind of a... hissing sound."

"I hear nothing," says Henry.

"Maybe I'm just losing it. Let's go."

After some time, the group plops down to take a break. The blazing sun peers through the thick canopy in random, scattered patches of light. The heat and humidity are so thick that, in these spots of light, it looks as if there's steam.

David moves to examine the satellite phone, but feels his stomach gurgling. He reaches into his pack and pulls out one of the very last protein bars that he has left. He opens it and goes to take a bite, but a gut feeling stops him. He looks over at Dee and sees the look on his face. His wide eyes remain locked on the protein bar. David promptly hands it to the malnourished boy who seems to devour it within thirty seconds. He looks in his pack and hands Dee another one, wanting to give him the rest but also trying to keep in mind what they may need as time goes on.

While Molly and Avery pause to rest along a trail, Anne tries to talk to Dee. The battered researchers feel an uneasy sense of relief coming back, knowing that they've put substantial distance between them and the prying eyes of Van Vuuren and his men.

David fumbles with the satellite phone, unable to turn it on. He sulks quietly to himself, but little by little his anger begins to show. He worries that they may have trekked into the jungle for no other reason other than to get away from rogue humans. "Come on, goddammit!" he says under his breath. He resorts to holding it above his head and pounding on it. Finally, it powers on.

"Guys, this thing's in business! Took me forever to get it going so the battery must be almost spent. Might only have a couple minutes or so talk time."

"Make the call now!" demands Avery.

David, already ahead of him, pulls up the extension to the US Embassy in Cameroon. The group springs into action. Powering up the GPS, Molly and Anne gather around David. Henry, even though he has no service on his regular smartphone, also pulls up the phone number to reach the US Embassy in Yaoundé, which he has saved to his phone. David hits dial.

Henry holds his hand, balled up into a fist, at his mouth, "Please dear God, please dear God, please dear God! Please dear-"

"Hello?" somebody finally answers after an unnerving amount of rings.

David and the others near him regurgitate everything as fast as they can talk: relaying their exact coordinates, Paul, the bite, the pirates, the fight, the gunshot wound, their satellite phone that could die at any moment, everything.

The operator makes sounds as if she's scribbling down notes. Finally, after a short reprimand for crossing into the Congo, she tells them what they're all dying to hear: "Help is on the way."

The group thanks her profusely and then ends the call, cognizant of their battery and overjoyed that the phone made it through to the end of the call. David moves to power down the sat phone.

"Well done, you guys. I think we're over the hump," says David with an exhale.

"*You* well done!" says Anne. "Thank you for what you did back at the river."

"It…" says David, wishing she hadn't brought it up and feeling like anything but a hero. "It was nothing."

"We're not out of the jungle just yet," says Henry. "I don't know about you guys but I am so goddamn thirsty I'm about to start slicing vines to see if they have fluids."

Henry points over to young Deion, and David realizes they all haven't had nearly enough water. Though he didn't bring it up, he started feeling painfully thirsty long ago, followed by dizziness and lightheadedness, not to mention tiredness. Henry continues, "Dee, right? I don't think Dee has had any water." He looks at him and they notice that he seems to be staying closer and closer.

"Are you thirsty, little dude?" asks Henry. Dee nods his head.

"Come on. I think I spotted a creek a little ways this way," says David.

Trekking over a hill along the game trail, sure enough, the group comes across a large body of water ... a pond. The open area surrounding the pond offers some but little relief from the extremely thick, suffocating jungle. Despite this, huge trees have grown massive branches that extend out over the pond, providing some shade. Vegetation grows straight up out of the pond reminiscent of bamboo shoots. The area is infested with gnats, water striders, and other tiny insects, including a few dragonflies.

Anne sticks her hand in the murky water and waves it back and forth to get rid of any unwanted debris and water striders, then shows Dee how to use the Lifestraw. The boy gulps his fair share and then one by one, the adults take turns.

David gags on the awful taste of the water, wishing to a god he doesn't believe in that they had gotten some more of their water jugs off of their boat before it exploded. He feels the urge to throw up but forces himself to hold it down. *At least it's safe now to drink. At least we have water at all.* The only one who seems unbothered by the taste of the water is Dee. This gives David pause. He watches Dee and wonders if anybody else in their group realizes just *how* much they take living in a "first world" country for granted.

"So how's our 'help' getting here?" asks Avery.

"She didn't say," says Molly.

David chimes in, "Well, I say we watch each other's backs and stay put. All we can do now is wai—"

A loud and sudden *SPLASH* in the water right next to them interrupts him and sends them all to their feet. They look around frantically, then down at the shallow pond water at the object that seems to have come from out of nowhere to scare the shit out of them.

"Jesus *Christ!*" one of them shouts.

"Can't catch a *damn* break!" says Henry.

They take another look at the object as the water mellows out. Their eyebrows draw inwards as their faces shift from startled to confused. Avery looks at the others and then cautiously reaches down to pull it out of the water.

The object is a large steel toe boot, belonging to none of the members of the group. A flabbergasted Avery turns the foul-smelling boot right-side up, revealing a large hole where the steel-protected toes sit. David reaches out and Avery hands it to him. He notices some strange material on the boot that he can only describe as wet, white, and stringy.

Raising the boot skyward to hold it above his head, a beam of sunlight shines right through the inch-or-so thick double hole that runs through it, indicating that whatever it was that pierced the steel toe part traveled clean downwards to pierce the sole as well, leaving a second, slightly smaller hole on the bottom.

"What... the... fuck?" says David quietly. The group looks up slowly, almost in sync, to the tree branches above them from where the boot fell.

What they see above them gives them shivers.

Enormous amounts of thick, intricate web sit right above them over the edge of the pond that they hadn't noticed until now. Molly slowly points up at the webbing with her index finger,

"That... was holding... this?"

"Can we maybe leave the pond now?" Anne asks, monotonously, like a frightened child.

They quickly vacate the area, heading back in the general direction of where they made their precious S-O-S call. Henry sees Avery examining the boot again. Avery's eyes squint as if he's found something.

"What is it?" asks Henry.

"Something's written here on the inside of the tongue."

"What is it?" presses Henry.

"Looks like a name," says Avery. "'N. Boku.'"

Anne feels her anxiety rising again, like she's going to have a panic attack, "I don't like this, you guys." Her breathing and heart rate begins to accelerate, "I don't like this one bit."

"It's going to start getting dark in a few hours, we need to find a place to hunker down and wait for our rescue. Why we didn't demand a timeline from her I don't know," says David.

"Preferably away from giant scary webs," says Henry, visibly afraid.

"I concur," says Molly, "I already couldn't get the image of Paul's venom-ridden body out of my head. The way he looked, when I... discovered him."

Molly feels the guilt once again and fights her emotions, then adds, "But then we just *had* to see that."

Not even fifteen minutes of walking back towards where they made the call, they pass through a slightly shaded area and lose sight of young Deion. He isn't behind them like he usually is. Nor is he next to them.

"Dee?" says David, looking around. A rush of worry suddenly surges through his body. "Dee? Deion!" he shouts.

"Where are you, kid?" shouts Henry at the same time.

"Guys!" Molly says, pointing to their left.

In a small opening between the trees, Dee stands looking up at something that draws his attention with a look of fear on his face not seen since David glimpsed how Dee looked at Oskar van Vuuren. It's as if he doesn't even hear their calls. The group hustles over to where he's standing.

"Dee! Don't stray too far—" says David, trailing off as a petrified look envelops his face as well. Dee turns and runs right up to David, holding him by the waist. David awkwardly comforts the boy with his left hand, rubbing his back. Using his right hand, he furiously rubs his eyes, as if what he's seeing may be an illusion. Except everybody in the group sees it, starting with Dee and ending with Avery, helping Henry limp his way over.

David's heartbeat accelerates. He suddenly feels a surge of adrenaline fall over him not unlike the one right before the encounter with the pirates.

In the thick labyrinth of spider web in front of them in the tree, running from the base of the tree up to the canopy lies the cocooned, mangled, and completely *drained* body of none other than the owner of the missing steel toed boot.

He has several sets of double-puncture wounds that are visible even under thick layers of webbing that encase his body like a mummified Egyptian artifact. The look on the face of the individual is a look of horror. His mouth sits wide open and his eyes have been seemingly hallowed out. Nothing remains of him except an empty shell of skin and bone.

His shriveled, colorless, dark gray body is so decayed that David can't tell for sure whether the victim was male or female, though the large frame indicates to him, most likely, male. His clothing is rotten and disheveled, but the opposite boot—matching the one from the web at the pond—remains on one of his feet.

The group, mortified and utterly speechless, looks around and above them. While there is webbing in the canopy as well, the majority of it sits closer to the ground or in between trees, resembling nets. Only now does the group realize that there are other, non-human victims cocooned in the vicinity as well: other large native game of varying sizes, including what appear to be some antelope and baboons. The sheer size and girth of the web is stunning enough to the group without having discovered a *full grown human man* wrapped up in it.

Anne feels sweat run down her head as she feels like she might spontaneously and involuntarily faint right then and there.

Henry forgets entirely, for a moment, the pain in his leg... and feels the sensation of phantom itches "crawling" all over his body. He's not the only one who feels the urge to squirm.

Avery, shocked beyond belief, croaks meekly, "I knew we shoulda' went to Canada instead."

7

THE GROUP WASTES NO TIME IN PUTTING DISTANCE BETWEEN themselves and the labyrinth of cocooned victims. They move through the thickets of vegetation, hearts racing, anxiety levels through the roof.

"We need to get out of here, now!" cries Avery. "Please, please, please, right now!"

"And go where?" says Molly. "We already put out our coordinates!"

David holds young Deion tightly by the hand, not wanting to let him stray from the group again after what they just found.

"Have you ever seen or heard of anything like that before?" says David with a shakiness in his voice. With his right hand he holds the AK-47 under the magazine, while holding an eager Dee's hand with his left. All timidity about staying within arm's reach of the group seems to have left Dee by now.

"I heard of a giant 'swarm' type web in Texas a few years back that covered multiple clusters of trees. Might've even been a few acres. But ..." Anne says. "But I've *never* heard of a person being preyed on like that." Anne's face turns pale.

Henry winces along with each rapid and labored footstep, moving faster than he has since before getting shot in the leg. Avery and Molly do their best to support him by the arm, under his shoulder. However, any consideration for the effectiveness of Anne's bandage staying on is eclipsed by their desire to flee the area.

Henry lets out a moan of pain and chimes in, "That... bastard... must've been at least 180 pounds. How many of them must it have taken to... ?" he says, gasping for air. "We are in way over our heads here!"

"Now tell us something we don't know," says David.

Henry looks at him and then the others as if seeking validation, then it occurs to him. "We get the fuck away from here and then we call the embassy again to give them different coordinates!" Henry looks around frantically, "We have to! Otherwise we're gonna end up like Paul!"

"Shut up, shut up, shut up!" cries Anne, covering her ears and trying to hold down a full blown anxiety attack. Molly moves to comfort her.

"I'm with Henry," says Avery.

"There's only one problem!" says David. "We very well might not be able to get the sat phone on again. After how long it took the battery to do its thing the last fuckin' time, I think it's a miracle we were able to make that call! Besides, if we stray too far from this area we risk missing our rescue altogether!"

Dee looks up at David and his face turns sour. Before they know it, the boy is crying. David and the others notice, and David immediately forces himself to put the composed facade back up.

"Hey, hey. Hey now," says David, kneeling down so that he is at eye-level with Dee. He sets the Kalashnikov down with care to make sure that the barrel stays pointed away from any of them. He gently places his hands on Dee's shoulders.

"We're going to figure this out, okay? And we're going to make sure we all get out of here, safely, okay? That includes you, little man." David gently uses his index finger to raise up Dee's chin so that his eyes look into David's.

"I promise. You will be okay," he assures Dee.

"Nobody … Nobody has ever made a promise to me that they kept," Dee says back to him with a sniffle. "Not since my parents."

David feels his heart break a little at these words. He looks up to the group and they peer at him and the boy. Molly nods slightly. David looks back to Dee and says the only thing that comes to mind, "Well, hey, there's a first time for everything." Dee seems to be comforted by these words.

David picks up the rifle and the group urgently moves on with Dee close in hand.

Power walking through the jungle, Anne says, "We have to try to contact them again. We have to try."

"Do you think they'd think we were pulling a prank or something if we told them about the cocooned man? They'd think we were nuts." replies Henry in a non-argumentative tone.

"No, we definitely don't tell them. We make up something else. Anything else," she retorts.

"Why didn't any of us think to take pictures?" says David.

"Camera's busted," Henry says.

"We still got our phones, dingus," Avery says to Henry.

Henry exclaims, "Do *you* wanna go back there to snap a few?"

"It won't matter with the service out here anyhow. Unless you plan on airdropping them to the embassy in Yaoundé," Molly says sarcastically. She continues, "Either way, help is on the way, guys."

The group comes through a slight clearing in the foliage and comes across yet another game trail, far from the view of any ominous spider webs. She looks around them and then proceeds, "If we stray too far though

… David's right. We risk missing them altogether if we stray too far from those coordinates."

"Give me the phone," says Anne. "I'll do it. I'll get it back on and make the call."

David reaches into his pack and pulls it out. He does a double take to make sure that they're in the clear away from any webbing, and then looks to Anne, "It's all yours. Doesn't hurt to try. Here, get it going and then give them new coordinates."

"I'll get the GPS back up," says Molly. David leans over to give Anne the satellite phone, when a deafening *BANG* comes out of the jungle and a bullet slams right into the sat phone, shattering it into pieces as it flies out of David's hand.

Narrowly missing Dr. Hale, Babila Kumba immediately yanks back the bolt-action mechanism to chamber the next round in his scoped Legend Heavy Sporter .458 Lott. The enraged pirate reveals his position after what must've been hours upon hours of secretly following them through the jungle, hell bent on avenging his brother's death.

The group springs to life. Running as fast as they can along the game trail, they hear another shot ring out from Babila's high-powered hunting rifle. Feeling his own pulse in his head pounding, David feels the literal wind of the massive bullet streaking past his head, narrowly missing him again by mere inches.

With Babila closing in behind them, David yanks Dee by the arm to shield him from getting hit in the back. The group flees, a pack of helpless prey being hunted by a vengeful predator. They bob and weave, and David suddenly overhears the desperately fleeing Henry, hopelessly trying to contend with his injured leg, while Avery and Molly desperately help him along to keep up.

Babila, with a bandage on his head from getting hit by the rock, surveys the fleeing group and makes a decision. He takes the crosshairs of his rifle off of zig-zagging David and points his weapon at the most helpless member of the group: Henry. Babila smiles maniacally as he pulls the trigger, blowing a massive hole right through Henry's back and out the front of his chest as he gurgles his very last, inaudible, word.

"Henry!" cries Avery.

Molly, knowing full well there's nothing they can do about Henry, yanks Avery off of him.

"No, No I have to... help! No!" screams Avery.

"He's gone, now move your ass!" shouts Molly, yanking Avery away with all her might. Babila shouts, proudly, "I'm gonna kill you all! Agghhhh! I'm gonna skin you alive, Hale! I'm gonna skin you alive... for Beza!" He follows the group in hot pursuit, cognizant of the fact that he only has one bullet left. He bellows out, "And you too, boy! You're dead, you little traitor! Oskar sends his regards!"

Dee screams upon hearing the words.

The group comes upon a clearing with their hunter in hot pursuit. David looks to Molly, Anne, and Avery and pushes Dee in their direction,

"Watch him, dammit!" he shouts. They take the boy and David spins around, yanking his AK-47 up. He lets loose with it, firing a burst of automatic rounds in quick succession towards Babila. Babila dives behind a tree, unharmed. David looks to the others, "GO!" he shouts. They do as told and continue to flee.

"Hey, you son of a bitch! I'm right here!" yells David to Babila, waving his hand to get his attention onto him and away from the other four. Not thinking straight, David sees a slight movement in the tree next to where Babila hides, and lets loose again; firing the AK-47 until the assault rifle clicks out of ammo.

"Fuck," David says to himself, turning tail and heading directly into the jungle, opting to carry the expended Kalashnikov with him. Babila hears this and dives back out from behind the shot up tree, centers his crosshair directly on the back of David's fleeing head, and squeezes the trigger.

David feels the powerful wind of the bullet again pass directly over his head as he drops to the ground, instinctually, barely missing having his head blown off by a round that's designed to bring down elephants. David pays no attention to the scrapes and minor cuts from "dolphin-diving" into a prone position on the ground.

Babila thinks for a moment that he's gotten him, grins, and then sees David get back up, running again deeper into the jungle. David hears Babila let out an almost inhuman-sounding yell of frustration.

Babila yanks out his bushwhacking machete and drops the ammo-expended rifle, chasing after his brother's killer in hot pursuit. With the heat over 100 degrees and with a humidity level in the mid-high 90s, David begins to huff and puff and *gasp* for air as he runs through the jungle, desperately pushing vines and branches out of his way as he goes. Babila begins to do the same, jumping over rocks and following David, his anger fueling his body.

The sounds of the jungle go unnoticed as the sounds of the two of them gasping for air drown out chirps, shrills, and hisses. David loses his footing and trips momentarily. Getting back up immediately, he springs forward. Babila closes in, careful not to trip on whatever object his prey just tripped over. Babila gains ground. David turns tail, realizing they must be hundreds of yards now away from the others, and hurls himself over an overturned tree trunk. Babila follows him, his will to kill David matching David's will to survive this and get home to Alex.

Finally, David comes up against a thicket that's too impenetrable for him to pass through. He looks back at his pursuer. Babila takes a breath and lunges forward. Not thinking to flip open the bayonet on the AK, David decides to pivot and runs the other way back to the game trail just in time to miss another lunge of Babila's machete which severs a vine right where David had briefly stood.

Feeling like his heart might beat right out of his chest, David runs with all his might. He is slowed ever-so-slightly by the guilt that crosses his mind. Perhaps he could've done more to prevent Henry's death. Shoving the thought down, he continues. Babila follows him through the jungle, desperately wanting blood.

The two finally come across the clearing, and David locks eyes with the others. Hating himself for a split second for accidentally leading Babila right back to them, he wastes no time in joining them to get away. Babila lets out another frustrated yell, and Molly grabs David by the arm and shouts to the group, "Move it!"

Pursuing them around a bend along the trail, Babila—no longer cognizant of his surroundings—runs right through a single strand of web running along the game trail, connected from a large overgrown tree to the other side of the path. He is now a mere inches away from slicing at one of them with his machete.

A massive, brown, tarantula-looking spider the size of a *grown man* springs out of the brush and pounces on Babila... pinning him down with its massive bristly-haired legs and body, and driving its nine-inch banana-sized fangs right into his stomach like warm butter. Babila shrieks in pain and horror. A spurt of blood erupts like a volcano from his mouth.

The group of five, shocked, take in the sight for a second with eyes and mouths as wide as a full moon, and then run.

Anne Matthews screams so loudly that birds fly away from the nearby canopy.

8

OUT OF THE CORNER OF DAVID'S EYE, HE CAN SEE BABILA DESperately reaching for his fallen machete. Blood spurts out of his mouth as he makes sounds that can be translated into any language: agonizing pain.

Reaching above his head as far as he physically can while pinned down on his back, Babila secures his machete using his middle and index finger and pulls it closer. He desperately begins hacking at the giant spider on top of him.

Chop!

Keeping Dee in front of them at all times, David and Molly and Anne push him along to keep him running... taxing the malnourished child to his physical limits. Avery barely manages to keep up.

Chop!

"Arrggghhhh!!"

They can hear Babila screaming in agony behind them.

CHOP!

One last look over her shoulder before losing sight of Babila - and the man-sized arachnid that ambushed him - and Molly gets a glimpse of Babila hacking off one of its front legs.

"Don't stop! Move!" yells David.

The group runs... and runs... and runs. They sprint back into the thick jungle away from the game trail. Pushing aside lush vegetation and remaining ever-vigilant of any spider webs, the group finally comes out into a clearing on a hillside where they keel over from the exhaustion of so much running.

Molly puts her head between her legs and begins huffing and puffing.

Anne heaves, and then throws up the bile of her empty stomach and begins crying. She uses her own clothing to wipe away snot.

Dee, surprisingly composed, makes his way towards Anne and puts his hand on her back to comfort her. His touch sends a jolt of fear through her body, which startles Dee. David can tell Dee immediately second-guesses his decision to try to comfort her. But in the split second that it takes Anne to turn around to see who it is, she melts into the young boy's arms and the two hold each other while she cries. David looks up at Avery, who's been trembling since Henry was killed.

"Avery," David motions to him.

Avery avoids his touch and begins trembling over his own words, "We. We. We, we, we, we were supposed to hit up my cousin's wedding together. Me an' Henry. You know that? He was ... He was supposed to be my plus one. Can you imagine that?" Avery's eyes well up with tears and his face turns sour. "Fuck. Fuck me, fuck this place," he says, still trembling.

"I am so sorry, Avery," whispers David, drained and feeling defeated. Avery's trembling sadness descends into full blown panic as the words pour out of his mouth, moving a mile per second.

"How, how, how is this possible? We're so screwed, man. We are so fucked. That thing. Did you see the fangs on that motherfucker? We're so fucking dead; we're dead; we're gonna die out here. Together. Us five. We're gon' die out here, and then, and then, nobody's gonna find us, and then—!"

"Avery," Molly finally interrupts him, motioning to Dee who is becoming visibly afraid again. However, Avery does not stop rambling. About Henry. About the giant spider. About almost getting shot himself. About everything. His words become unintelligible as they pick up speed. While Avery rambles, the rest of the group remains speechless.

"How, how…" Avery says, "That thing back there. It's literally impossible, right? Right?" Come on, you guys are the experts. Tell us something! We're gonna die out here! All of us, yeah! We gon' die! Us, the child, and—"

"Avery!" asserts Anne, shutting him up. Now it is her turn to comfort Dee.

"What… was that thing back there?" Molly asks nobody in particular, speaking slowly and monotonously from the physical exhaustion.

"A f—," David rubs his eyes and face, not entirely sure that what he's seen isn't just a bad dream or a bad drug trip from something he doesn't remember using. "A freak of nature," he says. "Spiders can't physically get that big, it's impossible. It is literally, *physically,* impossible."

"Apparently not!" shrieks Avery.

"I only specialize in cetaceans," says Molly. "But from what little I know about spiders, and other invertebrates, they're not supposed to be able to get that big because there's not as much oxygen in the atmosphere today as there was during the Carboniferous Period 300 million years ago."

Molly looks up at the others with wide eyes and an open mouth, questioning her own words as she speaks, "Spiders, in particular… nobody has ever been able to produce proof of a spider bigger than a dinner plate. Like you said, David, it *should* be physically impossible."

"I remember hearing about this thing called a Coelacanth," says Anne. "A super rare fish that they thought was extinct for millions of years.

Until one day it just showed up! Off the coast of South Africa or something like that. Maybe this is like that."

"This... this is a way, *way* bigger discovery," says Avery, possessing little scientific knowledge but stating what they're all thinking.

"So is this, what, another Coelacanth?" Avery asks.

"I don't think so," says David. They all look at him.

He continues, "I'm no paleontologist but I know for sure we've never seen anything like this in the fossil record. There were giant sea scorpions about 400 million years ago during the Silurian Period, but nothing like this." He pauses, and looks back up at them and continues, "I think we're dealing with an entirely new species all together," he says with a haunted-ness in his tone.

"First Paul, now this thing. How did we get 'lucky' enough to first discover a potentially new spider species that's *super* venomous," says Molly sarcastically. "Then come across a tarantula with a five fucking foot leg span?" She cannot believe her own words as she speaks them.

"This place. This jungle," says David. "Like Paul said, before we bamboozled him into taking us here—"

At this, Molly bows her head and swallows yet another wave of guilt.

"—because of the political instability here, few outsiders ever come through here. Few... people at all, even, maybe. This place is like Papua New Guinea in how remote it is. Shit, for all we know we could be the first people to ever set foot here. There are vast areas of this and every continent that are unexplored, especially in regions with tropical rainforests."

"I don't subscribe to pseudo-science," says Molly sternly, as if protecting her reputation before proceeding. "But... I've heard, when I was a kid, stories of big game hunters in colonial-era Africa talking about mysterious creatures that they came across. Same thing in North America, Asia, virtually every continent. And how a lot would keep it to themselves for fear of being called a nut job."

"Yeah, yeah. Fuck, man. If that fuckin' thing's real, then what the fuck else might be real?" yelps Avery with a crack in his voice,

"Sasquatch? Fuckin'... Loch Ness? How 'bout that Mexican bloodsucker thing? Who the fuck knows at this point? I certainly don't!" he says, getting more and more animated in his words. "How 'bout the characters from 'Monsters, Inc.', huh? Who knows, ha! Who cares! Come on down and we'll feature you on 'Good Morning, America!' Or hell, the 'Steve Harvey Show', even!!"

Avery catches himself beginning to panic again and checks himself with a few long, deep breaths while he holds himself up with his hands on his knees. The group takes a long moment of silence.

Finally, "That thing back there is going to rewrite everything we know about zoology," says David.

"Yep, and, what are we gonna do about it?" Anne says. "We can't just sit here." She stands up tall and continues, "I don't want to scare Dee either—no offense, Avery—but we are stranded at these coordinates now in the middle of the jungle with no communication. No more lucky satellite phone. Nothing. Just a homicidal maniac and... yeah."

"'Least it pounced on the maniac," Avery says quietly to himself.

"I don't do spiders, okay, I don't fuck around with that. After this trip I'm sticking with cats and dogs. So I say we get our shit and get as far away from here as possible," says Anne.

"What?" says Molly. "Don't be crazy! We'll miss our rescue!"

"Fuck the rescue!" says Anne.

"What are we going to do? Just walk all the way to Yaoundé? That would take literally weeks! Maybe months! We'll be dead from malaria or worse!" exclaims Molly.

"I'm willing to take the chance!" argues Anne.

"Well, I'm not! We're not trained to live off the land," she retorts. David and Avery look at each other, both of them unsure of where they stand on the matter. Molly and Anne go to town.

"Maybe," smirks Anne. "Maybe if you hadn't said what you said to Paul, we wouldn't even be here!"

"YOU bitch!" Molly snarls. "You pressured him, too, and you know it!"

David and Avery get up, ready to break up their inevitable fight.

"*Stop it!*" says a child's voice. They all turn and look towards Dee. He is surprised by his own confidence. "My father said a boat divided will most certainly sink."

Molly and Anne take a beat, humbled. Molly immediately regrets calling her a bitch.

"He's absolutely right," says David. Avery kneels down to the boy and asks him point blank what *his* opinion is on what their next step should be.

Dee hesitates, and then finally says, "My family and I mostly lived off the river. My parents and siblings were... we used to fish... until..." Dee suddenly looks very sad.

He finally looks up at them and finishes his thoughts, "I don't know enough about living in the jungle. I think... I think we should wait for rescue to arrive."

"We need to find a place to hold out for the time being and watch each other's backs," says Molly. The group gets up to leave, having finally regained their composure, when off to their right they hear a loud *SNAP*.

The leaves and foliage stir, and the haunting figure of Babila Kumba— somehow still alive—stumbles out of the jungle like a zombie struggling to walk. Avery screams, as surprised by the sight as the rest of them.

Babila's body is in horrendous condition. A look of distorted rage flashes on his face when he sees David, and he makes a move like he's about to shout profanity at him, but instead a thick, viscous gooey substance pours out of his mouth with blood mixed in with its contents.

Dee whimpers like a frightened dog at the sight, and cowers behind David and Molly, who promptly cover his eyes so he can't see the horror in front of them. A foul stench suddenly hits their noses: the same putrid stench that David smelled when Paul had died.

Babila's symptoms are just like Paul's in every way... except much, *much* worse. Huge purple boils envelop his body like a medieval bubonic plague victim... like Paul's, only bigger. Some of them have already popped with pus. All over, his veins are bright purple and his eyes completely bloodshot, with no more white showing. Babila's stomach looks corroded away and split open, with exaggerated tissue disintegration far worse than that on Paul's left forearm. Next to the necrosis, the two-inch-thick puncture holes of the spider's fangs are still leaking blood profusely. He seems like he's "here" mentally but also "not here." In his hand, Babila clings to his machete with just two or three fingers barely holding on. The machete has a strange yellowish substance on it, indicating that he managed to fight the arachnid off.

David, Anne, Avery, and Molly watch in absolute terror. David's eyes are wide and he covers his mouth, while his other hand holds Dee behind him and makes good on himself mentally, swearing to not let Dee see any more than he already has.

Babila's eyes widen and he lets out an ungodly scream of excruciating pain as the venom ravages his body. David realizes the only thing that has driven this automaton to their location is his insatiable desire for revenge.

In a twisted way, at this moment, David does not feel anger towards the Congolese river pirate criminal, just sadness. David speculates Beza must have been this man's younger brother; perhaps whom he may have even helped raise, and that this man really, really, *really* loved his baby brother.

Babila lunges toward them and they promptly back up several steps away. Babila gives it his all but instead of lunging towards them, he face-plants into the dirt, too weak now to stand. Paying no mind to the dirt and plant matter in the ground rubbing up against his insides, Babila musters every ounce of willpower he has as begins to drag himself along by his arms, hands, and nails.

"YOU!" he shouts. "You... took... him... from... me!"

Each word is met with gurgling and slightly more liquid regurgitating from his mouth.

"YOU!... PAY!... YOU MUST... PAY!"

Babila reaches his hand up in the air towards David, desperately trying to get at him. His every cell fueled now only by his sheer hatred ... right down to his rabid-looking red eyes.

David swears that he can see Babila's arm swelling worse and worse by the *second* as he claws at the air at him. Just then, he begins violently twitching and seizing, as if having an extreme fit of epilepsy or Parkinson's shakes. His cries of anger turn into literal cries of agonizing pain as the venom ravages his body. He wails and swipes one more futile time towards David.

Reaching out with all the might he has left, Babila succumbs to the insidious effects of the spider venom and dies with his hand *still* reaching out, his eyes and rage *still* locked on David. After a few seconds, the pain vanishes as his lifeless body finally ceases moving.

We're in hell, David thinks to himself as the group urgently moves with their stuff to put distance between them and the deceased pirate, still not 100% sure if he killed the giant spider or just fended it off. *There has to be more of them out there,* David thinks to himself, much to his dismay.

It's getting dark out, so the group uses their flashlights to comb every square inch of the area as they proceed with caution. By now, *getting shot by pirates or poachers sounds waaaayyy better than dying the way that poor bastard did,* Molly thinks to herself, beginning to wonder if Anne was right earlier. As of now, watching out for strands of random webbing and avoiding spiders is the group's first and only priority.

Anne fights to compose herself, fighting down a full blown panic attack every couple of minutes—knowing full well that she will be going into debt to go to therapy when she makes it back—if only to get the image of Babila dying off of the perennial screen of her mind.

Avery gives David a break from holding Dee's hand, and the two walk side by side with the others. David leads the way, with the bayonet of his AK-47 pointed out and ready to be used at a second's notice. The darkness of night falls.

"We need to find a place now to build a fire," says Molly.

"Yes, we'll take turns in pairs staying awake like a night watch," adds David.

Molly speaks, "Don't you think we sh—"

She is interrupted by the ghostly sound of a grown woman *screaming*, coming from what sounds like the other side of the valley ...

"Wait, you all heard that, right?" says Avery, frantically.

They again hear *that* strange scream from the distance. It is unmistakably human ... but it's certainly not any of them ... nor any marauding pirates.

9

"OKAY, OKAY, I'VE GOT ANOTHER ONE," SAYS JIMMY LEUNG. "IF this doesn't get you then nothing will."

The other two look at him. "Boss," as her nickname goes, rolls her eyes in anticipation. A shit-eating grin forms on Jimmy's face, and he carries on.

"A woman walks out of the shower, winks at her boyfriend, and says 'Baby, I shaved down there. You know what that means, right?' He looks up at her and says, 'Yeah, it means I gotta call a plumber in the morning to clear the drain.'"

Patrick Wright busts out laughing, cackling, while Boss slowly shakes her head.

It's been a few days' ride on the river now since these three private military contractors were hired by the US Embassy to find and retrieve the distressed film crew from the Curiosity network. Jimmy Leung and "Boss"—as her buddies refer to her, or sometimes "Boss Lady"—both know each other from their time spent serving in the US Marine Corps. Patrick Wright served in the US Army Rangers. While she and Jimmy don't know him as well as they know each other, this isn't their first "op" in the region, and the three of them have gotten well-adjusted to completing various private military contractor jobs with each other.

Boss stretches her limbs and takes in the humid air, and then for the seemingly millionth time inspects her KRISS Vector submachine gun. At five feet, seven inches tall, with olive brown skin, chestnut hair, and almond brown eyes, she is beautiful, but fierce, a true force to be reckoned with. While she doesn't like to talk about her accomplishments overseas during her tours, the nickname "Boss" is one that she earned. Jimmy knows her actual name, but is well aware of how she earned her nickname, and gladly refers to her as such. Patrick falls in line. Although Patrick, like Jimmy, at first found her extremely attractive, he has since transitioned from that original lust to the platonic friendship that now exists. Although he considers whether or not Boss would make a good "friend with benefits," he doesn't dare ask her this. Jimmy, on the other hand, nowadays views Boss like a sister.

Their boat is a more modern model compared to the one that the film crew traveled on, so they move faster in reaching their destination with a little more horsepower. Having crossed the Cameroon–Congo border recently, they are even more cognizant now of human threats rather than just animal ones. Jimmy suddenly twitches and slaps his own neck hard, killing a mosquito. He pulls out his big canister of bug spray, and the three take turns applying.

"All right fine, I've got a few," says Patrick. "But we need to hear some from you, too, Boss. It's only fair. I've got my share of memes but that shit won't pull up on my phone with the service we have out here." He goes on, "A man and a woman start having sex in the middle of a dark forest. After like ten minutes, the man finally gets up and says, 'Damn I wish I had a flashlight.' The woman says, 'Me too, you've just been eating grass for the past ten minutes!'"

Boss holds back her laughter, trying everything to keep her facial muscles from showing amusement, but it's no use. She starts laughing, and Jimmy's laughter only intensifies when he sees that *she* is finally laughing.

"You guys are excruciating," she says. "But, whatever, here's one."

"What did Bo Peep say to Woody when he caught her in bed with Buzz and asked her 'What're you doing?'" Jimmy and Patrick perk up waiting for the answer.

"Umm... you have a *friend in me*?"

Patrick and Jimmy erupt into nasally laughter, almost falling out of their seats.

Even though their destination is more remote than usual, the three believe that this will be an easy snatch-and-grab job.

"Probably just a couple more bumbling idiots who strayed too far off course," Jimmy said when they were first given the coordinates and the details by the embassy in Yaoundé. Despite this, the rescue team was adamant about going in armed, after hearing that the American citizens in question had had a run in with some local criminals. Piracy and militia activities are not unheard of in this region of the world.

After "recovering" from Boss's joke, Patrick examines his M4 Carbine assault rifle. He checks his rifle's ACOG scope and foregrip again and again to pass the time, but the heat bothers him. Waving away some flies, he leans forward and asks, "Tell me again why they couldn't just send us in by helicopter to get these people?"

"Area's too thick. Literally. The jungle is too thick where we received their coordinates," says Boss. She checks their navigation system and realizes they are getting close.

"Listen, ladies," she says.

"Shit talkin's fun and all, but don't forget that we're here to do a job. The Republic of the Congo is politically volatile and you both know that."

She rolls her eyes, "Just too bad those we gotta go in and babysit didn't know that."

This elicits a grin from Patrick and Jimmy.

"So I want to be ready in case anything goes south. I don't do surprises. I don't fuck with them. Y'all feel me?" The two men nod subtly with their eyelids, and she sits, content.

As the day goes on, the evening sun slowly turns into a magenta hue over the river, creating a stunning view that reminds Boss just how beautiful Africa really is. She is relaxed, and watches the water the way she used to when she was a child sitting on their pier as the sun would set. The water seems to move slightly in the distance, and she rubs her eyes to make sure that they're not playing tricks.

They're not.

Suddenly, she realizes that the disturbance on the water ahead of them is not the sun, the tide, or even a crocodile or a hippopotamus. It's another boat.

"Boys," she says calmly, as they perk up and see it, too.

Despite being the one navigating their boat, even Jimmy was completely zoned out before she brought it to their attention. They can now hear the motor of the oncoming boat. This is in contrast to the primitive hollowed-out canoes used by indigenous fishermen. Before long, its passengers come into view. The oncoming boat passes right by them and swings around making an abrupt U-turn.

"What d'ya think they want?" asks Patrick as the three watch.

"I don't know. Just be friendly. Keep the guns hidden for now. I'll do the talking," says Boss.

"*We* will," insists Jimmy. "Together!"

"Whatever," she says. The men on the other boat pull up, waving the three rescuers down. Jimmy kills their engine and they slow down, until the two boats are neck and neck with each other. The men on the boat abruptly toss three large ropes with hooks tied to them, hooking their boat onto the rescuers' boat without their consent.

"Whoa, whoa, whoa, now!" says Boss loudly, raising her arms. "Yes, you may. Go right ahead. Thank you for asking," she says sarcastically. Jimmy wonders whether or not she realizes that she doesn't sound friendly at all.

The man—the only white man on the boat amongst several Congolese men—looks at her with astonishment.

"Well, well, well. I'll be goddamned." He looks at his co-passengers, then back at her,

"I guess it's just... raining pretty women around here lately. But you... My God, you are beautiful."

Standing on the opposite boat with four Congolese river pirates, Oskar van Vuuren stands there eye-humping the female rescuer who leads the team of three on the outsiders' boat.

"Sorry, big guy, I'm also gay," she shoots back with a fire in her eyes. Jimmy and Patrick both know this is a blatant lie, and one that they are happy to go along with.

"Oh!" says Van Vuuren. "My apologies. You must understand, I'm sure you can understand, we don't get many women on our river. None of your... caliber."

Boss feels a bit of throw up rise to the back of her throat.

"What can we do for you?" asks Jimmy, warmly.

"Well, boss, we'd like to know—"

Van Vuuren is interrupted by Jimmy pointing to their leader, "She's the boss!"

Van Vuuren laughs, "Oh course she is. I should expect nothing less." He looks back at his buddies, then back at the three rescuers with an ominous look.

"Then... *boss*..." he says to her this time, "The real question I have is, what can my men and I do for you?" Boss smiles, unsure what he's getting at. He proceeds, "Because this is our river, after all. Since you fine people are on *our* river, how can we be of service?"

"Let us know where the big game is and let us get on our way," says Boss.

"Ah, you three are hunters? We come across those from time to time. Most of 'em don't give us any trouble. But every once in a while ... a bad apple ruins the bunch." Van Vuuren's face lights up as if there were an actual lightbulb over his head.

"Speaking of bad apples," Van Vuuren says with an inquisitive smile, "Don't suppose you kind folks have seen any other... *Westerners*... around here, have you?"

Jimmy and Patrick glance at each other. Boss immediately suspects the worst. She purses her lips as if to fool the man into believing that she's thinking his question over.

"Think we might've seen a group of them pass us by. At least a couple days ago," she says. "Back on the D'ja. Must be a ways north by now. Why? They give you any trouble?"

Kumni Mwanda, Van Vuuren's second in command, steps forward and says, "Let's just say, my dear, they have trouble coming to them."

"I see," she says. "Well, I wish you guys luck with your... entrepreneurial ventures. If you don't mind, though, my men and I are going to politely give you your hooks back, and we're going to be on our way."

She and Patrick move to grab the pirates' hooks off of their starboard side.

"Hey now, I thought we were just getting to know each other." says Wanjala Killian as he looks down to the now-visible stock of his AK-47.

Jimmy's and the others' adrenaline go into overdrive at the sight. Suddenly Boss is aware of the firearms that the men have hidden on board, ready for use. All of them are Kalashnikov model assault rifles. Another pirate, Kwabena Basinge-Guillot, puts his hand on the grip of his pistol ... the same model Colt M1911 handgun used to put a bullet in Henry's leg days ago. Van Vuuren puts up his hands as if to communicate "looks like we're at a crossroads here." He grins that signature wolf-in-sheep's-clothing grin of his.

"I think we can work something out," Van Vuuren says with a growing smile on his face.

"We don't have any money on us," says Patrick, annoyed.

"Of course, of course, nobody ever does!" says Kumni. "But there are other ways."

"Like what?" says Jimmy. Before the pirates can answer, Boss shakes her head and looks right into Kumni's eyes.

"Listen... friend." she says very sternly yet calmly, deliberately using the word "friend" in a sarcastic and borderline hostile way. "When I was in the Middle East... I stopped counting how many insurgents I killed after I reached a hundred."

The pirates look surprisingly intimidated by this.

She proceeds, "We are not the Americans you're looking for. That's your first reason to leave us be."

"Wait a minute!" Van Vuuren interrupts her with a finger. "I said Westerners. I didn't say Americans, specifically."

Boss pivots back to what she was about to say, realizing that the man is connecting the dots.

"Your second ..." she looks up at every one of the pirates, taking the time to make eye contact with each one of them before finishing her sentence. "Your second reason to leave us be is because there's more to us than meets the eye."

Kumni and Van Vuuren look her up and down, salivating like a lion looking at a zebra steak at the thought of what she might look like naked. Van Vuuren bites his bottom lip,

"That's exactly how we want to see you."

Suddenly Jimmy swings around his FN SCAR-L assault rifle and points it directly in Van Vuuren's face, bringing the pirates' collective maniacal laughter to a screeching halt. Before the Congolese pirates can swing their AK-47s and AK-Ms up to shred Jimmy's body, Boss and Patrick have *their* automatic weapons trained on the rest of them as well.

Stunned by the speed of the outsiders, and seeing their firearms, a wide-eyed Van Vuuren realizes that they are most definitely not here to hunt big game. Nobody in their right mind would go to Africa to hunt with military-grade automatic weapons.

A long and tense standoff ensues, with the Congolese men watching as their leader just stands there, staring defiantly into Jimmy's eyes. Finally, Van Vuuren and Kumni look at each other as if making an unsaid decision, then back to Boss and the other two.

"Let 'em go," Van Vuuren says quietly. "They're not worth the trouble."

One of the pirates, Unathi Andile, says something in French to Kumni and Oskar, angrily pointing at Jimmy. He then switches from his regional French to English with a thick accent.

"Him! You! You must be here to pillage the continent! Just like the whites!" Unathi says.

Being no stranger to anti-Asian discrimination, Jimmy bites his tongue and just keeps his SCAR trained on the men.

Van Vuuren shoots Wanjala a look, and he steps forward. He raises his hands to show the three that he's unarmed, and then leans over to grab their hooks back. Before they know it, the pirates' boat is detached from theirs and headed off down the other side of the river, leaving the three in peace. As she keeps her eyes and weapon locked on them as they leave, though, she catches a glimpse of the pirate leader spitting off his boat in a blatant show of disrespect.

"That was close," says Patrick. Boss scoffs, unimpressed,

"Those guys are pussies compared to the insurgents we used to deal with in Iraq and Afghanistan. He and his cronies can take their tiny dicks and fuck *all* the way off."

Jimmy smiles at this, and they resume their voyage down the river. They quickly return to normal, albeit keeping a watchful eye behind them to make sure they're not being followed by any other boats. Boss, irritated, reaches for her prized possession. She pulls out her windproof Butane Blowtorch and lights a cigarette. It's an older model, lacking a childproof safety mechanism.

Jimmy looks at her and shakes his head, "Thought you said you quit that shit."

"Look, I'm trying. Hold up, do I report to you now?" she says with raised eyebrows.

"It's only 'cause I care." Jimmy says. Boss takes several puffs, then looks back to her friend.

"Hey man," says Patrick. "Let the woman live!"

"Yeah," smirks Boss. "You heard him, Jim, let the woman live!"

"That's exactly what I'm trying to make sure of!" he retorts. Boss just smiles a bit.

"Fine. You have my word this time. As soon as we get back. I mean it, this time. Monday. On Monday, I quit!"

Jimmy smiles at her words, content, but secretly telling himself he won't be holding his breath. The group cruises along while Boss enjoys her smoke.

"Okay, I've got one more before we reach shore!" says Jimmy, returning to his upbeat self. The two look at him. Boss smirks, half annoyed and half amused.

"I saw this one online … A man and a woman are having sex. She's riding him."

"Here we go again," sighs Patrick.

Jimmy resumes, "Suddenly their young son barges into the bedroom and sees them in action. He's mortified. He runs out of the room. The mom is hysterical, wondering how they are going to explain this to their son. Her husband says, 'Leave that to me.' After insisting that they approach him together to talk about it, the mom looks at their son and says, 'Sweetie, what you saw was just me jumping up and down on your dad's belly to help him flatten it out! It's for his health!' The son looks up at her and says, 'Awww, Mom. You're wasting your time! Because when you're not here, the nice neighbor lady comes over and gets on her knees to blow it back up!'"

Patrick spits out the water from his canteen and the three laugh like hyenas.

Coming around a bend in the murky river where the mist is thick and the green foliage on either side particularly dense, they see traces of smoke rising up in the air. The amount is infinitesimal, but just enough to catch their attention.

"We're here," says Boss as she looks at their GPS. Jimmy slows the boat down drastically. Slowly coming into view on the opposite side of some thick trees, they can clearly see a destroyed boat. It either caught fire or there was an explosion on board. Judging by the looks of the charred boat, Patrick estimates that whatever happened to it occurred several days ago at least.

Jimmy guns the motor again and the three deliberately "beach" their boat on shore like a beached whale. Knowing full well that if a monsoon breaks out, the river can easily gain a few feet of water level … they drag it high enough onto the shore so that the Sangha River will not steal it back, no matter how high the tide gets. They gather their weapons and gear, and are greeted by somebody who takes them by surprise.

Stepping out of the jungle, making no noise, and over an hour early, stands their contact. The noticeably short man is dressed in a tattered button-down shirt and shorts that look like they could be either cargo or basketball shorts. A multilingual indigenous man from the *Aka* or *BaAka* tribe—who looks strikingly healthy despite his advanced age—he says nothing until Boss and the other two sling their firearms over their shoulders and reach out to shake his hand. Jimmy is surprised that the "pygmy" man does not wear more "traditional" clothing, like a simple cloth over his groin. *Isn't that how uncontacted people dress?* he wonders to himself. He waves these thoughts away, trying to focus on the task at hand. The observant and reserved man takes Boss's hand, shaking it lightly,

"I am Obasi." he says warmly, but with no smile. "I will be your guide." He gently puts his right hand over his heart.

Boss takes an immediate liking to his grounded, centered energy and says, "This is Jimmy, and this is Patrick. They call me "Boss" or "Boss Lady," but you can call me whatever you'd like. Thank you so much for taking the time."

Obasi bows his head slightly in a respectful nod.

Dang, she must really like him if she says he can call her whatever he wants! Patrick thinks to himself.

"The Embassy in Cameroon already took care of your payment, right?" she asks Obasi.

"Yes," he says quietly.

Patrick likes to give people nicknames, and he obviously couldn't give Boss one because she already had one. But he already wants to nickname their guide "Church Mouse" for his reserved demeanor, although he wisely does not voice this aloud.

"Good," says Boss. "If it's okay with you, Obasi, we'd like to get a move on. It's a bit of a trek to their coordinates... the people who got lost in there apparently... if they are still alive, then they've been out here for a long time."

Obasi bows his head again to communicate that he understands, and the four promptly get going.

Carrying nothing except for what might be in his shorts pockets, Obasi leads the pack and moves astonishingly fast through the thick jungle, compared to his younger counterparts. He routinely has to look back to make sure the three outsiders are keeping up. Night falls and the group of four pitch camp, the three rescuers discussing what they may find when they reach the coordinates and what they're going to do when they get back to civilization. They decide to carry on at first light. Swapping stories and more adult jokes at their campfire, Obasi peels a piece of fruit and eats it silently while intently listening to the others. Patrick wonders if he doesn't like the themes of their raunchy humor, or perhaps just doesn't understand their banter, *or* if it's just simply a cultural thing. Regardless, Obasi sits with them saying nothing as the others snicker and pass the time.

"Hey, Obasi," says Jimmy. Obasi looks at him. "I want to be sensitive and all, so I'm curious, is 'pygmy' an offensive word?"

Obasi pauses momentarily, "Not nearly as offensive as the Bantu treating us like dogs." His answer floors the group, as they realize that their knowledge of regional human rights violations is pathetic at best. Boss comes to the rescue and changes the conversation.

"You've got us beat in many ways, Obasi," she says.

She then turns to Jimmy, "For example, our old CO would kill us if he saw us today and saw how out of shape we've become!"

"You got that right," says Jimmy, looking down at the ground.

"Ooofff," says Patrick, as if the words metaphorically stung a bit.

"Mine, too."

The next day, the group is nearing the remote coordinates when the three suddenly realize that Obasi has wandered off, no longer leading the way. They spot him nearby and approach.

"Obasi?" asks Boss. "Did we go the wrong way? What's the matter?"

She looks at him and sees a look of fear on his face that she's never seen from any of the local people, neither from here nor any other region of Central or Western Africa. Dreading to see what he's looking at, several possibilities race through her mind. *What if it's one of the people from the film crew dead or something? Even hanging?*

She turns her head, and the four of them see something hanging, all right, but it's not a dead person.

"Fuckin' A," says Jimmy, astonished. "Don't wanna meet whatever made those!"

Looking in front of them, the group of four sees a thick pattern of girthy spider webs interconnecting several trees in the jungle head. The sight gives Boss the heebie-jeebies, though she tries to hide this.

"Remember that picture that surfaced online years ago when some soldiers in Iraq caught that massive spider-looking freaky thing on camera and everyone thought that there were giant spiders in the Middle East?" asks Patrick.

"Yes," says Jimmy.

Patrick continues,

"And then they analyzed the photo and it was just two regular sized spiders at an odd angle?"

"Yes," says Jimmy. "Camel spiders. Ugly little shits. I know that video of one eating a lizard on the brick wall was real! Yuck."

"We used to hear about them all the time overseas. I never saw one— luckily," says Boss.

"I'm just saying, maybe this is like that where, it's not one big web but a bunch of small ones that morphed into one? Just saying is all," Patrick says with a shrug.

"I don't know, and as long as there's none crawling on us, I don't care. Just keep your bug spray handy," Boss says confidently as she holds her Vector up against her collar bone and carries on walking confidently. She and Jimmy and Patrick again stop when they realize that Obasi is practically shivering ... frozen solid.

The look of fear on his face gets worse and worse. Boss takes a final puff from the stub of her cigarette and smashes it with her foot before approaching him. She can *almost* notice an imperceptible shaking of his head. His eyes are wide.

"Obasi ...?" Boss says warmly. He says nothing.

"Obasi?" She repeats herself. She gently puts her hand on his shoulder, startling the hell out of him. He flinches at her touch like a timid rabbit. She then makes out the sound of something he keeps saying under his breath; quietly, four syllables, and getting louder and louder as he repeats the word or words over and over again.

"*J'ba FoFi.*"

10

"WHAT'S HE SAYING?" JIMMY ASKS.

Boss listens to Obasi again. He is clearly spooked. Through his thick accent, she attempts to ascertain his words, "Cha-Ba Foo-Fee? Ja-Ba Foo-Fee?" she says.

"J'ba FoFi," repeats Obasi, to nobody in particular, scared out of his mind.

"Probably just some local superstition," says Patrick, borderline annoyed. He fidgets with his M4 carbine, not one to be able to stay still for very long.

"I'm with Patrick," says Jimmy. "I'm sure it's nothin'. Now let's get this show on the road. Quicker we get them, quicker we get back!" At this, Patrick and Jimmy eagerly motion to move on, but Boss Lady does not budge.

"Obasi, is everything okay?" she asks. Obasi snaps out of his trance-like state and frantically looks at the others.

"We go no further. We turn back. Now."

"What? Why?" says Patrick.

"You wouldn't believe me," Obasi says with wide eyes. "We leave now."

Boss and the two men are taken back by his sudden change in demeanor from the calm, almost shaman-like man who they followed out here into the steamy jungle.

"Obasi, I'm sorry," says Boss awkwardly, trying to remain gentle with her words. "But... we've already been paid. There are people out here that need our help. We're very close! We're only an hour or two trek away from their coordinates!"

Obasi puts his hands over his chest,

"If it's mating season..." he says ominously, looking at the web and then at her. "It won't matter. They would already be dead."

He says something under his breath in the local Aka language that they cannot understand. His tone is frantic, as if he's saying a prayer of sorts.

"Mating season?" smirks Jimmy.

"Yeah, where's my invite??" says Patrick. Boss shoots him a look for his ill-timed humor. He looks away. Jimmy stifles another shit-eating grin and the two men exchange a quiet fist bump.

"Obasi, my friend, we need you for just a little bit longer. Please?" Boss asks him.

Obasi slowly shakes his head.

"I'll talk with our point of contact with the embassy," Jimmy finally chimes in.

"We'll see that they double your pay. All in Central African Francs."

Jimmy looks to the others as if looking for agreement, knowing he just committed to this without discussing with the others. It occurs to him that they aren't paying Obasi's "stipend" anyway, so they likely couldn't care less what the embassy needs to work out.

"We get them and then we leave. No delay," Obasi finally says.

Patrick smiles and says, "Thank you. Don't worry, nothing in this jungle can withstand the kind of lead we're packi—"

"Three times, though," Obasi interrupts him, something that the man of very few words has never done before. "I want your people to increase payment by three times. Not two. For my people."

"Done. Now let's move." Jimmy says.

Suddenly the sound of somebody *screaming* off in the distance rings out through the thick, steamy jungle.

"Oh my god," says Patrick.

"Move it, now!" orders Boss. "Could be one of ours!"

Obasi leads the way, but with a hesitation now in his steps that allows his younger, Western counterparts to keep up with him without breaks. They push past thick vines and shrubs. Coming across an opening with tall grass, the four move with haste past a stream with several bushes all around it.

They enter another thick patch of jungle yet again, proceeding towards where they heard the sound of the person screaming. Boss suddenly throws her fist up to bring the group to a halt.

"You hear that?" she asks quietly.

Ever so slightly, off in the distance, they hear a strange noise that Obasi quickly identifies as the sound of an antelope in distress.

"Probably something preying on the poor bastard. Let's go," she orders.

Coming over a hill where they must use all four limbs to navigate their way through the dense foliage, the frustrated rescue party starts to question their own ears.

"Where the fuck?" asks Patrick. "We all heard that. Whoever that was shouldn't've been this far away! We are *at* the coordinates. Where did they go?"

"Timid fucks," smirks Jimmy.

"Fuck it," says Boss. She unslings her submachine gun off of her shoulder and puts her hands up to her mouth and bellows at the top of her lungs,

"HELLO! WHERE ARE YOU?!"

Obasi quickly moves to stop her, frantically shaking his head, as if calling out to them is suddenly a bad idea now. Boss feels the frustration rising inside her. She composes herself and takes a deep breath before speaking ... but she is interrupted.

The group hears another haunting *scream*, this time accompanied by the sound, again, of an antelope in distress. The two sounds are much closer now and coming from *right* over the other side of the hill. They turn towards each other with wide eyes and say no more.

Dashing their way through the jungle, they push past yet more and more vegetation. Patrick thinks to himself, *Sweet Jesus, there ain't this many trees in the entire Middle East.*

This would be the last thing that Patrick thinks to himself before slipping off the edge of a muddy ravine that none of them had seen. Not watching his footing well under the thick undergrowth of the foliage, Patrick loses his balance and starts tumbling down the hill. He rolls, and rolls, and rolls, getting banged up and scratched on various shrubs until he lands right into a mass on the other side of the hill, of a texture that he's not familiar with.

"Patrick!" yells Jimmy.

"Hold on, we're coming down to get you, brother!" shouts Boss. She, Jimmy, and Obasi start clumsily making their way down the other side of the hill to help their friend, desperately trying to avoid being taken by either gravity or any slippery slopes like he was.

Having landed face first, Patrick winces and raises his arms, until he's in a sort of a push-up position on the ground. He struggles to get up and wonders if he's broken something, until he realizes that that's not the case. Upon looking up, a part of him wishes that he had broken a limb instead.

Raising his head, Patrick realizes that he's fallen into a "minefield" of enormous, thick, girthy spider webs. He freaks out.

Thrashing like a fish caught in a net, he desperately tries to get to his feet and get out of this minefield. He slips on the slippery, muddy ground beneath the webs and lands on his ass like a disgruntled circus clown right back into the webs. Finally managing to get to his feet, he furiously tugs at the web that clings to virtually every part of his body, including his face.

Having almost reached him, Boss notices out of the corner of her eye the petrified look on Obasi's face. A worried look forms on hers, and she traces his gaze down to what he's looking at. About ten yards away from Patrick, four huge, hairy spider legs begin to emerge—one at a time—from a hole next to the thick underbrush alongside the minefield. Her eyes widen and her eyebrows tough each other. Then another leg emerges. Then another.

"You gotta be kidding me," says Jimmy as he sees it, too.

The image strikes fear into him, looking eerily similar to a "facehugger" crawling out of its "egg" from the Ridley Scott movie "Alien," which scared the hell out of him when he was young.

"*No* fuckin' way," Boss says under her breath.

Patrick gets the webbing off of his face, allowing him to see the four-foot tarantula emerging from nearby. Nearly pissing his pants, Patrick starts freaking out. "Ohhhhh, fuck that! Fuck that!" he shouts, desperately trying to move away, like a stuck animal trying to wade its way out of a thick tar pit. His frantic movements send vibrations to the spider's tarsal claws on the end of its legs, causing its instincts to kick in and sending its predatory "curiosity" into overdrive.

"Here!" shouts Boss.

She grabs her Vector submachine gun and tosses it to Patrick below. He catches it with his one now free hand and flips the safety off. The giant four-foot behemoth—all eight legs showing clear as day now—skitters towards Patrick at astounding speed. It leaps straight into the air to pounce on the entangled man when Patrick shreds its body in mid-flight with a loud burst of automatic fire.

Boss grabs Patrick's M4 that fell nearby and swings it up to center the sights of the ACOG scope on yet another gigantic spider emerging from the underbrush. It's on the other side of Patrick and also has a four-foot leg span. Holding the foregrip with her left hand, her right trigger finger squeezes down and, while looking at it through the scope, sees the giant spider's body shredded by her bullets right at the arachnid's carapace. Off to her right-hand side, she hears the faint sound of bullet casings hitting the shrubs.

Patrick, terrified and still thrashing about in the web, forgets momentarily his training to conserve ammunition and fires *way* more than is needed at the spider that very nearly pounced on him. With the four-foot hairy brown monster tarantula having been dispatched, he watches in horror as its body slumps onto its back and its massive eight legs twitch as they curl inwards towards the rest of the body. Even in the chaos, Patrick can clearly see the fangs on the dead arachnid angled towards each other to form a 'V'-shape, each at least five inches long, and pointed inwards in a curve to look like what he imagines the main claw on a velociraptor's toe would look like.

"Hold still! Hold still!! The movement... !" Obasi says, trying in vain to instruct Patrick.

He doesn't listen. Jimmy checks that the magazine in his SCAR-L is ready to go and, like the other two, switches off the safety to full-auto.

"I'll go get him!" says Boss. She motions to Jimmy's assault rifle, "Use that damn thing and cover me!"

Jimmy shoots her a frantic look, "No! You'll get trapped too! I'll do it!" he shoots back.

"We really gonna do this right now?" she snaps. "I'm in charge here!"

Jimmy disobeys her, hustling down towards the minefield of webs, but not before his quick-thinking sisterly figure wrong-foots him.

"Oh my god, look, another one!" she shouts, pointing behind Jimmy. Jimmy swings around faster than a bat out of hell and realizes a second later that she did that so that she could jump into the minefield to help Patrick first. Jimmy's eyebrows curl.

"You crazy woman!" he yells.

Swinging his SCAR up to watch their surroundings, he covers them as she wades her way through the webs until she can reach Patrick. She's astounded by how much she has to strain to move through them. Grabbing Patrick by the hand, she tugs on him.

"No more jobs here, please!" he says, looking at her in horror. "I need to get out of here!"

"And *I* could use a cigarette!" she says, panting as she yanks him towards her.

Suddenly, Jimmy is distracted by an insidious *hissing* sound in the brush nearby, taking his and Obasi's attention off of Patrick and Boss. At that moment two more spiders of gargantuan proportions spring out and attack the two struggling to get free of the web. Their bodies are massive, the size of dogs. Both tarantula-like spiders come out to a leg span exceeding four feet, but not bigger than five feet.

Jimmy frantically keeps his eyes peeled for whatever had made that hissing sound, while simultaneously trying to cover the other two nearby. One of the eighty-pound arachnids skitters over to Boss and leaps right onto her like an ambush predator. She catches it in mid-flight by two of its front legs, by its femurs, and—as if in slow motion—narrowly misses having her *eyeballs* pierced by its massive fangs. Its chelicerae incisors snap and reach at her face ... her face right up to its hideous "mouth." She screams in terror, something that Jimmy *never* saw her do during *either* of their tours together in the Middle East. She desperately holds it away from her as its surprisingly powerful legs keep hooking at and grabbing at her, trying desperately to deliver its venom so that it can enjoy this long-overdue meal.

Behind her, Patrick contends with the other spider. He manages to stick the barrel of the Vector right up at an angle into the arachnid's "mouth" and pulls the trigger, spraying bits of frothy yellow matter into the air. He kicks at the dead arachnid furiously to get it away.

"Kill it!! Kill it!!" screams Boss to anyone listening.

"I can't get a shot!!" cries Jimmy, unwilling to risk shooting her by accident. At this moment he hates her for putting herself in this situation, and wishes that it was him instead. Patrick grabs the abdomen of the five-foot tarantula and pulls on it. It is incredibly strong. Boss swears that she can see a small droplet of venom on the tips of each fang like giant hospital syringes.

Finally, the combined might of him pulling and her pushing gets the freakish arachnid off of her. Tossing it as far as they can, this gives Patrick and Jimmy the full "one Mississippi" second that they need to absolutely obliterate the spider with their automatic weapons, without risking hitting their friend. Quickly reloading the Vector, with Jimmy reloading his SCAR, the two finally pull themselves loose from the minefield. Obasi watches in horror, able to do nothing except feel glad that their ceasing movements in the web most likely won't attract any more of them.

Boss takes back her Vector and Jimmy tosses Patrick his M4 Carbine.

High up in the canopy, another specimen slowly but surely descends on the group of four like a slow-moving sky lantern descending to earth by the strand of web coming from its spinnerets. They do not realize its presence above them. This one is a solid two feet in leg span; most likely an adolescent male, with a slight purple coloration on its abdomen. The jungle here is mostly shaded over. The behemoth arachnid's legs grasp and grab at the open air as it descends towards them ... their bodies getting bigger and bigger as the movement below draws it closer and closer.

They look up just in time to see, for a split second, the black silhouette of the eight-legged demon illuminated against the few rays of sunshine that peer through this section of the canopy.

They move to react but it's too late. The giant arachnid lands directly on top of Patrick and moves to deliver its fatal dose. Swinging madly, Patrick avoids having his neck bitten, but the spider's massive fangs sink deep into his right arm.

Patrick lets out an ungodly screech from the pain, and throws the arachnid off of him. The three raise their rifles and empty their magazines into the spider's body, shredding its two main body parts—its abdomen and cephalothorax—until not even its eight pebble-looking black eyes are visible.

"Arrrrgggghhhh!" Patrick gasps, grasping the bleeding bite area on his arm. A *searing* pain immediately travels in both directions of the bite area, moving down to his hand and up towards his neck simultaneously.

Mortified, Obasi looks down at the red blood-soaked fangs on the ground that used to be attached to the monster spider. He points to Patrick's arm and says something in Aka which the group does not understand. He repeats himself, but it's no use.

"I... we... need to go," says Patrick, clenching his teeth at the pain. Jimmy quickly wraps up the gushing bloody bite holes on Patrick's upper arm, much to Patrick's discomfort. Boss pulls out their GPS and demands that they move away to an open area where nothing can crawl down and surprise them from the canopy above.

Patrick moves to take his first step since shooting up the arachnid. Everything becomes suddenly blurry as he falls to the ground like a bad drug trip gone dangerously wrong. From his perception, his fall feels like it's happening in slow motion. He feels immediately delirious and feverish.

The other three rush to his aid, but his condition worsens by the minute. Boss looks at their GPS.

"We are *at* the coordinates," says Boss. "Who was the one that screamed both of those times? Where'd they go? They had to have heard those gunshots. If they're not here, then—"

"Then *fuck* 'em!" croaks Patrick.

"Damn right," says Jimmy. "We are in way over our heads here!"

Jimmy holds Patrick by his arm underneath his shoulder. Obasi helps to keep him upright as well, on the opposite side. Boss takes point with her weapon ready to fire at a second's notice.

With every passing second, Patrick can feel his sensory perceptions becoming more and more overloaded. The slightest sounds are excruciatingly loud now, and even the slightest glint of the sun's light hurts his eyes. The volume of the group's talking becomes distorted, and he also experiences sudden changes in depth perception.

The stench coming from Patrick's bite wound is nauseating to both Jimmy and Obasi. Even Boss can catch a whiff of it every now and then. They move as fast as they can with their injured friend until they're out in a grassy clearing where they feel a little less surrounded.

"On second thought ..." says Patrick, short of breath. "We've come all this way. We... we should try to..."

"Try to what?" says Boss. "They're nowhere to be found."

"Speaking of screams and missing people. I don't know about you guys but I haven't seen any antelope either. Just big fuckin' spiders! Am I trippin' balls? No gorillas or chimps or anything! How's this even possible?" Jimmy says. His words go unheard.

Patrick suddenly clenches his whole body from the searing pain, and begins motioning to his chest like he's having a hard time breathing. He starts furiously taking off his clothes as he sweats profusely. Catching on that he feels overheated, Boss rips open his shirt and the sight sends shivers down their spines. Patrick's veins and skin turn a bright purple, especially at his major arteries. A labyrinth of bright purple veins begins to appear, contrasting against his pale skin and getting darker and darker ... seemingly with each passing second. His arm where he was bitten has already begun swelling to massive proportions. The areas of his heart and jugular veins look like they are about to thump right out of his chest and neck. Even his eyes begin changing color. He heaves, and vomits. Boss puts her hand on his forehead and feels that he has a dangerously high fever. Patrick begins to look even more pale than he was before, and despite how hot he is, the violent chills start.

"We need to get him help immediately!" shouts Jimmy. "We must go back!"

"It's at least a two-day walk back to our boat. He won't make it in time if we carry him. We need to get help sooner than that!" shouts Boss.

"They just *had* to send us in by boat! Fucking brilliant!" he shouts back. "If we were flown in by chopper we could have five times the supplies! Maybe some antivenom!"

"There is no cure for the bite of this animal," says Obasi, quietly, in a sobering tone.

Boss composes herself and leans over to Patrick, who by now is too weak to even sit up on his own. Looking at her helpless friend, she suddenly feels a rush of emotions that she does not permit herself to feel. She was about to ask him, "Patrick, my guy, is there *any* chance you can walk if we assist you?" but she pulls her head out of the clouds and realizes the answer: absolutely fucking not.

"Patrick?" she asks him, more like a warm nurse than a stern fox hole buddy.

"Can you ... do you ... tell us what you need." She immediately hates herself for choosing such useless and unhelpful words of support. Patrick gurgles some nasty fluid and tries, desperately, to speak. Nothing audible comes out of his mouth. Jimmy leans over with her and they can only make out the sound of one letter coming out of his mouth, and can only hear it when they put their ears right up to his mouth.

"H– h–."

"Help," Jimmy says with a sobering look on his face.

The following words come out of Obasi's mouth the same way almost all of his spoken words do, except even more quietly than usual: "The best thing we can do for our friend is keep him as comfortable as possible."

It is getting dark again. Not even a half hour has passed and the purple, viscous boils have already begun forming on Patrick's body as they carry him. Boss and Jimmy take turns helping Obasi carry Patrick, while the other covers their front and rear guard with a fully loaded weapon ready. Having combed the area thoroughly and shouted "Hello! Is anybody out here?" several times, they have given up on finding the lost members of the doomed documentary film crew.

They start making their way back to their boat, but will soon need to stop, lest they trek through the thick jungle with just their flashlights in the pitch darkness. Patrick has slipped out of consciousness, but his breathing persists ... shallow and labored, like somebody that should be hooked up to a ventilator machine. The sight terrifies Boss, although she would never admit it. Jimmy on the other hand is more of an open book.

"Of all the fucked up things that I've seen in my day," he says with a shakiness in his voice, looking at the insidious effects of the venom on their buddy.

"I've never... ever... seen anything like this."

Suddenly, the jungle goes dead quiet. Boss quietly instructs Obasi to gently set Patrick down, and her and Jimmy's training kicks in. She raises her weapon. She and Jimmy use their firearms and their flashlights to comb the area all around them, including above. The jungle going silent prompts them to suspect the worst. "Hope for the best, prepare for the worst," her dad always used to tell her as a child. And after what happened earlier back there, she genuinely has to work up the courage to shine her flashlight above them. She takes a deep breath, counts down from five, and then does so … no spiders. Thank God. Only more overgrowth in a steamy jungle that manages to stay hot and humid even at night. A few long minutes pass. The only thing they can hear for the longest time is Patrick's labored breathing.

"Boss!" Obasi says. They look at him, then up to where he's pointing.

Far off in the distance, a small glow draws their attention. Jimmy and Boss look at each other, then to Obasi.

"Campfire," Obasi says.

Jimmy looks to her, "What'd you say, Boss? Could be more thieves. Militia. Who knows."

"Or they can help us help him," she replies. "C'mon. We'll take our chances."

Picking Patrick back up, the three use the remainder of their energy to carry him towards the ominous glow. Before long, they come to the entrance of a cave nestled in the jungle. From their angle, they can't see who, if anybody, is in it until they get right up to the entrance. Finally, the moment arrives. Setting Patrick down just outside the cave and moving quieter than mice in a church, Obasi stays close by while Boss and Jimmy ready their weapons up to their shoulders.

Fearing the possibility that there may be "undesirables" such as more pirates inhabiting the cave, they tighten their grips around their firearms and flip the safeties off. Exercising proper trigger discipline, Boss creeps right up next to the entrance. Glancing back to make sure that Jimmy's ready, he taps her on the back and the two spring into the mouth of the cave in a manner similar to "breaching" a door in a combat zone.

The group of five in the cave falls over themselves from being startled so badly. Hearts pounding, sweat racing, it takes a solid second or two for the chaos to settle down.

"Who the heck are you guys... ?" Dr. David Hale asks, sheepishly.

Boss and Jimmy lower their weapons, seeing that they are unarmed and helpless. The group of five in the cave, four Americans and a small African boy, look like they've been through hell. They look shaken, hungry, and exhausted. They look like they've seen a ghost, as Jimmy's mom used to say.

She and Jimmy immediately recognize his American accent as a non-local and look at each other, amused.

"I'll be goddamned," Boss says. The group in the cave waits bashfully for them to answer David.

Jimmy continues, "I don't suppose you guys are from the Curiosity Channel, are you?"

"Yes, yes!" says Dr. Molly Hendricks.

"We're your PMC rescue force," says Boss. "Congratulations."

Anne Matthews raises her hand to speak, "We've ... we've been held up here for so long now. We've just been staying in this cave. We were wondering if you guys were coming at all!" Anne raises her hand again, as if to get out an afterthought, but Boss shoots her trigger finger up in her characteristic way to stop her.

"Hold up," Boss says. "Then which of you was screaming?"

The film crew survivors look at her, puzzled.

Boss continues, "If you've been here this whole time—"

She looks at Jimmy mid-sentence, confused, then says, "Then who was the one who *screamed* earlier? Over there?"

The film crew looks bewildered. Finally, young Deion speaks up.

"That ... that wasn't us."

11

PATRICK WRIGHT REGAINS CONSCIOUSNESS A FEW HOURS later, while it's still dark out. Shooting up into a quasi-seated position inside the cave, the stench of his swollen bite wound is suddenly accompanied by the far-worse sounds of the pain in his body manifesting. Excruciating waves of pain shoot from his upper arm and pulsate throughout his body, one after the other.

Immediately leaping to their feet and turning on their flashlights, Boss and Jimmy and a few others rush to his aid. But aside from waiting by his side, there's nothing they can do. If David didn't know any better, he would think that Patrick's behavior was something out of a demonic possession movie. Patrick twitches and yelps, but the forming purple boil on his neck prevents him from being able to say a word. Molly moves to cover Dee's eyes from seeing Patrick in the state that he's in, as if there's any of the child's innocence left to be protected.

"We need to give him something, damn it! Anything!" yells Jimmy. Waiting and hoping that they wouldn't need to resort to it, Boss pulls out one of only two vials of morphine that they brought with them and jabs it right into Patrick.

"I'm so, so sorry, Patrick," she says, in a gentle and sad tone.

"We shouldn't have ..."

Boss catches herself from saying what she, Jimmy, and Patrick all felt: that they shouldn't have come out here. She catches the gaze of the helpless African boy looking at her and wonders, if he wasn't here, if she'd have it in her to finish her sentence and let everyone hear that she feels they weren't worth coming out here for. The very last thing she expected was for one of her men to have to go through something of this magnitude. Although she and Jimmy bicker all the time, he is absolutely right about one thing: they are in way over their heads out here.

A boil on Patrick's chest next to one of his major arteries pops to the tune of a quiet, squishy sound and foul-smelling pus oozes out. David takes in the sight, wretches, and then vomits the contents of his empty stomach all over the floor of the cave. Boss looks at him and rolls her eyes wide enough to make sure that he can clearly see her do so. As far as she's concerned, he and his crew are the reason Patrick is in the condition he's in.

Just then the morphine seems to level Patrick out and he stops thrashing about so wildly. He attempts in vain to speak, but he simply cannot. Jimmy holds his hand and reluctantly brushes Patrick's hair back, trying to comfort him while simultaneously avoiding the nasty boil forming on his forehead. The sight makes him and Boss feel nauseous too, but they'd never admit it.

"It looks like it's... helping," says Anne sheepishly, feeling just as useless as the other "doctors" in the cave.

Anne speaks too soon. Patrick suddenly springs back to life and wails in agony. Anne covers her mouth and begins to cry, overwhelmed by it all. The bite wound is so swollen on his upper arm that it looks as big as his thigh, and jagged like a rocky surface. By now, his entire arm looks ready to burst. Even though Patrick has necrosis decaying away his tissue at the immediate puncture holes of the bite area, it's the swelling that is far worse. Boss swears that she can even see—and *hear*—the "contents" in Patrick's arm. If Patrick was his normal self, she and Jimmy know that he'd make a joke, probably something like "Contents under pressure!" and Jimmy would laugh while she would slowly shake her head.

Patrick's wail reaches a breaking point, and his entire right arm *POPS* from the swelling like a balloon, sending bits of it spewing in every direction like a meaty, moist little frag grenade. Boss and Jimmy furiously wipe bits of Patrick's flesh from their eyes and mouth, and a wide-eyed Anne screams bloody murder. Boss's anger reaches a breaking point.

"Shut up!" she yells at Anne. Looking back at Jimmy and then back down to Patrick, her anger turns to sadness as she realizes that she will never, ever be able to smirk at one of her friend's lousy jokes again. Patrick dies just a minute or two later.

Boss slumps back, stunned and unwilling to comprehend what has just happened. She pulls out her butane blow torch and lights a cigarette, taking a long and angry puff before exhaling. Compared to the smell of the body, the stench of her cigarette is nothing. A long moment of silence befalls the inhabitants of the jungle cave. David leans forward to speak, but Boss shoots her hand up at him before he can.

A long few minutes pass, and then young Deion finally says something to Jimmy and the tough lady that accompanies him, "We are sorry about your friend."

Boss composes herself and looks at him.

"They never told us you all had a child with you," she says solemnly. "They probably woulda' paid us more. That raises the stakes. Any child, U.S. citizen or not." She turns her gaze towards her fallen friend, killed by something far worse than any bio-chem weapon that she knows of that's been created in a laboratory. "Would've... paid *him* more," she finishes.

"He tried to warn us," Jimmy says, looking over at the oldest member of the two groups. Obasi looks at the others with the same reserved look that he almost always has, and says nothing. Whether positive, negative, or neutral, his expression is unreadable. Jimmy goes on.

"We came across a bunch of enormous webs on our way out here, and he tried to warn us. We should've listened."

"We…" Molly chimes in quietly. Everyone looks at her. "We should've listened to our guide as well."

Remembering who she is, Boss grabs Patrick's M4 and rises to her feet,

"But that doesn't matter anymore," she says. "All that matters is what we're going to do about it. You all need to get home, and we need to get back to normalcy," she says looking back at Jimmy and Obasi.

"Sooner we get back, the sooner we can all get back to our happy little lives," she concludes with a sarcastic and irritated tone.

Falling back asleep after Patrick's gruesome death is an impossible and daunting task. A few hours pass by while the two groups get to know one another. Boss seems to share a soft spot for the boy, to which none of the others are allowed the same luxury. She is the one most closed off to sharing about herself, or about anything, which doesn't surprise Jimmy at all. After what's transpired, small talk is a welcome distraction for all except her. David periodically zones in and out of the conversation between the others.

"I be petty, bruh. White people age like fruit!" Avery says to Jimmy, with David missing out on the prior context. He mentally zones out again and then "rejoins" them a few minutes later.

"Before I joined the marines," Jimmy goes on. "I was broke as a joke. I had to live in somebody's garage for a while."

"Yo, that's hella dope, though!" Avery exclaims. "I've been watching these garage-transformation-into-bedroom time-lapse videos on YouTube! Neat stuff!"

"Yeah," Jimmy says casually. "My ceiling fell on me."

Finally, the slightest hint of sunlight begins to illuminate the cave in the wee-morning hours. Boss's tough and intimidating exterior keeps the others from making much chit-chat with her or asking her many questions.

Finally, David leans over and asks her, "I'm sorry, I never caught your name. I'm David. We really appreciate you guys coming out here."

She looks at him, entirely uninterested in conversation.

"You can call me Boss," she says.

"I'm... I'm sorry?" David asks.

"You heard me," she says matter-of-factly. "Everyone else calls me that. Why not you?"

David tries to pivot from the awkwardness, "Well, I mean, I thought that ..."

"You thought what?" she says incredulously. "That's not a request. *You* can call me Boss."

David doesn't know what to say. Before he can speak, she is at it again.

"You guys said you're doctors, right? In... what was it, marine biology?" she says.

"Yeah," says David.

"Man..." Jimmy interjects. "They couldn't have had us rescue spider doctors? Or venom doctors? Whatever that's called. Or! Even regular injury doctors!"

Jimmy's words take Boss's right out of her mouth as he catches on to what she's getting at. The embassy isn't paying them to be polite, after all.

"What do you want us to say? We're sorry for your coworker!" says David defensively.

"That's *friend*," says Jimmy.

"We are sorry for your friend! Do you think we wanted any of this?" he snaps back.

"You say you're doctors," says Boss. "So that means you got your Ph.D. in marine bio, right?"

David opens his mouth but Boss cuts him off again.

"Perfect!" she says. "You refer to me as Boss, and I'll call you... Ph.D.!"

"Wait, no... college. You are 'College.' Nice to meet you, College, I'm Boss!" she says, wrapping up her words with a self-assured grin. Jimmy leans over and they give each other their "handshake," starting with a swipe and ending with a fist bump. David and the others are floored by the rescuers.

Some ray of sunshine she is! he thinks to himself, frustrated. *Un-believable!*

Molly tries to come to the rescue and acknowledges the elephant in the room that nobody else wants to: the awful smell.

"Hey, uhh, I think I might still have some of that Pepto Bismol," she says to David, trying to lighten the mood. Suddenly she cringes internally, fearful that their ex-military rescue team will take offense to her making a remark about the smell of Patrick's body, but to her relief this elicits no such response.

"Yeah, I just might take you up on that," David says. "That ride out here in that contraption they called a van, bouncing and banging back and forth on that dirt road... that should've been the first red flag. Couldn't keep anything down!" The members of the film crew chuckle a bit. Boss and Jimmy look at each other, and she shakes her head.

"My grandma must be worried sick," rambles Anne. "I hope that my boyfriend is helping my brother take care of her... I'm sure he is. He's the best. My brother is one of the last people that we would ask to take care of her. Hopefully my boyfriend is making sure that he's not throwing parties in her house. God, my brother's immature."

Her words are sobering to the group, who realize that they are days overdue from arriving at the Yaoundé airport.

"Yeah, me too," says Molly. "Not about the grandma part. But... my friends are gonna be worried about me. I'm not supposed to be alone for too long... not since…"

Molly ceases her sentence, but David knows that she's talking about whatever emotional and mental hell that she's been through since losing her wife.

"I just don't want them to think that I've done something stupid," Molly says, hanging her head down, seated in a criss-cross-apple-sauce position.

"My parents won't suspect anything for a long time," says Avery, trying to cheer everyone up. "Maaaaaaan, me and Henry, we was always out travelin'. They prob'ly think we decided to go to some rager in Europe and that I'll be back shortly!"

His glee is felt by all except for David.

"I... umm," he says, trying to conceal his uneasiness.

"I was supposed to be back by now. We were scheduled to get back just in time for my son's birthday." The group can hear the struggle in his voice, and they listen intently.

"I almost didn't take up the offer to come out here because of how close it was. His... eighth birthday."

David shakes his head, trying to keep himself together, before speaking again.

"My old man never kept his word with me. It's all I ever knew. And... I promised that I'd be back in time for Alex's birthday. I don't even know what day it is anymore, but I broke my word. I ain't there. I don't even wanna know what he and my sister must be thinking right now."

Boss looks at him, showing him the first and only hint of warmth thus far.

"Nobody's perfect," she says.

"I told Patrick I'd be buying drinks when the three of us got back."

Jimmy nods solemnly. David appreciates her words, offering him a hint of sunshine through his legions of internal guilt. Obasi and Dee follow along with the conversation, staying close by each other. Other than David and Molly, Dee has taken a liking to the shy, gentle, elderly Aka man, although the two haven't exchanged a single word yet.

"Let's get you guys home then, already," says Jimmy. "We'll do everything we can to get you back to your boy," he says to David.

To this, David takes a deep breath, sighs, and then nods in appreciation. Dee looks up at David, and David notices a sad look on his face that he cannot explain.

"You okay, kid?" he asks him gently.

Dee looks at David and then bows his head, unresponsive. Suddenly it hits David. *How stupid can I be?* he thinks to himself. If Dee pulls through with the rest of them, as David is determined that he will, he has no luxury of family left to go home to. In the dim light of the cave, David can see a single tear run down Dee's face. Dee, so young and so sweet, reminds David again of his own son, and it takes all of David's willpower not to scoop up the boy right then and there in embrace. Instead, he motions his arm outward, inviting the boy in. Dee accepts, and the two hug each other awkwardly.

Molly is the only one that manages to doze back off. The sound of water droplets slowly falling to the ground, deep inside the cave, puts her mind at ease as she drifts off.

The afternoon sun arrives in full force, as does the return of the steamy, humid heat.

"It's time to go," says Boss, as she sits up from a prone position.

"We need to get a move on. Let's just pray to whoever-the-hell that those assholes didn't discover our boat by now and steal it."

"Or siphon out our gas," adds Jimmy.

"Wait," says Anne, still sitting. "I wanna go as much as all of us do, but, what if they're out there? Those pirates? What if we run into more of those spiders??"

"J'ba FoFi," Obasi says, politely correcting her.

"I'm sorry?" she asks him.

"J'ba FoFi," he says again, sounding out each syllable.

Boss looks at her, "That's the phrase he kept saying when we first came across the webs. The big ass ones. Must be a... local euphemism?" she asks, turning back to Obasi.

"No euphemism. It is the name for a very real animal. J'ba FoFi. My people, and others in these regions... we've known about these creatures for as long as we can remember. One generation after the other has spoken of them. They are much, much bigger than any others like them. They are ambush predators, and use strands of web to hunt along game trails. They are very, very dangerous. Their bite has a 100 percent mortality rate. But I've never encountered one myself until yesterday. Sometimes, we and others living in this jungle will even build our homes in such a way to keep them from wandering in at night. The elders often insist on it while the younger ones ignore their warnings. They can take children in the middle of the night... but as we have all seen, they do get big enough to hunt fully grown men. My people talk of this creature being once very common, but are now a vanishing animal."

"Good," interjects Avery.

Obasi continues,

"This area must be one of the last areas where they live that hasn't been... what is the Western word... deforested?"

The group takes in his words. Anne knows full well that, if this had been told to her before seeing the monstrosity that pounced on Babila, that she—a fully educated researcher—would've written off Obasi as "talking about some kind of regional myth with no substantial evidence to support it beyond esoteric folklore about the metaphysical."

"Hey," says Jimmy to the group. "It's time to go. You heard the Boss Lady. Can somebody wake up Molly?"

Boss pulls out another cigarette and lights up while everyone grabs their stuff. She kneels down to pick up Patrick's M4, says a prayer to nobody in particular, and then stands up.

"I probably shouldn't do this, but, which of you is most reliable with a firearm?" she asks, exhaling a long drawl. The group looks around awkwardly and centers their sights on David, their de-facto leader.

"Ummm," he says awkwardly.

"College!" she says. "But you have an AK! Great weapon, by the way. Not as accurate as an M16, but super durable and reliable. That baby won't let you down." Boss turns to see who else is willing to handle their third gun.

"It's out of ammo," David says sheepishly.

Boss sighs. "You're killing me, College. Fine. Here. Don't point this at *anything* that you don't want to destroy! Even if it's empty. Even when the safety's on. Got it?!" she barks.

He nods and takes her Vector submachine gun.

"Wait a sec!" he says. She turns back around.

"Just to be safe... let me use that one instead," he says pointing to the late Patrick's M4 in her hands. "Promise me you won't laugh... promise? It's just... I recognize that one from a bunch of movies. Wouldn't that be safer? I don't even know what using this one looks like!" he says to her sheepishly.

She rolls her eyes and looks down at Dee, who looks up and gives her a nod of approval.

"Fine. Here," she says, giving David the M4 and taking back the Vector. He passes the AK-47 to Anne, who volunteers to take it. Boss points her finger right in David's face, "If you graze any of us, I'll shoot you myself," she growls.

"You got it, Boss," David says. Boss gives him an approving, but fake, smile. She turns around to face the others.

"Did nobody hear Jimmy? His vocal cords work perfectly fine. He said, 'Can somebody wake up Molly?'" Boss turns around and becomes aware of Obasi pointing at a sleeping Molly.

"What?" Boss demands.

That look has returned to Obasi's face. He points to the sleeping scientist, and the group turns to see a spider—exactly like the one that bit Paul—crawling over her as she sleeps. Its prickly legs start at the back of her head of hair and slowly crawl up, exposing its whole body as it crawls over Molly's face. It is the exact same kind that bit Paul: yellow with a purple abdomen, only this one is a solid nine inches in leg span.

Its bodily shape looks strikingly like a Giant Golden Orb-Weaving spider from Australia. Its prickly legs cover Molly's entire face, as its keyboard mouse-sized abdomen comes into view to cover her forehead.

The remaining members of the group shoot to their feet and try not to panic at the sight. Avery suddenly gains cat-like acrobatic reflexes.

"Quiet!" orders Obasi with a loud whisper.

"The movement. If it feels movement, it will bite more likely."

The group freezes. Anne and Avery use all their willpower not to start freaking out right then and there. Anne covers her mouth. A determined look forms on Obasi's face while the others back away. He grabs a large stick and slowly approaches the sleeping, unsuspecting scientist to knock it off of her. But before he can reach the stick far enough, Molly opens her eyes.

Having her peaceful dream interrupted by the sight of the arachnid's fangs and chelicerae "incisors" twitching about right up in her face, and suddenly feeling the sensation of its prickly legs, Molly screams bloody murder and the arachnid is tossed off of her.

"Ahhhhhh! Fuck! Fuck! AHHHH!" she screams, thrashing about and feeling the phantom sensations of creepy crawlies all over her body. She nicks herself a few times on cave rocks during her meltdown, as Anne and Avery desperately try to calm her down.

"I can't do this! I can't do this anymore!" Molly shouts hysterically as the group stumbles out of the cave. They flee as fast as they can into the broad afternoon daylight of the jungle, as the illusion of the cave's "safety" is shattered by a creature a fraction of their size. Then Obasi, taking the lead again, says something that confirms David's suspicion.

"Baby! That was just a baby! A hatchling!"

Hearing confirmation that the species of arachnid that gave Paul a slow, agonizing death from one little bite is the *same* species that grows large enough to ambush and overpower a grown man only makes Molly more hysterical. She thrashes about and starts peeling off clothes as she orders the others to check her for unwanted arachnids on her person. They check her and themselves and their surroundings. Nothing. Not even spider webs. Molly hyperventilates and stumbles into a thicket of vines, which sends her into another downward spiral of panic. Anne, usually the panicked one, grabs Molly by the shoulders and shakes some sense into her. Obasi holds Molly still and examines her all over her face, forehead, neck, everywhere…

"You weren't bitten. Consider yourself very lucky." he says with a stern, fatherly tone.

The group scurries through the jungle. David and Boss take point with their weapons, while Jimmy holds up the back with his to make sure they're not being followed. David checks, what seems like every five or ten seconds behind him, to make sure that Dee is still there. The adults surround him as they travel, not unlike a herd of elephants protecting a calf.

"Hey! We've heard that weird screaming sound, too!" exclaims Avery. "The one that you asked us about last night. The one that the kid said wasn't us. We've heard it, too. Like a person! Usually it sounds like a woman, but occasionally a man, too! There could be others out here. What if there are others?"

"Did you radio in for a separate lost group?" demands Jimmy, looking over his shoulder at Avery.

"What, no! We told you, it's just us. We don't know who that is, but... we've heard her out here!" he says, looking around and waiting for Boss or Jimmy to answer him.

He continues, "What if there's a missing person out here? What if she needs our help, too?"

"Then she better get lucky and find us real damn fast!" says Boss.

"Bet you this God-forsaken place is just *cursed*!" cries Molly, who has still not regained her usual composure.

"There's someone else out here," David says to himself under his breath.

The group comes around the bend and passes a thick swamp. Next to it, they observe large, deep imprints in the mud which resemble cracked saucepans.

"Elephant tracks," says Anne.

"C'mon guys, let's pick up the pace!" says Boss, who doesn't give a damn about wildlife tracks ... until she sees two other types of tracks.

Stopping to examine them, she comes across sets of human shoe prints alongside something else. Dug into the mud, small prints can be seen scattered in much greater numbers than the elephant and human prints nearby. The prints resemble what you would imagine it would look like if somebody took a two or three-inch thick stick and poked holes in the ground like polka-dots. Boss examines them, and then looks up at Obasi.

"What was it you said... about mating season?" she asks him. Obasi says nothing, knowing full well that she and the other outsiders get it by now. Scurrying through more and more jungle to get away from the giant spider tracks, the group keeps moving until Boss throws her fist skyward. Some of the group reacts properly, while some others do not understand her signal. She flattens her hand out and lowers her palm so that it's facing the ground.

"Wha- What's going on?" asks Avery out loud.

"Shut up!" Boss whisper-shouts to him. Jimmy comes up from behind the clueless man and shoves him by his shoulder to the ground. Now concealed like the others, Avery now hears what caught Boss's attention to begin with ... voices.

A ways ahead of them on the other side of the gully, several hurried voices move through the trees. All men, and definitely as many of them as in their group, if not more. No female voices. They all speak French or another local language. The group turns to Boss and Jimmy, and she raises her trigger finger to her two lips ... the universal signal to be quiet. She and David look to young Dee to make sure that he understands. He nods timidly.

Suddenly, the barrel and circular front sight of an H&K G3 assault rifle comes into view, followed by its handler. A tall Congolese man raises his rifle and scans the shrubbery ahead of him. After a few tense seconds, he is summoned by a voice that both the rescuers and the rescuees alike recognize, much to their dismay, despite the voice speaking French ...

Dee personally recognizes the voice immediately and stifles his own crying.

"Wait a minute!" the voice shouts, now in English. He barks an order in French and steps forward with his fully loaded AK-47. He steps closer ... and closer ... and closer. David feels a trickle of sweat run down his leg. Peering through the tall grass, Jimmy can clearly see Oskar van Vuuren a mere three yards from where David and the boy are hiding in the shrubs.

Jimmy's eyes widen, and he raises his SCAR, slowly and quietly, until he has a clear shot at the pirate leader. He waits tensely to see if Van Vuuren will discover the civilian and the child. Should the second call for it, he would only be one of many men that Jimmy Leung has killed over the years, albeit the first one that he's killed outside of formal active duty service. Jimmy's finger hovers over the trigger, when Van Vuuren turns right towards him.

For a split second, Jimmy thinks he's been spotted, but then the sweaty pirate leader keeps scanning his eyes across the gully. Van Vuuren wipes his forehead and flicks the sweat off of his hand, returning his right hand and trigger finger back to the trigger. He pauses again ... scrunching his nose and taking deep, dramatic inhales through his nostrils, as if he can smell something unusual.

Finally, he turns away towards a section of the jungle where none of them are hiding. Behind him though, a group of a solid dozen pirates fan out into the jungle, all of them armed with Kalashnikov assault rifles except for the one with the G3. Every one of them searches for the posse of outsiders that killed one of their own and foiled their efforts.

Just our fucking luck, David thinks to himself as he tries desperately to keep his breathing quiet. Without warning, Van Vuuren sprays a hail of bullets into the shrubs, firing off at least fifteen automatic rounds from his clattering AK.

Dee squeals, terrified, and David covers his mouth to silence him just in the nick of time. Van Vuuren's men don't react to the loud gunfire, don't even seem to flinch ... as if they're used to these random outbursts. Luckily, nobody was hit by this burst of fire.

Just as the pack of pirates begins to wander off, the log that Avery's crouched on, hiding him behind the shrubs, comes loose and rolls down the hill. Avery slides, helplessly exposing himself. Van Vuuren and his men turn around, stunned at the sight.

Boss thinks to herself, *Fucking useless!*

"That's them!" Wanjala shouts, pointing straight at Avery. One of the pirates raises his AKM and Avery yelps in fear, but not before Jimmy blows a hole right through the pirate. The dead pirate and his AK tumble to the ground, and a massive fire fight ensues.

Van Vuuren swings up his AK-47 and furiously shoots at Jimmy, but Jimmy dives behind a thick tree suitable for cover. Dee screams and covers his ears in the ensuing chaos, crying. Getting shot is not what Dee is afraid of. He is deathly afraid of ending up back in the "care" of Van Vuuren and his right-hand man, Kumni.

David promptly hands a crying Dee off to Anne, who gets him to cover. She pushes him away with one arm while the other holds the completely empty, but bayonet-tipped, AK-47. Molly hides with Avery while David tries to clear a jam in Patrick's M4. He becomes frustrated, panicked even. Banging on the rifle, he finally pulls himself together and realizes the rifle has the safety turned on. Flipping it off and yanking back the charging handle like he's seen in several movies and games, David points and shoots.

He kills one of the pirates, and in response at least four of them turn their automatic weapons on him, firing on his position even though they do not know exactly where he is. He yells in fear and dives into a large slope in the ground, providing cover for him. He hides in the hole as bullets pop into the dirt and whistle all around and above him ... some of them landing way too close for comfort.

Their gunfire is drawn away towards two much, *much* deadlier targets. The pirates disperse as the two devil dogs fire on the woefully untrained and unprofessional marauders.

Boss snaps out from behind a tree and skillfully dispatches two pirates with her Vector in short and controlled bursts of fire, cutting up their chests, while Jimmy holds his own just as well. The clattering of the pirates' AK's versus the distinctly different-sounding three round bursts of the trained professionals' NATO-issued weapons can be heard for miles around in the Congolese jungle. The pirates indiscriminately shoot up vegetation and vines as they attempt to take out the outsiders.

Completely distracted by the danger in front of them, none of them see Van Vuuren and his closest men sneaking up on them from behind. The three armed members of the group—Boss, David, and Jimmy—realize too late why the pirates in front of them have ceased firing. Without warning, Van Vuuren uses the butt of his rifle to bash the back of Jimmy's head. The marine's vision turns starry as he tumbles to the ground, with only his elbows breaking his fall. David feels the hot barrel pressed up against the back of his neck.

"Hands up, cocksucker!" Van Vuuren snarls. "We got some catching up to do!"

He takes his steel toe boot and kicks David downwards onto his stomach. David desperately tries to get away, but Van Vuuren kicks him right in the gut. Coughing and in pain, David lays there helplessly in a fetal position. Van Vuuren kicks him again, over and over again until he's bleeding, much to Dee's horror.

"What's wrong, Doc? You got off just fine with one of my men! Hey, did you know that Beza was Babila's younger brother? Did you know we practically raised that kid?" he says again, furiously kicking the marine biologist again in the sternum.

"Stop it, please stop!" Molly wails for the carnage to stop, but Van Vuuren and the other pirates just laugh with delight, seemingly unfazed at all that at least four of their "friends" were just killed in the shootout.

Boss desperately tries to take back control of the situation. One of the pirates grabs her, but she quickly twists his arm into an arm bar and then trips him; disarming him, putting him on his ass, and turning her weapon on him in a matter of seconds. But it's no use. At least four pirates point their weapons at her, screaming at her to surrender. She glares defiantly into the eyes of Van Vuuren as his men encircle her, and then finally drops her submachine gun, never taking her defiant glare off of the pirate leader.

He smiles back at her, then turns his attention back to David. He kicks him again, and David coughs a small amount of blood.

"No!" cries Dee, giving his position away nearby. Van Vuuren and Kumni look at the boy, surprised.

"Well, well, well," Van Vuuren says. "I love family reunions! I see you made yourself a little friend, doc." He looks maniacally at the small African boy. Kumni raises his hands at the boy and beckons him.

"Deion! Come on, man. We missed you! What, you didn't miss us? That's too bad 'cause we gotta catch up!" Dee's crying intensifies at this.

David, having no strength to plead with their tormentors, says nothing as Wanjala Killian yanks him up to his feet.

Unathi Andile grabs young Deion by the back of his neck, separating him from Molly, Anne, and Avery.

The armed pirates lead the overwhelmed and outnumbered group of eight by gunpoint to a nearby opening between several overgrown trees where the group desperately tries to keep their hands raised in surrender, hoping that the pirates will spare their lives. Van Vuuren looks at the boy and then kneels down to him, while his cronies keep their weapons trained on the other seven. Then he notices Obasi, the Aka man that he's never seen before.

"And who might you be, old man?" he asks Obasi, the only one there who maintains a calm composure. Obasi does not answer him, maintaining a healthy posture as he sits on the ground while the others are kneeling.

"Hello? You deaf or something?" Kumni demands. He and his "superior" piggyback off of each other's hateful energy.

"You wanna die out here with these losers?" Van Vuuren says to him.

To this, Obasi looks up at the man, "Death is just another journey of life," he says in a calm and yet defiant tone that floors everyone.

"No!" David croaks to himself, tasting his own blood and fearing that they are going to murder the old indigenous man. Van Vuuren, frustrated by not getting a rise out of Obasi, looks angrily at one of his men. The pirate punches Obasi across the face, causing his nose to bleed slightly. Van Vuuren turns his attention back to the child and shoves his finger in his face.

"You… I believed in you, kid. You could've been one of our best. But you just… couldn't forget, could you?" he says smugly. "I've told you before, Dee, this is a dog-eat-dog world. Predator or prey! Don't you get it? And you had the chance to be one of *us*!" he snarls at the boy.

"We gave you a chance… to be a predator. To not just survive here but to *thrive*… I, yes, *I* gave you that chance! And you threw it right back in my face. Well now you are going to die with these miserable fucks. YOU, boy, will die as a coward for leaving us. Yes. But also, as a traitor. Not as intruders, like *these* miserable fucks, but as a *traitor.*"

"Leave… the kid… alone," croaks David weakly, still feeling the pain in his abdomen. Van Vuuren stands up to talk again, but Boss snarls at him.

"Oh my God, would you just shut the fuck up already? You really like to hear yourself talk, don't you, tough shit?" she says right to Van Vuuren.

"Oooooooohh!" the other pirates snicker. Van Vuuren looks down at the woman, but instead of shooting her he glances at Kumni, the closest thing that he has in this small world of his to a friend. The two don't even need to verbally communicate their intentions. Kumni reaches down and grabs Dee, yanking him up by his ear as the child screams. This riles the group up, but the pirates shove their Kalashnikovs in their faces and yell at them to stay in line.

Kumni starts hitting and kicking the child over and over and over again. He hits, not hard enough to cause permanent injury, but hard enough to cause substantial pain and further torment for the captured Americans to watch. Dee yelps with every blow like an abused puppy, powerless at the hands of his tormentor.

"Stop! Stop!" Avery and the others plead, as Kumni viciously hits and kicks the helpless boy.

"Hey, real talk," Kumni looks at the Americans. "You wanna know why this boy's so afraid of us?"

He looks to Van Vuuren, as if asking for permission with his gaze, and the pirate leader shrugs his shoulders as if to indicate "Tell 'em, I don't give a shit."

Kumni's words that follow send chills down every one of their spines, including the battle-hardened combat veterans, and possibly even a few of the newer pirates ... though they wouldn't dare voice their objections. "My boss here... my partner, we hadn't seen a woman in so long when we raided the boy's boat. I'm sure you can understand. But instead of killing the boy, we thought maybe he could be of use to us. They do the same thing to condition child soldiers to turn on their parents. Where we made the mistake was making it way too obvious that we in fact were the ones responsible. We 'took' the boy's mother."

David, Boss, Molly, and Anne feel the rage rising up in them as they watch Kumni recount Dee's traumatic background simply for the sake of tormenting him.

"I tried to kill the boy, just like his father and siblings, after Oskar was finished with his mother. But he wouldn't allow it," he looks to his superior.

"Hey, we all make mistakes!" Van Vuuren says with zero remorse in his smug look. Kumni looks down at the bruised boy right in the eye and continues. "We should not have spared you all those years ago when we raided your family's boat."

Dee heaves, crying hard, but by now no tears are left to come out. David feels the pain in his body being replaced by anger and adrenaline. Boss snaps and starts screaming at the pirates.

"FUCK YOU!" she yells at Van Vuuren and Kumni. "You sick, twisted sons of bitches! Fucking COWARDS! Fuck you! FUCK you!"

"I would love that, honey," Van Vuuren says. He nods to two of the pirates, and they grab her by each forearm and yank on her to remove her clothes. Anne bursts into tears, fearing that she and Molly will be next. Boss spits in one of the pirates' faces, and he hits her. She struggles with them. David watches in horror, knowing full well that if he charges them again that they will not end up so lucky this time. Jimmy turns beet red with anger, ready to erupt like a volcano at the sight of the two men trying to rape one of his closest friends. The pirate who hit her, Kwabena Businge-Guillot, and the other pirate manage to get her vest off. Then Kwabena pulls out a knife and starts trying to cut away at Boss's top and belt.

Boss seizes her opportunity.

Grabbing Kwabena by the wrist, she twists it with all her might, breaking it. Kwabena *yelps* in pain, and then Boss—now wielding his knife—stabs Kwabena right in his Adam's apple, slicing the blade right up his neck to just below his chin.

The pirate gurgles blood out of his mouth and his clothes are immediately soaked red from his own fluids running profusely from his sliced open neck. He desperately reaches for something to sit back on with one hand while he grasps at his throat with the other, falling on his ass and gurgling some more. Jimmy knows that he will be dead within minutes. Shocked, the other pirate leaps back away from her like a timid mouse. In the split second that this unfolds, David swears he can even hear the other pirates gasp a bit.

Kumni's and Van Vuuren's eyes widen in surprise at the speed that she manages to turn the tables on Kwabena.

"ENOUGH!" barks Van Vuuren. "I've had enough! Kill this bitch! Kill them all!!"

The pirates keep their weapons trained on her and the other seven, including the child, but do not fire. Van Vuuren, furious, remembers that many of his men don't speak English. He barks the order again in French, this time speaking for longer and apparently adding an additional instruction or two that the Americans cannot understand.

"You idiots!" he screams at them, then says the rest in French. The Congolese men begin beating at all seven of them with the buttstocks of their rifles, beating the crap out of all of them except for Boss herself.

"You see this? You kill him? Now they suffer because of you, devil woman!" Kumni shouts at her. She begrudgingly drops the knife, hoping that that will get them to stop hurting the others. Finally, she receives a beating from the vengeful pirates, as well.

"Good! Very good! That's enough, now." Van Vuuren instructs his men, in French.

"Kill them all," he says with a smile. The pirates raise their Kalashnikovs to execute the group for the final time, when all of a sudden they hear a bone-chilling *scream* ring out from the jungle.

That ominous scream again ...

Both groups suddenly realize that they are *not* alone ... and the scream came from the brush extremely close by.

Right next to them.

12

ALL OF THEM SLOWLY TURN THEIR HEADS TOWARDS THE DIS-torted, human scream coming from the thick jungle foliage right next to them.

An eerie shadow unlike anything they've ever seen makes its way towards them, moving slowly and methodically. The shadow almost reminds David of the time he saw the shadow of an enormous octopus wading through the shallow water near the beach. But the scream …

The scream was definitely a woman in distress … the same one that they've been hearing periodically that allows them to stray, mentally, from hard evidence and into paranoid superstition over *who* out here could be making those sounds.

Perhaps, the jungle *is* haunted.

A branch of some kind? David wonders as he and the others watch as the figure causing the shadow slowly reveals itself.

The entity *screams* again.

Almost human.

The shadow of a giant, man-sized spider with a six-foot leg span comes into view through the foliage, and the pirates' faces begin to look sour.

Another scream.

An enormous, hairy, brown spider leg steps out from the shrubs.

Another scream.

Then another leg.

Then another.

Then another. Pushing the shrubs aside.

Within the span of an extremely tense few seconds, slowly the giant man-sized arachnid reveals itself ... stepping out of the thick jungle until its hideous shadow is replaced by the body and legs from which the shadow originates.

The origin of the sound.

Coming into view, all the humans can clearly see the massive arachnid revealing itself ... one leg at a time until they can clearly see its face: eight eyes, enormous and bulbous chelicerae, banana-sized fangs, pedipalps, and its "mouth" where *the scream is coming from.*

Logic fails David as the wide-eyed, almost trembling marine biologist realizes that it's the adult J'ba FoFi that has been "screaming" all this time. Somehow ... some way ... they have evolved the ability to "mimic" the sounds of their prey in distress.

Out of the corner of his eye, he can see sheer terror on Boss's face.

"What the f—" Van Vuuren croaks, horrified.

"Mother of God, shoot it! Shoot it!" he yells. He, Kumni, and every one of the pirates turn their attention away from the captured outsiders and raise their guns to shoot the giant spider, when a *chorus* of screams and hissing sounds begins all around the flabbergasted humans.

A woman screaming.

A man screaming.

An antelope in distress.

Even the sounds of various other, local animals in distress that only Obasi recognizes.

All mixed in with the sounds of woodpecker-like "clicking" and hissing.

Then *several* giant spiders emerge from the thick jungle all around them, surrounding both groups of terrified humans like a pack of hungry velociraptors.

The yells of some of the terrified pirates, moments earlier carrying themselves like hardened criminals, can be heard from every direction ... drowned out only by the haunting mimicry of the eight-legged jungle monstrosities.

The flash of their muzzles from ensuing gun fire can be seen reflected in the first J'ba FoFi's glossy-looking eight eyes, as chaos ensues.

"Ahhhhh!!" shouts Kumni as he unleashes a hail of automatic fire from his Kalashnikov, killing a couple of the giant spiders just as they were about to pounce. The captured Americans quickly snatch back their firearms, but the pirates don't even notice. Completely distracted by the freaks of evolution all around them, both groups of humans spring into action as sheer adrenaline rushes through their veins.

Obasi, just as horrified and taken aback by this discovery, shouts something to the others in Aka.

"What?" shouts Boss. Obasi course corrects and switches to English.

"Back to back!" He orders. Obasi, Boss, David, Jimmy, Dee, Molly, Anne, and Avery huddle together with their backs touching, allowing the armed members of their group to see—and shoot—in all directions as dozens upon *dozens* of adult J'ba FoFi spring out of the jungle to attack both groups of humans.

Van Vuuren's and Kumni's "leadership" falls by the wayside as the pirates fail to work together the way the outsiders do. One of the pirates drops his guard for a split second and looks back towards the Americans, as if he's about to suggest to his buddies that they do the exact same thing.

Just then a J'ba FoFi specimen with a body as big as a Rottweiler pounces on the man from behind and drives it's nine-inch fangs into his upper back's trapezius muscles. The fangs pierce him on either side of his spine and narrowly miss severing it. The man screeches in pain and in horror with an ungodly look on his face as the spider drags him off into the depths of the jungle ... using either its sheer strength, or its webbing, or both ... to drag him.

Dee and a few of the film crew survivors cover their ears at the deafening sounds of the automatic gunfire all around them.

Another adult J'ba FoFi, easily with a six-foot leg span, pounces onto another one of the pirates before he can swing his AK-47 towards it to shoot. Wrapping its hairy brown legs around him in mid-air, the massive arachnid sinks its fangs into his neck before they even hit the ground. Spurts of blood gush from the puncture holes in the man's neck like a schoolyard drinking fountain.

"Shoot! Shoot, goddammit!" Van Vuuren shouts, desperately trying to compose himself and his men. Kumni and Van Vuuren get separated in the chaos, but the Congolese pirates and their leader empty their magazines into the cephalothorax and abdomens of multiple specimens, and for a time they seem to gain the upper hand. Several spiders are slaughtered in the torrent of 7.62 x 39 ammunition fired by the humans' Kalashnikovs.

David fires the 5.56 rounds from his M4 at anything that moves in the brush around them, while Boss skillfully dispatches a couple of J'ba FoFi with her Vector. Jimmy points and shoots again, and again, and again with his SCAR, and they reload their weapons as quickly as they can. Molly furiously uses the AK-47's bayonet to swipe at oncoming spiders. Anne and Obasi do everything in their ability to shield and comfort Dee, who has practically shut down from the overwhelm of it all.

The group of Americans hears that *hissing* sound coming from right over their heads.

They look up just in time to see another six-foot specimen fall down right on top of them, breaking up their "back to back" maneuver as it lands. It turns to attack Anne, but Obasi grabs the AK-47 out of Molly's hands and stabs the monstrosity right in its hideous incisors. The spider skitters off, injured.

"Thank you, thank you, thank you, thank you!" Anne cries as Obasi nods to her and then tosses the AK-47 back to Molly. She catches it back using both hands and willingly gives it back to Anne so she can coddle Dee. Suddenly another spider, this one with a five-foot leg span, squares up with Molly. The marine biologist is distracted by the horror in front of her, as she ushers Dee away to join the other adults behind her.

Bullets whistle all around as men are hunted by the man-sized arachnids. The noise of the chaos becomes so deafening that Molly can almost hear the sounds of—or at least imagines hearing the sounds of—bullet casings "clinking" together as they land on the ground. She swears that she can even see the chelicerae of the spider in front of her "tingling" in vibrating motions as it emits its freakish hissing sound at her.

Suddenly, something on the other side catches Dee's attention.

The boy runs up to David and Boss and frantically tugs on them until he gets their attention. They look at him and he points to an opening where the "ring" of giant spiders surrounding them now has a break in its armor.

David and Boss look at each other in a split second, no words needing to be said.

"Move it!" she orders. The group of seven makes a run for it, sprinting as fast as they can. They bob and weave and maneuver their way through the thick jungle away from the J'ba FoFi and the other humans.

In the chaos, Molly does not hear them moving on and stays distracted by the colossal arachnid which seems smart enough to take its time and size her up, rather than just mindlessly pouncing. She pelts it with rocks and empty assault rifle magazines, as the other seven slip away without checking to make sure that everyone is following along.

Molly looks around frantically as she realizes that she is all alone. Both groups of humans have split off, with the survivors escaping one way and the pirates fleeing another way. Dr. Molly Hendricks descends into a full blown mental breakdown as she realizes that the only living things around her now are a few adult J'ba FoFi up in the canopy, slowly descending down to her by the webbing of their spinnerets ...

FAR REMOVED NOW, THE OTHERS KEEP RUNNING. BOSS LOOKS back at her friend to make sure he is with them. She is relieved when she sees Jimmy sprinting alongside them, struggling with his own exhaustion but still maintaining proper trigger discipline like she does. Obasi is still the fastest out of all of them, while Dee remains the slowest.

"This a good time for one of your stupid ass jokes?" Boss shouts at Jimmy.

"Not the time, Boss Lady!!" Jimmy yells back. "Writer's block!"

After several hundred yards of running as fast as they can, Anne lands her foot wrong on the uneven ground. The young researcher rolls her ankle and tumbles into some vegetation. The others stop and hurry back to help her, when Anne shakes the dirt off of her face and suddenly becomes aware that she is not alone.

"Wait," says David incredulously. "Where's Molly?"

His words go unanswered as the group is again distracted by Anne's misfortune.

Noticing too late the hissing, "clicking" sounds coming from the shady underbrush in which she has fallen, Anne's two eyes meet the glossy, black eight eyes of another massive J'ba FoFi adult. The ravenous giant lunges at her with its front legs, ensnaring her the way a regular-sized tarantula would a small frog. She screams loud enough to cause pain for her vocal cords as the spider ensnares her limbs with its webbing - much like a hog tie - and drags her off.

"No!" shouts David, as he raises his M4 to fire.

Jimmy shoves the barrel of his gun away from Anne and the spider and barks, "No! You don't have a clean shot! You'll hit her!"

"Fuck! Fuck! Fuuuuuuuuck!" bellows David, melting down. He continues, "I should've fuckin' done it! If the bullet killed her at least the spider wouldn't!" he yells at Jimmy.

"How do you know?" Jimmy argues back. David's anger reaches a breaking point, and he snaps at the Marine, turning the "real" doctor tables on him from earlier.

"And how would YOU know?" David snarls and postures at Jimmy.

"Are YOU a doctor?"

"Ya know, we didn't have to come save your sorry ass!" Jimmy snarls back, turning bright red with anger. David points back at where Anne was dragged off.

"I could've saved her if you hadn't stopped me!"

"You couldn't even save yourself!" Jimmy barks. The two men almost come to blows, before Boss and Obasi break them up.

"ENOUGH!" Boss shouts. "Enough goddammit! There's nothing we can do about it now!" she shouts at David. She turns back to Jimmy, stopping him before he can swing at the civilian scientist.

"Knock it off, Jimmy! Bro... BRO! That's enough! You're a Marine, for Christ's sake! Act like one!" The two men take a moment and cool off, before Dee interjects.

"Where is the other dolphin lady?" he asks. "The nice one?"

David nearly collapses, wanting to pull his own hair out at the realization that Molly has gotten separated from them. His internal guilt never ceases. David tries to hold himself together.

"One of those things must've gotten in between her and us," he says, trying not to break down. "Neither of them fucking deserved it."

ON THE OTHER SIDE OF THE JUNGLE VALLEY, VAN VUUREN and his men comb through the thick vegetation, watching intently for monster spiders while trying to get as far from the area as possible.

"Kumni!" shouts Van Vuuren. "Mwanda! Mwanda! Where are you, you idiot?"

"What should we do about him and the others, boss?" one of the scared Congolese pirates asks Van Vuuren timidly. Van Vuuren hesitates for the slightest moment. He feels deeply concerned about Kumni's whereabouts, but would never allow his men to detect this. He swallows his emotions.

"Fuck 'em," he says, matter of factly. "There's nothing we can do."

FAR REMOVED FROM HIS PARTNER AND THE REST OF THE pirates, Kumni stumbles out of the jungle. He picks himself back up and attempts to reorient himself after taking a tumble down a ravine. Having gotten separated from the others during the chaos, he tries to maintain his composure as he realizes that he is hopelessly lost. About a half hour has passed since they became surrounded by J'ba FoFi.

Kumni attempts in vain to retrace his steps through the thick jungle to get back to Oskar and his men. He knows full well that being alone in the jungle is a death sentence. *Better to get back to the others, even if I risk running into more of those eight-legged devils.* He kicks and thrashes in frustration, dusting himself off after his tumble. He breathes deeply and looks around. The area is thick, steamy, and hot ... but now even more misty.

Through the thick mist, Kumni freezes in fear as he hears a rustling in the bushes ahead of him next to a fallen tree. The rustling gets louder, and Kumni nearly pisses his pants as he remembers the fangs on those spiders back there. He takes off running again, limping this time from the soreness of having tumbled down the ravine moments earlier. He runs through a stream and finally spots the opening to a place where he can take refuge ...

A cave.

MEANWHILE, THE GROUP OF SIX SURVIVORS KEEPS PLUGGING along but have slowed down considerably. They make their way towards the river, where they pray that the rescuers' boat remains there intact. Every one of them feels sore, exhausted, and painfully hungry and thirsty. An interstellar headache ravages David, due in no small part to the lack of adequate water and food intake. His clothes already feel like they fit much more loosely around him, and he wonders if anyone else has a searing headache. *Never, ever, ever, ever* he swears to himself. *If I make it back, I will never take modern luxuries for granted again.* The pain in his head is matched only by the pain from his abdominal area from getting the shit beaten out of him. He gently rubs his stomach and the temples of his head, and groans quietly.

Another ruckus of hissing nearby snaps them back to attention.

"It's them," says Boss. Obasi looks around.

"This way, follow me!" he says.

The group runs again, away from the tall grassy clearing where they fear that a J'ba FoFi is sneaking up on them. They enter a large pocket of foliage and then come upon another grassy clearing, where Obasi centers his sights on a large tree.

"Climb!" he says, urgently motioning to the tree. "Climb! And then hold still! No noise! No movement!"

The group does exactly as told. Boss and Jimmy sling their stuff over their backs and make quick work of the tree. David wonders if they had to do a lot of wall climbing together in training. The two Marines and Obasi, exhausted, nonetheless muster even more energy to help the others climb up high. At David's insistence, Dee gets pulled up into the tree first ... something which Boss happily agrees to. Then Avery. And finally, David.

Even though Obasi makes clear that the tree serves only as temporary protection, there are no J'ba FoFi, and their noticeably thick webbing is nowhere to be seen on it. This particular tree is isolated from all the others nearby, sitting by itself in such a way that the arachnids wouldn't be able to reach it from any of the other trees.

This gives the group a desperately needed sense of relaxation not felt since the night prior, when Patrick was unconscious in the cave. Every one of them melts into the tree as they soak in even the slightest moment of relief.

"You know, it's ironic," David whispers softly. "You know who else used to cower in the trees? Millions of years ago to escape prehistoric predators?"

Avery and the others look at him.

"Our primate ancestors."

David looks over to the battered, abused boy, who looks back at him. If David hadn't been with him the last few hours, he would be wondering right now why Dee's eyes look red and sunken. It wouldn't take a rocket scientist to be able to see that the sweet boy had been crying for hours. Boss looks at the boy, as well, and her heart breaks a little as she remembers what those horrible men back there put this sweet boy through.

Boss glances up to make sure that no one is looking directly at her, and she allows a singular tear to escape from her eye. She wipes it away and looks away from the boy, not wanting to get emotional in front of the others. She considers faking a sneeze ... just in case anybody saw that tear. *That way I can say I have allergies. Yeah, allergies!* she thinks to herself. But then she remembers what Obasi said, about how movement and noise attracts the spiders. She swallows her pride and decides against faking a sneeze.

Without even fully realizing that they are both trying to comfort the boy, David and Boss reach to hug him at the exact same time, coming awkwardly close to hugging each other by accident instead.

"Oh, uhh, my bad," David says to Boss.

"It's okay, College," she says gently. "After you."

Alex's father takes the kid gently by the arm, and notices one of Dee's many scrapes and bruises. Focusing on the big one on his arm, he looks at the boy. "You've had a rough day, bud. Haven't you?"

The boy's brown eyes simply look up into the eyes of the fatherly figure. David gently tries to clean the wound on the child's forearm.

"It's okay now. I... I promise. Remember what I said... First time for everything. I don't know how, but... I'm going to make sure that you get out of this okay."

David looks up and notices Boss observing their embrace. He looks at her, then back down at Dee.

"We all will."

Dee gives them an almost imperceptible grin, and then curls up next to David. Within minutes, the exhausted child is out like a light.

"Sweet kid," says Jimmy. David looks over at him with a lingering tension.

"I'm ..." Jimmy hesitates. "I'm sorry about your friends."

"Thank you," says David, inhaling and exhaling slowly and deeply. "Molly must be out there still. She... could be. But, Anne..." he sighs.

Avery chimes in,

"I've seen some crazy shit over the years, but who in the hell coulda' anticipated this?"

Boss raises her eyebrows in a show of agreement.

"Damn," continues Avery. He pivots to a lighter tone. "I could really use a double cheeseburger right now. Extra steak-cut fries and a coffee milkshake. Or strawberry!"

The group groans unanimously, salivating at the image of the meal that pops into their heads.

"Dear god, yes," Jimmy says. The only one who doesn't groan with delight at the thought is Obasi, as he's never had the luxury of such a high-calorie, fattening meal like this one. Boss pulls out her canteen.

"I have something for you guys. Share it out. I think this is all we have left until we take that straw and get to another water source."

She takes a tiny sip and passes the very last of their drinking water around, and the group's thirst is temporarily quenched. She pulls out her blow torch lighter and lights up a long overdue cigarette.

"Save some of that for the kid," she adds. She takes a few long puffs.

"For when he wakes up."

MINUTES BEFORE OBASI INSTRUCTED THEM TO SCALE THE tree, Kumni Mwanda, all alone on the other side of the valley, entered the cave …

He wipes the damp, cold sweat off of his forehead. His heartbeat accelerates as he enters the dark and obscure cave. However, the fear of the rustling that he heard outside trumps his fear of the darkness ahead. There's a strange smell ahead, becoming more and more prominent as he gets closer. Kumni can't exactly put his finger on it. It's almost as if it smells like candy. However, this somewhat-sweet smell is not pleasant. The moisture of the cave smells like puke to Kumni. He heads deep enough in so that he can still see his surroundings, albeit not very well. The light at the end of the cave's tunnel dims as he gets further away. The temperature of the rocky, moist cave is only a little bit cooler than the steamy jungle outside.

Fuck me, Kumni thinks as he contemplates his next move. The fact that his rifle got lost during the tumble is not lost on him, as he feels completely naked without any form of protection besides his bare hands.

A loud screeching sound coming from outside the cave sends chills down his spine. The screech-like sound is accompanied by a long and rhythmic sound that he can only describe as continuous clicking sounds, mixed with a low frequency *purring* sound eerily similar to that of a domestic cat.

"Ohh, shit," Kumni cries, as he rapidly steps backwards, further into the moist darkness. A loud *CRUNCH* sound below his shoe startles him, as he realizes that he's just backed into—and crushed—something delicate. Even with shoes on, the sensation of the crunching sound shoots up his body, and the hairs on his legs stand up.

Kumni stifles a yelp as he looks down, bewildered. Another trickle of sweat runs down his forehead and into his eye. Looking down at the floor of the cave, Kumni realizes that he's accidentally backed up into a bunch of strange looking objects in a cluster that he doesn't recognize.

He rubs his eyes to adjust to the dim light, and begins to make out the shapes of several large clusters of peanut-shaped pale white and yellow *eggs* on the ground.

A nest.

Kumni shivers with terror as he watches a few of the peanut-shaped eggs in the closest cluster break open, as tiny little spiderlings, bright yellow in color with tiny purple abdomens crawl out of their shells. While the rest remain dormant, a few of them skitter away ... disturbed by Kumni stepping on their brethren.

He struggles to compose himself, trembling, as the once tough river pirate sees ... and *feels* the prickly *sensation* of ... a bunch a baby and adolescent J'ba FoFi descending from the wall of the cave to the top of his head and to the ground below. These older sibling spiders range in size from two inches to a solid twelve-inch leg span. The smaller ones maintain their yellow and purple coloration, as the others look more brown and hairy the bigger they get.

Even in the poorly lit cave, Kumni can see the strands of web coming out of them as they descend, with their eight legs grasping and grabbing at him below. Kumni freezes in fear, unable to move. He feels a warm stream run down his leg, and a dinner plate-sized J'ba FoFi baby brushes its hairy front legs against his bottom lip. Unable to close his wide open mouth from the sheer fear, the man twitches, ready to sprint out of the cave.

Still paralyzed, he prays. He crosses himself and then kisses the cross that he wears around his neck, scared out of his mind.

But then he hears the hissing.

Right above him.

Slowly turning his body to look above him, Kumni can now see the shadow of the massive appendages above him twitching slightly in the poor light. Legs. A six-foot adult specimen dangles from the ceiling of the cave above him.

Kumni screams and takes off running, running as fast as he can and shaking off the babies as he makes his way to the exit of the cave. The light at the end of the tunnel beckons him, and he runs as fast as he can ...

... directly into a strand of webs. Ensnared at the one-way exit and struggling frantically, Kumni shrieks and fights tooth, claw, and nail to get free. But it's no use. Even amidst the chaos, he realizes that the giant arachnid outside the cave deliberately set a trap for him after he wandered inside.

"Help! Help! HELP!" he cries out in vain, as he hears the hissing adult behind him getting closer and closer and closer. Her hissing sounds morph into clicks, and then back to the original hiss. The giant arachnid rears up on its front legs and spins the pirate leader a few times, rotating him like a rotisserie on a rotating spit to make extra sure that he is trapped in her webs and not going anywhere. The feeling of the prey being wrapped up stimulates her pedipalps and she brushes them against him. She feels the closest thing that she can to ecstasy.

The giant spider holds him in place as he whimpers, terrified.

Kumni's life flashes before his eyes. He remembers one of the many things that he said to the little boy, Dee ... one of the many things told to the boy to justify his and Van Vuuren's twisted treatment of him and others whom they came into contact with: "Vengeance is in the creator's hands."

The J'ba FoFi takes her sweet time, knowing full well that her prey isn't going anywhere. She angles herself just at the right angle, and casually sinks her steak knife-sized fangs deep into Kumni's chest cavity. He feels *all* of it. Blood soaks the thick webbing. The adult backs off of him, and a few young ones of various sizes crawl on top of him.

Feeling the effects of the insidious venom at the exact same time that he feels the young ones crawling all over him, Kumni begins to feel a third sensation—as the smaller ones begin biting him all over his body and face. The adult female spider's brood slowly begins to consume him alive. Purple boils already begin forming on him, as the venom injected into his chest has almost instantaneous access to his heart and vital organs. His chest turns purple along with his veins, and his eyes change color. He can even feel the beginning staging of necrosis, as the venom eats away at his chest tissue like acid. His insides slowly become liquified, and the hungry babies dig in.

Kumni Mwanda whimpers again; quietly, softly, for the final time.

13

THE SUN SETS A STUNNING ORANGE HUE OVER THE CANOPY and the grasslands, as it gets dark once again in the African jungle. The base of the tree in which they remain hidden up high slowly begins to darken as the shadow envelops the tree, yielding to the setting sun over the horizon. Birds and other wildlife can be heard all around, albeit faintly.

"You know," David says to Boss, "All things considered, I think this is one of most beautiful places that I've ever been to. It's, like... I feel like it needs to be appreciated. Like the Amazon, it's one of the last untouched areas where biodiversity rules over man."

Boss listens but doesn't know how to respond. She considers his words to be rather awkward and dorky, but is slightly intrigued. She cannot think of anything to say, so she just shrugs her shoulders.

"Sorry," continues David. "I'm just a nerd is all. Always have been. Especially about ocean life and the mammals that inhabit our oceans. I've never even been in a fist fight prior to all the stuff that's gone down out here. I was always one of those good kids that liked to stay out of trouble."

Boss thinks this over, then responds, "I can't relate. When I was a kid I was suspended so many times for getting into fights with school bullies."

David looks at her, listening intently.

She goes on, "They were always bigger than me. The bullies, I mean. Almost all of them were boys. But... one thing that the school didn't seem to care about was the same reason I never felt bad for getting in trouble over it. Because I only ever got into fights when I was standing up for those who were getting picked on."

David takes this in but can't think of what to say next.

"Sorry," she says. "I've always been like that. I can't relate to textbooks or science-y stuff like you can."

"No, no, that's awesome!" says David. She looks at him inquisitively.

"I mean," he says, trying to course correct. "It's awesome that you'd stand up for the other kids. Especially when the mean kids were bigger than you. I never had the guts to do that as a kid."

She listens. David goes on.

"We... we need more people like that in this world. Willing and eager to stand up for what's right."

At this, Boss grins and looks down. "And you're not just a nerd," she adds. "Or, maybe you are. But who cares? We need nerds who know their shit."

The two of them glance at Dee, who remains asleep curled up next to David in their "section" of the tree, leaning against the base of a thick branch.

"Tell him about when you first heard of the Corps," Jimmy chimes in.

Boss chuckles a bit. "When I was in grade school," she says, "there was this bully. He always dressed well and you could tell he was from an uppity family. Anyway, one day he and some other kids started picking on a kid who had recently worked up the courage to come out of the closet. Poor little shrimp of a guy. When they came after him in the school parking lot next to the gymnasium, he didn't stand a chance. I laid into the son of a bitch, and even scared off his buddies who were also picking on the kid. He cried like a punk bitch by the time I was done with him. Me and the LGBT kid became good friends after that."

She takes a beat, thinking over the memory before continuing with her story,

"There were several adults on the other side of the parking lot when it happened. Even some faculty. That's the only reason that the bully got in trouble, too. There were security cameras all around, but the school was too cheap to get them fixed. Or maybe they just didn't have the funding, I don't know. They didn't catch anything. I did ultimately get in trouble for laying into that kid, but not as much as usual ... only because the adults saw how badly he beat the kid that they were picking on. Afterwards, somebody on campus who I'd only seen in passing—who apparently had witnessed me intervening—walked up to me. Later, I'd learn that he was a military recruiter. He had seen it all. He walked up to me, trying to hide how impressed he was, and said, 'Young lady, I think I have a career option for you.'"

"That was my first intro to the Corps."

David listens, fascinated. "What happened to the bully?" he asks her. Boss looks up at Jimmy, knowing that he knows the answer.

"Actually," she says, "he was supposed to be expelled because of it. This wasn't the first time he'd hurt someone. The year prior, he had sexually assaulted a female student. But, get this... he received suspension rather than expulsion for one reason and one reason only: his rich lawyer parents threatened to sue the school district and they caved in."

"Wow," David says, shaking his head in disgust. David, knowing full well the humble childhood that he was born into, would've never been able to "buy off" a chance like that. His disgust intensifies. *If I, a Black kid, had done that ...* he thinks to himself, *I probably would've gotten far worse than expulsion.* David considers sharing this, but doesn't want to interrupt her story.

"Yeah," Boss continues, "so from then on it sort of became my M.O. to keep people like him in line."

David nods his head in approval. A feeling of appreciation catches him off guard.

"Boss?" he says.

"Yes, College?" she replies.

"Thanks for coming for us. Thank you both. I don't know if anyone's said that yet, but, thank you. And I'm sorry about your guys' friend, too."

She and Jimmy say nothing, but they look happy to hear these words.

Suddenly, David's mind spirals down a rabbit hole of worry for the status and whereabouts of his colleague and fellow Ph.D. marine biologist. *Anne is certainly a goner* he thinks to himself, remembering how she was dragged off into the underbrush. *But Molly?* The thought of whether or not she—out there all alone and separated—is okay or not sickens him. Then he remembers the Pepto Bismol that she kindly gave him on the group's ride out here, and he can't contain himself anymore.

"I know we're supposed to be quiet, guys," he says to everyone in the tree, abruptly pivoting the vibe.

"But, Molly could be out there. We didn't see her get taken like the others were! What if she's close enough to hear us? What if she hears us calling out for her and can join us?"

Boss and Jimmy say nothing. Avery nods in agreement. Finally, Obasi chimes in, "That is a risk you must decide for yourself."

After some short debate, they begin calling out her name.

"Sorry, bud," Avery says to Dee. Even though he got to nap for a few hours, the sounds of the adults calling out into the night wakes him up.

"MOLLY!" Avery shouts.

"MOLLY, WHERE ARE YOU?" follows David. Several long minutes pass by while they call out her name. They take a long moment to listen ...

for anything. Her calling back. Footsteps. The sounds of the grass parting ways while something moves through it. Anything.

"Nothing," Obasi says with a sigh.

"We can try again when the sun comes back up," Boss says. "If she's smart like you, she's hunkered down somewhere and not traveling at night. C'mon, we should all try to get some r—"

Suddenly the tree branch holding Boss's weight snaps before she can finish the word. David's lightning fast reflexes kick in, and he grabs her by the forearm just in time before she plummets to the ground. She holds onto his wrist and forearm, dangling above the ground. The others spring into action as they help David pull her back up.

Even though David knows that she totally would've survived the fall, he takes a moment to tease her.

"I thought... " he says, trying to steady his breathing after the sudden rush of adrenaline, "I thought *you* were here to rescue *me!*"

"Uh huh, shut up," she says, shooting him a look while she huffs and puffs. David laughs and, much to his relief, she begins to laugh as well. Obasi and Dee even smile. The group laughs together ... the very first time that any of them have laughed or even smiled in a very long time. Boss shimmies herself until she feels secure by the much larger branch on which she now sits. She takes a deep breath, holds it for several seconds, then releases it slowly as her heart rate begins slowing down little by little after the fall.

"Where'd you learn to move like that?" she asks David.

"My son, Alex," he says. "He was a toddler not too long ago. Little shit he was, he got into everything! Nothing was safe from him climbing up. There were a couple times I caught him when he fell off the furniture. One time out of a tree house, too!"

Resting her head against the abrasive surface of the tree, Boss begins to feel her eyelids getting heavy ... when something wakes her right back up. At first she simply sees the shadow of it. She turns on her flashlight and sighs in relief.

In front of her, crawling along the surface of the tree is an itsy bitsy spider. It's tiny ... even smaller than most household spiders. Its coloration indicates that it's definitely not a J'ba FoFi hatchling.

"What is it?" Avery asks rather frantically. All of them look at her.

"Don't worry it's not one of them. Just a regular little spider," she says. She looks at it up close and scoffs.

"Fuck off," she says to it as she flicks it away with her trigger finger.

"Wish it was that easy with the other ones," Avery says, cringing.

"Hey, one can dream!" says Jimmy. "Just gotta get on their good side, you know!"

Boss smiles at him. His sense of humor never ceases to entertain her. Whether her fellow Marine's jokes make her belly laugh, make her groan with irritation, or somewhere in between ... she is nonetheless entertained and amused by Jimmy's ability to keep things lighthearted.

"Okay, so I got an idea," Jimmy says. The others look at him, at first taking it seriously.

"To get the big ones on our side. We gotta schmooze them up a bit. Romance them, you know?"

Boss rolls her eyes and shakes her head. Dee listens to Jimmy, amused.

"We write 'em a love letter to woo them. Hear me out," he continues.

"Dear spidey,"

"Is this a letter to Peter Parker, or to these things out here?" David says playfully.

Dee laughs at this. Jimmy proceeds,

"Dear spidey, I love you. I love everything about you. I love the sensation of... all eight of your legs when you're with me. I love peering into all eight of your eyes. I love the home that you've built with lots of love. And by love, I do mean sticky!"

Dee eats this up, as if he's never heard an adult making jokes for years, if not, ever.

"I love... all three thousand of your children," Jimmy says, putting his hand out as if to make an effeminate gesture.

"I love when we are together, spidey. I love when my children are with yours. I promise to gift you all the flies. It'll be like 'Lord of the Flies' when we are together... or, umm, antelope. Yes, I mean antelope!"

Boss groans out loud so that Jimmy can hear it. Dee eats it up, though. Obasi looks at Dee laughing, and the old man cannot help but smile at the boy's delight.

"Now, spidey," Jimmy concludes. "Please don't eat us! Love always, us."

Dee claps his little hands together, and the others join in, trying to keep their sounds to a minimum.

"That should work, right?" Jimmy asks.

"Oh, yeah," says Boss. "Your best work yet."

The group sits in silence for a few minutes, when David finally speaks up.

"You know, I have a theory about how they've gotten so big." The tone suddenly shifts from playful to serious again, but the group listens to him intently.

"I... I'm not an Arachnologist, so take this with a grain of salt. Or just tune me out 'cause this isn't my field of expertise..."

The group keeps their attention on him, waiting for him to continue.

"But I think I saw one of them... I could be totally wrong, but I think I saw the bodies on one of them rising up and down slowly, as if it was inhaling and exhaling. I don't know much about spiders or other invertebrates, but from what I've heard, spiders and scorpions don't have lungs the same way that we do. Their respiratory system is totally different. Their 'book lungs' don't expand and contract like ours do. And that's the main reason why they're not 'supposed to' get bigger than the Goliath bird-eating tarantula from the Amazon. I mean, that's still a big fuckin' spider—pardon my French—but it's nothing compared to…"

David hesitates, and then continues his train of thought.

"Invertebrates got much bigger, 300 million years ago, than they are today because there was *so* much more oxygen in the atmosphere back then. The surplus of oxygen during the Carboniferous allowed them to grow bigger. So I think… if what I saw is true… then this specific species of arachnid has lost their 'book' lungs and evolved to have lungs very similar to ours. That's probably why this species has been able to get around the size-oxygen barrier. But… but that still wouldn't explain the exoskeleton barrier. I really have no idea. All of this is just a theory."

The group never takes their eyes off of him.

"I don't know about this one either, but…" David says, as his tone becomes even more uneasy.

"This might also explain how they've evolved to be able to make vocalizations, too."

A troubled look forms on Avery's face. David continues.

"I've definitely heard of birds being able to mimic the sounds of other animals, especially in Australia. But this… man, I don't know. I would almost think that these spiders would also have needed to evolve vocal cords to be able to emit sounds from their mouth! But… who knows. I certainly don't."

The group sits in sobering silence. Just then, David realizes whose opinion he should really consult: the one man amongst them who knows these parts better than all of them combined. David looks over at Obasi, and asks him gently, "Obasi?"

The old Aka man, deep in thought, looks back at him.

"Are you aware of these spiders... these... J'ba FoFi, are you aware of their ability to... mimic noises? Has anyone ever spoken before of their ability to scream?"

Obasi just looks at him, perturbed. "Never," he says. "I've never seen anything like it."

Some more time passes as the group sits in silence. By now, it is pitch black outside. They can barely see the outlines of each other, let alone a few feet in front of them. This terrifies David. But at Boss's stubborn insistence, even he caves in and allows himself to get some badly needed rest. After a long while, he finally drifts off.

DAVID WAKES UP AND FINDS THAT HE HAS A KINK IN HIS NECK ... he fell asleep in the living room chair again. After yet another argument, the last place he wants to sleep is in the bedroom with Angie. David murmurs about the kink in his neck, and gets up to grab a cold beverage out of the refrigerator. By now, their son Alex should be sound asleep in his bedroom, and so the two no longer need to tiptoe around the house. Their old house.

"Angie?" David calls out from their kitchen. "Hey, Ang'? Where's that permission slip for Alex's thing?"

"What thing?" she barks at him from the bedroom.

"What'd you mean, what thing?" David says. "He has a field trip tomorrow! For his class. Every kindergarten class is going to the museum!"

"Yeah, and they need us to write another check for it!" yells Angie. "That's more money that we don't have!"

"This is the only time this year that the class is going!" he retorts, irritated. "You're telling me we ain't gonna send him over fifty bucks? C'mon, Ang'."

"Jesus CHRIST, David!" she barks. "We're still dealing with your student loans! And for what? You barely make enough for us to stay alive!"

"I am NOT in the mood, Angie!" he yells. Any concern about Alex not hearing their argument falls away as the married, albeit dysfunctional, parents square up... yelling at each other from separate rooms.

"You never are!" She yells. "It's only the end of August, and every time that kid comes home, that goddamn school wants another deposit, or supplies, or a fee of some kind. Fuckin' teachers getting off on it!"

"They make even less than I do! Then WE do!" David says. "You wanna be stingy, fine! I'll fuckin' pay for it!" he yells at the closed bed-room door.

"You wanna talk about stingy?" Angie snaps back at him from the other side of the closed door.

"Refusing to pay for the tab for your drunk ass friends doesn't make me stingy!" he snaps back. "Now who's being irresponsible?"

Angie screams, hitting the wall and then screaming over and over again into her pillow:

"I can't! I can't do this no more!"

David angrily slams the refrigerator door shut, and talks himself down from chucking the bottle of Corona at the wall. He takes several long, deep breaths and then counts to ten. He presses the ice-cold beer against the kink of his neck and then opens it, taking a long gulp before setting it on the counter. It's 1:00 o'clock in the morning, according to their stove. David closes his eyes, takes another deep breath, before turning around.

Startling him out of his skin, David realizes that Alex is standing right behind him in the living room next to the kitchen.

"Jesus!" David says, taking a breath after jumping a little from being startled.

"Alex, bud, what are you doing up? You have a big day tomorrow. Do you know how far past your bedtime it is?"

His son says nothing, maintaining a blank, ghostly expression on his face.

"Alex…?" David says.

Alex slowly raises his left arm until he is pointing to his parents' bedroom. His index finger, pointing at the door, trembles.

"Something's wrong," Alex says, frightened, his eyes never leaving the gaze of his father. A concerned look forms on David's face.

"Alex… are you okay?" he asks his son.

"Something's WRONG!" the boy says. Just then, Angie screams bloody murder from inside the bedroom.

"Ang'? Angie!" David lunges over towards the master bedroom, and is stopped by the sight of bright red blood flowing out slowly from under the door.

"Oh, God," David says with weak knees as he attempts to open the door. It's locked, as per usual from the inside whenever Angie is mad at David after an argument. He yanks on the door handle. She screams again.

David kicks in the door and turns on the light. A large, strange bulbous shape lies under their blankets and comforter. David runs over to yank the blankets off of his wife in distress. It is *not Angie*.

Rising up from under the covers, a massive tarantula-looking spider—an adult J'ba FoFi—gets up on its eight legs and slowly turns around towards David, who is petrified with fear. The arachnid rears up slightly and opens its mouth … where the sound of *Angie screaming* can be heard coming out of its hideous oral opening. The spider's fangs quiver. David backs up against the wall of their bedroom, terrified. He looks at the monster spider and composes himself as best as he possibly can.

"Angie? Honey? Are… are you in there?" he says, weakly.

The J'ba FoFi's chelicerae quivers, and "Angie"—trapped inside the hissing creature—lets out another scream at her husband before it lunges at him. Barely dodging out of the way in time, David screams and runs out of the room to grab Alex so they can get out of there. Alex *isn't* there. He scans the living room … nothing.

"Alex?" Alex! Alex, goddammit, where are you?!" he shouts, desperately looking everywhere he can for his son. Then he hears the pitter-patter. Coming out of the bedroom, the six-foot monster spider skitters along the living room wall as it charges at David.

David, running away from the creature as fast as he can, can hear Alex's voice coming from everywhere and nowhere at the same time.

"Something's wrong!"

"Something's wrong, Dad!" Alex's disembodied voice shouts to him.

"DAD! Something's wrong!"

David realizes the one place that his son likes to hide when he's afraid of something or something is going down. He turns tail, wrong-footing the giant arachnid. Running to their back sliding glass door, David opens it and slams it shut behind him before the spider can follow him outside. Pounding against the sliding glass door with its enormous legs, the spider struggles but it's no use.

Just then, the desperate J'ba FoFi rears up on its back legs and drives its fangs straight through the thick glass. The two fangs poke right through it as easily as two steak knives poking through a sliding screen door. Despite this, the Congolese Giant Spider is still unable to open the door or get through the glass. David scurries over to the tree in their old backyard ... to Alex's treehouse where the disembodied voice seems to be originating from.

"ALEX!" he shouts. "Hold on, son! I'm coming!"

He hastily climbs up the makeshift wooden ladder and pokes his head inside the treehouse. What he finds inside sends shivers down his spine.

Sitting in his treehouse criss-cross apple-sauce, a venom-ravaged Alex looks up at his father. The boy has red eyes and his veins are a bright purple. He has purple boils forming on him in real time. His limbs are swollen and jagged. He opens his mouth to speak, and a viscous liquid pours out. With his mouth wide open from shock, a tear rolls down David's trembling face at the sight.

David begins to hear the sounds of something—or multiple things— skittering around on the grass in the backyard, at the base of the tree below him.

"You," Alex wheezes to his father. "You messed it all up. You... were... too late."

Suddenly, the skittering and pitter-patter sounds get louder, and louder, and louder ... until David can't bear it anymore. He covers his ears with both hands and screams for it all to stop.

DAVID GASPS AS HE WAKES UP FROM HIS NIGHTMARE AND clutches his chest, desperately gasping for air and nearly falling out of the tree himself. He realizes that he is not at their old house, but still sitting in a tree ... in the little-explored jungles of the Congo, in the pitch darkness.

He inhales and exhales hard, relieved, but drenched in sweat.

His relief lasts mere seconds. Down below, David sharpens his attention as he realizes that the pitter-patter and skittering sounds from his nightmare weren't just in his nightmare: It's on the ground below them ... coming from nearby bushes and vegetation.

"Fuck me," David whispers to himself.

"Guys!" David whispers, loudly, attempting to wake the others. It doesn't work. He repeats himself, louder,

"Guys! Wake up!" he whispers as loudly as he can. With his nightmare still fresh in his mind, David thinks that his ex-wife would not make it very far out here, as she seemed incapable of keeping her voice down when needed. What flashes much more fresh, though, is the realization that this is not his nightmare. This is *real life*.

"Wake up, damn it!" he says. Finally, the others begin to stir. Boss is the first one to snap awake and notice the sporadic sounds of something—perhaps even multiple things—skittering in the tall grass below the tree.

"Get your weapons ready," she says.

"What is it?" Avery asks out loud at a volume that's definitely not a whisper.

"Shut up!" Jimmy whispers at him angrily. Avery acquiesces.

"I don't know about you but I'm low on ammo." Jimmy whispers to Boss.

"We'll do the best we can," she whispers. Just then the pitter-patter suddenly gets louder, and then ... nothing.

The group waits in silence for what feels like an eternity.

Nothing.

More waiting.

Finally, Boss decides to pull out her flashlight, something she wonders why she didn't do immediately upon hearing the noises. Mentally, she blames the fact that she's still waking up for "not thinking straight." She fumbles around her pack in the pitch darkness until she gets a grip onto her flashlight. It won't light.

"Can't see shit!" David whispers.

"That's what she's working on, hold tight," Jimmy whispers back. Dee makes a sound and Obasi promptly, albeit gently, instructs the boy to make no noise and keep absolutely still.

Boss bangs on her flashlight. It still won't turn on. Becoming frustrated, she shakes it a bit and then bangs on it again. It finally turns on, illuminating a *massive* J'ba FoFi below them at the base of the tree. Avery stifles his own scream. The monster arachnid sits there with its two front legs and pedipalps reared up; mouth, chelicerae, and fangs showing clearly in the beam of her flashlight. It's the biggest one that they've seen yet, and it made absolutely no noise in the last several minutes as it snuck up on them. The beam of her flashlight even reflects slightly against its black, glossy, fangs. Jimmy postulates that it may have been attracted by the sounds of them calling out for Molly earlier.

Then they can hear it.

The arachnid only now begins emitting its signature hissing sound, like a crocodile perched along the edge of a river with its mouth open. A terrified David wonders if it's smart enough to have stayed quiet until discovered. *This ain't no nightmare, this is very real*, he thinks to himself as his blood runs cold with fear. The group, frozen in fear, watches as the J'ba FoFi stays perfectly still for a long few seconds. It keeps its appendages reared up, frozen in place like a statue.

Then, it begins to move.

Despite its enormous size and weight, the arachnid's eight legs begin moving in unison to scale the tree. All concerns about whispering are left in the dust as the group scrambles to figure out what to do. Obasi, Jimmy, and Boss are the only ones who maintain their composure. David, who ran out of ammunition for his M4, doesn't even bother reaching for it. Boss raises her Vector, and Jimmy his SCAR-L, to eviscerate the giant. Jimmy pulls the trigger to the sound of a very distinct click. Out of ammo. Boss fires on the spider, but her weapon *jams*.

"I'm out!" says Jimmy.

"I need to clear a jam!" exclaims Boss, beside herself.

"You gotta be fuckin' kidding me!" Jimmy says, beginning to feel panicked. The J'ba FoFi moves closer and closer like a menacing elevator, ascending slowly up the tree.

"FUCK!" shouts Boss, unable to clear her weapon jam.

"Kick at it or we climb higher!"

Obasi quickly grabs the AK-47, the one originally wielded by Van Vuuren, and flips open the bayonet at the tip. He looks over at Boss, who can see his quick-thinking despite how dark out it is. David keeps Boss's flashlight pointed at the adult J'ba FoFi. Their heart rates accelerate as the creature's hissing gets louder and louder the closer it gets. Its incisors quiver with excitement as it looks at the smorgasbord above it.

Boss and the others attempt to, but realize quickly, that they simply cannot climb any higher to avoid the spider.

In a burst of courage, a determined look forms on Dee's face, and he reaches for the pack which used to belong to the pirates. The adults do not notice this. He feels around in the bag until he can feel what he is looking for. The child clunkily pulls out an enormous revolver—one that he stole from Van Vuuren and his men—and uses both of his small arms to aim straight down at the giant spider.

BANG!

The group jumps out of their skins at the ear piercing sound of the gun shot, which must be audible for miles around in the dark jungle. Dee is taken aback by the revolver's insane recoil, in which the gun almost hits him in the face. He centers himself and shoots the spider again right in its face. Recovering in between each recoil, he shoots it again and again, using all of his strength. One of the bullets lands directly into one of the spider's main eyes, and it "pops" a yellow, gooey bullet hole where that eye once was. The spider makes a slight "shrieking" sound. After four shots, the boy's arms and hands are trembling from the revolver. On the fifth shot, the hairy man-sized arachnid shrieks again and loses its grip on the tree ... falling back to the ground with a thud. Grasping and grabbing at the air with its enormous legs, the J'ba FoFi struggles to turn itself right side-up. Back up on its feet, the giant spider's hissing, clicking sounds morph into another faint "shriek" of pain as it wanders off, injured.

The adults, dumbfounded and astonished, look at Dee and the smoking revolver in his hands. It is just starting to get light enough out now where they can see a bit better. Jimmy puts into words what they're all feeling.

"Holy shit!" he says, with a demeanor of relief. "Well done, kid! Thanks!"

14

"I DON'T LIKE IT, OSKAR," WANJALA SAYS TIMIDLY TO THE MAN who he answers to, as he feels the sweat forming once again on his head.

The Congolese river pirates have not been the same since the gully. Most of them still remain wide-eyed. Some of them pray. Not the toughest among them can believe that they were attacked by man-sized tarantulas ... not even Oskar van Vuuren. Prior to this, he swore that he had seen it all. These giant spiders—with the most poisonous venom ever concocted by nature and a size that allows a fully grown specimen of their kind to overpower a grown man—gives these men *pause* ... whereas their guilt for their past crimes, or lack thereof, never could.

"Boss?" croaks Wanjala. Van Vuuren does not respond. He sits there on the log, AK-47 in his lap. He strokes his weapon slowly as if it were a cat sitting on his lap. His composure is that of an alpha lion at rest. He is the only one of the group who doesn't seem bothered by what they're about to attempt.

"Boss, please, I...We..." Wanjala continues.

"WHAT!" Van Vuuren finally interjects, sharply, breaking his thousand-yard stare. He looks to his acquaintance.

"Do you have a million dollars?" He then looks over to the other pirates. His friends. One by one, he looks them in the eye, but each one sheepishly looks away to avoid making eye contact.

"How about you?" he says to another individual. He gets no answer.

"Or you?" he says again to Unathi.

Nothing. Finally, Van Vuuren realizes that he might be pushing them too far, and consciously forces himself to mellow out his tone. Returning to a warm tone to emphasize camaraderie, he continues.

"Brothers," he hesitates before continuing. "I don't like this any more than you guys do, but think of our options. We've lost so many men. We have no means of sustaining ourselves! I know it's crazy... but... just *one* of these things captured alive could put seven damn digits in our pockets!"

The other pirates nod timidly in mixed agreement. Van Vuuren goes on.

"Even a dead one should put money in our pockets! But... alive?" Oskar mimes the action of clutching someone's hair as they give him "good head" with a look of mock ecstasy on his face.

"One of these things alive could be easily worth a million dollars. Think of what the Congo government would pay for it. Or, fuck 'em... think of what some billionaire bastard would pay for it just because! One of those assholes who's wasting their fortune to go to outer space!"

"Or... or..." An idea flashes into Van Vuuren's mind that makes him salivate. He snaps his fingers.

"The venom on those motherfuckers... think of how much a foreign power would tip us off for that succulent shit! Think about how they'd wanna weaponize it or something!"

Wanjala and the others look at him and begin to feel sold again on his vision.

"You're right, Oskar. I'm sorry," Wanjala says.

"No, no, no, no, no—!" Van Vuuren says. He stands up and slings his AK onto his back. He walks over to Wanjala and Unathi, and puts his arms over both of their shoulders in a show of affection for his buddies.

"Don't be sorry, brother. Don't be! I'm scared, too. And you all have a right to be."

He holds them close, one on each side like an older brother trying to comfort his younger siblings. Van Vuuren continues on.

"But we've dealt with something far worse than this. Other men."

This seems to put Unathi and Wanjala at ease.

"And if they give us any more shit," Unathi says, raising his Kalashnikov assault rifle, "We'll show 'em what we're really about!"

Van Vuuren grins and wonders if anyone else can see through his cheesy and blatantly obvious faux-courage, but he says nothing. *They don't need any more doubt*, he reminds himself.

"Gentlemen," Van Vuuren says, almost like an afterthought. "You know that I'll look after you. Us. We have always looked after each other. Now if the Kumba brothers can show us how it's fuckin' done, then goddamn it we can do this!"

The group moves into position. A few pirates pull back the charging handles on their AK-47s, even though Oskar instructs them to resort to live fire only as a last resort. It's been a while since they heard the unmistakable hissing, clicking sounds coming from the massive hole in the ground. The hole is large enough to hold an entity out of a Stephen King novel, and these Congolese men clearly recognize it as a tarantula burrow ... only this one is exponentially larger. Several of the pirates hold a large net, ready to ensnare whatever may skitter out of the hole at a moment's notice. The net is large and thick, and strong enough to hold a wild boar in place, but the men still tremble at the thought of its massive fangs slicing right through it. The possibility of the creatures shooting urticating hairs at the men is also completely lost on all of them except Van Vuuren. He knows that old world tarantulas do not "shoot" urticating hairs; however, this is a new species which has thus far defied everything that the men hold to be true about the natural world. At this point, Van Vuuren realizes anything is possible, but he does not share this with his men for fear that this will serve as a chicken exit for them.

Nearby at a mere fifty or so yards, an unpaved road runs through the dense jungle. It's the only "road" in this area for miles and miles in any direction, and the haunting sounds coming from the giant burrow have the pirates convinced that a J'ba FoFi has built a home here near it. They move into position with a long, skinny tree branch, the vibrations of which they intend to use to entice it out of the burrow.

Unathi feels his heart rate accelerate as he turns his head slowly to his right, craning his head at something that's caught his eye, but forgets to adjust his Kalashnikov to point in that direction. A mere thirty yards to their right, on the dirt road, a strange-looking animal comes into view. Unathi's blood runs cold.

That ain't no monkey or jungle cat.

Horrified, he observes as the gigantic tarantula-looking spider crosses the road. As if the arachnid can suddenly sense their presence, it turns and looks at him. In this moment, he would swear that the arachnid is looking at him and *him* alone. The other pirates have yet to notice.

"B-b-brothers?" Unathi rasps. Before they can turn their heads, the sound of a loud rustling rings out from the forest to their left and behind them. Their attention is turned away from the burrow ahead of them.

"Fuuuuuuuuuuuck," croaks Wanjala.

I count at least three! Van Vuuren thinks to himself, tallying the one they can see on the road with the sounds of the loud rustling around them.

"Back to back, brothers! We can do this. I believe in all of you, and we only need one!" he barks at them. They quickly fall into line. With their backs clustered together, the men tremble in fear with their weapons pointed in all directions of the thick steamy jungle. Held together by the fear of their leader, the fear of the spiders, the fear of looking like cowards, and the fear of returning "home" empty-handed and broke, the men fight off the urge to run away.

Wanjala barely looks up in time to see the twitching appendage above them.

Illuminated momentarily by the sun's rays, the spiny, prickly six-foot arachnid falls on top of the terrified men. They squeal and scatter as the giant spider breaks up their back-to-back maneuver. This one is not hairy like the others ... and it's not moving.

Several of them fire on it, shredding it apart with automatic fire.

"Save your goddamn ammo, you imbeciles!" Van Vuuren barks, as he realizes that the eight-legged apparition that fell on top of them—even touching them with its prickly surface as it fell—is not a live spider.

It's a spider's *molt*.

Almost in unison, the weak-kneed men with their hilariously worthless "net" look up to the thick webbing high above them that they hadn't seen until now. Above them, moving slowly across her webs in the canopy, they see the original owner of the exoskeleton. Having just molted, she is vulnerable but is the largest one that they've seen yet.

One of the pirates points his H&K G3 up at her and fires over and over and over again. She shrieks and her legs twitch and flail in all directions until the bullets from his rifle split open her abdomen, causing her yellow, gooey insides to spill out onto her webbing and trickle down onto a few of the pirates below.

"Alive, you moron! Alive!" Van Vuuren shouts furiously, as he shoves the young Congolese pirate who shot her up. Stumbling back and then falling to his ass, the man's eyes look up to Van Vuuren. The barely 18-year-old Congolese man looks at him, terrified and trembling. Looking down at his subordinate, Van Vuuren looks into the eyes of a frightened boy, rather than a hardened criminal. Although he cannot put it to words in this moment, the Congolese "pirate" is stunned by what comes out of his mouth next, putting to words what the group is beginning to think.

He has failed them.

"NO! I can't! I can't do it!" he says, trembling. Furious that this isn't going as planned, and that he was just disobeyed, Van Vuuren bends down and yanks the boy back onto his feet. He takes the boy's weapon and shoves it back into his shaking hands.

"We work together or they'll pick us off! Shoot *only* as a last resort and get that net ready!" The others comply, but Van Vuuren's spell is broken when one of the pirates, Masamba Lafleur, is suddenly snatched up into the trees by an adult male specimen. Not as large as his dead mate, the male nonetheless ensnares him with his web and skillfully pulls him up into their domain. It all happens too fast for Masamba or the others to react, and the five-foot giant sinks its fangs into the screaming pirate. Chaos ensues as the men abandon their leader's insane plan to capture one alive.

Another human-sounding scream pierces through the foliage directly behind them, and the men begin firing at it and in all directions. Bullet cases pelt the soft ground below them, as giant spiders emerge from the brush ... as if they'd been lying in silence waiting for intruders or prey to wander into their domain.

We're outnumbered, a flabbergasted Van Vuuren realizes, too late, as his men are picked off one by one.

One pirate is pounced on and brought to the ground by a J'ba FoFi. Next to him, Wanjala and Unathi watch in horror as yet another one of their buddies is impaled.

Two fangs pierce through the back and straight out the front of another man next to them. This spider must have descended upon him, upside down by its web, before biting him with its banana-sized fangs in his back. The fangs pierce straight through the pirate's lanky, twig-thin mid-section out the front side, as blood spurts from his mouth. The petrified look on his face sears into their forever memory as they spring into action to fight for their lives.

Emptying his magazine, Van Vuuren quickly reloads his AK-47. Clicking another mag into the body of his weapon and then yanking back the charging handle, he shoots up another arachnid before it can skitter towards him. His men quickly reload as well. Trees are pocketed with bullet holes, and vines are shredded, as the terrified men spray automatic fire from their clattering Kalashnikovs into the jungle around them.

"Go! Go!" Unathi shouts, and the pirates take off into the jungle to get away. Looking over his shoulder, Wanjala can see a giant spider emerging from the huge burrow, the one that they were trying to coax out. Van Vuuren, irritated that his men took off without him calling the shots, reluctantly runs after them in order to not get left behind. More spiders are killed in the continuing clusterfuck, but the men realize they are becoming dangerously low on ammo.

Before they know it, only Van Vuuren, Wanjala, and Unathi remain. Desensitized now to the deaths of his friends, Van Vuuren pays no mind to this. Hearing the sounds of more skittering and hissing and clicking following them through the jungle, Van Vuuren turns back and barks at the other two men.

"Cover me! Cover me, goddammit! I'm out!" Wanjala and Unathi turn and fire into the foliage behind them as they cover their leader. Having lied to his men about running out of ammo, Van Vuuren gasps for air and charges up the hill ahead of him to get away ... leaving the other two to act as his rear guard to contend with the menace.

They catch on to this, and turn back to catch up to him. Climbing up through a particularly steep part of the hill where the foliage is especially thick, the three men practically have to use all fours to move through the mud to get any higher.

Just as they are about to crest the hill, Unathi trips a strand of web in the underbrush. An enormous J'ba FoFi begins to emerge, one leg at a time, as the exhausted pirates muster all of their energy to keep going. Suffering with their muscles pushing past their breaking points, the men do their best to crest the hill. Even though it's just a few yards above them, it feels like an eternity away.

Responding to the stimuli of the tripped web like a cat hearing its bell-tipped toy, the freakishly large spider skitters at a blistering pace up to Unathi and grabs him. It's two front legs wrap over both of his shoulders from behind, like an Olympic wrestler, with its pedipalps wrapping around his neck. He screams and tugs frantically to get away.

"Unathi! Brother!" Wanjala yelps as he turns back and nearly rolls back down the hill in his desperation to help get his friend free. Van Vuuren hears all this and looks back at the two of them, hesitating.

Van Vuuren grumbles, frustrated, then finally decides to help. Rather than diving to help Unathi like Wanjala did, Van Vuuren watches his steps carefully as he slowly makes his way down to them. Wanjala tugs Unathi by his right wrist, and Van Vuuren finally reaches out his hand to grab Unathi's left wrist.

Before their skin can make contact, the J'ba FoFi rears its cephalo-thorax up. It's chelicerae quivering with delight, the monster spider sinks its fangs into the back of Unathi's neck. Immediately twitching, gurgling blood, wide eyed, and possibly even paralyzed ... Unathi Andile makes an ungodly sound of anguish before being dragged away by the hungry spider into the underbrush to be liquified and devoured.

"Aaaaaaaaaaaaahhhhh!" Wanjala shrieks in terror. He and Van Vuuren charge up the remainder of the hill, with him following his "superior" behind him every step of the way. Van Vuuren raises his AK-47 and fires at the spiders coming up the hill behind them. In the chaos, Wanjala realizes that Van Vuuren lied about being out of ammo, but doesn't have the air in his lungs to bring it up until later on when they can rest.

After about fifteen shots fired in three round bursts, Van Vuuren kills at least two J'ba FoFi—smaller four-footers—but then his rifle clicks.

Having run out of ammo for real now, he turns back and reaches the crest of the hill with Wanjala.

The two look over the other side and see a small embankment of the river below. The water looks deep enough for them to safely jump, but the two men hesitate.

"What if we hit something? What if we break an ankle on an underwater rock?" Wanjala asks frantically. Before he can answer, Van Vuuren abruptly looks behind them and can see at *least* three or four J'ba FoFi specimens making their way up to them ... getting closer, and closer, and closer.

Van Vuuren snaps himself back into reality, as he ponders Wanjala's question. He takes a big, deep inhale, then exhales slowly before speaking.

"That's a chance I have to take."

Wanjala catches his wording.

"I?" he says back.

Just then, Van Vuuren kicks Wanjala in the back of the knee and shoves his last living "subordinate" back down the hill from where they just climbed up. The pirate "leader" watches as Wanjala is pounced on by three J'ba FoFi simultaneously. The arachnids tear him apart limb by limb like a pack of wolves as they fight over who gets the spoils. Wanjala Killian screams bloody murder from the pain and disbelief.

Van Vuuren does not have the balls to look him in the eye.

Turning back to the river embankment below the drop off in front of him, Van Vuuren carefully moves to slide on his butt down the other side. He slides too quickly, and the wet leaves and mud below him give way.

Tumbling down the hill, getting scratched up along the way as he tumbles, Van Vuuren is pulled by gravity until the husky man makes a big *SPLASH*...

Plunging right into the water below.

15

EARLIER, THE SOUNDS OF SEMI-AUTOMATIC GUNSHOTS FROM the pirates fighting the J'ba FoFi off in the distance temporarily pulled the attention of the survivors away from their troubles ...

"College," Boss says, with a subdued tone. She pulls out one of the last of her cigarettes and lights up.

"Yes, Boss?" David replies.

"You're smart... I think." She looks at him and Avery. Avery puts his hands up, self-conscious, and says, "Don't look at me, I'm just an assistant!"

Boss chuckles, amused. She continues on, "What're the odds that those are coming from the same assholes who tried to fuck with us?"

Before David can answer, Jimmy chimes in, "High. We haven't seen anyone out here besides them in days. Very high."

He looks at Obasi, and the man of few words nods in agreement.

Everybody in the group of six feels like hell. The onset of dehydration hit them a long time ago, followed shortly thereafter by the beginning stages of starvation. The ones least affected are Obasi and Dee, as they're used to eating substantially less than their counterparts from the

West. However, even they are beginning to feel painfully thirsty. The lack of adequate hydration causes all six of them to experience lightheadedness, headaches, and more; helped in no small part by the blazing sun and rampant humidity.

Obasi periodically reminds the group to stay quiet, and that they should consider themselves lucky that so far only one J'ba FoFi found them and has tried to reach them.

Earlier, Avery recited some of the lines that he remembers from one of his favorite movies, "The Lion King," in which Timone and Pumba show a young Simba the hidden world of nutrition from insects. On a few occasions thus far, Avery can be heard reminding the group, "Hakuna Matata!" as they are forced to palate the few bugs and grubs found in the tree. This, once again, is of little bother to Dee, and no bother to Obasi, who has grown up getting his protein from this abundant and sustainable food source, in which he believes the rest of the world should catch up.

Unfortunately, the fact that they're stuck in a tree means that they cannot simply overturn a wet log somewhere on the ground to get at more grubs. They are completely reliant on what they can find in the tree, and that food source has run out long ago. David knows full well that this lack of sustenance issue is nothing compared to the more immediate threat of dehydration. The others are keenly aware of this, too.

Finally, Boss purses her dried, crusty lips and says, "We need to move on. We haven't seen one of those things in at least twenty-four hours. If we stay here for much longer, we'll end up dying of thirst. We're starting to push our luck."

The others look at her.

"We've been pushing our luck ever since we crossed the border. Fuckin' smart, huh," Avery says.

"That shit's in the past, let's focus here," she replies.

She looks at Jimmy, "What're you thinking, dude?"

Jimmy looks down at his weapon and back up at her.

"Out of ammo. Out of options...You're right. We move on."

"Yo," says Avery, "Why didn't y'all bring more bullets and shit?"

"We were expecting to run into nothing at best or a few local militants at worst. Some people come with a lot less. You should be grateful," says Jimmy.

Avery awkwardly tries to backpedal, "Oh, I ... I am, man. I was just curious!"

Off in the distance, the sounds of automatic gunfire make themselves known.

"Look," says Boss with a sense of urgency in her voice. "We can only survive about three days without water, and we're pushing it! We make a run for it now while those bastards are off causing a ruckus!"

She turns to Obasi.

"Yes. Yes, the movement." he says.

She smiles with a determined, almost angry look on her face.

"I rest my case, then. Now who's with me?" she says.

She looks into the eyes of the other five, one at a time. Jimmy and David, a few days earlier ready to strangle each other, look at her and then at each other and tip their heads slightly in a show of goodwill.

"It's your call," Jimmy says after a long pause to his fellow devil dog. Boss takes one long, tense, dramatic puff from the stub of her cigarette and tosses it to the ground.

"Let's go," she says.

The group moves as fast as they can through the tall grass and shrubs. Leading the way is Jimmy, holding the bayonet of the AK-47 in front of him and ready to slash at anything that moves. On his side, he has tucked away the revolver that young Deion used two nights prior, which has just one single bullet remaining.

Obasi, Dee, and David follow directly behind him. Dee clutches the old Aka man's right hand, while his other hand holds David's left. The two men usher the small child like parents trying to bob and weave their way through a crowded theme park. Except the crowds of people are replaced with tall grass, bushes, and numerous other types of jungle vegetation; the noisy rides replaced with the sounds of crickets, frogs, and myriad other jungle critters. Behind them is Avery, who remains the most skittish amongst them, even more so than the child. Finally, Boss brings up the rear. She is armed with her Vector which she estimates contains just half a magazine of ammunition. *Better something than nothing,* she thinks to herself.

Despite navigating through the thick foliage and being exhausted, Boss and Jimmy insist that they continue carrying their packs of stuff on their backs just in case they need those bare essentials.

Suddenly, Obasi stops.

Scanning the jungle ahead and to their right, he looks at Jimmy and waves him over, as if he's just recognized something.

"What's up?" Jimmy asks, but Obasi says nothing. He motions for Jimmy to take Dee's hand and take his place, and then reaches his hand out for the Kalashnikov. Confused, Jimmy hands it over and Obasi steps to the front of the group to take the lead. In its place, Jimmy pulls out the revolver that was tucked into his belt. Still, Obasi says nothing. He shields his eyes from the sun with his left hand and scans the area.

"Obasi?" David asks. He stands up straight and then looks back at them.

"Follow me," the man says softly. The group follows him into one of the densest clusters of trees yet. The trudge through this stretch of jungle is especially harsh. The group heaves and gasps for air as Obasi leads the way, using the AK-47's bayonet to hack a path through the vines that block their movement at every turn. Boss can't tell if it's getting dark already or if the shade from the canopy overhead is just blocking out the sun, but it is especially dark here. Dee flinches and, for a moment, David and the others panic at the thought that a J'ba FoFi spiderling might be on him. Dee waves his hands around.

No spiders.

Being swarmed by mosquitos, the boy flinches in all directions to get rid of them. Pretty soon the others are doing so as well. David even uses his pack to swing at an especially large mosquito that keeps trying to land on him. He swats it away and it lands on a vine nearby.

"We need to watch out for malaria or whatever the fuck else these little shits could be carrying!" Boss says, waving the mosquitos away. She pulls out her canister of bug spray.

"Here," she says. She sprays them all down one by one and they lather up, starting with Dee. The combination of the chemical smell of the bug stray, the oppressive heat, and the suffocating density of the foliage and its humidity make it even more difficult to breathe. Even Obasi struggles.

Finally, after what feels like forever, he breaks one more vine with the bayonet and the group stumbles out of the jungle. Disappointed that it's not the Sangha river, but relieved at the same time, David and the others look to see what the Aka man has led them to: a creek.

Miserably thirsty and drenched in sweat, the group dives to their knees to splash water on themselves like elephants. Unlike the pond where they found the poacher's punctured boot, this water looks surprisingly, refreshingly, clean. One by one—starting with the child—the group passes around the Lifestraw and their thirst is quenched. Only David and Boss are left in line, ready to drink. She tries to hand it to him.

"Here," she says. "Go ahead."

"No, no, no," David says, panting. "Ladies first."

She gives him a look. "I love the "Titanic"-style chivalry, but it's fine. You're a civilian. Drink."

"No, no," David replies, waving it away. "I insist. Ladies first."

"Age before beauty!" she says, borderline annoyed with him.

"Nope," says David, sharply.

"For once, *you* get to follow an order!" he says to her, satisfied with himself.

Her eyebrows rise up as if to say "Oh, really?" She finally acquiesces, trying to hide how flattered she feels. She drinks and then hands the straw to David.

After a long while of rotating turns drinking the creek water, the group rests. Even though they've been "sitting" in a tree, the use of uncommonly used muscles and awkwardly lounging on the tree's branches means that they haven't been able to properly rest for days. The six melt into the soft, cool ground and seem to forget what could be lurking all around them.

Jimmy, amused like Dee by David and Boss Lady's exchange, cranes his head down to make eye contact with the marine biologist to get his attention. David notices. A shit-eating grin forms on Jimmy's face like he's done something mischievous. Jimmy's eyes look towards Boss, who's not paying attention to their silent interaction. Jimmy motions his head towards her, and raises his eyebrows twice. The questioning look on Jimmy's face is an unmistakable "Ooh, la, laaa." An oblivious David, also saying nothing, finally catches on and shakes his head quickly. Jimmy gives him a look which screams "Uh huh, sure." David again stifles a laugh and shakes his head. Jimmy raises his shoulders like, "Oh well!" David realizes that Avery and Dee have been watching them. Avery looks at Boss, who's resting, to make sure she's not looking. Avery looks at Jimmy, smiles mischievously, and nods his head quickly. Amused, the two of them silently gang up on David, who keeps shaking his head "No." The two men enjoy messing with him. None of them say a word.

Boss rustles through her pack and pulls out her blow torch lighter. She grabs another cigarette and lights it, with her back still turned towards the others.

Embarrassed, David seizes his opportunity. He points at her and pantomimes her smoking, then waves in front of his face to show the other men that he's serious ... quietly communicating that he can't stand the smell of her secondhand smoke. Jimmy and Avery don't buy it. The two grin at each other and at David and try not to laugh. David cringes and rolls his eyes, waving them away like pesky flies. Obasi sits with the boy, momentarily content.

Before they know it, darkness has fallen and they decide to get a move on towards the river rather than hunker down for the night. They kiss the creek goodbye before they go ... drinking so much water that they have to piss like racehorses every ten minutes and feel bloated from their water intake. Luckily, they also stumble upon some more grubs for sustenance.

"At least we're losing some weight!" Avery jokes, as the group slips into the night with their equipment and flashlights in hand, feeling much better and following Obasi along the way.

HOURS LATER, AWAY FROM THEM, THE NOISE OF THE JUNGLE late at night starts to wind down.

Something's coming.

Moving haphazardly through the jungle ... exhausted, depleted, helpless, nearly dead from drinking contaminated water, and having totally and completely given up hope ... another two-legged animal plugs along, all alone. She moves along, not sure whether she is more tired physically or more tired emotionally.

She is in a horrendous mental state, and has been ever since she got separated from the others. Possessing no resources, weapons, or even a compass, she is hopelessly lost. Every leaf and branch touching her or even the slightest gust of wind moving the greenery terrifies the once-astute marine biologist. Off her prescription medication now for a long time, Dr. Molly Hendricks moves through the dark jungle. She is unrecognizable now, with her cheek bones showing and her hip bones jetting out against her pants, which barely fit around her rapidly shrinking waistline. Her hair is matted and full of God-knows-what. She longs for the most basic necessities, including one luxury—the thought of which only worsens her mental state—a shower.

The once-tough, composed scientist who had the guts to stand up to Van Vuuren and his cronies now shudders. She loses her footing and falls face first onto the ground. Adding soreness to it all now, Molly breaks down. She sobs into the dirt, clenching her head of hair so hard that she very nearly pulls some of it out of her head. She heaves, and sobs, and heaves again.

It's over, she thinks to herself. *I'm going to die out here.*

She musters her strength and sits up, still crying as she forms herself into a criss-cross apple-sauce position. She slouches, and reaches for a device that she used to rely on to do absolutely everything: her smart phone.

Worthless now that it, like the others' phones, hasn't had a signal out here for as long as they've been out here, she recalls an app that doesn't require service to function. She feels another wave of emotion fall over her as she thinks of her loved ones back home, how much they mean to her, how worried sick they must be for her, and how she will never see them again. Tears run down her face, and her breathing trembles. She opens the "voice memo" app and hits the red record button.

"This… Hey, guys. It's me. It's Molly," she says with shivers and trembles in her voice.

"If you find this… if you're listening to this… I'm so sorry. I'm not going to make it out of here. I always wanted to go to Africa, but…"

"I think… I think this is where I'm going to die." She begins sobbing again, before composing herself as best as she can. "Don't come looking for me. There are too many of them out here. Avoid… avoid the trails. Avoid the webs. They use them like tripwires to hunt."

"Avoid the jungle. Avoid all of it. Just don't. Don't... come... looking for me. I can't bear the thought of... of anyone else dying because of me. I am the reason that we strayed too far off course. It's all on me." She trembles in between sobs.

"Mom, I want you to know... I know that we haven't always seen eye to eye. And I know that... that... that you don't believe that I'll be going to heaven with you because of who I love."

"But..." A particularly strong sob makes its way up her throat.

"But I want you to know that... I forgive you. I know you and Dad pretty much hate each other, but you guys gave me your all. And, Mom, I know you did your best. I... I... I love you, Mom."

"Dad," she pauses before speaking again, covering her mouth and overcome with emotion,

"You have no idea how much you mean to me. You aren't just my dad... you're my best friend. And I'm going to miss you so, so, so much. If you ever feel sad or lonely, just know that I'm there with you always. Think of me when you visit the beach, or the water. Thank you for putting me before your religious beliefs. You saved me more so than any single living person, and I love you, Daddy."

"Jeanie, Austin, Rich, Hailey... you guys are the best friends that I ever could've asked for. You were there for me when others were not. You guys are the only reasons I didn't choose to join Debra immediately after she passed... and I'm very thankful for you four. I love you guys so, so much."

"If you've found this out here... get out now. And avoid strands of webbing along the game trails." Molly curls up into a fetal position, holding her legs tightly into her chest. She takes a pause, and then croaks, "Debra ..." she says out loud to herself, with the voice memo still recording. "Debra, my love... I'll be with you soon, honey."

Suddenly, a loud rustling sound right behind her in the thick foliage snaps her into a state of returned adrenaline. The sound is accompanied with the sound of a branch *snapping*.

Dr. David Hale and the five others rush out of the jungle, scaring the daylights out of Molly. It takes a moment for her to recognize their voices in the dark night of the jungle, but they shine their flashlights on her and Molly is overjoyed to be reunited with them.

She drops her phone and "flies" towards them. She lands into David and Avery's outstretched arms and hugs them tightly.

"Molly! Molly! Molly, thank God!" cries David as he embraces his colleague. Molly cries ... but this time it's a different kind of cry. A joyful cry. Hope.

"Queen!" Avery squeals. "We thought we lost you for good! Girl, I'm so happy you're okay!"

"Okay is... definitely a euphemism for it," Molly says to her friends. She looks at the group of six and smiles. Her smile only intensifies when she sees that little Deion "Dee" Loemba is okay and safe with the group.

"I'm glad you're okay, bud!" she says to the scrawny boy.

Dee smiles, and hugs her around the hips. Boss and Jimmy look at each other, and smile. For the first time thus far, the tough PMCs feel warm and fuzzy about coming out here to help these people. Obasi also smiles.

"I am so, so sorry about getting separated," David says somberly. "We felt awful about it."

"It's okay," Molly says.

"We've been calling out to you for days. I'm so sorry that we left you out here alone," David says.

"It was an accident. It's okay now!" Molly insists, wiping away her tears.

"Wait," she then says, looking around. "Where's Anne?"

The others look around at each other. Avery bows his head and looks at Molly, then slowly shakes his head. Molly's heart sinks and she feels bad for the argument that she and Anne got into. She reflects on their researcher friend for a moment, hating herself for not doing more, but then pushes the thought away.

"I thought I was going to die out here," Molly says.

David inhales and says gently, "I... I heard some of what you said just now. While we were coming up to you. We... I... want you to know that we got you." David squirms a bit, feeling anxious about his words and wondering if anyone else thinks they're cheesy.

He composes himself, "That moment, when we were about to be executed by those pirates back there... I thought about my life and my contributions. More specifically, I thought of my son." David holds his hands tightly into his chest, trying not to get emotional.

"Alex. My Alex... is about to turn eight years old. Well, *was* about to turn eight. His birthday has passed now. I swore I'd be back in time for it and it's the first time I've ever not kept my word with him. These guys set me straight, though. Even though I still feel bad... it's not like I intentionally missed it. Anyway... I know you don't have kids, Molly. But, I for one don't have the luxury of giving up. And neither do you."

David pauses to look at Boss and Jimmy, who listen to him proudly.

David continues, "And they don't either. These tough fucking marines. With the shit they've been through, they wake up with morning wood harder than anything we've been through."

The group laughs, and Boss rolls her eyes, once again secretly flattered. David resumes speaking, "What I'm saying is, they don't have the luxury of giving up. I don't have that luxury. Goddammit, my son is only eight years old and I'll be *damned* if he loses another parent!"

Molly looks at him, saddened, "I'm so sorry, David. I had no idea."

"Oh, his mother's alive as far as I know," David says. "But she's MIA. She took off on us. She's a deadbeat... Ha... surprise! The more you know about me."

Dee looks at David with a mix of emotions, as the American man reminds him of the same essence and love that used to radiate from *his* late father. David looks at the boy and smiles, beaming with love, as the boy reminds him of Alex back home in almost every way.

"So let's—" David and Boss say, in unison, unplanned, at the exact same time.

"After you, College," she says.

"So let's go home!" David says, finishing his sentence. Molly looks as if she is about to burst into tears of joy, yet again. Amidst the sheer relief of being found and reunited with the group, Molly completely forgot to end her voice memo recording, but does pick her phone back up off the ground.

She stands up straight: shoulders back, chest out, and chin up. Her posture in this moment is better than it's been in several days, even since before their flight from the US.

"I will not give up hope," she says triumphantly, with a renewed spirit.

They notice, too late, the J'ba FoFi sneaking up on her in the tall grass.

The hairy, brown, six-foot spider ambushes Molly, pouncing on her from the overgrown grass behind them. It grabs her with its legs and subdues her in less than one second. Screaming so loudly that her vocal cords start sounding choppy, Molly thrashes about, but is helpless. Boss, Jimmy, and Obasi raise their weapons to fight it off, when four more spiders lunge at the group from all sides.

"It's a goddamn ambush!" David screams, as he shields Dee from another J'ba FoFi. The spider's fangs narrowly miss him and the boy. He kicks at it furiously as he holds the frightened boy back. Boss desperately raises her submachine gun to blast the J'ba FoFi that's dragging Molly away, but another one leaps out of the tall grass and she is forced to adjust her fire to kill it. Obliterating the arachnid, she turns her attention back to Molly ... who has now vanished.

"NOOOOOO!" Boss yells, enraged. She switches to full auto and fires on the hissing spiders attacking the group. Within seconds, her ammo has completely run dry. Obasi stabs a J'ba FoFi specimen nearby, and he fails to see another large spider sneaking up on him.

Boss tosses her Vector at the spider and it lands on its abdomen, distracting it for a moment. Before the pissed-off adult J'ba FoFi can square up with a now completely unarmed Boss, Jimmy pulls out the revolver and shoots it right in the eye. The eye pops a meaty, moist pop and the hairy brown giant gives off a faint shriek. Obasi turns towards it, and in under two seconds thanks the marines with his facial expression, then furiously stabs the spider right in its face. The J'ba FoFi wanders off, but soon collapses to the ground from the bullet and bayonet stab wounds to the face, dead. Its giant legs quiver and wrap inwards as it expires.

"Molly! Molly!!" David screams, in vain.

Avery, backing up slowly into a thicket of foliage, notices the clicking and hissing sounds coming from right behind him too late. He looks back, and up ... just in time to see the wide open mouth of an adult J'ba FoFi. Its mouth looks like a black hole with red fibers lacing it all around like the prickly parts of an artichoke heart. The giant spider pins him down with its body weight and uses web from its spinnerets to hold him in place. Avery screams in terror.

Turning his head back and forth, Avery's screams go unanswered and his prayers unheard; as more giant spiders emerge from the dark jungle to prey upon the human survivors. David, Boss, and Jimmy shine their flashlights all around them to see that there are *way* more of them surrounding them than they realized. They shine their flashlights frantically, blinded by the darkness around.

"Heeeeelp!" Avery cries out. The young flamboyant party animal is cut off, as the J'ba FoFi pierces his chest with its nine-inch fangs. An excruciating pain travels through Avery's sternum as he can actually *feel* the venom moving like an invasive species into and through his body. He quivers, and the hungry spider pierces him again ... and again ... and again. Blood trickles from every new puncture wound. The spider hastily begins to wrap up Avery—still alive—in its webbing, cocooning him and then dragging him off, kicking and screaming.

"Move it, MOVE IT!" Boss screams. "GO, NOW!"

The frantic movement of their flashlights through the tall grass illuminates a few more incoming spiders, and David, Boss, Dee, Jimmy, and Obasi take off running as hard and fast as they can.

As the frightened group barely escapes with their own lives, they have no time to mourn Avery and Molly. In the chaos, they cannot even hear *her* screaming ...

After having been dragged off, *still alive*, into the dense jungle nearby, the giant tarantula-looking spider drags her into a massive fifteen-foot web that connects two trees on either end. Screaming and thrashing, Molly gives it her all. The giant spider rears up and pushes her farther into the sticky, inescapable web like it has dozens if not *hundreds* of times with local game. Molly thrashes like a stuck fish in the gooey, silky, and impossibly strong J'ba FoFi webs.

It's no use.

Her phone falls out of her pocket in the struggle, dangling in the webs. The giant spider uses its front legs to start cocooning her. Rotating her rapidly as it wraps her up like a mummy, the spider quivers with the closest thing that it can feel to human-like delight. It hisses in her face as it spins her around and around. It wraps her up like a rotisserie on a rotating spit, over and over and over again until the webbing envelopes her mouth ... muffling her screams.

Her phone drops to the ground with the voice memo *still recording* as she gets cocooned alive. Within seconds, only the squishy sounds of the cocooning web itself can be heard on the memo.

16

THEY RUN AS FAST AND AS FAR AS THEY CAN THROUGH THE dark jungle until there's no more air left in their lungs. It's a miracle that none of them lose their footing on a rock, twig, or any other of the myriad underbrush terrain obstacles. They make it out of the clearing, begrudgingly realizing that the tall grass is just as dangerous as the dense jungle.

Nowhere is safe here.

David keels over, supporting himself by holding his knees. He forces his head to stay raised in order to allow the oxygen to better enter his burning lungs. He pants, in disbelief.

"They're... they're gone," he says.

"Avery... Molly... all of them. They're all... gone!"

"Shh!" Boss heaves, using all the air left in her lungs to quiet them and leaving David no time to mourn the others. She and the others listen intently, desperately trying to keep their heavy breathing sounds to a minimum.

"Do you hear that?" she whispers. Then, David hears it. Then Jimmy. Then the child. The look on Obasi's face indicates that he's heard it for as long as Boss Lady has. If David hadn't been out here in this hellhole, he might even delight at the sound of what he would otherwise assume to be the sounds of a loud woodpecker going to town on a tree.

The clicking sounds coming from the Congolese giant spiders turns into their unmistakable hissing.

The noises get louder, and louder, and louder. They are *all* around them. David clutches tightly to Dee, and he wonders if there really is no hope. *This could be it,* he thinks to himself. *So this is how it ends, huh?* He forces himself to course-correct his thoughts. *Alex still needs his daddy.* Dee clenches his lips, trying not to make a sound despite being scared out of his mind. Before Boss can signal them, Obasi does it for her, motioning with his hands and fingers to hunker down and stay quiet. Flashlights off. They do so.

The chorus of hissing and clicking sounds is strangely rhythmic, as if the spiders are communicating with each other. The survivors instinctively huddle up against each other, back to back, the four remaining adults shielding the child and trying their best to put on a brave face.

Fuck, I'd much rather be in Afghanistan right now, Jimmy thinks to himself. He is sure that his closest friend and soul sister would agree in a heartbeat.

Their heart rates accelerate. With no guns or weapons of any kind, they sit there completely vulnerable ... ready to fight to the death with their bare hands. They wait, and wait, and wait.

Nothing.

The chorus continues, albeit not as loudly. It's impossible that the spiders aren't aware of their presence. David is certain of this. Whether by sight, sound, smell, or vibration of their very breathing, he knows that they are sitting ducks.

More time passes by.

Nothing.

Wondering now if the spiders are testing or toying with them, Boss tenses even harder, waiting for the attack. She knows how the saying goes, "If it's going too easily, you're walking into an ambush." They wait in silence, hunkered down until the noise finally stops. For a moment, the jungle is dead silent. So much so that you could hear a leaf drop. After a few long minutes of waiting in silence, the sounds of the jungle, teeming with night-life, begin to return as if nothing had happened.

The sun is ever-so-slightly beginning to brighten the sky, but it's dark enough out to be considered nighttime still. Obasi looks at them and whispers, "We move quietly to the river."

Before they can leave the area, they become aware of a very faint sound which is definitely not one of the jungle's frogs croaking or crickets chirping. Dee hears it first. Still holding David's hand, the boy pauses for a moment and scans the tree line at the base of each tree nearby. Then they hear it, too.

The low, pained, murmuring sound draws them to a cocooned animal stuck in a labyrinth of leftover J'ba FoFi webbing at the base of a large tree, where a game trail runs next to it. David quickly realizes that it's no animal.

"Aidez-moi," the man says, struggling to get his words out.

He is barely audible, and the state of the J'ba FoFi venom makes it excruciatingly painful and nearly impossible to speak. Cocooned like a housefly, the Congolese pirate Masamba Lafleur looks at the five survivors with desperation.

"Aidez-" he croaks, choking on the boil that forms on his neck.

"-Moi. Aidez... moi." The group quietly makes their way to him. He looks at them wide eyed and gurgling on the fluid coming out of his mouth. Red eyes and purple veins cover his body to accompany the swelling, just like the others prior.

"We should help him," David whispers.

"He's been bitten. Let's go. He's a goner," Jimmy whispers back.

"We oughta put him out of his misery," Boss adds. Obasi looks at the pirate, who days earlier was ready to shoot them, with pity.

Masamba struggles to breathe, and croaks again,

"Aidez... Moi!"

"What's he saying?" David asks.

Dee looks at the suffering, dying man. The boy's kind and gentle nature overtakes him, as he forgets all the times that Masamba, just like the other pirates, never bothered to intervene whenever Oskar or Kumni would mistreat him.

"Help," the young boy says. He looks up at the adults around them. "He's saying 'help me.'"

Boss and Jimmy look around, anxious and irritated. "We don't have time for this!" she whispers loudly.

David does not pull the child away, though. He examines Masamba, and becomes aware that the man is completely incapable of moving. By now, the once-squeamish scientist has become desensitized to the sights and smells of the J'ba FoFi venom wreaking havoc. He examines the bite wound, where the tissue decay eats away at Masamaba's back. Masamba trembles in pain. David can clearly see where the stalactite-sized J'ba FoFi fangs pierced the man's midsection ... traveling straight through his oblique muscles and severing the man's spine. Masamba sits, paralyzed by the unlucky angle of the spider's bite, with his body in horrendous condition. He even sits in his own excrement in the web. The smell of *that* alone makes the group gag.

"He's paralyzed," David says, somberly. "We gotta do *something* for him."

Masamba utters again ... slowly, quietly, whimpering like a dog in his cocooned shell ...

"Aidez-moi," he croaks. The effects of the venom worsen before the group's very eyes in real time.

Suddenly, the group hears a loud rustling moving through the underbrush nearby. The cadence and frequency of the steps indicates clearly that whatever makes the noise possesses more than four legs ... and it's *big*. Masamba becomes aware of the sound, too.

"Tue-moi!" he says strenuously. "Tue-moi!"

He switches from regional French to broken English in his desperation. "Kill me! Please, kill me!" he says again and again laboriously. David looks for an object nearby, but Boss grabs him and shoves him along to flee with the others.

"No time!" she orders, whispering loudly and prodding him along.

Stepping ominously, casually, out of the jungle, the giant spider wanders with its eight legs moving in tandem to where its prey lies cocooned at the base of the tree. The group flees the area and scales another tree close by to hide from the menace. Still, they can clearly see Masamba's eyes moving independent of his paralyzed body. His eyes look up at them, and they can see that they are filled with tears.

They momentarily lose sight of the man-sized tarantula as it passes behind a bush. Moving past it and back into view, they can see the spider's incisors quivering. It climbs on top of Masamba until its hairy legs are on either side of him. The spider's mouth, chelicerae, and fangs quake with delight as it plunges its eight-inch fangs into the dying pirate. The sound of the creature piercing his midsection sounds like an eggshell getting cracked on the side of a kitchen pan. This time, however, the spider does not release him. Masamba flinches with a petrified look on his face.

The group hiding, watching it all unfold from the tree nearby, is forced to stifle their own gasps at what happens next.

Covering Dee's eyes, the group watches in horror as the spider feasts on Masamba's liquified innards. The spider drains his body through its fangs. David swears he can even hear the slurping sounds of the man's liqui-fied organs draining. The slurping, slushy-like sound makes David feel like he needs to blow chunks. Even the Marines are mortified. Jimmy swears that the sight looks eerily like a scene from a nature documentary that he saw as a kid ... where the British narrator shows a goliath bird-eating spider, the "largest spider in the world," consuming a bird. Despite Dee's protests, David refuses to take his hand off of the boy's eyes.

Masamba's eyes remain trained on the group. His mouth opens wide as he twitches. He starts to lose color, and his skin contracts, shriveling up into a matted gray color not unlike elephant skin. His life force disappears. The sight reminds Boss of a scene from a movie where a perfectly pre-served body, which looks like it had only been dead for a day, immediately changes form and decays away due to its first exposure to air in hundreds of years.

After several long minutes of feasting, the J'ba FoFi removes its fangs and casually wanders off, satisfied and feeling full ... leaving behind the hollow, weightless shell of bone and skin that used to be Masamba Lafleur.

"Good riddance," Obasi whispers. Jimmy finds the timing and choice of his words uncomfortably humorous, as he chokes down an untimely laugh.

The morning sun arrives, and the group decides that it's safe to move on. They climb down from the tree and start trudging along, following Obasi's direction, but a worrisome thought catches Boss off guard.

"Wait a minute," she says. "Our boat has been left unattended now for a long time. Assuming it's even where we left it along the bank of the river... do you think somebody's probably fucked with it by now? Maybe Van-Very-big-asshole or whatever the fuck his name is?"

"Oh, fuck," says Jimmy. "She's absolutely right."

He looks at the others and tries to salvage the look of defeat on their faces. Even though Obasi does not rely on getting back to the boat as they do; the kind, old, local man nonetheless feels sorrow for them.

"But hold on," Jimmy continues. "Unless they, or whoever, used their boat to tug it along, our boat should still be there. After all, they would need our key to get it going."

David looks at him, surprised and confused by this.

"Wouldn't they just be able to hotwire it or something?" David asks.

"No," says Jimmy. "Luckily we came in on a newer model that won't activate without the key being in the immediate vicinity. Kinda like those newer cars."

"No way," says David, relieved.

Jimmy goes on, "It's quite brilliant, really. It's highly unlikely that someone would've stolen it. So... we get back and we get the fuck outta here."

"Whoa, whoa, now!" Boss exclaims. They look at her as they keep on walking,

"Pardon me for shitting on your parade, being the pragmatic one here, but our boat is still gas-powered. It's not like we can paddle our way back to Cameroon. And it's been sitting there for how long?"

She looks at Obasi and softens her tone, "Obasi... what're the odds that someone has syphoned our gas by now?" Obasi looks at her, concerned and dumbfounded. He is not the only one, however, who hasn't thought of this dilemma.

After a pause to think, "High. Very high," the Aka man says softly.

"Fuck," David says with a sigh. They keep moving though, keenly aware that numerous dangers can be lurking around any of these leaves and shrubs. David still can't believe that man-sized spiders are one of them.

Obasi suddenly raises his gaze back up at the others, "I have an idea," the Aka man says. "There is an abandoned outpost near here. Just a few hours walk. Hopefully it is still there." He points in the general direction of where his memory recollects that it's located.

"There, we will hopefully find your gasoline."

An unpleasant feeling washes over Boss. She is keenly aware that, by now, any chance of Obasi receiving the extra payment that they promised him is highly unlikely. Obasi does not seem bitter about this in any way, and that makes her feel even worse about it. He has more than delivered on his promise, and yet here he is still; willing to help these outsiders who, without him, would be hopelessly lost in all the greenery. For centuries, people like Obasi and other indigenous groups like his have been taken advantage of and mistreated. Yet he still helps them, willingly, out of the good of his heart.

And then, she thinks to herself, *then* we *as a society have the audacity to call* them *primitive and savage.* In this moment, the Marine's heart swells with a bittersweet gratitude for their old, short, local friend. Her thoughts race on. *Maybe it's* our *so-called "civilized" society, where people only help each other if they "owe" them something, that's the "savage" one.* She smiles with a deep inhale, vowing to do everything in her power to uphold the deal, and then resumes following them along.

It's late in the evening by the time they reach the rusty old outpost in the middle of the jungle. Sure enough, it is there.

The group comes up to a rusty old gate, and David is surprised to see that even a gated fence was once constructed here. The gate holds within it a shack, and both the gate and shack have overgrown vegetation all around it. The large shack makes up a majority of the outpost's structure. The outpost is almost entirely made out of wood, except for some rusty window frames with still-intact, albeit filthy, glass panes.

The group walks up to the entrance, where the gate is still shackled shut. The exhausted adults look at each other to see who's going to pick the lock, and all eyes fall on Boss and David. She looks at Jimmy.

He scoffs playfully and says, "You can't expect the Asian guy to do everything!" he says, joking. She laughs and looks back.

David looks at her, "After you, Boss?"

"On your six, College," she replies.

David waves his hand towards the rusty lock on the gate as if he were politely gesturing her towards it.

"Beauty before age," David insists.

Boss grins and rolls her eyes.

Before she can grapple with the lock, the group looks down and sees Dee already fumbling with it. The boy casually takes the lock off, which they now realized was just hanging there, unsecured. He opens the gate and looks up at them with a self-assured smile.

"Actually, allow me," the boy says gleefully. The adults look at him, amused and dumbstruck.

"Oh!" David says.

"Well, then!" Jimmy says. They follow the child inside and maneuver their way through some weeds to get to the entrance of the shack. Not wanting the boy to get scratched, and fearing tetanus, Boss steps ahead of Dee and turns the knob before he can. She opens the door, but the sight of something in her peripheral vision snaps her back into adrenaline and she shoves Dee behind her.

"Get back!"

Pointing the AK-47 bayonet at the thing that they hadn't noticed until now, she and Obasi see that it's not a spider, even though there's a ton of webbing.

"No J'ba FoFi," Obasi says. Despite his advanced age and short stature, he never fails to make the group feel safe, even if just by his tone. In front of them, cocooned and still moving, is an antelope. No spiders to be found anywhere around. She exhales deeply as she lowers the bayonet and flips her hair back.

"Poor bastard," Jimmy says casually.

Obasi does a double take at the cocooned animal.

"This..." he says, "This is different."

The group is taken by surprise when Obasi calmly takes the AK-47 out of Boss's hands and plunges the bayonet into the antelope without warning. Thinking at first that he did it to put the suffering animal out of its misery, David watches uncertainly as Obasi digs into the cocooning with his bare hands and starts pulling the sticky webs apart. He struggles with it, but piece by piece he is able to get the web separated from the now-dead antelope. He strains as he pulls with his legs and back to drag the animal over a few feet where he then proceeds to examine it.

Finally, Jimmy asks, "What're you doing, man?"

Obasi says nothing and continues. The group watches him intently as he examines every square inch of the animal's body. Then, Boss realizes what he's looking for and begins thinking what Obasi's thinking.

"It hasn't been bitten," she says, surprised.

"Exactly," replies Obasi.

"I mean, I guess it makes sense," Jimmy says inquisitively.

"Perhaps they prefer to drink the insides of their prey fresh," David says, casually with his arms crossed.

"Maybe... maybe we're not all that different after all," Boss says. Her interesting choice of words is sobering to the group.

A metaphorical lightbulb turns on over Jimmy's head and his tone gains a pep in its step. "If it hasn't been bitten, then... ?"

"Yes," says Obasi softly, two steps ahead of them. Obasi instructs the others to get a fire started before the sun starts to set. Boss and Dee do so, while Jimmy and David search the rest of the outpost.

Much to their relief, the two exhausted men discover more than enough gasoline for the return journey ... two whole barrel drums plus several cans. All of them are full. Beyond relieved and amazed by their luck, the street-smart Marine and the book-smart scientist even hug each other in a moment of celebration, in which nothing at that moment matters other than their respite.

David even looks his new friend Jimmy square in the face and says to him enthusiastically, "I think our luck's turning around, my guy."

The group salivates as Obasi skillfully prepares and cooks the antelope over the fire for the insatiably hungry group.

"Never thought I'd be eating antelope!" David says.

The vibe of the group is better than it's been in a while. They fill their stomachs as much as they can until night falls, and then they go back for seconds, and thirds, and fourths ... until they are stuffed to the gills. Exhausted, they hunker down inside their newfound shelter at the outpost, and stay the night.

David is seconds from falling asleep, when he notices that Dee is still awake whereas the others are out like lights. David sits up onto his right elbow, and then all the way up until he is facing the boy. The look on Dee's face reminds David of the first time that the group met him. He looks scared, timid, and desperately in need of somebody, anybody, to give him the love that every child deserves. David turns on his flashlight and scooches towards the child.

"Hey, little man. What's wrong?"

Dee bows his head and his bottom lip quivers, "They used to tell me that I would slow them down. That I was a burden. Is this... is this all my fault?" the kid asks him, saddened.

"What?" David gasps.

He catches his volume and looks over to make sure that he didn't accidentally wake the others. He scans the room. He did not. He turns back towards Dee.

"What, no! Of course n- absolutely not! Why would you even think that?" he demands of the child.

"Well..." Dee says, "The mean guys used to make me feel like I was a problem. I'm sorry if I did anything to hurt you guys."

David's heart sinks at the abused boy's words. *There isn't a damn thing that those motherfuckers didn't take from this child!* David thinks to himself.

"Dee, look at me!" he commands. Dee looks up at him and fights the internalized emotional abuse controlling his quivering bottom lip.

"Deion Loemba, you are NOT a problem. You are NOT a burden. And absolutely none of this is your fault. They are the problem! Those mean guys... THEY are the problem. Not you! Do you understand me? Not you!"

Dee grins from ear to ear at his words.

"And," David adds, pointing his index finger at the boy to get his point across, "And, you are STRONG. You are BRAVE. I know you are."

David gently holds Dee's shoulder and continues, "I made you a promise, and I intend to keep it, little man."

Dee looks up at the man who he's beginning to see as a father figure now.

"You have." Dee says, beaming. The two hug each other tightly, and within minutes they are both out cold, sleeping harder than they have in a very long time.

Dawn arrives.

Dreaming peacefully for the first time in as long as he can remember, Dee slowly opens his eyes. He feels relaxed and more at ease than ever, hiding out with these nice people in the middle of the jungle. The soft morning light envelopes the outpost. For the first time in weeks, it's not miserably hot and humid already this early in the morning.

He rolls over, and the boy's peaceful, relaxed feelings are shattered.

Rubbing his eyes quickly as he looks at the ominous shadow covering the thin window, Dee contemplates his next move. Still half asleep, he can clearly see the adolescent J'ba FoFi covering the thin windowpane on the outside of the shack. Its grotesque eight-legged shadow spans an enormous two feet in total. Small for J'ba FoFi standards. Dee sits up and stares at it, scared and wide-eyed. The sight is similar to that of a regular-sized spider perched on a camping tent, from which its shadow can be seen from the inside. Only this spider's shadow is exponentially larger.

"Guys?" he finally croaks, uneasily.

"Guys?" he says, louder. He shakes the others hard until they begin to stir. David slowly peels his eyes open, turns to look at whatever has Dee spooked, and shoots to his feet once he realizes. Wide awake now, Boss, Jimmy, and Obasi snap to attention as well. Jimmy speaks but Obasi shoots his hand up like a school crosswalk guard to silence him.

"Shhh, my friends," he whispers. "No movement."

They do as he says, and they watch the adolescent J'ba FoFi intently. After a while, it slowly crawls across the window, out of sight on the wall. The fear of not being able to see *where* it is now is even worse than seeing it covering the window.

They remain in silence. Before Obasi can say anything, the group hears a thumping sound on the outside of the outpost. This one is faint. And then they hear another thump, and another, getting louder.

On edge enough already as it is due to the presence of the "small" one, the group shudders with fear as more, and more, and larger J'ba FoFi specimens swarm the outpost. Any attention paid to remaining quiet falls by the wayside. The giant arachnids crawl around the outside of the structure, some skittering quickly while others move slowly, besieging the human survivors' shelter while searching for a way inside.

"Find anything you can use to defend yourself!" orders Boss. They scramble to grab any sharp or blunt objects that they can to use as makeshift weapons. David feels something hairy tickle him from behind.

"AAAH!" David yelps, startled out of his mind, as an enormous leg belonging to an adult specimen snakes its way through a small opening in the flimsy wood and touches him. The leg made no noise as it entered from the outside, but the sensation of the hairs brushing down David's neck and back scare the shit out of him and nearly cause him to piss his pants. He takes the AK-47 bayonet and stabs the hideous leg. The spider shrieks faintly and the leg retreats to the outside again.

"Keep it together, College!" Jimmy says, now using Boss Lady's nickname for him.

"Have that furry fuckin' leg foreplay tickle you and see if you keep it together, man!" David exclaims.

The hissing sounds begin. Dee grabs a blunt object as well and stands with the adults ready to fight, but they shimmy him behind them. Another adult spider punctures a pair of holes through the wood of the structure with its fangs, scaring the daylights out of everybody inside including the Marines. It bites through the flimsy structure again and again until it begins to create a hole through the wood.

Before they know it, the arachnid has created *such* a large hole in its desperation to get to its prey, that its entire pedipalps reach through and "grasp" like giant "feelers" at the stuffy shack's air inside. The group cowers from the spider working its way in until their backs are pretty much up against the opposite wall, where they can hear and even feel the sensation of another one crawling around the structure on the other side.

The J'ba FoFi's hole is so pronounced now that it sticks its entire cephalothorax inside ... mouth, chelicerae, fangs, eight eyes, and pedipalps reaching in.

Suddenly, a quick-thinking Boss realizes that she may have a trick up her sleeve. Her eyes widen with the idea, and she springs into action. Grabbing her big bottle of bug spray that none of them have thought to use, she shakes it furiously in her hand. She grabs her blow torch lighter with her left hand, whips her head around and says to Jimmy and David, with a shit-eating grin, "Consider yourselves *lucky* that I put off quitting smoking!"

She turns towards the hissing spider and lights up the blow torch ... spraying the arachnid right in the face with her DIY flamethrower.

The arachnid shrieks in pain and immediately abandons trying to get inside the shack-like structure. Satisfied with herself, she turns back to them and holds her arms out, knowing full well that they're just as impressed.

"Holy shit, woman!" David squeals.

"That's *Boss!*" she corrects him.

"Holy shit, Boss Woman!" David exclaims with a nod of approval at her quick thinking. Before long though, they can see Obasi's nose twitching. Then, they smell it, too …

Smoke.

Fire.

Boss's "plan" works a little *too* well, as the group begins coughing and choking on air, realizing quickly that the burning giant skittering around on the outside has caught the structure on fire.

"Wait! The gas, the gas!" Boss screams. "We need the gasoline!"

She, Jimmy, David, Obasi, and even Dee dive into action to haul the barrel drums and cans of gasoline outside the outpost before they catch fire and explode. One by one, they escape as the structure is completely enveloped in smoke and flames.

"Shit!" David says, realizing that they left a gasoline can still inside.

"We have more than enough!" shouts Dee, and he pulls furiously on David to get him outside. They flee the rusty structure just in time before a loud explosion from the can inside, igniting, destroys the entire outpost in a *SWOOSH*-sounding inferno of flames.

"Holy SHIT!" yells Jimmy, looking like he's ready to lose it.

"Snap out of it, soldier!" Boss says, pushing him. "Keep your head in it!"

The group realizes that they're outside, where just a few minutes ago they were trying to avoid at all costs being eaten or worse: bitten.

"Back to back," says Obasi. The group waits outside the burning structure, huddled back to back with their primitive "weapons," ranging from the Kalashnikov's bayonet and her DIY flamethrower at best to a large rock at worst. They wait.

Nothing.

Relieved that the fire has driven away the besieging spiders, but utterly disappointed that their newfound safety shelter has been destroyed, they hurriedly discuss what to do next. It's getting lighter and lighter outside. Their debate rapidly turns into a full-blown, panicked argument. The only one who does not take part in the verbal clusterfuck is Obasi, as he begins to zone out with his eyes drawn to something nearby.

Their arguing voices seem to get quieter in his head as his eyes fixate on what he believes—what he hopes—he might be seeing in the nearby underbrush. Obasi's eyes widen with sheer excitement as he comes to life, pointing.

"Look!" the otherwise quiet man says giddily.

Before the other four can turn to look at him, another nauseating *scream* comes out of the dense forest.

17

A MASSIVE, LONE J'BA FOFI SHOOTS OUT OF THE FOLIAGE.

David, Dee, Boss, and Jimmy make a break for it. The spider's tarsal claws sense the vibration of their movements through the ground, sending its instincts surging through its body.

"Mother of God," yells Jimmy, "let us *rest!*"

The four quickly notice that, oddly, Obasi is not following them. He stands there like a statue, and becomes an obvious target for the arachnid.

"Obasi! Obasi!" the three adults shout at him, beckoning him urgently to follow them. They wave him over frantically.

"C'mon! What the fuck are you doing?!" Boss shouts at their local guide.

Despite the danger, the Aka man *refuses* to budge, fixated on a strange-looking exotic plant in the ground near them that he hadn't noticed until just now. Obasi turns his head and shoulders back to give the others a solemn look.

"It's okay, my friends. Everything's going to be okay."

He rubs the balls of his feet into the ground as if he's about to take off running to home plate. Fearing what the old man thinks he could possibly be doing, Boss goes after him.

"NO!" shouts David. The marine biologist intercepts the charging Marine, grabbing her and fighting to keep her from running towards the old man. She is incredibly strong, and it takes everything that David has to hold her back. Realizing that Obasi won't budge, he knows in his heart of hearts that it'll be *him* that the spider gets ... or *both of them* if she tries to save him.

Boss furiously fights David to try to get out of his arms but finally caves in and follows the others away, needing to be tugged on by David in order to betray her conscience. The four run to a nearby tree and quickly scale it, with Jimmy helping the child up and David busy trying to keep Boss Lady from doing anything brash.

"Get the fuck off me, College!" she snarls, terrified for Obasi's life and sick to her stomach that they're not doing more to help him. David turns to make sure that Dee is firmly with them, and safe.

A triangle forms with the survivors in the tree, their local guide—whom Jimmy believes has lost his mind—on the opposite side, and the giant spider in between them all like a twisted game of monkey-in-the-middle. The spider hisses, quivering, and charges ...

Obasi sprints as hard as he can and dives into the dirt of the exotic plant, plunges his hands into the plant itself, and begins at once to rub a slimy, syrup-like material all over his body, face, and limbs. But then he feels a pit in his stomach when he realizes that the spider's not going for him.

It's going after the *boy*.

Unbeknownst to Obasi, just two or three seconds prior, Dee slipped on a wet branch and fell right out of the tree ... landing painfully on his ankle in the process. Obasi's blood runs cold and his eyes widen as he watches the J'ba FoFi closing in on the helpless boy.

"DEE!" the adults in the tree shout.

They dive to the ground, paying zero regard to the soreness in their knees caused from landing on the ground the way they do. The J'ba FoFi stops, distracted by a sensation unknown to the humans, but that gives the adults the extra second that they need to reach the boy.

Panicked, David leaps down to grab the child. Boss and Jimmy begin chucking rocks at the overgrown, freakish, tarantula-looking abomination. The spider raises its front legs up, ready to pounce.

Obasi, determined to keep the child safe, rises up from his squat in the mud. In a fashion unlike *anything* the group has ever seen from the old, quiet, indigenous man; Obasi bellows a mighty yell and begins furiously yanking on a strand of spider web. The strand looks exactly like the one that Babila Kumba ran through on the game trail, but this one is much longer, connecting Obasi's location all the way to where the monster spider sits, ready to pounce on the others. He yanks on the rope-thick silk with both hands, with more fury than any man Jimmy has ever seen using "battle ropes" at a gym.

The J'ba FoFi again rears up at Dee and the others, with its front legs and pedipalps in the air and quivering fangs showing clear as day.

But then, it senses the moving web. Unable to resist its instincts, the spider turns around and shoots right up to Obasi, skittering until it is a mere five feet away from him.

Obasi ceases yelling and freezes in place ... dead quiet and still as a statue. Having gotten Dee safely back into the tree, the four watch in horror as the spider moves in for the kill.

Except, it doesn't. It just ... stops.

The wide-eyed group cringes, certain that the J'ba FoFi will bite or maul their local friend any second now. Obasi swallows his fear and glares defiantly into the creature's pebble black eight eyes. *Something's wrong with it,* David thinks to himself, puzzled, as they watch the standoff.

The adult J'ba FoFi specimen twitches slightly and starts crawling right up to Obasi, one hairy leg at a time. The arachnid moves cautiously, inquisitively, towards the man until Obasi is forced to move from a squatting position onto his hands and rear-end, scooting back until the foliage is too thick for him to scoot back any farther.

The spider proceeds forward slowly, until its eight eyes are *right* up to Obasi's. Its face, mere *inches* away from his.

With their faces close enough to touch, the spider gives off a low-frequency hiss which sounds eerily similar to a cat's purring. By now, it's practically on top of him. Seeing them like this, even Dee can see that the adult J'ba FoFi dwarfs Obasi in comparison.

The spider "feels" him with its hairy pedipalp appendages, stroking his chest, arms, and face like a grandmother who hasn't seen her grandchild in a while. The hairs feel more prickly than they appear. It continues "feeling" him with its appendages; slowly, methodically, and stifles another hiss ... as its curiosity finally ceases.

It twitches, as if it's about to sneeze, and then retreats off of the man.

It lets out another purr-sounding hiss, the sound of which morphs into a series of woodpecker-like clicks as it wanders away from Obasi.

Stunned and astonished by what has just transpired, the group in the tree watches the spider and the old Aka man, who continues to remain still, until the spider has completely wandered off, disappearing into the thick jungle.

Boss is the first one to get down from the tree, thumping to the ground and walking over to Obasi with the backdrop of the burning, smoking outpost behind her. This time, David doesn't lift a finger to stop her. Jimmy follows suit. David leaps down and then reaches his arms up to help Dee get down safely as well. Internally, David's relief that Obasi survived is rivaled only by how flabbergasted he is.

Obasi stands up triumphantly, with his shoulders back and chest out. In that moment, Dee swears that the once-reserved, seemingly timid, and, what one might even call "meek" man looks as if he's gained a foot in height. A smile appears on his face, illuminated by the rising, now-bright sun.

David breathes heavily as he feels his adrenaline cooling off for the umpteenth time. He looks at Obasi with a new-found sense of respect.

"How... how did you do that?"

Boss puts her hand on Obasi's shoulder,

"It's this," she says. "Whatever this slimy stuff is. It... It's like it couldn't see him. And he knew it!"

"No," Obasi says quietly, but sure of himself.

The group gathers around him, impressed by his ingenuity and intrigued by the tricks up the man's sleeve. They listen intently, like children gathering around to listen to the wisdom of an old master.

"It could see me just fine. They can't stand the *smell*."

"My people have known this for a long time. I took a great risk... I wasn't completely sure until just now. But now I am. This material acts as a natural repellent." He wipes a glop of the substance off of his arm to show them.

"And it can only be found by digging up that plant," he says, pointing to the now-destroyed exotic botanical where he got the goopy substance.

"When I saw it, I knew I had to try. I've been keeping my eyes open for it all along, but this is the first of it that I've seen out here. You're fine to rub it on as long as you don't ingest it. But, there is a catch. The plant is extremely rare. We will keep our eyes open for more along the way back to the river. I think I might know where some more of it is growing, *if* we are lucky. *If* it's blooming."

"Only one way to find out," says Boss. The others nod.

The group says nothing, but takes it all in. They sit in Obasi's radiant aura until the old man simply smiles and says, "We must go."

18

HER PRIMAL FEAR HAS NEARLY CAUSED ANNE MATTHEWS TO lose her mind. She sits in complete darkness. Although she can't see anything around her, she can feel *everything*. The soft, wet soil on which she lays would be almost tolerable if she didn't feel the sensation of a baby J'ba FoFi crawling on or over her every few minutes.

She's paralyzed with fear.

Trembling in the darkness, she regains consciousness after an undetermined amount of time. She has no idea where she is. The last thing she remembers, she was fighting for her life in the thick, steamy jungles of equatorial Africa. Remembering the monstrosity that snatched her, and too scared to move, Anne sits in the pitch darkness where she can only hear three distinct sounds.

The first is her own labored breathing. The trembles in her inhales and exhales can be heard echoing nearby, wherever she's at. The humidity here, wherever she's been taken, is even worse than compared to the "usual" jungle. She can't see a thing.

Secondly, she hears the clicking sounds.

Their clicking sounds.

Every few minutes, the once-adventurous and bubbly researcher can hear not just the pitter-patter of creatures moving through the darkness, but their signature clicking sounds as well. The haunting sounds coming from the creatures sound like an uneasy mix of a house cat purring and a woodpecker on a tree. Even in her deteriorating state, Anne knows full well that this definitely isn't her beloved cat, Lasagna, from back home. Should she ever get back to him, she'll *never* be able to listen to the sounds of him purring the same way ever again.

Thirdly, she hears the moist, squishy, almost meaty sound of nearby creatures using their titanium-strength web to line the area and wrap up dead or dying prey. To her left, she swears she can hear something—an animal, maybe—struggling as it gets cocooned alive.

Though she doesn't realize it, above her something releases its grip from the ceiling and slowly begins to descend down to her using the spinnerets of its abdomen to harness the thick web. This specimen is only a foot-and-a-half in leg span, just old enough to begin losing its yellow and purple coloration and begin taking on the hairy, brown complexion of an adult. This J'ba FoFi, no longer a baby, feels the vibration of her breathing below.

This prey is alive.

This prey is *fresh.*

Anne's already cold blood runs ice-cold when she can feel the giant spider's hairy front leg touch her face in the pitch black darkness. Before she knows it, all eight legs release from the arachnid's web strand. The eighteen-inch tarantula-like spider sits perched directly on her trembling face. One of its legs tickles her ear lobe. She inadvertently releases the contents of her bladder, as tears form in her eyes. After a solid thirty seconds, the young arachnid climbs down her body and off of her. As it passes, she can hear the faintest little "hissing" sound as it crawls away casually.

Finally, she works up the courage to attempt to move. She tries to raise her right hand, then her left. She starts softly, but applies more and more pressure as her frustration builds. It's no use.

She's already been cocooned.

The moldy, cotton candy-like smell of the webbing is almost as bad as the smell of what else litters this dark area: dead and decaying cocooned prey, spider droppings, clusters of peanut-sized J'ba FoFi eggs, and the subtle, unpleasant smell of exoskeleton molts.

All thoughts about her loved ones back home race through her traumatized mind. Despite the unbearable sensory torture that she's going through by being taken here in the dark, she feels no pain in her body. *I haven't been bitten yet*, she realizes, though this thought allots her zero relief.

She flinches in her cocooned prison at the wretched sound of an adult J'ba FoFi screaming like a banshee nearby. Anne's fear overloads her body. She wretches, vomiting all over herself.

Not since getting dropped off for daycare, for the first time when she was a toddler, has Anne vomited due to fear. Suddenly, a new noise befalls her dark surroundings.

Thump.

In that moment, back in the daycare play yard, all she wanted was for her mother to come back and get her.

Thump.

She wanted her back so desperately that she made herself sick.

Thump, thump.

The sounds of the daycare lady's footsteps walking over to pick her up—and little Anne in that moment realizing it wasn't her mom—made it all worse.

Thump.

In this moment, Anne Matthews reverts back to the little girl deep inside that's been suppressed for decades of adulthood.

"Mama," Anne croaks in the darkness.

Thump, thump, thump. Nearby, the footsteps of an adult J'ba FoFi become louder and louder on Anne's damaged psyche as it seems to tip-toe its eight legs closer and closer to her in the pitch darkness.

It moves up on her until she can feel its bristly hair touch her arms and face. Then, she feels its enormous incisors brushing against her face.

She tenses every muscle in her body, but she simply cannot move.

Without warning, the giant spider sinks its fangs into her solar plexus. Anne's scream rings out through the pitch darkness, bouncing and echoing off of walls that she cannot see. She screams so loudly that even the adult spider is put off.

She coughs blood and immediately feels the searing pain of the fatal J'ba FoFi venom traveling through her body. She feels a phlegm-like substance travel up her esophagus until she heaves and throws that up, too. Immediately, the sensory torture becomes far worse as her senses go into full-blown deterioration. The warm sweats, even inside her cocooned prison chamber, turn cold. She starts shivering from the sweats, and becomes even more delirious than she already was. Even though she can't see her own body, or even the webbing itself, she can feel her abdominal area getting larger and larger.

The *swelling.*

Shooting pains travel through her body to accompany her chills, and she experiences the worst headache of her life, one that makes all those college dorm hangovers feel like nothing in comparison. She descends deeper and deeper into madness in the pitch-black darkness, as the venom ravages her body. In her right mind, removed from the danger, she'd otherwise be fascinated by the scene ... her inner high school theatre nerd self would think that it'd be fitting for a twisted Shakespearean style play.

"Mama," Anne whimpers.

The eighteen-inch juvenile spider from a few minutes prior suddenly rears up in the darkness and, following the example of its mother, bites Anne right on the forehead.

"MAA-MAAAAAA!" Anne screams.

The vibrations of her voice do the exact opposite of what she so desperately wants, and only speed up her misfortune. Nearby, other J'ba FoFi hear her and come crawling over. A twisted, sinister force has rung the dinner bell in this dark, wet realm teeming with giant spiders.

Anne begins to feel the *boils* forming on her body. They stink worse than her surroundings. As another adult spider reaches her, one of the boils on her chest pops, moist and meaty, and pus trickles out of it. On her forehead, another boil pops pus as well, and the liquid runs down into her eye. The adult spider "feels her up" with its hairy pedipalps, practically trembling just as much as she is. Rather than trembling from fear, though, this freak of evolution trembles from hunger and delight.

"Mama?" Anne says, deliriously.

"Mama."

Although she can't see them, the J'ba FoFi that bit her in the stomach, the one attracted by her movements, and the smaller one that bit her on the head, along with a few other specimens, all close in on her at the same time. Intuitively, Anne knows that she's dying. Instinctually, however, she keeps calling out for her mother.

The arachnids pierce her with their massive fangs and begin at once to liquify her insides for consumption, before the venom can even begin the process of necrosis. The pain from the venom is now eclipsed by the pain from feeling her insides getting sucked out. Anne, with no more energy or fight left in her, quietly whimpers for her mom over and over.

"Ma-ma..."

"Mama..."

"Mama…"

"Mama…"

She finally, mercifully, flatlines.

BACK IN THE JUNGLE, OBASI IS ALL-TOO-AWARE THAT THERE was only enough of the slimy "repellent" from the one lone plant for him to use on himself in the heat of the moment. They have yet to locate any more, but they desperately keep their eyes peeled for the life-saving plant. Earlier, he tried to rub some of it on Dee and the other three, but there simply wasn't enough to go around for everybody to be covered topically from head to toe. David describes the gooey, slimy botanical material as smelling sweet and oddly pleasant. It's not nearly as thin as water, but not quite as viscous as tree sap, either.

Boss and Jimmy take turns holding the AK-47 bayonet, while David and Obasi hold Dee closely at hand. They are forced to carry—whether by hand or worn over their backs like backpacks, or both—the gasoline needed for their escape. This need to carry their gasoline and remaining supplies has slowed their journey considerably, and they are again miserably thirsty and hungry. Obasi, however, insists that they are close to the river. Not wanting to jinx it, David bites his lip and refrains from saying that they must be "over the hump." They quietly trudge through the jungle, through dense brush and along game trails. With every step they take, they carefully watch the ground for any webbed trip wires. They are all too aware now of what hell awaits them should they accidentally trip one.

"Alrighty," Jimmy says, huffing and puffing. "I got another one for you guys. I can't promise that these are going to stay clean for much longer… I'm running out of family friendly jokes…"

"Excuse me, sir!" Boss says. "We have a kid here!" she exclaims, gesturing to Dee, which prompts a smile from the boy. The child looks up at his new friends and they smile back. David feels tempted to try asking again what Boss's real name is, but being the perennial introvert and shy man that he is ... he talks himself out of it. Jimmy goes on with his joke.

"How do you look for Will Smith in the snow? You just follow the fresh prints!"

All adults groan except for Obasi, but Dee laughs his head off, even though he and the Aka man have no idea who Will Smith is.

"A man walks into a library and orders a cheeseburger," Jimmy says. "The librarian says to him, 'Sir, this is a library.' The man apologizes and whispers, 'I'd like a cheeseburger, please.'" Dee eats his jokes right up.

"Hey, how 'bout you, College?" Boss says to him, looking back at the man who holds Dee's hand.

"You're a father. You must have a few good dad jokes up your noggin!"

She looks at Dee and winks. The child smiles and looks up at David with anticipation.

"Define... good?" David says.

"C'mon, outsider! Take your foot off the brake, the boy's waiting!" Obasi says, taking David by surprise. "Let us hear some!"

Until now, David wasn't even sure if Obasi was paying attention to their silly conversation. David clears his throat and tries to think of some from the past. As usual, he gives himself "analysis paralysis."

"He's right, pops, the kid's waiting!" Jimmy barks at David, teasing him.

"Okay," David says, as he composes himself while struggling with the drum of gasoline on his back.

"What do you call a winter contract?" David says. They look at him; Dee with the most excitement. "A Santa Claus!"

The boy laughs out loud, as does Obasi at the sight of Dee laughing. David drums them up.

"How do dinosaurs pay bills? Tyrannosaurus Checks!"

"Okay, okay," David says to Dee. "This one might be a bit dark, but I think you've seen it all by now, young fella." David waits for Dee's giggling to die down.

"What do you call a two-legged dog?" He looks at the boy, waiting for a guess. Then at the others. Boss shrugs her shoulders. He looks back down at Dee.

"Well?" he asks him.

"I don't know!" Dee says, smiling.

"It doesn't matter, that dog's not coming!"

Dee looks confused, thinks it over for a moment, and then gets it.

"Boooooo!" Jimmy groans.

"Man, that's fuuuuuuucked," says Boss, trying not to laugh. Dee giggles loudly, however. In this moment, it's this giggling that makes David's anxiety not care whether or not the adults found it funny. *The child found it funny and that's all that matters!*

Boss notices the interaction between David and Dee, and can't help but blush underneath all her sweat and accumulated dirt and grime from over the past several days.

"Hey," Jimmy says to her, noticing this. "You good, fam'?"

"I'm good, bro," she says.

Obasi insists on hauling an oil drum over his back, as well. Everybody has something taking up their exhausted hands, whether it's holding Dee's hand, holding the expended Kalashnikov, holding their stuff, or—most of all—holding as many cans of gasoline as their fingers can handle. Jimmy remarks that he's had a lot of practice, since his mom always hated making two trips to unload the car after a grocery run. Even Dee carries a bag of their remaining supplies with his free hand. Their fingers burn and their muscles ache. They collectively gave up on wiping the sweat out of their eyes long ago. Despite this, David keeps sharing his corny dad jokes and Dee keeps giggling every step of the way.

"Hey if you think the one about the dog is bad," Jimmy chimes in. "Then just wait until you hear this one…"

Suddenly, some rustling nearby shuts them all up and puts them back on edge.

They wait, unsure at first what to do.

"Set your shit down," whispers Boss. They do as told, setting the gasoline and other things down quietly while they keep their attention, and adrenaline, trained on whatever must've made that noise. Obasi, who's turn it is now to hold the AK-47 bayonet, keeps it ready.

The mid-day jungle goes dead silent.

Crunch.

Jimmy puts his finger up to his mouth. David does the same, looking at Dee. The child nods his head quickly, knowing to remain quiet. They hold still.

Crunch.

Stepping out of the dense jungle, and attracted by their noise, the moving object crunches over piles of leaves, the sound of which is inevitable despite the creature wanting to remain undetected. It is not a giant spider. It's a giant cat. And it's huge.

A leopard, David realizes.

The big, spotted cat makes a low-frequency growling sound as it trains its otherwise-beautiful yellow eyes on the group. Its ears and large, white, whiskers flattened backwards. David fights the urge to panic. While he is no expert on terrestrial predators, he knows roughly what to do if one encounters a mountain lion or a bear. Obasi, on the other hand, knows exactly what to do.

He spreads his limbs and begins at once to make himself appear larger than he looks. The cat must be especially ravenous, as it ignores their numbers and instinctually zeros in on the weakest member of the group: Dee.

This makes Boss's stomach churn as she mentally rehearses, as fast as she can, what she plans on doing if the cat doesn't back off. But before she can finish calculating how quickly she can get to the bayonet-tipped rifle should Obasi fail to use it, something happens.

The loose rock that Dee stands on gives way, causing the boy to stumble rapidly, sending the big cat's "chase" instincts into overdrive.

"RUN!" bellows David. He and the others get Dee to his feet and out of there just in time before the cat can pounce on him. The leopard growls and gives chase. The opportunity to scare away the leopard with intimidation is lost within milliseconds. Obasi knows, even with the adrenaline thumping through his head, that outrunning the leopard is a hopeless task. He picks up large rocks and begins throwing them at the cat and yelling as intensely as he can. His actions buy the group time to leap out of the way. The leopard goes after Obasi, but he brandishes the bayonet-tipped rifle to defend himself.

He doesn't have to.

Boss distracts the leopard by throwing a large rock at it, buying Obasi the time he needs to regroup with them.

"Down the hill, NOW!!" she shouts. The group of four charges as fast as they can down the slope, losing their footing but tumbling fast enough to narrowly avoid the leopard, which follows them down the hill in hot pursuit. The already-battered group suffers nicks and scrapes from various plant matter on the way down.

Reaching the bottom of the slope, all cautions around avoiding J'ba FoFi tripwires go right out the window as the group runs as fast as they can from the cat. On the way down hill, the cat must've inadvertently been wrong-footed, Obasi thinks, otherwise it would've surely caught up to them by now. Dee can practically feel his heart beating so hard that it just might burst out of his chest right then and there.

"What about the gas!" one of them shouts.

"We'll come back!" yells Boss. She and David hold Dee on either side, with their hearts pounding in their ears as well. Jimmy and Obasi lead the way.

Without realizing, Dee passes right through some thick ferns where he runs *right* through a J'ba FoFi tripwire running parallel to the game trail. The leopard is rapidly gaining on him and the two adults who are holding his hands.

"AAAAH!" Dee screams.

He sees a massive, eight-legged form shoot at him from out of the forest. The giant spider springs seemingly from out of nowhere and accidentally pounces right on the leopard, which runs right into its ambush path. The stunned group realizes that, ironically, the arachnid has saved them just in time before the leopard could make contact.

The leopard immediately reacts, grabbing the man-sized spider by one of its back legs and rag-dolling it off of its back. The spider cartwheels through the air and lands in the bushes nearby. It immediately turns itself right-side up again. The confused leopard looks around frantically, with both its predatory *and* defensive instincts clashing against one another ... not sure of which course of action to take.

The leopard growls and squares up with the monster spider. The leopard roars, and the spider hisses back at it, rearing its front legs and pedipalps straight into the air in a defensive display to send the cat a clear message: *Stay back or I'll fucking kill you.*

The two apex predators of the region square up, slowly encircling each other like alley cats having a standoff. While the leopard is clearly too strong for the adult J'ba FoFi to overpower, the cat instinctively knows to watch out for its venom.

The leopard lunges at the spider, swiping its huge paws and claws at the spider and hissing ... the cat showing a surprising level of fear.

The spider, with its injured back leg, rears up again into an attack position and hisses back at the big cat—its fangs showing clear as day, venom dripping from the tips like massive needles being prepped for injection.

The leopard lunges again, swiping and barely missing getting bitten by its equally fast opponent. The two lunge at each other like caged cobras unwilling to back down.

Unbeknownst to the leopard, another giant spider slowly creeps up behind it. Quietly joining the fray and working together like a pack, the second J'ba FoFi manages to get within just a few feet of the predatory cat. The arachnid moves slowly through the underbrush.

The leopard realizes the presence of the other spider too late; the J'ba FoFi springs forward and delivers its fatal bite right into the leopard's back hip. The leopard yelps from the pain and shoots around as fast as lightning to deal with this second spider.

The cat kills the spider, grabbing it with its jaws and tearing it apart limb by limb. For yards all around, the sounds of the spider getting mutilated can be heard like a leftover meal popping in the microwave as it gets overcooked. The cat tears into the spider's body—both to make sure it's dead as much as to satiate its hunger—as the original spider charges at it and brandishes its fangs. The leopard rips out frothy yellow insides from the dead spider's ruptured body cavity.

Instinctually knowing that it will most definitely lose in a face-to-face fight with the leopard, the first spider does not pounce like its dead kin did. The leopard, already feeling the effects of the sinister venom, realizes that a third J'ba FoFi has joined the fray.

The once-proud predator's growl turns from a roar into whimpering yelps of pain as the venom travels through its body. Outnumbered, outdone, and already doomed ... the leopard finally limps off.

By now, the five human survivors are long gone from the scene, back up the hill to grab their gasoline and get the hell out of there.

19

WITH NO TIME OR BANDWIDTH LEFT FOR JOKES, THE SURVI-
vors trudge along as fast as they can towards the river. A very familiar patch
of foliage comes into view, and David realizes that they're almost there.
Leaving himself no time to rest or celebrate, he presses on with Dee close in
hand. By now, Obasi moves just as slowly as the rest from sheer exhaustion.

The group comes to a clearing, and Obasi suddenly stops dead in his
tracks. Boss readies the bayonet-tipped Kalashnikov, fearing that he sees
something that they do not.

She's right.

Obasi turns towards them and slowly raises his right arm, pointing
at something in the distance that they can see by squinting their eyes. The
charred wreckage of the original boat used by the film crew ... and next to
it, lo and behold, the still-intact boat used by the rescue team.

"Our ticket home," David says, taken aback by how happy he suddenly feels at the sight. Obasi catches his gaze, and the aging Aka man
smiles with a youthfulness that David aspires to. Obasi points at their
boat again.

"This is as far as I go, my friends. I am also long overdue to get back to my family. Now, go. Go, and be safe on your voyage back."

He smiles at the outsiders, and especially at Dee. Boss suddenly feels a bittersweet wave of emotion flow over her. Everything has been about making it to this point. For some reason, she thought they would have more time to say goodbye to their new friend. Their collective desperation to leave this place is, for a moment, temporarily put on hold for their guide ... their friend.

"I...," Boss says to the man sadly. "I don't know what to say."

"I'm sorry about your friends," Obasi says. "If you feel sad for your friends, just remember: death is one of the most beautiful journeys there is to take." The group is moved by his words, and they embrace the man.

"I'm sorry I ... couldn't do more," Obasi adds.

David, dumbfounded by Obasi's even slight hesitation of whether or not he has done enough for them, says, "You've done more than enough. My friend. Thank you." Obasi tips his head slightly in a show of solidarity.

"It's been a pleasure, man," Jimmy says to Obasi, offering his hand. The Aka man shakes it gently and grins. Then he turns to Boss. The tough-as-nails woman who refuses to let people inside, not even so much as to know her real name, lunges at Obasi to give him a hug.

"Thank you," she says. "We'll never forget you, Obasi. And I promise... if we make it back..." She suddenly stops and corrects herself, intentionally trying to practice the "positive thinking" taught to her by Jimmy, even though a part of her still thinks it's all woo-woo nonsense. "*When* we make it back," she says, correcting herself, "the embassy will be notified of your service. We promise, you and your people will get the extra payment that we agreed to. And then some." Obasi tips his head again slightly at her.

"And... thank you," she adds.

Obasi would be remiss if he didn't acknowledge the barely ten-year-old Congolese boy by their side. He looks down at the boy and sees that he has tears in his eyes for the grandfatherly figure who's guided them all this way, with whom he doesn't want to part ways.

"And you, young man," Obasi says warmly. Dee charges at the man and hugs him tightly around his hips, and the two embrace. Moved by this, David swears to himself that Dee has gotten bigger since they first found him with the river pirates. This observation of the child growing takes David by surprise, reminding him of his own boy back home whom he misses dearly. In David's current state, Dee is Alex and Alex is Dee. The two represent each other.

And there's nothing that David wouldn't do for them both.

Still embracing the child, Obasi gently rubs a tear off of the boy's cheek then takes his time making eye contact with everyone in the group, one by one, before setting off.

"Hey, Obasi!" Jimmy says.

Obasi, about a dozen or so yards away from them now, turns back around.

Jimmy continues, "Dee here and I came up with one more for you for old times' sake."

Obasi smiles, listening intently.

"What'd you do if you get a cold?" Jimmy says. Dee looks at Jimmy, as if his expression is that of asking for approval.

Jimmy nods to him with a wink, and Dee gleefully adds, "You stand in a corner, obviously! They're 90 degrees!"

Obasi, taking after Boss, shakes his head and gives them a big thumbs down, with a huge smile on his face. He waves to the group of four, and they wave back. Finally, he disappears like a ghost into the thick jungle.

"Let's get you guys home," Boss says quietly, looking off into the distance at their boat along the shore.

Now in the home stretch, the four carry their supplies, including the barrel of gas previously carried by Obasi, through the remaining misty thickets. David hears some tropical birds singing in the canopy nearby. If he hadn't been out here for as long as he has, and fought numerous times just to survive, he otherwise would stop to take in the beauty. He does not.

About thirty minutes pass until the shore and their boat come back into view, this time only a few hundred yards away. The group is overjoyed when their exhausted feet sink into the muddy bank of the river where their boat sits. They run towards the boat, and Jimmy practically hugs it.

"I need to take a piss before we set off," says Jimmy. "If anyone else does, I'd say now's the time." Boss's attention is brought to her bladder; she didn't realize until now how long it's been since she's gone. She's not alone.

"I'm going over there," she says, pointing to the bushes where she'll relieve herself separately from the guys.

"Okay, make good choices! Don't fall in!" Jimmy shouts after her. David busts out laughing at this. He looks at the child.

"How about you, bud?" Dee thinks for a second and then nods his head. David raises his eyebrows to get Dee's attention before the child runs off.

"Hey!' David says after the child. Dee looks back but keeps moving.

"We won't look or anything, but don't go too far! Stay where we can see you!"

Dee gives him a big thumbs up and says, "I promise!"

David smiles, content.

Relieving themselves, Jimmy finishes before David does and says to him, "Good kid, huh? Way better behaved than I was when I was his age."

David nods, "Me, too."

Jimmy looks at him and snickers, "C'mon. The quiet kid you talked about who'd become a dolphin doctor? I doubt that! I bet you were the easiest kid ever!"

David contemplates this, knowing the Marine well enough by now to know that he only banters with people he likes. After all these years in a toxic marriage, David relishes the new friends that he's made in this hellish journey.

Relief from reaching the boat turns to sadness, as David realizes that they will all be parting ways when they get back to Cameroon's capital. *And, then what?* David asks himself. The sadness morphs into sheer gratitude and excitement that, soon enough, he will be back home with his son. He giddily plans to give Alex the most epic make-up birthday celebration ever, and to apologize profusely to him and Alex's aunty—his sister—for their worry for him. David wonders if they're okay. He sincerely hopes that they're not losing sleep over him, but knows that if he was in their shoes, that would be impossible.

His gratitude and excitement seem to simmer away, as the mist in this pocket of jungle along the bank of the river seems to darken over the place like ominous storm clouds. A terrible feeling suddenly washes over David. An intuitive feeling.

A gut feeling.

A *child's scream* rings out from nearby.

"Heeeeeeeeelp!" Dee cries out. David and the others snap to attention and spin around to see the boy getting dragged over the hill by something that they cannot see.

"DEE!!" David wails. He and Jimmy and Boss gain supernatural urgency as they sprint to the distressed child's location. They crest the hill along the shore and see a fully grown J'ba FoFi, easily a six-footer, dragging the child away. Then another hairy brown giant scurries out of their previously hidden subterranean burrow and grabs onto Dee as well. Dee screams.

"DEION, NO!!" screams Boss. They charge and furiously look for anything that they can find nearby to fend the spiders off, having foolishly left the bayonet on the boat. The two hissing, clicking arachnids wrap their powerful front legs around the boy's diminutive body and pull him into a burrow.

David lunges, landing in the shrubs and grabbing the boy by the hand. He and Boss tug on the boy with everything that they've got, but the spiders—hissing, and now unseen under the dense underbrush except for the tips of their hideous legs—fasten the boy with their spinnerets to resume pulling on their fresh, easy meal.

Dee wails, desperately holding onto the adults' grasp with sheer terror on his face.

"DON'T LET GO, GODDAMMIT! DON'T LET GO!!" shouts David. Dee looks up into David's face, and their eyes meet for a brief moment in time ... before David and the Marines lose their grip on the child.

"HEEEEELP!!" Dee screams, as the giant arachnids pull him into the pitch-black underground. Within seconds, his screams are no longer audible. David, shocked and in disbelief, looks at his surroundings to the sight of Dee no longer with them, having been taken just seconds before they were about to motor away *from this wretched place*. It all boils over for the marine biologist.

"No... No... No! No! NOOOOOOO!" David wails as he bursts into tears.

"We let it happen! We let it happen! *I* let it happen! They took him!" David explodes into sobs, practically burying his head into the wet mud along the shore next to the previously unseen spider burrow hidden in the underbrush.

Boss covers her mouth in shock and disbelief, trying to get ahold of herself. Finally, her tough exterior falls away as she, too, begins to cry over the loss of the child. Distraught, she and Jimmy try to console the civilian scientist. David stands back up and starts kicking branches, punching the mud, and cursing a higher power above, which he certainly believes has just spat on them.

"Why? Why him? Fuckin' WHY? Why, why, why, WHY!!" David wails at the sky above them. He grabs his midsection and slumps over in grief for the boy who means so much to him.

One final blow before they return home.

Boss rushes over to David and the two hug each other, distraught. All three of them are a mess. Suddenly, she brushes her hair away from her face as she realizes something that she hadn't until now. She grabs David by the shoulders, trying to get his attention.

"No, no, you don't get it. I promised him that—" David says, completely beside himself.

"SHUT UP and listen to me, College!" she orders, interrupting him. He looks up at her with red eyes.

Unsure of how crazy what's about to come out of her mouth is going to sound, she soldiers on anyway. "Don't you remember that antelope from earlier? The one that we found at that outpost?"

David's mind flashes back to the cocooned antelope which hadn't even been bitten yet, and it clicks. David's eyes widen and he looks into hers. She nods. David stands up.

"I'm going after him!" he declares.

"Whoa, whoa, whoa," says Jimmy. "I... I... that was only one time. Everything else we've seen. Every other time those things attack, they bite right away! If they've already bitten Dee then he's already lost!"

"That's a chance that I'm willing to take!" David barks. He looks at the two Marines so sternly that even they are caught off-guard.

"I'm going after that boy!" he says, pointing to the subterranean underbrush. "No matter how slim my chances are! No matter what the odds! I'm GOING, with OR without you two!"

The marine biologist promptly begins gathering up their last remaining flashlights that still have working batteries, and runs over to the boat to grab the bayonet-tipped AK-47.

"NOT without me, you're not!" Boss declares, stepping forward as if volunteering herself to her commanding officer for a mission. "I'm going, too. For Dee."

David's lips tremble, overcome with various emotions.

"For Dee," David repeats.

"I've got an idea," Boss says to him with a determination in her tone.

"HEY!" Jimmy shouts after them, cutting them off. They look at him. He puts both of his arms up to his sides in a manner that says, *Ya know what? Fuck it.*

"If *you two* really think that you're gonna risk everything and possibly get your asses killed, *all* to save that boy," Jimmy points back at himself, "... and *me* not get *any* of the glory..." Jimmy inhales deeply and exhales sharply, "... then you're both crazier than I thought!" he finishes, trying not to mirror their emotion. David and Boss look at him and then back at each other.

"Then where were we?" David finally asks the two of them, pulling himself together.

"Right," says Jimmy, with a shit-eating grin on his face. "I've also got an idea..."

The trio knows, full well, something that doesn't even need to be said aloud. Whatever plan they devise, it's going to require them to go straight back into the interior of the jungle from whence they just came.

20

"EVER SINCE WE SAW THE FIRST ONE, I'VE SUSPECTED THAT these spiders have some kind of underground dwelling that has allowed them to stay hidden so long. They must be at least partially subterranean, like trapdoor spiders," David says.

"I hate to agree with you," Jimmy says.

"We can't just charge into the nearest hole in the ground without any thought. It's suicide. But Obasi said something to me earlier that might get us some more of those miracle plants, if we're lucky. The kind he used back at the shack to hide his scent or whatever."

The three gather whatever supplies they have left, including the gasoline that they hauled out to the shore. They hide what they cannot carry under some thick foliage to prevent it from being stolen by any possible stragglers traveling down the river.

Jimmy pulls out a huge combat knife from his pants and studies it with a look of pity.

"Uhhh... better than nothing, I guess." he says.

"No way, bro. Nuh uh," Boss interjects. "We're gonna need to do better than a knife and an AK bayonet. We got two flashlights for the three of us. Good. But we need more weapons. Anything." She balls her hands into fists, trying to think up something quickly.

"Next time we bring more lead?" Jimmy asks, trying to lighten the mood. His attempt at humor fails. Just then, Boss peers over to the overturned tree nearby with several thick branches jetting out.

"Spears!" says David.

"Yep," she replies.

The trio hastily saws at the overturned tree, using the bayonet-tipped assault rifle that's out of ammo to sharpen the sticks until they have makeshift spears. The sun is beginning to set again, but the group doesn't bat an eye at this.

"What did Obasi mention to you?" David demands of Jimmy.

Just then, a colorful apparition in David's left peripheral vision catches his attention. Jimmy answers him, but David zones out, distracted like a dog watching a squirrel in a park. David walks towards the coloration peering out of the darkening jungle.

"What is it now?" Boss asks him. She and Jimmy look at each other and then follow him. Pacing into the dense foliage, David squints his eyes to try to get a better look. He pulls out one of their two remaining flashlights and turns it on. He is floored by the sight in front of him, unsure whether they're lucky to have discovered it now, or unlucky to have not seen it in time to prevent Dee from being taken.

Boss's eyes widen, and Jimmy blinks rapidly with an equally surprised look on his face.

"I'll be goddamned!" she says to the two men.

In front of them, dozens upon dozens of the strange, colorful, exotic botanicals, the *exact* same one used at the burning outpost by Obasi, sit there in full bloom for the taking. David still doesn't know what kind of plants these are, but their color and pleasant odor are unmistakable.

"What... are... the chances?" David exclaims. He then remembers having asked Jimmy what Obasi had mentioned to him about the whereabouts of this miracle "repellent" plant.

"You were saying, Jimmy?" he asks the Marine.

Jimmy, grinning from ear to ear in disbelief at the sight in front of them, laughs and says, "He said that they tend to grow alongside the shore of the river!"

The group wastes no time in gathering up as many of the botanicals as they can stuff into their packs. Awkwardly following Obasi's example, the three plunge their hands into the plants' oval-like "openings" where they dig out a treasure-trove of the slimy, gooey material. Rubbing the stuff on like sunscreen, the group applies the substance as thick as possible until they are covered head to toe in it. To anyone else, they would look like they're covered in green war paint.

Boss, leading the way in a manner that is *so her*, David thinks, squats down and starts crawling into the smelly, soft hole where Dee was dragged by the two monster spiders. Before the others can follow her, she retreats back to the surface.

"It ain't gonna work," she says, taking in the cool surface air.

"What is it?" David demands, terrified of what she could be referring to.

"They must've scrunched up their ugly ass legs when they pulled him down. The passageway is too narrow. There's no way we can fit down there."

"We've seen bigger holes out there!" she says, pointing to the dense jungle.

"C'mon. We search the jungle until we find one big enough for us to enter."

She and David accidentally say the words "big enough for us to enter" at the exact same time, unplanned, in unison. At this occurrence, she smiles at him and David feels the faintest sign of hope. The probability that Dee is still alive, however, and that David may have already failed him, sobers him right back up.

They help Boss up so she doesn't get nicked by the twigs, and the group proceeds into the thick jungle ahead of them. David turns on his flashlight.

"Save your batteries, only use them when you need to!" Jimmy says. Agreeing with him, David doesn't protest and promptly turns his off again.

After hours of desperately combing through the jungle, the group is hit with a god-awful smell that nearly keels them over. The origin of the smell, the smell that Jimmy compares to a decomposing animal that died in somebody's crawl space, eludes them. Boss trudges along, holding all her stuff just as the others do. Something in her right peripheral vision causes her heart to skip a beat. She turns her flashlight on and peers at it.

Hanging from the dark canopy next to them by a thick strand of web is a reddish-orange Columbia sportswear jacket. The torn up jacket swings ever so slightly, like a swing set at an abandoned playground. The sight gives the trio chills. David immediately recognizes the jacket.

"Henry," he croaks.

The two look at him confused. David carries on with his words, almost reluctantly.

"He was our camera person for the trip. The pirates shot him. All happened before you found us. The spiders must've gotten ahold of his body afterwards."

"L-lovely," Jimmy says.

The three stare at the hanging, webbed up coat. David turns his flashlight on as well, and the three thoroughly examine the canopy above them and the vegetation around them to check for giant spiders. To their relief, they see nothing. But then they are nearly swept off their feet again by the smell.

"What the actual fuck?" David says.

"Must be something dead nearby," says Boss. Her heart sinks when she realizes that that "dead thing nearby" could very well be the sweet child that was in their care. Without consulting the others, she clicks on her flashlight and rushes over to the origin of the smell. She shines her light on it. Even at night, the dense jungle is so hot, steamy, and humid that she can even see what looks like vapors in the beams of her flashlight, searching through the dense greenery.

"Oh thank God, thank God!" she says, exhaling with a sigh.

The source of the smell is not Dee. Catching up with her, David and Jimmy see it as well.

"Fuckin' A'!" Jimmy exclaims. The three of them hold their noses. The smell of what lies in front of them completely envelops the subtle, pleasant smell of the plants' slimy repellent.

It's the leopard from earlier.

The massive cat, with its weight easily in the triple digits in pounds, is partially cocooned, as if the J'ba FoFi started wrapping it up out of habit before realizing it was unnecessary. The cat's body is mangled and covered in gigantic pairs of one-to-three inch puncture holes, giving the trio shivers from the thought of just how those spider fangs must've *felt* upon piercing its flesh. Its spotted, beautiful coat is shriveled gray, wrinkled and tight like elephant skin, indicating that the cat's insides have already been liquified and consumed. It's impossible to tell if the J'ba FoFi tried to drag it or not, but David postulates that the cat was too heavy for the spiders to drag into their lair for consumption. So, like the pirate Masamba, the ravenous arachnids just ate it here on the surface.

"If you didn't know any better," David asks Boss, unsettled. "What would you say happened to this poor bastard?"

"Probed by aliens?" she monotonously responds.

"I'd say bitten over and over again by a saber-toothed cat," David says.

"The Devil himself," Jimmy says, the usually lighthearted man not joking around this time in the slightest. He looks up from the putrid-smelling cat.

"Let's go," he says.

A fine, bristly sensation brushes up against the back of Jimmy's neck in the dark jungle. The Marine gains lightning-fast, cat-like reflexes ... spinning around and looking up just in time to avoid a five-foot J'ba FoFi landing on him.

"Aaaaghh!" the Marine screams, and jumps away just in the nick of time before the spider's legs can grab at him. Attracted by the movement below, the giant arachnid had begun to descend to the surface below the canopy with its legs and pedipalp "feelers" reaching and grabbing at Jimmy below the whole way down as it descended.

Only now, the adult male spider starts hissing.

David and Boss charge at the monstrosity and start clubbing it with their sticks. They flip the sharp ends of their makeshift spears towards the eight-legged predator and start stabbing at it furiously. The arachnid shrieks, injured, but this only seems to enrage the monster spider. It skitters towards Jimmy and leaps up onto him, grasping him around the chest before the terrified Marine can push it off or dodge out of the way. Having no choice but to touch the hairy arachnid with his bare hands, Jimmy desperately holds it away from him *just* far enough so that its fangs can't pierce his chest cavity.

Jimmy screams, desperate, and is stunned by how strong the spider is. It continues to cling to its prey, desperately reaching at him with its trembling incisors over and over again in an attempt to bite. The spider *screams* its human-sounding scream right in Jimmy's face. David and Boss struggle to pull it off him. Finally having it by the legs, she and David keep pulling, allowing Jimmy's right hand to come free. It shoots a strand of web at his hand out of its abdomen, but misses ensnaring him. Yelling,

Jimmy pulls out his knife and starts stabbing the giant repeatedly, right in its eight eyes.

"AAAGH! Fuck you, fuck you, FUCK YOU!" Jimmy shouts, stabbing over and over again. Yellowish liquid from the arachnid's eyes squirt out like tiny, erupting volcanoes, and drip down into Jimmy's face with the same pace and consistency of hot sauce dripping out of a bottle.

The spider finally yields, but the furious human trio does not.

David takes the AK-47 bayonet, and the three stab the J'ba FoFi over and over again until they are 200 percent sure that its mutilated body has completely stopped moving.

Breathing heavily, the group checks their surroundings again for any surprise J'ba FoFi adults, adolescents, or spiderlings.

"FUCK that!" Jimmy exclaims, wiping the contents of the spider's inner eye sockets and yellow blood off his face. He tastes a sour substance and furiously spits the stuff out of his mouth, too. Boss and David check him thoroughly.

"You weren't bitten!" Boss exclaims, relieved.

"Thank Christ!" Jimmy says, still trying to calm down from cheating death. He looks at the thin layer of green "miracle" repellent slime that they had applied hours earlier upon discovering more of those rare plants. He sneers at it. Before he can bitch about the repellent not working, David catches on, wondering the exact same thing.

"Uhhh ... maybe we reapply this slimy shit every half hour. Just to be safe? And, like Obasi did, we have to stay still as best we can."

"MAN!" Jimmy scoffs,

"*You* try having one of those things try to seduce your ass and see if you stay still, man!"

"Touché," the marine biologist says to the Marine. They compose themselves again and carry on.

It isn't until the wee hours of the morning, while it's still dark out, that they find a tarantula burrow large enough for them to fit inside. They don't enter it just yet. David wonders if he's imagining the sounds of the jungle getting quiet, or if it's actually happening. As far as David is concerned, he doesn't care. Nor does he know what is real versus what isn't real anymore. David and Boss turn on their flashlights, dreading what is to come despite knowing exactly what they're up against.

At least... she thinks to herself, *at least we don't have fear of the unknown to deal with.* The beams of their flashlights follow some thick vines along the ground, slowly illuminating the massive hole in the underbrush, one that looks just like the one that Dee was pulled into, only bigger.

"Here," David says, pulling out his pack full of the plants. He grabs a gooey handful and starts to apply the material to himself again, covering the already-existing layer. He can't help but think of how similar this feels to applying sunblock before bathing in the scorching sun.

"One more application before we enter the furnace?" he says.

The other two gladly follow his lead, doing exactly as he does and rubbing on more of the slimy substance that should act as repellent for the J'ba FoFi.

Jimmy gulps. Suddenly, Boss's thoughts betray her. They *are* going up against the unknown here. Deep in those pitch-black catacombs beneath the jungle, where David suspects that the J'ba FoFi dwell, she has no idea what to anticipate. *There could be thousands of them down there for all we know! What if this "miracle" repellant goop doesn't work as well as it did for Obasi? What if Dee's not there at all? What if we all get eaten alive? Or die miserably from the venom?* The Marine descends a mental rabbit hole of *What if's*, just like the civilian casualties of this hellish documentary-turned-rescue-mission before her.

"Fuck me," she whispers so quietly that only she can hear herself. Her thoughts are interrupted by Jimmy.

"Hey, you guys," he says to her and David gently. They turn to look at him.

"I... I want you to know that I'm with you. Till the very end. But I also... I hate to have to be the pragmatic one. That's usually her role..." He motions to his best friend and fellow Marine. "But," he continues, "we need to be mentally prepared for the worst. For all we know, he could already be dead. It... could already be too late."

His words cut like knives for David and Boss, and to himself as well. Jimmy holds back his emotions, feeling guilty for sounding like he may be the least willing to attempt a rescue. David catches onto this, as Jimmy is unable to cover up his feelings.

Rather than arguing with him, David simply says, "I know, my friend. We both do. But..."

David also contends with the sudden rise of emotions inside of him. He feels a sob make its halfway up his throat. Boss lightly touches his shoulder. This time, he successfully pushes the sob down before it can finish making its way up.

He continues, "But if somebody was looking after my boy all this time, and they didn't at least try... then, well, if I were that person I wouldn't be able to live with myself. I'm going after Deion Loemba, no matter what the odds."

At this, David stands taller than Boss and Jimmy have ever seen.

"And we're with you every step of the way, brother," says Jimmy.

"Now... age before beauty!" Boss says to David. David shines his flashlight into the unsettling hole before them, taking a big gulp of surface air for the final time before their descent.

"Let's do this," he says.

21

BOSS HASN'T BEEN THIS UNSETTLED SINCE SHE WAS A MERE eight years old, watching the trailer of a scary movie. An R-rated movie. For weeks she had nightmares and couldn't sleep, terrified by what ravenous ghouls could be lurking in the dark. Her dad felt really bad about it all, and never anticipated that it would scare his baby girl so badly. After watching this trailer, she couldn't sleep for months without the covers over her entire body ... including at least a foot or two above her head. Dark corridors, dark rooms, and even the outline of her own mother sitting on the edge of her bed in a dark room scared the sleep out of her. From then on until adulthood, Boss would never, ever again be able to hear the song "Tiptoe Through the Tulips" by Tiny Tim without feeling unsettled.

Although Boss has come light years since then, the memory of it all returns from her subconscious with a vengeance. Except, this is not a movie theater with her dad by her side holding her hand. This is real. Very real.

This is the nightmare.

Covered in a thick layer of anti-spider repellant, they proceed into the huge spider burrow until the burrow is a full-on tunnel. The thought of how many passageways like this one remain undiscovered below their feet boggles David's mind.

Taking point with one of their two flashlights, David cautiously, nervously, scans the pathway ahead. The air is stuffy beyond belief down here, and the soil has a dank, damp smell that is unpleasant compared to surface soil that's just been rained on. Almost immediately, bits and strands of webbing begin to appear. These webs start out thin, but get thicker and thicker as they proceed further, and deeper, underground. Roots stick out from the ceiling of the tunnel, indicating that there may be enormous trees on the surface above them. Jimmy tries to occupy his mind so as not to think about how far they would have to dig through the soil above them to reach the surface. *A few yards of digging? A few floors worth?* He waves the thoughts away. The three are drenched in sweat, but the slimy substance stays on thick.

No spiders anywhere to be found. David, still taking point, comes to a drop off.

"Stop, stop!" he whispers to the other two, putting his hand up.

"What's up, College?" Boss whispers. David points his flashlight downwards, seeing that the "drop off" is only about six feet down. He looks back at the others,

"Anyone wanna take a turn taking point?" he whispers. Jimmy and Boss look at each other.

"You gonna make the Asian guy go first again?" he asks her, whispering loudly.

She shoots him a look, "Are you gonna make the *woman* go first again?" she claps back.

Jimmy rolls his eyes, knowing full well that his friend usually hates when men try to be chivalrous. He knows her well enough to know that she usually looks for any opportunity to show that she's able to do something; not only as well as the men around her, but better. And she always does, without fail. Jimmy makes a mental note to give her grief about this later. He takes the flashlight and jumps down, plopping into the muddy floor of the tunnel below. He shines his flashlight around in his left hand while holding his knife with the other. He holds the knife tightly in a reverse-grip, edge-out technique. He scans the tunnel ahead, and can tell that they are slowly going deeper underground.

"C'mon, we're clear!" he whispers up to them.

The two plop down one at a time. While the walls of the tunnel are large enough for them to crawl through without needing to maneuver prone on their bellies, they cannot stand erect, either. The need to bend over and slouch the whole way wreaks ergonomic havoc on the trio as they realize they are not quite as young as they once were. Not ten feet farther along, they see their first spider.

Jimmy immediately squashes it with his shoe. They examine it. It's only three inches at maximum, but bright yellow with a purple abdomen. Definitely a J'ba FoFi. The spitting image of the spiderling that killed Paul Lumumba.

"Awww, a baby," Jimmy jokes.

"Fuck that baby," David whispers.

"Let's pick up the pace, you guys," Boss whispers to them, urgently.

Concerned about the lifespan of their flashlights' batteries, the group begrudgingly keeps on, a non-decision since the tunnel would be pitch black otherwise. Boss comes up with an idea, though. Triggered by a craving for a long overdue cigarette, she lights her blow torch lighter to create a third albeit much weaker source of artificial light. She takes a deep breath from the stuffy, hot, damp underground air and bottles up her Titanic-sized craving.

A J'ba FoFi "purring" sound comes out from the pitch black recesses of the tunnel ahead. Despite this, they pick up the pace. Slowly waving around her lighter in the pitch-blackness, where only the beams of their flashlights are visible, she waves it back around to her left and suddenly sees an *enormous*, hairy, brown J'ba FoFi. The trio are not numb to the effects of the spider, as the sight causes all three to freeze in fright. After jumping, the trembling group slowly examines the eight-legged menace. Although it's not yet a six-footer, its body alone is the size of a small dog. With its legs added in, the tarantula-looking spider tops out at about four-and-a-half feet altogether. David shines his flashlight on it, and he feels the heebie jeebies all over his body. The spider sits on the side of the tunnel wall a mere four feet away from their faces. David takes a beat to observe the arachnid. Perched on the claustrophobia-inducing tunnel wall, he's amazed to see its body faintly expanding and contracting.

'I *was* right,' he thinks to himself. He watches it, wide eyed, half terrified and half fascinated by the spider that's evolved to have vertebrate-like lungs.

The group moves on. Soon another J'ba FoFi can be seen in the beam of their lights, moving along the wall. This young one is about a foot in diameter, the size of a large dinner plate. Then, they see another one. This one is bigger ... about the size of a catering tray. Their flashlights reflect off the spiders' eyes slightly. In areas where their flashlights aren't directly pointed, the arachnids' eyes, and *only their eyes*, can be seen moving through the dark like beacons on a black sea.

Before long, there are clusters of eight eyes every few feet or so amidst the darkness. Luckily for them, the tunnel is also rapidly getting wider and wider.

"I... I... I don't like this," Jimmy whispers with a tremble. Boss puts her finger up to her lips. David shines his flashlight up to her, and sees a baby J'ba FoFi crawling its way down her right shoulder. David stops her, and carefully uses his spear to brush it off. Boss amazingly maintains her composure. Jimmy checks the layer of slime repellent on his body every five minutes.

David fights to control his rectum, trying not to panic. Before they know it, the three have giant spiders all around them, ranging from babies to four-footers. Sure enough, the slime seems to be keeping the spiders' curiosity at bay. This, however, does not give the group an ounce of relief.

Suddenly, a big one descends via web from the tunnel ceiling right in front of them and they almost collide with its grasping hairy legs. Keeping as still as humanly possible, the three humans maneuver stealthily around the hanging arachnid. The faint sounds coming from the arachnids' mouths are getting more and more numerous: light hissing, clicking, and even purring sounds.

Great, Boss thinks to herself, *now I'll really never like cats.*

David suddenly feels a spiderling crawling across the back of his neck. Its prickly little legs send shivers down his spine.

"Guys!" he whispers to them, trying to emulate Boss's example and not freak out. It hits David that at any moment he could feel its little fangs jabbing into him. All it takes is one bite, even from a baby, to ensure that Alex never sees his daddy again.

Jimmy carefully brushes it off with the blade of his knife.

They continue along. David shines his light up at the ceiling and sees several J'ba FoFi spiderlings perched on their webs. He gulps and scans the beam of his flashlight to look right above his head, where he sees a J'ba FoFi hatchling crawling its way across a single string of web in the dark just above his face.

Taking the lead again with the AK-47 bayonet, David leads them to a fork in the tunnel. They study their two options.

"What does your gut tell you?" Boss whispers in his ear. David hesitates, running his hand over his head of hair which he is certain must be getting gray by the second. He can feel that his hair is noticeably longer now than usual, as is his facial hair.

"We go right," David says, hesitant and unsure of himself. Proceeding slowly down the right passageway, David's flashlight illuminates a seemingly impregnable labyrinth of giant spider webs. The mass looks laced over so thick that a four-wheel drive couldn't pass through without getting permanently stuck. On the other side of the webbing, they can clearly see the shadow of a gigantic, adult J'ba FoFi sitting right in the middle of the tunnel. Its appendages move slightly, as if it's grooming itself. It's easily a six-footer.

"Uhhhh," Jimmy whispers. "You were saying?"

"We go left!" says David. "Left was actually my first impulse," he whispers.

"Always trust your gut," Boss whispers. "It usually knows the first time."

They retrace their steps back to the fork and pivot left. The tunnel is increasingly getting wider and rockier. By now, this dark realm feels more like a cave than a dirt tunnel.

David loses his footing on some loose rocks, but quickly recovers and prevents himself from tumbling down into the black abyss. He struggles with everything he's carrying to maintain his balance. The cave seems to level out, allowing them to walk normally. By now, they can easily stand up straight. Boss shines her flashlight above them just to make sure they don't bump their heads on any stalactites.

The sound of a low-frequency hissing draws the beam of her flashlight. Shining just above her head and to the right, her light illuminates another six-foot spider crawling across the wall. It stops suddenly and turns towards them, causing them all to freeze in place. They watch the hairy giant intently, and it stares them down, seeing two bright sources of light in its vision. They can see the reflection of their flashlights in its black eyes. The arachnid's hissing sounds intensify, as does its curiosity. It picks up the scent of the slimy botanical on their bodies. The giant twitches a bit then, finally, wanders off.

The three exhale in unanimous relief.

A little ways further, the three come across a massive and wide-open cavern system. They scan their flashlights in all directions, astounded by this underground world that sits, undisturbed, right below one of the least-explored rainforests in the world.

"Unbelievable," Boss whispers. Scanning the area, they are amazed to see that there actually aren't that many spiders around. The evidence of their existence litters the area, however; they see no J'ba FoFi themselves except for a few random stragglers on the far sides of the cavern. Strange sounds that they do not recognize come from somewhere within the darkness, too far off for the light of their flashlights to reach. One of them, David recognizes, is the sound of an injured animal. The animal that they can hear is clearly in pain, and is definitely not a spider. *We've made it*, David thinks to himself.

The *hive*.

Without warning, David's flashlight dies.

"Fuck!" he says, catching himself and making a mental note to stay quiet. With Boss's flashlight being their only remaining source of light, since her lighter is too weak to make a difference in the huge cavern, they soldier on ... desperately searching for Dee or any signs of him. Her flashlight then illuminates a haunting sight.

A graveyard of dead, and *dying*, prey. Despite their apprehension never wavering, the three muster their courage and immediately get to work. They plunge their hands into the impossibly thick, sticky webs and start pulling apart as much as they can, as they examine the J'ba FoFi victims one by one. They uncover only dead and dying animals. The dead ones have either succumbed to the spiders' insidious venom, or have already been drained dry.

David uses his dirty fingernails. Barely able to see what's in front of him, since her flashlight can only shine on one place at once, he bends over and squints his eyes as he peels apart the cocooning. An antelope lies there dead, its insides sucked out by the man-sized arachnids. They can hear a spider hissing and "purring" in the darkness nearby, and the sound appears to be getting closer and closer. They pick up the pace. David pulls apart the silky webbing of another victim. This, again, isn't Dee.

Scaring the ever-living shit out of him, another cocooned antelope comes to life and wails, clearly experiencing the effects of the potent venom. The animal's body is in horrendous condition, and Boss remembers Obasi's chilling words from days prior: *There is no cure for the bite of this animal.*

She looks up and shines her flashlight on a slurping noise coming from the "graveyard" nearby. There, the three can clearly see a giant spider feasting on its victim, another wild animal. The critter shrivels up in real time, its skin turning grey and lifeless and elephant-like just as Masamba's did. They can see this even underneath the white webbing wrap. Boss notices that this smaller animal's insides are consumed faster than the full-grown pirate's were.

"We need to hurry up!" Boss whispers to the other two. They check themselves again, and feel the slimy repellent substance in an attempt to put their minds at ease. Nearby, more J'ba FoFi are either eating or preparing to eat their cocooned prey. The various prey that are still alive can do nothing but squirm in place. Crusty spider molts litter the dark cavern. Another unique and God-awful, unrecognizable smell is overwhelming to the group's nostrils. *Spider droppings?* David wonders.

Boss shines her flashlight over to see a sight that gives her chills. It is eerily similar to the famous viral video taken in the Middle East of an upside-down camel spider perched on a wall as it feasts on a lizard or a gecko. Her light illuminates a five-foot monster spider perched the exact same way. As it hangs from the rocks by its back legs, it feasts with its incisors on a fully grown dead and dangling pangolin.

The J'ba FoFi that are feasting look as if they're in a trance-like state of ecstasy, their chelicerae quivering with delight as they suck out the sustenance. The others draw their stalactite-sized fangs and plunge them into their squirming prey. One of them feasts on a duiker, a small antelope native to the area. It's impossible to tell which of these are already succumbing to the venom, and which hadn't yet been bitten.

David's heart sinks as he knows that their chances of success vanish with every passing minute. *WHERE THE FUCK IS HE?* His mind races. Finally, he can't take it anymore.

"We have to call out to him! We're not covering enough ground fast enough!" he whispers loudly to the others. They do not protest.

"Dee!" David calls out. "Dee, are you down here? Say something!"

"Dee!" Boss calls out.

"Deion Loemba!" Jimmy follows. They call out for him repeatedly, but can hear nothing. David and Boss start to feel desperate.

"DEE!!" they both call out at the same time, realizing quickly that their volume that time was recklessly loud. Without warning, a sound that David feels like he hasn't heard for an eternity sounds out from the "graveyard" of the rocky, webbed-up cavern nearby.

Music.

They follow the sound around a giant rocky pillar that connects to the cavern ceiling. They can clearly hear the song playing. Echoing throughout the cave, David recognizes the song, and he feels a pit in his stomach. Echoing off the walls of the cavern is none other than "Sympathy for the Devil" by the Rolling Stones.

Boss slowly, almost reluctantly, scans her flashlight to the source of the sound, until the three can clearly see the cocooned, dead body of the second-youngest member of their party.

Avery Chambers.

They see the faint rectangular outline of Avery's phone lighting up in his pocket, as it plays the song. Avery's favorite song is also his ringtone. How Avery's phone is getting a call down here is far beyond any of them.

The thought of Avery's worried loved ones, desperately trying to get ahold of him, sickens David. His phone rings again and again.

Woo! Woo!

They see the J'ba FoFi responsible for his death.

Woo! Woo!

Boss keeps the flashlight trained on it, and the frightened trio sees something that nearly causes them to blow chunks.

Woo! Woo!

Avery's petrified, dead face stares back at them in the darkness.

Woo! Woo!

It's the only part of him other than his arms that isn't completely wrapped up in the webbing. Right where his heart would sit, on the left side of Avery's chest, is a massive double-puncture hole with dried blood, indicating that the final J'ba FoFi bite pierced his heart with its right fang.

Woo! Woo!

The look on Avery's face indicates a gruesome and unimaginable death.

Woo! Woo!

Avery's face stares back, his mouth is wide open and his eyes look as if they've been hollowed out, drained away with the rest of Avery's insides upon being consumed by the giant arachnid.

Woo! Woo!

His terrified face indicates that he was still screaming when he died, and it even resembles the "Ghostface" from the "Scream" series.

Woo! Woo!

Boss and Jimmy shiver at the sight, despite being some of the toughest people they know. The presence of Avery's favorite song, for David, only rubs salt in the wound as the marine biologist remembers the once-vibrant young man's essence.

The cavern returns to its eerie, low-frequency chorus of hissing, clicking, purring, skittering, pitter-patter, cocooned prey squirming, and the occasional groaning from an injured or dying animal. The group moves on in dread.

Boss takes a long stride forward, and her foot lands in something that she immediately realizes is a piece of clothing. She shines her light and bends down to examine it. She picks it up, and then gasps a bit.

It's a piece of Dee's shirt, ripped and bloody. The Marine, with a tough, guarded exterior, feels a wave of sadness fall over her.

"What is it?" David demands, upon hearing the sound of her faint gasp. She holds it up to him and he examines it in the light. David holds it tightly, with both of his hands, as if he were grasping an old family photograph. He slowly brings the cloth closer to him, until he's holding it tightly to his chest like a football. Boss and Jimmy watch him.

David feels the hope vanish from his body.

His eyes fill with tears, and he quietly breaks down crying. Pretty soon, Boss is joining him as well.

David chokes on his words. "It's all my fault. I failed him. I was... too late."

He heaves, trying to keep the sounds of his crying to a minimum. The same woman who scolded him upon their first meeting gently takes him by the face and then hugs him tighter than he's ever been hugged in his life. She squeezes him, and tears creep out of her eyes as well.

"No. It wasn't your fault. We all let our guard down. You..." she says, trying to hold herself together, "You did your best... we all did." The two embrace each other, and then Jimmy embraces the two of them. The three hold on to each other in the dark cavern. Boss can faintly hear David saying something to himself, under his breath.

"Oh, Alex. Alex... Alex..."

"C'mon," Jimmy says, feeling defeated. "Let's get you home to your boy."

The three pick themselves up and David wipes away the wetness from his face, taking some of the slimy repellent with it. Following her lead, the trio slowly begins to make their way out of the cavern.

Walking across cocooned prey, and feeling the crunching of bones under their feet as they go, Boss picks up a sound that she doesn't recognize.

"SHHH!" she orders, sticking her fist into the air. The cavern is silent now.

"Do you hear that?" she whispers to them.

Jimmy and David zero in but hear nothing.

"No, nothing!" David whispers back.

Boss flinches and turns around, hearing it again. "You didn't hear that?!" she says again, louder this time. She frantically scans her flashlight over the graveyard of cocooned death. Then, David and Jimmy hear it, too.

"Help."

The faintest little voice can be heard coming from the darkness.

"Heeeelp," the voice croaks again.

"Oh my God!" David and Boss say out loud. It's a child's voice. A boy.

"Oh my God, Dee!" the three yell out. "Dee! Deion! DEE!"

The three come to life, yelling as loudly as they can and searching.

"David?" the voice croaks.

"DEE! DEE, WE'RE COMING!" David shouts. They follow the voice, running as fast as they can over the sticky cavern's obstacles, until her flashlight comes across young Deion Loemba's face illuminated a few dozen yards away from them.

Her relief plummets when she sees what's near him.

A massive adult J'ba FoFi makes its way over to the cocooned boy. The arachnid doesn't skitter quickly. It walks casually. Even at a casual pace, the man-sized spider covers a lot more ground with its eight legs working together. The three human adults surge into a frenzy of adrenaline and nearly fall over themselves as they make their way over to try to intercept the arachnid. The spider makes its way towards Dee, fangs drawn.

Even though he's stuck, the boy strains his head and eyes to move just to the left until he can see the eight-legged menace approaching him. It's *closer* to him than the mysterious voices with a flashlight. Despite the trance-like, shocked state that Dee is in, his eyes widen with fear. Dee recognizes the giant spider, the exact same J'ba FoFi adult that he shot in the face with the revolver while they were perched in the tree. Even in the dark catacombs, he can see the arachnid's large, missing eye. It hisses at him with hunger, drawing its venom-dripping fangs, coming to within just a few feet of him.

Resisting the urge to scream at the hairy arachnid giant, the three adults reach Dee just in the nick of time before the spider can plunge its fangs into the boy. David plunges the tip of the AK-47's bayonet into the spider's German Shepherd-sized body. Boss adds a plunge with the tip of her spear and Jimmy adds to the assault with his combat knife. The three adults go ballistic on the overgrown tarantula, clubbing it and stabbing it with the fury of a hundred lifetimes. They stab it over and over, splitting it open until its yellow innards are visible. The spider shrieks in pain and its legs curl up, dead.

The group listens intently, relieved to have fended it off just in time but now concerned that its noises may attract more of them.

"Oh my God! Oh, thank God! Thank God!" David lunges at the boy, furiously pulling apart the webbing all around him until the child is recognizable again. The three desperately untangle the boy from his cocooned, mummified bodily prison. They check him for any bite marks. David feels his spirit soar with relief when they see that there are none.

Dee does not recognize them.

Stuck in a state of shock, the three try to get his attention.

"Dee? Dee! Dee, it's us! Dee!" The boy simply stares into the void, emotionless.

They finally resort to gently shaking the boy to get him to snap out of his trance-like state. Suddenly, Dee comes to life and starts to panic, thrashing and screaming with terror as he remembers where he is.

"They're gonna kill me! I'm going to die! HELP MEEE!" cries Dee.

"SHHHHH!" the three adults say in unison.

"Shhh, shhh, shhhh..." Jimmy whispers to the boy.

"We're going to get you out of here!" Boss says to him. "We need you to be strong, now, okay?"

"Ahh, who are we kidding?" David whispers to him quietly with a smile. "You're stronger than all of us combined."

"Yep!" Boss says.

This seems to reassure the boy. Dee's eyes become red as they fill with tears.

"You came back for me..." he says softly.

"Of course we came back for you!" Boss says. David looks Dee right in the eye, holding the boy's gaze with his hand against his face.

"Hey, I told you! First time for everything!" David says to him.

By now, there really isn't anything that David wouldn't do for him. Although he doesn't ask her, he is sure that the previously gruff "Boss Lady" feels the same way.

The group pulls out what little they have left of the botanicals from their pack and hurriedly rub on as much of the slimy, repellent material onto the boy as they can to mask his scent.

They pull Dee up and pull hard to get the remaining webs clinging to him off his back. David picks up the exhausted child, and Boss leads the way with her flashlight. Jimmy covers their six with the bayonet-tipped AK. The group of four trudge along through the darkness, and David ignores the soreness in his back from carrying Dee and his remaining supplies. Boss leads them to take the arduous journey back out the exact way that they came in, when she sees something that catches her attention.

Light. And it's definitely not from an artificial source.

High above them near the ceiling of the cave, where some rudimentary vegetation grows, she and the others can make out the faint look of a tunnel on the far side ...

"There!" she whispers to them, pointing up at it. Dee and the two men look up, seeing the exit which leads to the surface daylight above.

"That's our ticket out of here!" David whispers.

"I concur," says Jimmy. "There were too many damn spiders on the way in here! Might not be as lucky on the way out!"

Boss studies their path ahead with her flashlight. Other than the surface light peering in faintly above, indicating that nighttime has ended, her flashlight remains their sole source of light in the steamy, damp cavern.

"Look," she whispers to them, pointing at a slope with an approximately 45-degree angle. "That rocky pillar up there is angled just enough where we can climb our way out. Then, uhhh..."

"Then we cross that there!" David chimes in, pointing at a large, over-turned tree that, miraculously, seems to have created a makeshift "bridge" between the rocky pillar and the far side of the cavern ceiling, which would be impossible to access without its presence. On the far side lies the tunnel-looking passageway where the light shines in slightly.

"Feels like we're climbing that fuckin' Mordor mountain!" Jimmy whispers as they make their way up the rocky surface.

"You mean, Mount Doom?" Boss whispers back, scoffing and trying not to chuckle at him.

"Yeah, whatever the fuck!" Jimmy whispers. The only one who doesn't get the reference is Dee, but the elated boy couldn't care less. No longer able to carry him, David and Boss take turns holding Dee's hand as they ascend.

"We were so worried about you, little man! We were worried sick!" Boss says to him.

Dee smiles at her.

"Yeah, we were a hot mess!" David says. "Gosh. You are never leaving our side again, dude!"

Dee smiles at them, and ponders his next words.

"You guys are the best friends I ever had," the boy says to them.

At this, their hearts melt.

The four reach the overturned tree. On the other side: salvation. Adding heights to his list of many fears, David tries not to think about how far off the cavern floor the perched tree sits.

"On me, boys," Boss says confidently. She grabs the tree's roots and pulls herself up. The tree's trunk looks thinner up close, and the eons of dampness in the cavern have caused it to start rotting in some places.

"What's the hold up?" Jimmy whispers from the rear. Boss studies the tree in front of her, also making a mental note not to look down. She turns back to David, Dee, and Jimmy.

"We need to take this nice and slow," she whispers. "Hold on tightly to each other."

One by one, the group mounts the rudimentary bridge and starts inching their way across. The faint light on the far side of the cavern, where the morning sun is slowly getting brighter, calls to them.

The group is taken aback by just how few spiders they've actually seen in this vast underground area. It feels as if there were more of them in the tunnels that there are here. Boss has always wondered what crawling through the rat tunnels must've been like for American GI's in Vietnam.

Now, she has an idea of it. The last J'ba FoFi that they saw was the one that was about to kill Dee.

Even so, this provides little comfort for the group. Occasionally, they can hear *that* indistinguishable pitter-patter of skittering giants coming from the otherwise pitch-black darkness of the cave.

Thank God for Obasi, David thinks to himself. *Without him and these plants, those things would be on us right now like moths on a lantern.*

"C'mon, bud," David says to the child, holding his hand tightly. By now, all four of them fight to maintain their balance on the rickety trunk, moving inch by inch.

David continues, "We're in the home stretch."

Boss puts another foot forward. She desperately tries to keep her flashlight at an angle where the others behind her can see their own footing. She struggles to see what lies ahead of her, or even how far across the tree they are.

Her flashlight misses an especially rotted part of the thinning tree trunk.

SNAP.

Without warning, the trunk of the "bridge" snaps and the four lose their balance. The four go tumbling down with all their stuff, falling and landing in a small body of water at the bottom of the cavern below with a loud *SPLASH...*

... and accidentally washing off all of the spider repellent.

22

THEIR PLUNGE INTO THE WATER BELOW RINGS OUT, THE sound bouncing off every corner of the cavern. They can't see a thing. Boss splashes through the water to grab her flashlight, still turned on and floating on the surface.

"Dee?" David says frantically. He quickly finds the boy.

"Dee? Guys? Is everyone okay?" Boss exclaims.

"Holy shit!" says Jimmy. They clutch the boy and each other, the shaken four up to their necks in the murky water. The cave goes dead quiet. Too quiet.

They hear a faint *scream*, coming from far off in the cave.

Then, a faint *hiss*.

Then, *another scream*.

Then, louder hissing.

The human-like sounds chill the group to their bones, as if it was the dead of winter in this triple-digits humid African jungle cave.

Another scream. Another hiss. Another scream.

Then another and another and another ... the screaming and hissing sounds starting off isolated and then turning into a full blown *chorus* of screaming and hissing within the cavern ... one by one, getting louder and more numerous, and becoming *noticeably closer.*

"Go to Plan B!" quick-thinking Boss says, whipping around and pulling out a gallon of gasoline from her soaked pack as she stumbles out of the water.

"C'mon! Move it! And get out of the water!" she orders. "You too, College!"

David and Jimmy quickly catch on and follow suit with their packs. The three furiously pour a ring of gasoline around their position using the gallon-cans recovered from the outpost.

"Dee, stay close to us!" David shouts as he shakes the now-empty can of gas and tosses it into the darkness.

David, Boss, and Jimmy haul the barrel drum that they brought along, the one that Jimmy has had tediously strapped to his back this entire time, and move to the next phase of "Plan B." Catching on to what they're doing, Dee runs over amidst all the screaming and hissing coming from the pitch black cavern. With his heart racing, the kid helps them tip over the container of gas, allowing its contents to leak out, running into the pond water next to them and seeping into the soil.

"C'MON!" Jimmy shouts, and they frantically ascend to a safe section of cavern dirt where there is no gasoline poured on the ground.

The hissing and screaming is only getting louder and more numerous, coming towards them like a menacing tidal wave in the pitch-black darkness. Dee nearly wets himself at the thought of just how many of those things they might've accidentally disturbed.

All of a sudden, the loudest *hiss* that they've heard yet in the horror chorus of the last minute sounds out, and it is *right next to them.*

Boss pulls out her blowtorch lighter and flicks it on, turning for a split second towards the others.

"I could still use that cigarette!" she shouts.

She pulls her arm back and chucks her favorite lighter, hurling it towards the screaming, approaching J'ba FoFi specimen right next to them.

The massive arachnid is immediately engulfed in flames.

The spider screeches in excruciating pain as it gets burned alive.

The fire spreads to form a half-ring of protection around the group, shaped like a crescent moon, narrowly separating them from the oncoming spiders. The fire spreads to the gasoline in the pond, creating a massive inferno that makes the temperature in there even more unbearable than it already was.

The cavern comes to life as the fire illuminates everything inside with a *SWOOSH*, revealing *not dozens, but hundreds,* of four to six-foot J'ba FoFi spiders that were closing in on them in the dark.

Now, their hearts really skip a beat.

"MOVE IT!" David screams. Hearts nearly pump right out of their chests as the four desperately try to scale the rocky wall. Boss and Jimmy grab a few burning branches from the fire to use as makeshift torches. David rushes to grab one as well.

"NO!" Boss screams at him. "GET DEE UP TO SAFETY!"

She and Jimmy furiously yell and wave at the spiders, not unlike Neanderthals desperately trying to fend off prehistoric predators. Dee climbs as fast as he can, and David pushes him up the rocky, web-filled slope.

"GO!" Boss shouts at David, but he doesn't listen. With Dee having climbed to safety, he also grabs a burning "torch" and starts fanning back and forth at the hungry spiders.

"You are stubborn, College!" she shouts.

"I learned it from you!" he shouts back, waving another J'ba FoFi off with his burning branch. They yell with fury and wave their torches fiercely.

"CLIMB!" screams Jimmy. Boss gives him a booster lift under his shoe, using her hands, and the Marine makes quick work of the rocky slope, getting up to Dee. He reaches down to help David and Boss.

"COME ON, GODDAMMIT!"

The scorching fire lights up the cave as brightly as daytime, and it keeps most of the hungry arachnids at bay. Boss and David contend with the stragglers, fanning them away as best as they can before turning their backs on the oncoming swarm.

"Guys!" Dee screams down at them. He and Jimmy pull with all their might, helping David and Boss to get up to them. The group of four climbs to safety on the other side, now having only their legs to kick at the approaching spiders below them to keep them away.

Finally, the group pulls off the impossible and scales the remainder of the cavern wall, now no longer needing to worry about tumbling back down into the fire or the hungry hive.

They book it, running as fast as they can towards the well-lit outside, maneuvering around rocks, webbing, and more cocooned bodies—animal and human alike—on their escape out.

"C'mon, we're almost there!" Dee shouts to the three adults, who need to hear the encouragement by now just as badly as he does. The skittering and screaming and hissing follows behind them, all the way to the exit.

Boss accidentally runs straight into a maze of webs that cover the tunnel, blocking them from escaping to the surface. She fights like hell, but immediately finds herself hopelessly entangled and stuck. She thrashes, and can nearly feel her heart about to beat right out of her chest, but it's useless. The more she fights, the tighter the web's hold.

The other three turn back, and desperately pull apart the webbing to try to get her free. They even resort to using their teeth to pull it apart.

Screaming can be heard loudly behind her, getting closer.

Unable to turn her head around, the other three look behind her to see the shadows of dozens of man-sized arachnids making their way towards them. Their hideous eight-legged bodies move towards the exit amidst the backdrop of the bright cave that's still burning brightly behind them.

Boss erupts into a fit of coughing, as the smoke from their fire starts catching up to her. Before long, all four of them are coughing like crazy.

"GO!" Boss shouts at them, rasping her way through coughs as she sits there perched in the web, completely stuck.

"I said... GO! Take the kid and fucking GO!"

"NO!" David, Jimmy and Dee all shout at her in unison.

"I'M in charge, here!" she screams.

"You can take that order and SHOVE IT!" Jimmy claps back. "One for all, all for fucking one!" he barks. The tidal wave of spiders closes in, with the leading J'ba FoFi a mere five or ten feet away from her.

Finally realizing that they will never get her free in time, David thinks on his feet. Remembering that Boss mentioned earlier that she carries a secondary, backup lighter for her smokes, he shoves his hands into her pockets, frantically searching each one until he finds it. It takes all his strength not to get *his* hands caught in the webbing as well.

He grabs Boss's other lighter and his can of bug spray, and furiously shakes what's left of it. He aims and sprays the incoming giant spider right in the face with the tiny, improvised flamethrower. It shrieks and backs off, buying them a few extra precious seconds.

"We're not leaving you!" David exclaims, trying to control his coughing.

Jimmy and Dee tug furiously, while David torches the webbing all around her ... taking great care not to burn her. They work like hell to get her free.

The spiders are catching up to them again, but this time, the can of bug spray has run out.

Just as a six-footer is about to pounce on her, they finally get Boss free. The group sprints like hell to the exit, coughing and sputtering as they go, until they are nearly blinded by the morning sun. They continue coughing uncontrollably on the surface, but refuse to stop moving.

"Which way to the river?" says David.

"I... uhh... shit!" says Jimmy. "Sure would be nice to have Obasi here!"

Boss tries to say something, but the combination of years of smoking plus the smoke from the cavern wreaks havoc on her lungs. The three try to rub her back while keeping her moving along with them. They move quickly through the jungle. It takes her a few minutes, but her coughing finally subsides. Jimmy checks on Dee while David consults Boss. He continues to rub her back, and she looks up at him.

"Thanks for... for not leaving me behind." she says bashfully. "I really thought for a sec there that you guys would have no choice."

"Never," David says to her, grinning from ear to ear.

"We need to keep moving!" exclaims Jimmy. "Those things could be on us at any moment! They could be anywhere!"

"Anyone know which way to the river?" David repeats. The group ceases talking, but keeps moving, realizing that they have no idea where they are now. This thought is sobering to the three adults, but not to Dee.

"Friends!" Dee exclaims. "There is a cliff near here! Old friend told me about it! We can go to high ground, and we'll be able to see the river from any direction! We might even be able to see the boat!" The adults look at him, impressed.

"He's right! He's right!" exclaims David. He and Boss look at the boy, proud of him.

In the slightly overcast morning sun, none of them sees the J'ba FoFi spiderling crawling across David's pack. He reaches his hands up to the left strap to swing his pack farther backwards to create some more comfort for his sore body, and the baby spider awkwardly makes its way onto his hand.

David, exhausted and partially covered in lingering webs like the rest of them, doesn't feel the prickly legs of the newborn spiderling on his skin.

"You lead the way, boss man!" David says to the boy.

The spiderling suddenly follows the instincts that it's born with, and bites David right on his left hand in between his thumb and index finger.

"GAAAAGH!" David screams, violently shaking the spider off and then stomping on it. David stares wide-eyed at the bite. Boss, Jimmy, and Dee gasp upon realizing what has just transpired. David trembles in place, and the look of dread and terror on his face descends into full-blown madness.

"No! No! No, no, no, NOOOOOO!" he screams. He balls his bitten hand up into a fist so tightly that his veins look like they're going to pop out of place. He clenches his jaw.

"NOOOO!" Dee shouts, and then bursts into tears as he runs over to hold David around the hips. Boss covers her mouth, shocked. David heaves, and his distraught turns into an uncomfortable laugh.

"So... so this is how it ends, huh?" David says, utterly defeated. "After everything... all this time. This is how it ends." Thoughts of Alex back home race through his head as he examines the bite that they all know is 100% fatal.

Alex. Sweet, sweet Alex. Not one to be included by the other kids in school, and now, he will sit at *home* alone *as well as* in the school cafeteria. The emotions fall over David. *Will my sister even be able to raise him? How could I let this happen? First he loses his mom... and then, his dad?* David's thoughts spiral downwards, and tears creep out of his eyes. The group looks at him and at each other, hopeless.

"I'm so sorry, Alex. Bud, I am so, so sorry," David says, out loud this time. He looks at Dee, Boss, and Jimmy and says, "One final nail in the coffin for this fucked up trip, huh?"

Suddenly, Boss's eyes widen. She looks at Jimmy. Without consulting him or David, she grabs Jimmy's knife and—without hesitation—hacks at David's left hand. David jolts, and wails in agony. She hacks at his left wrist over and over until his hand comes off completely.

It all happens so fast. She did it so quickly that one would think that she had used a katana. David's eyes widen even farther, and he stares at the profusely bleeding stump where his left hand used to be attached. Jimmy and Dee are just as surprised by this quick-thinking and boldly audacious move on her part.

Shock traveling through his body, David's mouth slowly opens ... slowly, trembling; then the next scream comes out. Never in David's life has he experienced this much pain. The pain is excruciating, but even in this wretched state, he and the others know that Boss just saved his life.

David's stump bleeds profusely, shooting blood all over himself, his clothes, the dirt at his feet, and on the others. Now, it is Dee's turn to babysit *him*. Deeply empathetic to the pain that David is feeling, Dee holds him tightly and tries to console the man. Jimmy rips off a long piece of cloth from his worn out shirt.

"I'm sorry. I'm so, so sorry! It was the only way!" Boss says to David, holding his face in between her hands. "Maybe... just maybe you'll thank me later!"

"It..." David says to her, his voice trembling as if he had hypothermia. "It... it was the only... way."

Dee tries to comfort David, while Jimmy and Boss try to apply a tourniquet to his arm in an attempt to slow down the blood loss. The act of tightening the tourniquet sends waves of unbearable pain throughout David's phantom hand, arm, and body.

"Hey! I got to tell you, bro, after all this shit you've pulled. I gotta say you would make one hell of a Marine!" Jimmy says to him, trying to encourage him.

"Damn right," Boss agrees.

"Now, hold on tight," says Jimmy. "We're gonna need to tighten this, okay, man?"

"AAAAH!" David screams, over and over again with each tighten of their crude tourniquet.

The three carefully help get David back up to his feet. Jimmy leads the way, bushwhacking a trail through the dense jungle with his bare hands while Dee guides the group to their destination. Dee and Boss hold David on either side of him. Boss practically carries David with his right arm wrapped over her neck and shoulders. Dee splits his attention between trying to comfort his friend, and helping Jimmy to navigate. They trudge uphill through the jungle, David using all his willpower to keep up with them. He grunts and groans in excruciating pain. On a particularly steep and wet slope, David's legs give out from underneath him.

"Go... go on." David groans, miserable. "Go on without me. Get..."

"No!" Boss says to him firmly. The three of them look at David like it's the stupidest thing that they ever heard anybody say in their entire lives.

"Get to safety... get... get the kid to safety," he croaks.

"Would you shut your yap?" Boss interjects. "Do you really think after all that that we're just going to leave you here?"

"Crazy scientist," says Jimmy.

"Crazy outsider," Dee piggybacks.

"It... it hurts like crazy," David winces.

"Rest for a sec. I'm going to get a fire going," Boss says.

"But, it's almost midday?" Dee asks, innocently. Boss inhales deeply and lets it out with a sigh.

"I know," she says. Suddenly, David and Jimmy catch on to what she's up to. David's pain intensifies just at the thought.

Boss pulls out her remaining pack's supplies and grabs a large rock. Then she finds something in her pocket that she forgot about: her second, and last, vial of morphine.

"This'll help," she says, taking it and jamming it into David's left shoulder.

David yelps, "Aaagh! A little warning would be nice!" he says with a wince.

She uses the rock to smash open the canister of bug spray. Smashing it open, she is able to extract the very, very last of it, pouring about a tablespoon's worth into the dirt. But then, a dilemma.

"Fuck," she says quietly, attempting over and over again to flick on her secondary lighter.

"My lighter's all out. Fuck!"

"Good! I think it's Monday by now…" Jimmy says, remarking about her previous promise to quit as soon as they got back from this op.

"Now? Really?" she says to him. But then Jimmy pulls out his own lighter. Boss looks at it and at him, surprised. She knows full well that he's not a smoker.

"How did…?" she starts to ask him. Jimmy shrugs.

"You never know. Better to have it and not need it I guess."

"Tell you what!" she says to him, smiling as she takes it. "You're a pain in my ass sometimes but you are one resourceful S-O-B!" She nods approvingly at her foxhole buddy, and he winks back.

Boss makes a small fire in the dirt and turns back toward David. They all look at him. David's face turns pale. He knows even the morphine flowing through his veins will not stop the agony ahead.

"Let's... get this over with," David winces. He pulls up his shirt with his right hand and balls it up to fit in his mouth. He reaches his still-profusely bleeding arm over to them.

"Good idea," she says. "Bite down on that."

"Bite on it as if you were a hungry spider!" Jimmy jokes, trying in vain to lighten the mood. David shakes his head rapidly, his shirt tucked into his mouth, muffling the words,

"Uh uh, nuh uh! Not funny!"

The two adults grab an extremely nervous David, and Dee cringes in anticipation.

Using all their might to keep him in place, Boss and Jimmy shove his amputated hand into the fire to cauterize the wound. David screams so loudly through his "gag" that it hurts Dee's little eardrums. After a hellish few seconds, they release the man.

David bites down on the gag hard, wincing so intensely that they can see the veins in his head and neck. His face is beet red. He drops the gag and lets out the most agonizing yell that they've ever heard.

The pain is so excruciating that David nearly passes out. Delirious, his only reprieve at this moment is that there are no symptoms of the J'ba FoFi venom present. *She really did save my life,* he thinks. The delirium intensifies, and he nearly passes out again.

"Hey you! Hey! College!" she says to him, tapping his face to keep him awake.

"How are you doing?" Dee asks him.

"I..." David croaks. "I... I'd... I'd much rather be... on that dirt road. In that van," David heaves and throws up the contents of his empty stomach, overwhelmed by the pain of it all.

Despite his attempt to lighten the mood, Jimmy feels awful for the man.

David remembers a historical event that he read about a long time ago online. He remembers how surprised he was by what unfolded, and was even more dumbfounded as to why it was never mentioned in any class in school.

Perhaps, David thinks to himself, *perhaps Belgium's King Leopold II would be laughing right now. Perhaps he would be laughing from his pedestal in hell, at the irony of yet another Black man getting his hand chopped off in the Congo.* David can picture it in his mind: the evil, murderous tyrant that history forgot, laughing at the scene with a fat cigar or a lavish pipe in his hand.

"We need to move. Those spiders can still be anywhere," Boss says. They help David back up onto his feet again. Even though the morphine is kicking in, David feels extremely lightheaded. Boss, Dee, and Jimmy lead him through the jungle as fast as they can possibly move. The terrain is flat for a while, but before long the group finds themselves trudging through an incline. Their severe thirst and hunger wreak havoc on them with every excruciating step.

Despite this, Dee continues to bravely, and confidently, lead the way.

If David could show the child a snapshot of where he was when he first met him, timid and nervous as a Chihuahua, and compare it to the young man that he's already turning into now, he would in a heartbeat. Even in his current state, David beams with pride for the boy. In a bitter-sweet thought, he conjures up an image of Dee's late family. And with this, he knows in his heart of hearts that Dee's family would be beyond proud of the young man that he is becoming, despite overcoming shocking odds. For the first time since discovering that the boy was still alive in the cavern, David smiles.

At least an hour passes before they reach their point of high ground, overlooking the river basin. The exhausted group trudges forward, slouching like zombies... but excited at the same time. After what feels like an eternity, they have finally made it.

The two exhausted Marines, the child, and the civilian scientist scan the river with squinting eyes, covering their eyes from the late morning sun above the otherwise beautiful jungle.

"LOOK!" Dee shouts, his excitement carrying their eyes over to a tiny black dot in the distance. Sure enough, alongside the shoreline, the rescuers' boat sits in view.

"There it is!" Boss exclaims with joy. Now they know exactly which direction to head to reach their boat and return home.

The group's collective excitement is so intense that their vibrations practically radiate in every direction off the cliff where they remain perched. David and Dee hug each other tightly, and then Jimmy and Boss do the exact same. Overjoyed, the group throws themselves at each other, giving each other giant hugs one at a time. The vibe is different now. No longer is it dread. It is now relief. For a second, David even forgets the pain from his left limb. They all feel so happy that they feel as if they could cry, especially Dee.

"We're almost there!" Jimmy says. "C'mon, let's g—"

BANG!

BANG! BANG!

The deafening sounds stun the group silent, scaring the daylights out of them and interrupting Jimmy. The ear-piercing gunshots come from the jungle directly behind. Jimmy Leung looks down at the three bleeding holes in his chest.

His body slumps over, dead.

23

"JIMMY? JIMMY!" BOSS SCREAMS, DIVING DOWN TO JIMMY'S body and displacing dirt into the air. She shakes him violently, desperate to get some kind of a response. He is gone.

"No... no, no, no, no!" she wails, exploding into sobs over him.

David urgently grabs onto Dee with his good arm and holds the boy close; shielding him, both of them shocked by what just happened. David scans his eyes upwards to the jungle behind Boss and Jimmy.

Slowly stepping out of the jungle; ragged, injured, and scruffy with messy hair and unkempt facial hair... Oskar van Vuuren stands there with a smoking Vektor SP 9mm pistol and a crazed look on his face. He steps out onto the boulder just in front of him and then jumps off it, plopping down right in front of them only a few yards away.

"You didn't think you three would get away that easy now?" he says to them.

"Aaaaaaaagh!" Boss screams. She gets up from her murdered best friend and charges his killer like a freight train. Van Vuuren casually raises his handgun.

BANG!

"NO!" shouts David.

Van Vuuren's bullet casing flies to his right, into the thick foliage next to him, and Boss is stopped directly in her tracks. She falls backwards, feeling the virulent pain from the gunshot wound in her shoulder. She gnashes her teeth, furious and crippled by the shot.

Utterly defeated, she musters her energy to crawl over to Jimmy using her non-injured arm, taking him by the forearm.

"I'm so sorry," she whispers to him.

Van Vuuren turns his attention to David and the child, and raises his weapon with an insidious smile on his face.

"WAIT! Stop! Don't!" David shouts, shoving the terrified boy behind him. The presence of his long-time abuser immediately restores the child to his former self, the one that David and his colleagues first met.

"Please, stop, please! Leave him alone. It doesn't have to be this way," David pleads with his hand raised in the air to try to de-escalate the man.

"Please, just let him be. He didn't want any of this. None of this is his fault! It's my fault! Please, just leave the child alone and take me instead!" David begs, desperately pointing to himself while using his amputated hand to try to keep Dee safe. Boss winces and grabs her shoulder, rising to her feet to join David and the child.

"You," she says to Van Vuuren. "You could take off right now and start over as if nothing had ever happened. You can leave the boy in peace. It... doesn't... have to be this way!" she says, wincing.

Van Vuuren looks at the two of them like they're out of their minds. His eyes widen, as if in disbelief. He laughs, uncomfortably.

"You two really think it's that easy?! You two think I can... just... walk away? This. This place. This life! This is all I know! This river, *my* river. This is all I've known for as long as I can remember!"

"It doesn't have to be this way..." David says in a gentle tone, trying to appeal to his better nature.

"Just leave the boy alone," Boss says. "Oskar," she says.

Van Vuuren looks at her, as if he's stunned that she referred to him by his first name.

She continues, "You could start over. You could even settle down with someone, I don't know! But there's more to all of this besides..." She hesitates.

"She's right," David says gently. He holds his good hand out as a show of good will.

"You, and the boy, and us? We could all go our separate ways and you could completely start over. You really can! You can take good care of yourself."

Van Vuuren looks at them, stunned by their words, and shakes his head. His eyes glance away for just a second, and then they find their way back to the three in front of him. His hand trembles slightly.

"I've been taking care of myself since I could barely walk," Van Vuuren croaks.

"You think I can just walk away from all of this?" he says, his expressions getting bigger and bigger.

"You think I can just... what'd you just say, settle down with someone?" He bursts into wheezing laughter and keeps the loaded pistol pointed directly at them. "It's a fantasy. That's a goddamn farce! No, no. I stay in my lane. I do what I do. And I survive. I take care of myself! It's not like anybody else volunteered for that role!" he snarls at them.

Van Vuuren pauses, as if he is actually allowing something new in; then his face turns red and sour again without warning.

"I do what I must," he says. His lower jaw jets out as the anger fills his face.

"And you know what? I regret nothing. Nothing!" he exclaims.

The thought of the people throughout Van Vuuren's life who have taken advantage of him flashes across the screen of his mind, and his blood begins to boil. Then, like an addict being given a taste, his mind lights up, remembering how good it feels to take rather than to be taken from.

"I regret nothing," Van Vuuren reiterates softly to the distraught trio. His insidious gaze turns down to the boy at David and Boss's hip level. Dee shivers when their eyes meet. Van Vuuren smiles at the child.

"You know, if it really *was* my destiny to be wronged at every turn, then... if it was between your mom and I..." he says, waving the pistol, "then I'm *glad* that it was her and not me," Van Vuuren says, taunting the child.

Dee feels the rage rising inside of him as his eyes fill red with tears from the memory. David and Boss listen, mortified. Van Vuuren leans in closer, as if he's about to reveal to the child a secret.

"And I *enjoyed* her, too."

Dee loses control, screaming at the fully grown, armed man as if ready to charge at him,

"I HATE YOU!" the child screams at him at the top of his lungs. Van Vuuren raises his pistol to kill the barely 10-year-old boy.

"NO!!" David and Boss scream, desperately trying to shield the boy. Van Vuuren begins to squeeze the trigger, but the gun does not fire.

Van Vuuren's face goes from "smiling" with scorn, to confusion as he turns his arm holding the pistol. He turns it slowly until the pistol is being held at a sideways angle.

Van Vuuren's eyes widen, and the rage boils up inside of him, as he examines a small wooden *arrow* that plunged into his right forearm before he could shoot.

He looks around, wondering where it came from.

Astonished, the maniacal man looks back up at the trio on the edge of the cliff with a psychotic look on his face. He points again to finish the three off once and for all, when *another* arrow comes from out of nowhere to land directly into his back.

Van Vuuren bellows and whips around, enraged and unhinged, yelling and shooting randomly into the thick jungle all around him with no target in sight.

David shoves Dee to the ground, and he and Boss seize their opportunity.

The injured madman pops off at least four shots from his handgun before the injured David and Boss tackle him with all their remaining might. Boss struggles with her pained shoulder, as she goes for the pistol itself. Van Vuuren yanks before she can get it out of his hands, but she holds his arm in place as they yank back and forth.

David punches Van Vuuren over and over again, unable to land any critical blows with the three of them tussling and moving around too quickly. Van Vuuren raises his leg and kicks David in the solar plexus, knocking him a ways back.

Boss manages to get the gun free from Van Vuuren's hands, but he maneuvers just at the right angle and the pistol gets tossed to the side, away from both of their grasps. Boss grabs Jimmy's knife and stabs Van Vuuren, going for his chest but accidentally stabbing the maniacal man right through the palm of his left hand. Van Vuuren howls with pain and elbows her in the face, then goes after the gun.

Recovering immediately as if his elbow were a mere mosquito bite, she savagely goes for his legs, tripping him to the ground just before he can reach his loaded pistol. She climbs her way up the husky man and grabs onto the arrow in his back. Van Vuuren yelps in pain as she uses the lodged arrow to pull herself up, and then digs it with all her might into the flesh of his back.

He howls in pain, reaching around behind him, desperately trying to get her to stop.

David, back on his feet, dives for the gun.

Van Vuuren furiously pulls the arrow from his forearm out and, spinning around, jabs it right into Boss's shoulder where the gunshot wound is. She yelps in pain.

David grabs the gun but Van Vuuren tackles David's right hand, gripping the pistol, just before the exhausted civilian scientist can point and shoot. Van Vuuren twists his arm and takes the pistol from his hand. With every twist and coil of their savage hand-to-hand fight, the excruciating pain from David's amputated hand pulses out again and again throughout his body. They fight dirty: tooth, claw, and nail.

Van Vuuren shoves a weakened David away with all his might, just as Boss leaps up on top of him.

The Marine grabs the arrow out of Van Vuuren's back and nearly drives it right into his neck, before the man twists just at the right angle to avoid having his jugular vein impaled. Boss snarls at him, all her hatred for the loss of her best friend boiling over. She goes after him again and again, thwarting him from pointing his pistol to end David and Dee's lives.

Van Vuuren squares up with her and grabs the barrel of his pistol, spinning it around in his hand and then pistol whipping her right in the face. She goes down for a split second, taken by surprise from the pain in her nose. Van Vuuren whips her again with the pistol, yelling and swinging as hard as a pitcher at a baseball game, landing the grip of his handgun right into the back of her head and knocking her unconscious.

"No!" David shouts.

Van Vuuren turns to square up with David, opting to enjoy beating him to a pulp rather than shooting him outright. David trembles as he stands to his feet, and Van Vuuren charges at him. The two men swing at each other, both of them injured and both of them fighting ungracefully. Severely weakened from the excruciating pain, exhausted, and down one hand, David is almost immediately overpowered.

From the side, Dee watches, searching for a rock or a stick or anything that he can use to help his friends.

Van Vuuren lands one blow after another onto David, punching him over and over again in the sternum and face. David catches a glimpse of Dee and coughs up blood. Van Vuuren savagely puts David into an arm bar and punches again. He then grabs David by the shirt and knees him right in the face, sending him seeing stars all the way to the ground.

"Don't," David croaks weakly to Dee, coughing up blood as he looks at the terrified boy.

"Run," he says to the child, wincing.

Dee starts to cry, knowing there's nothing he can do to help his friends in their losing fight.

David grabs onto a large piece of tree trunk in the dirt nearby, and swings it up as hard and fast as he can, smashing it into Van Vuuren's temple with a yell. Van Vuuren stumbles around for a bit, dazed.

In retaliation, he grabs David's left wrist ... where his hand used to be ... and shoves it down into the dirt before savagely stomping on the stump. David lets out a long and agony-ridden wail, the pain so great that he nearly begins crying himself.

Utterly defeated and breathing heavily and raspily, David watches helplessly as Van Vuuren stumbles toward him and pulls his pistol back out. He cocks back the charging handle and plops down on one knee next to David, pleased with himself. David feels the warm barrel of the pistol pressed up against his skin as Van Vuuren puts the pistol directly to his forehead.

"Goodbye, Dr. Hale," he snarls.

The bullet *barely* misses David's head as Dee, less than a third Van Vuuren's size, tackles his abuser in a furious yell, narrowly saving David's life.

Van Vuuren and Dee stumble over towards the edge of the cliff. The kid kicks and screams, but his courage is short-lived. Van Vuuren immediately shoves the kid onto his back, pins him down and goes for the boy's throat. Using both of his hands, Van Vuuren chokes the squirming boy with all his might. The sweat from his forehead drips from his enraged face down into Dee's face, as he attempts to choke the kid to death. Dee's face starts to lose color. He flails, desperately, unable to get the grown man off or even to call for help.

David looks over at the two by the cliff's edge.

Emotions that David didn't even know he was capable of feeling surge through him, as he watches what the abuser is doing to the sweet, helpless child who he has come to love as his own. David musters *every ounce* of his remaining strength and willpower as he stumbles to his feet, seeing the boy pushed to within an inch of his life through David's now-blurry vision.

With a triumphant war cry worthy of 10,000 Vietnam-era war flicks, David charges Van Vuuren with everything he's got left, shoving him off of the boy and sending him toppling over the cliff.

Boss comes to, grasping her head as she rushes to the aid of the boy who's desperately trying to get his breath back.

David, having nearly gone over the edge of the cliff himself, tugs and tugs with his legs and right arm until he manages to pull himself back up to where gravity won't work against him.

The three hear a noise, and look down.

Van Vuuren has not fallen off the cliff.

He dangles primarily by one hand, desperately clinging onto the rocky surface, his injured bloody left hand barely able to hold on. Below him is a long fall to the rocky ground and jungle vegetation. Van Vuuren looks up at the three of them, wide-eyed and desperate. He pants, terrified and straining to hold on.

"Help! Help me! Help me!" he pleads with David and the others above.

"Hey, you were right! We can all go our separate ways peacefully and call it a day! Yeah? Come on now!"

Boss resists the urge to spit in Van Vuuren's face from above. She moves instead to comfort an inconsolable Dee, who is still trying to catch his breath. David just stares down coldly into the man's eyes. Suddenly, the three above can hear the unmistakable sounds coming from the jungle below them at the base of the cliff.

Pitter-patter.

Skittering.

And finally ... *hissing.*

Van Vuuren hears the sounds, too. He trembles and whimpers. He looks down terrified, and then back up again. He feels his grip slipping, and desperately takes a different tact.

"Come on, help me up!" he scoffs. "You... You wouldn't want the kid to see a man die, now, would you? C'mon!"

Van Vuuren hears the hissing coming from below getting louder and louder. His eyes widen. "Don't let the kid see a person get killed by the monsters!" he shouts up to David.

David looks at him from above, hesitates, and then turns his head back to look at Boss and the child, as if asking for permission. Boss catches his gaze and then slowly redirects it, with her eyes, to the traumatized boy next to her until she and David both look at him. Dee looks back at David, who slowly shakes his head.

David takes a big inhale through his bleeding nose and gives Dee an almost imperceptible nod. David turns back and, although painfully exhausted, reaches out with his good hand to help Van Vuuren up. He reaches, and the once-proud pirate leader desperately holds on, dangling while David secures him. Upon securing his hand, he uses his overtaxed arm to pull himself and Van Vuuren close enough together so that their faces are mere inches apart. Van Vuuren struggles desperately with his other limbs to try to get back up. David then looks down into Van Vuuren's face and says, solemnly, "*YOU* are the only monster here."

David lets his hand go.

Van Vuuren yells, reaching out to grab David in pure rage as he tumbles down the cliff wall. The fall takes several seconds, and a loud CRACK can be heard by the three above upon his impact.

Shivering, trembling, and in shock, Van Vuuren slowly sits up to see that both of his legs are broken, bones sticking straight out of his flesh. His eyes widen and his mouth slowly opens, before letting out an agonizing scream. He turns bright red, and hopelessly attempts to get up. Another *crack* can be heard as he makes a futile attempt to shimmy himself around. The excruciating pain surges through his body, and his howls can be heard far in all directions.

He isn't going anywhere.

Then, he hears the sounds.

Van Vuuren whimpers in pain and fear as he can hear something, multiple things, rustling around in the bushes nearby. The foliage seems to come to life. Then, the sounds become more and more clear.

The cadence of the skittering has to belong to something with more than four legs. Definitely not two. The hissing and slight purring sounds are unmistakable. Then, the terrified man sees a hairy, brown spider leg step out of the thick foliage. Then another leg, then another, and another. His already lightning-fast heart rate accelerates.

"No! No, no, no, no, no, NO!" Van Vuuren whimpers.

One by one, adult J'ba FoFi gather around him, emerging from the jungle and forming a ring of giant spiders around the helpless man. Van Vuuren swings his head back and forth at the six-foot arachnids. He looks up at the cliff edge above him, trembling and scared out of his mind, and feeling his hatred boiling over.

"You," he whimpers, looking up at David. "Hale," he whispers, looking like he's ready to combust.

"HALE!" he bellows, his voice becoming raspy and throaty.

"HAAAAAAAAAAALE!"

The giant tarantula-like spiders gather around their easy prey, surrounding him like a pack of hungry wolves and closing in on him, taking their sweet time. Van Vuuren begins to cry, his tough exterior facade falling away like a house of cards.

He remembers his pistol. He considers using it against the oncoming arachnids, but can see clearly that there are *dozens* of the hairy eight-legged menaces. Trembling with tears and a snotty nose, he promptly puts his pistol right up to his temple and pulls the trigger.

Click. Out of ammo.

"AAAAAAAAHHHH!" he screams, terrified and unhinged, as the spiders reach him and begin to climb on top of him.

Without warning, an inhuman *howling* sound rips out from the jungle nearby.

The spiders immediately and simultaneously come to a halt. The arachnids hesitate for a moment, quivering with hunger and instinct. Strangely, the spiders unanimously back off him. Van Vuuren trembles underneath the horde of giant spiders, watching, dumbfounded.

What are they doing? Why did they stop? David wonders from above.

Then, they hear the *howling* again. This time, it's ear-piercing for Van Vuuren.

In a show of unusual intelligence, the J'ba FoFi begin to yield to something moving toward them through the brushes. Something enormous. David, Dee, and Boss watch from above in pure horror as that "something" steps out of the foliage and the spiders down below yield to the biggest J'ba FoFi specimen that they've seen *by far.*

The mama.

She is dark chocolate brown in color ... so dark that she's almost black. She easily exceeds a whopping nine-foot leg span. But there's something else about her, something different than the other spiders. Even from high up above, the three survivors watching can see that her abdomen is jagged and textured strangely. Its coloration is a strange, creamy yellowish swirl. Then, he and Boss realize why her abdomen looks "off."

"Holy mother of God," she says to David.

On the ground, Van Vuuren is still unable to see why the spiders have suddenly stopped and backed off him. One by one they yield until her enormous hairy legs come into view. She is so large that she could easily fill an empty Jacuzzi, no problem.

It is only now that Van Vuuren, trembling and scared out of his mind, can see that she has *hundreds* of J'ba FoFi spiderlings *completely covering her abdomen*, all bright yellow with little purple abdomens.

Van Vuuren descends into utter and complete madness at the sight, scrunching up his face and crying a snotty cry. Boss watches his face from above. She knows that if her old CO were here, he'd say that Van Vuuren is crying "like the punk bitch that he is."

The mama steps over the sobbing man, one leg at a time, bringing her face right up to his. Her glossy and enormous set of eight eyes peer into his with a haunting level of intelligence. She rears her moist incisors and cephalothorax up, and *screams* the species' signature humanoid scream inches from his face.

"AAAAAAAGH!" Van Vuuren screams in sheer terror, releasing the contents of his bowels and bladder while his bottom lip quivers. The mama's scream is so intense, coming out of the prickly, artichoke heart-shaped hole that is her mouth, that Van Vuuren can feel it like a light, warm desk fan on his face. The man and the mama spider scream simultaneously.

She waves her venom-tipped, dripping fangs over him. They must be at least twelve inches long, and still as sharp as when she herself was a spiderling. She opts not to bite him, wanting to keep him fresh for her young.

The nine-foot J'ba FoFi turns her body slightly at an odd angle, as she unleashes her brood on him like a swarm of skittering locusts.

The J'ba FoFi spiderlings swarm all over him, covering every inch of his body and biting him repeatedly. Van Vuuren feels *all* of it, like little burning thumbtacks digging into his skin from head to toe. He nearly loses his voice, screaming more intensely than anyone Boss has ever heard scream in her life. Van Vuuren flails desperately, trying to shake them off, but it's useless.

Already bitten in hundreds of places, the venom *immediately* begins changing his physical appearance. His veins swell bright purple and the pain of the venom entering his body in so many places simultaneously matches the level of pain from his broken legs. The spiderlings keep biting him and swarming him, with dozens of them having already found a comfortable spot somewhere on his body in which to begin liquefying and consuming him. They crawl up and into his clothes and into every nook and cranny.

Many of them find their way into the open wounds on his legs where flesh and bone stick out. Van Vuuren looks up at the heavens, screaming bloody murder under the sweltering sun. The spiderlings crawl into his wide-open mouth, slipping in like a multi-lane highway merging into a one-lane tunnel. He screams and twists and coils and hums in pure terror.

The effects of the venom from the bites covering his face and body begin to intensify. Small purple boils and swelling begin to form, and even his eyes begin turning red until there's no white left around his pupils. His mouth and tongue and airway immediately begin swelling from the bites inside his mouth.

The three watch in horror with their mouths covered, flabbergasted, as the newborn J'ba FoFi feast.

The wide-eyed man-turned-spiderling buffet slumps back, with his eyes still open, twitching. He twitches again and again, no longer screaming. The twitching continues, as if having a seizure in a catatonic state.

A few seconds later, Oskar van Vuuren meets his end.

24

DAVID PULLS HIS BATTERED, BRUISED, PAINED, AND exhausted body over to Dee and Boss. Upon reaching them, he gently puts his hand up to examine Dee's bruised throat. The child only now begins to breathe normally, having returned from the brink of death. Boss grasps her shoulder and David gently rubs the back of her head where she was struck. She and Dee, in turn, examine his left stump. The three hold each other tightly for several long seconds, breathing heavily and still coming down from another adrenaline high of terror.

"Wait a second," David says.

Almost as if in unison, the three look up and examine the area around them, insatiably curious to know where those arrows came from. They hear a rustling in the shrubs nearby, and Boss assumes the worst. She and David motion for Dee to stay put. They stand up weakly to get a better look.

The shrubs rustle again.

Stepping out of the jungle with a bow and a quiver full of arrows, covered from head to toe in the native spider repellent, stands Obasi.

The old Aka man, fit, lean, healthy and sharp-as-a-tack as ever, looks at the three and a huge smile forms on his face. Behind and all around him, at least two dozen more people peacefully step out of the thick jungle.

The people. *His* people. Historically referred to as "pygmies," Obasi's people gather around him and the trio of survivors. The ultimate survivors themselves, they look at the battered Westerners with curiosity and a radiating feeling of benevolence.

"OBASI!" Dee exclaims with joy, taking the word right out of David and Boss's mouths before they can say the exact same thing.

"I thought ... my friends could use some help!" Obasi says warmly.

"When I heard the screaming and the gunshots, I knew. This is my people. We are the BaAka," he says, putting his hand over his chest exactly the way that he did when he first met Boss and her crew.

She and David now fight to contain their relief and excitement, but Dee springs to his feet and runs without a second thought into Obasi's wide-open arms, giving the older man that saved their lives an enormous hug.

As his people emerge from the jungle, the trio can see that they carry a hunting net with bushmeat, and several of them have bows and arrows. A couple others have spears. Some of them have fine line tattoo-like markings on their faces. All of them have little hair or are bald altogether. They begin to smile warmly at the outsiders, and David can see that many of them have filed, sharpened teeth. They are dressed ranging from traditional, tribal clothing to very little clothing. Several are topless. Along with the two dozen or so Aka, there are a few parents amongst them: fathers, carrying their babies. Every single one of them is covered head-to-toe in the same slimy, botanical material that the J'ba FoFi can't stand.

"I..." David says, exhausted and having been to hell and back. "I don't know what to say."

"I do," Boss says, walking up to Obasi and giving him an enormous one-armed hug, shielding her pain-ridden shoulder. Side by side, the Western woman towers over him.

"Thank you," she says. "Thank you so, so much." David embraces Obasi as well, thanking him and the others as profusely as she. The aging man examines David's amputated wound.

"Come now, let's not delay," the Aka man says to them. A female member of his group kindly gestures to a male member, and he promptly brings over a bag stuffed with something that smells rather pleasant. The young Aka man opens it up.

Reaching in, Obasi and two other members of his tribe help Dee, David, and Boss to apply a thick layer of the repellent slime as well. As Boss runs the material over her body, she feels a wave of relief wash over her. Dee and Obasi start playing with each other, teasing and trying to rub some of the miracle material in each other's faces ... much like two friends trying to "get" each other by smearing whipped cream in the other's face. Dee giggles freely, and the adults smile at him.

Wanting to join the fun, the small toddler in the arms of another Aka father, the oldest baby in their group, grunts to be let down. His father lets him down, and the child slowly starts waddling over to the older child, Dee, like a drunken penguin learning how to walk. Dee smiles, and walks up to the child. By comparison, the now-liberated Congolese boy towers over the indigenous toddler. The toddler coos and starts giggling at Dee. He reaches out to Dee like an older brother, uttering an Aka word that only Obasi and his people understand. The toddler's father smiles.

"He wants you to pick him 'up!'" Obasi says. Dee looks up at him and Obasi, as if asking for permission. Obasi and the child's father nod.

Dee picks up the child and the two hit it off immediately. The sight melts David and Boss's hearts. Never before have they seen the abused, traumatized boy beaming like this. *It's almost as if,* David thinks to himself, *he has a family again.*

Boss's mind drifts in a similar direction. After the roller coaster that she's just been on, she reflects on her life, what's important to her, and, possibly, why she was meant to be here. She feels sad about Jimmy, realizing that if he was having similar thoughts that she'd just give him a hard time and call it all kumbaya. Her mind drifts back to Obasi and these people who saved their lives, even though they didn't have to. *These people are so warm. So loving. And we've only just met them. They look so ... happy. Maybe ... maybe our society's idea of what riches and happiness is has been wrong all along.* Boss surprises herself with her own thinking, knowing that her best friend would be proud of her.

"Jimmy..." she whispers softly. Nobody hears her. She turns back and walks toward the cliff's edge to her fallen brother. The friend who she expected would outlive her by a wide margin.

"Jimmy," she says, kneeling over his body. David, Dee, and the others notice her. One by one, they make their way over to her. David gets her attention by gently putting his hand on her non-injured shoulder, and she turns up to look at him. She rises from Jimmy's body where she was holding his hand, and David hugs her tightly. She melts into him. For the first time in years, she lets her tough, invincible, exterior wall fall away as she sinks into David's chest and mourns her friend. David holds her tightly, and one by one the Aka console her as well, gently placing hands upon her shoulder and back.

It isn't until hours later, after Jimmy has been properly buried in the soft soil nearby and Obasi has said a traditional BaAka prayer over him, that Boss accepts food from the tribal members. She, David, and Dee are miserably hungry and thirsty. Upon Obasi's insistence, the trio devours as much of the Aka's cooked bushmeat and edible roots as their stomachs will hold. David and Boss try to pace themselves, feeling strangely like they are taking advantage of them by accepting their food. They have already lost so much to outsiders over the centuries. The Aka, on the other hand, insist.

Obasi and his people lead the exhausted group through the jungle to a clean water source, and the grateful trio drink as much water as their bodies can handle after so much time feeling parched.

David stands up and wipes the water away from his mouth. Boss does the same. Dee finishes drinking last. He cups one more big gulp of water into his hands and sips. He gently rubs the remainder from his wet hands along his throat to soothe his bruises. David, Boss, Obasi, and the tribe let him take as much time as he needs.

Dee looks up and sees David's hand reached out above him, beckoning him. Dee smiles and takes his hand. Holding David's hand on one side, and Boss's on the other, with Obasi and his people acting as escorts, they begin their short journey back to the boat. Dee and the two adults couldn't care less about the slimy, weird texture of the repellent on each other's hands.

Finally, exiting the thick, steamy jungle, they come over a ridge and their boat comes into view. It sits there, glistening amidst the backdrop of the early evening sun along the river. The sight is absolutely stunning. After everything that they've been through, the boat is even more beautiful to behold.

The Aka help them load the boat with their few remaining belongings. Two other members of the tribe help Boss fill the boat's gas tank up with gasoline. They store the leftovers on the boat under a tarp, giving them more than enough fuel for the return trip to Cameroon.

At last, it hits David like a bullet train that it's time to say goodbye. He turns to the aging Aka man, the man who has come to be their friend.

"How can we thank you? How can we repay you?"

Boss listens intently for Obasi's answer. The old man turns to look at his people all around them. The sight of them puts a warm grin on his face, like a dad or a grandfather watching his family gathered for the holidays, beaming with happiness at *their* happiness. He ponders David's question.

"I promise we will take care of the payments to you and your people with the embassy," David says. "But, is there *anything* that we can do to thank you?"

Obasi turns back to David.

"Never tell anyone what happened here." The two adults stand at attention. Nearby, Dee plays with the BaAka children and babies, happy as can be.

"If the world finds out about the Great Spider, then there will be people all over this place," he explains. "Scientists and poachers, and adrenaline junkies from around the world." Boss and David nod to him. Obasi continues.

"As unforgiving as this place can be…" He turns and looks at his people playing happily with the children, their children giggling with delight.

"This is our home. This jungle," he gestures to the natural beauty all around them. "This is our home. And we love it very much. And, if you tell anybody what has happened here, we could lose our way of life."

David and Boss are floored by his words, having fully expected him to say something else, such as "double the payment" or "free crops from nearby farmers for a year." Instead, the outwardly focused man gives them one final, and humble, gift to part with.

"Thank you," David says, at a loss for words.

"You have our word," Boss says to Obasi, offering him her pinky. He looks at it quizzically.

"What is this?" Obasi says playfully.

"Oh," Boss chuckles. "Sorry, it's just a thing that we do sometimes when you are making a promise to somebody. I used to do it all the time with my dad. He taught me that your word is your most sacred honor. And, I know it's kind of cheesy, but, to remember him, I like to carry that on." Obasi smiles big, and offers her his pinky finger in return.

"You have our word," David reiterates. Not one to be a touchy-feely person, David surprises himself when he dives in to give Obasi an enormous hug, simultaneously trying not to get emotional. Boss follows suit.

"Thank you, good friend," she says to the elder Aka man, trying not to get emotional as well. A look of warmth radiates from Obasi's face and that of several other Aka teens and adults listening in on the group's conversation.

Obasi nods his head very slowly, with a smile, as if bowing his head at them. David and Boss turn back to board their boat in order to part ways for good, when they both seem to realize something at the exact same time. A lingering thought overtakes the two of them like a torrent of rain in the wet season, and they turn back to look at the boy whom they saved.

Dee continues to play with the other kids, happy as can be and completely oblivious to what is about to transpire. David wonders if he subconsciously knows, or if he's just happy again and doesn't realize it yet. He looks at Dee, playing with the toddlers, so happy and so sweet. He sees Alex in that boy. And, like Alex, there's nothing that he wouldn't do for him. David swallows the tension in his eyes and throat caused by the realization. Dee is going to have to make a choice.

Without any words needing to be spoken, Obasi catches onto this. He watches the child playing with the younger members of his tribe and beams with pride. At the same time, he sees the looks on David's and Boss's faces, and feels solidarity as well.

"I can take him," David finally croaks. "I will gladly watch over him. I can raise him... but..."

David pauses as Obasi and Boss listen to him. David bows his head and continues, "But that has to be his choice. I only want what's best for him."

Obasi smiles at him, and Boss looks at the marine biologist, the civilian scientist whom she first judged to be weak and lame. Now, the woman who misjudged David looks at him with the utmost respect. She smiles, as well. Obasi nods his head, and he looks over to Dee.

"Young friend!" he says, waving Dee over to them.

One of the Aka mothers with the group watches Dee happily bound over to Obasi, David, and Boss. He reaches them along the shore, and she can see the three adults bend over a bit to talk with him. They usher him to a log nearby, and the four of them sit down to have the necessary conversation with the child. Although she can't hear their words, the Aka mother can see the happiness temporarily leave Dee's face, upon realizing that he has a choice to make, and that his newfound friends will be splitting up. Her heart melts for the boy, but she and the other Aka give the group of four their space.

As the sun slowly begins to set, a long and heart-centered conversation happens here between the three adults and, above all, with young Deion himself. About his fate. He's already been through so much as a child; they feel terrible giving him even one more burden to bear.

"Dee," David says softly to him, trying to respect his boundaries.

"You can come with me, you know. If you want. My son would enjoy having a brother. He's… he's always asked for one. But that has to be your decision. Not mine. You could come with me, and, well, I'm no millionaire. I'm still paying off my student loans for goodness sake," David chuckles awkwardly.

"But… I would do everything in my power to give you a good life. You could come live with me and Alex in the United States. You can have a family again. Or, or, I could even watch over you while we wait for another loving family to adopt you? Maybe, maybe one with two parents?" David tries so hard not to sound too eager, deciding to suggest the option of him being adopted by "another" Western family as a cover to hide how badly he wants Dee to go with him.

"Or," David says. "Or you can stay here." David looks up at Obasi, and the old man nods to confirm what David already suspects: that Obasi and his people would gladly take him as well.

"It's up to you, little man," David says, trying not to get emotional.

"You can stay here with these wonderful, doting people as well. They are more generous than any other group of people I've encountered. And, I know this place... this land... is your home, too."

"Dee?" Boss asks the child. He looks at her.

"Do you... do you have any other family left here?" she says, hating to have to ask the question, but also knowing that it's necessary. Dee thinks of the "mean guys" and, sadly, shakes his head.

"No," he says softly, looking at the ground.

David, Boss, and Obasi look up at each other and take a deep inhale through their noses from the difficult conversation. Dee looks at the boat, glistening along the shore and ready to take them home. Then he looks at the children playing nearby.

"Either way," Obasi says. "No matter what you choose, you have a family again." Dee looks back and forth at both groups, soaking in their radiant energy for several minutes. David, Obasi, and the others watch him.

Dee peers off into the distance, looking across the river ... and makes his decision.

25

THE BITTERSWEET PAIN IN DAVID'S HEART NEARLY ECLIPSES the physical pain from his amputated hand, but he knows deep down that Dee's decision is the best choice for him. Choosing to stay with the BaAka, Dee struggles with his emotions. He looks up at David and Boss, hugging them tightly.

"You guys are the best friends I ever had," he says to the two adults, tearfully.

"Will, will I ever see you again?"

"I don't know for sure, bud, but... I would very much like that," David says, trying to hold himself together. He fears that if he shows too much sadness, the boy will go back on his own decision—perhaps the first decision that he's had the power to make independently—out of guilt. David refuses to allow this to happen to the child, and holds down his emotions.

"I would very, very much like that," David says again. Down on one knee, David notices that Dee seems to stand taller than he did when they first met in this very spot along the river. Where Dee once stood at David's eye level when he was kneeling, now it seems that Dee stands just above him.

"From what you've told me about your family, I know in my heart of hearts that they would be so, *so* proud of you right now, for the man that you are becoming." David says. "I know I, for one, am."

Dee smiles and wipes a tear from his face. Boss kneels down as well and takes Dee by the shoulders.

"Hey, you," she says to him. "I want you to know, *you* would've made one heck of a Marine. I'm proud of you, too, young one. And we meant what we said back there. You are stronger than all of us."

Boss playfully boops his nose.

David and Boss both notice the setting sun.

It's time.

"Take..." David says, barely holding his emotions together. He looks at the young man with red and moisture in his eyes, "take good care of yourself, bud."

Dee rushes into David's arms and the two hug each other tightly. David fights the tears down, as does Boss. Dee, however, doesn't bother to fight his.

Boss takes her turn, hugging the child more tightly than she's hugged anyone in years.

"I love you, bud," David forces himself to say, overcoming the strange Western notion instilled in him from birth that it's "weird" to say that to anyone other than your spouse and immediate family.

"I love you guys, too," Dee says, hugging them both. Dee breathes through the shakiness in his voice and looks at his friends. "I know it's been hard... but..."

Dee searches his inner depths for the words.

"But I'm glad you guys came out here... because... because you saved me."

David and Boss's hearts melt. Obasi listens in, trying not to get too emotional himself. He observes the American man in action, far removed from his own son, and yet loving this one as his own. Obasi gently places his hand over Dee's shoulder.

"I promise to look after him," he says, gently. Obasi hesitates, but then carries on with his words.

"I... I lost my grandson a few springs ago. And I see so much of him in you, Dee."

The Aka man turns to look at his Western friends and his tone becomes more serious.

"I promise to look after the boy. I give you my word. He *will* be loved with us," Obasi says, embracing Dee's shoulders.

Obasi reaches his pinky out to his new friends to give them his word, and David immediately takes it. Then Boss does, as well.

"Take care, my friends," he says to them. Obasi sees the pain on David's face.

"My friend!" he says with a smile, catching David's attention as he's walking away.

"We BaAka have a reputation for being some of the best fathers in the world. *You* would've made a fine BaAka man." David takes this in warmly.

He and Boss feel no animosity or spite for Dee choosing to stay with Obasi and the Aka, only sadness that they must part ways and happiness that the boy is finally with loving people. David simply grins. The Marine and the marine biologist, who risked absolutely everything to save the life of a boy who they will likely never see again, board their boat and part for the final time amidst the evening sun, setting over the river.

Standing side-by-side with Obasi, a look of sheer concern flashes across Dee's face. Just as Boss turns on the boat's motor, Dee sprints forward to them. David, never losing eye contact with the boy, hops out of the boat and meets him along the shore. The two hug each other as tight as can be ... one last time.

"I'll never forget you, David," Dee says to him.

David replies, "I'll never forget you for as long as I live, Dee."

Only now does David allow a tear to roll down his face. Boss hops out of the boat and hugs the child as well, one last time. Boarding the boat, David and Boss part with extremely heavy hearts.

They watch the Aka as they get smaller and smaller and smaller upon drifting away. Dee, never taking his eyes off of David and Boss, waves to them as they depart. So does Obasi. Before long, the two survivors can see Obasi and the whole tribe waving goodbye to them. Boss lightly guns the motor, sending them in their desired direction along the river, working their way north to the border with Cameroon.

Obasi and Dee gently take each other by the hands, the old man the grandfather Dee never had. As they wave, Obasi embraces the tearful boy by his side. David never takes his eyes off of Dee, and vice-versa. Despite the lump in his chest and throat, David beams with happiness for the boy. He looks over at Boss and can tell she feels the same way.

The group on the shore gets smaller, and smaller, and smaller. Still they continue to wave, with the red-eyed David and Boss waving right back. The evening sky turns a beautiful orange over the Congo river basin, as Dee and his new family disappear from sight.

With the jungle surrounding them on both sides of the peaceful, flowing river, and the temperature dropping to a comfortable level, the sole survivors of each of their parties sit in silence together.

David struggles with the searing pain, although the lingering effects of the morphine help him. They both know that they will need serious medical care immediately once they get back; him for his amputated hand, and her for her shoulder and concussion. In spite of the immense physical pain that the pair struggle with, a sense of relaxation flows over them unlike anything that they have felt for a very, very long time.

Suddenly, David becomes aware of how closely they sit near each other. Their boat moves down the river, and the two of them find themselves huddled up near the stern, exhausted. Boss becomes aware of their close proximity as well.

"Sorry," David says to her softly. "I know I stink."

She smiles slightly, exhausted herself.

"It's okay," she says playfully. "I stink, too."

"Hey, Boss. Can I ask you something?" he says to her.

"Sam," she says, softly.

David's eyes perk up.

"I'm sorry?"

"My name is Samantha Jimenez. But... Everyone close to me calls me Sam," she says, bashfully. David looks at her and, despite his pain and exhaustion, a huge smile begins to form on his face.

"Nice to meet you, Sam. I'm David,"

"I know," she says, teasing him. "You told me, remember?"

David's lips form an 'O' shape, too tired to laugh with his body.

"Ohh yeah, that's right!" he croaks, grinning from ear to ear at her and trying not to chuckle at himself. Sam tries to compose herself, but then starts laughing. Within seconds, the two of them are laughing together.

"It's nice to meet you, too, David," Sam says warmly.

"Now tell me another thing that I don't know," he says.

"Well, I've been thinking for a long time now that I'm overdue to come home. Back to the U.S.. I just don't know where to land, ya know? I've been out here taking PMC jobs for so long that I ... I need a taste of home again," Sam says.

David hears every word that she's saying syllable by syllable, but at the same time he doesn't hear her. He feels like he cannot hear her. A new feeling washes over him. One that he hasn't felt in a long, long time, and never this intensely. He listens under the evening sky as Sam continues to tell him about herself.

In this moment, he realizes how deeply his feelings run for her. This absolutely gorgeous woman, loyal to a fault, who has put her life in harm's way numerous times in service to others. A woman who risked her life to help him save this child whom they only just met. A woman who sticks up for the underdog in any and every situation. He fears that she is way out of his league, but he can't help himself. He listens to her, enamored.

She goes on, but can see that he's a bit distracted. She smiles and laughs a bit. He does as well, until they're both laughing just for the sake of laughter. Despite how much their injured bodies hurt, the laughter helps the pain. And laughing together multiplies that benefit.

She catches him staring at her, and her thoughts begin to race. *Would a guy of that caliber ever go for a girl like me?* she wonders, as she realizes her feelings for him. This incredible man, who risked his own life to save that boy. Who was ready to go down into the darkness all by himself to do it if need be. Who steps up to the plate at every turn. Who keeps his word. Who was willing to stand up for those getting picked on. Then, shyly, she gently brushes her beautiful chestnut hair behind her ear.

"Now tell me something *I* don't know," Sam says to him.

"All my life, I loved the ocean. I always felt drawn to the water. And I've known for a long time that I wanted to be a marine biologist. And, I did it! You know all that. But... as I get older, I realize that getting some fancy degree and getting my dream job, that wasn't the end-all-be-all for me in life," he says.

She looks upon him, awaiting the rest of his thoughts.

"Being a dad is," David says. "My boy is the best thing that ever happened to me. I wasn't ready for him. I suppose nobody ever really feels ready, you know? But Alex has helped me re-learn something that I had lost for years. For decades! He helped me re-learn joy. Just pure joy. The lessons that he's taught me, while I've had the privilege of being his dad, those mean more to me than a degree ever will."

"I saw this thing online one time," Sam says. "It was a meme or something. And it was of a father and his son. In it the kid said something to the effect of, 'Please pick me up, Daddy! I love it when you hold me!' And the father in the graphic says, 'Oh, son, if only you knew how much *you* were holding *me*.' Is that true?"

Sam looks at him for confirmation. David smiles, beaming with excitement to get back home to Alex.

"Every word and then some," he says.

Sam zones out for a bit, pensive, but happy, before speaking again.

"I... I have no idea what that's like, having a kid of my own. That joy that you speak of. But, a part of me has always wanted to find out."

David looks into her eyes, and she into his. He feels butterflies in his stomach. Before he knows it, both of them are leaning forward, having unknowingly scooted closer and closer to each other for the past several minutes.

David very nearly kisses her, but stops himself, deciding that she's too valuable not to take things slowly. Secretly disappointed that he didn't follow through, she looks down and sees that their hands are within mere centimeters of each other, their pinkies nearly touching. Sam hesitates, but then remembers *I'm a Marine, damn it! Just do it!* She feels butterflies in her stomach.

Simultaneously, David works up the courage within. *C'mon, dude, you dove into a cave full of giant spiders. Now be brave!*

Their pinky fingers meet in unison as they both reach out for the touch. Before they know it, her left hand and his right are completely interlocked. She takes a big, deep breath and exhales into him, snuggling up against his body. He does the same. The two beam with elation, nothing further needing to be said.

After a long pause in conversation, Sam says, "Sorry to ruin the moment but, God damn do I crave a cigarette!"

David busts out laughing, causing his left limb to hurt even worse. At this moment, though, it is worth it.

"Do you... have any left?" he asks her, wincing.

"No," Sam says. Her demeanor changes slightly as she feels herself getting emotional again.

"Even if I did," she says to him, quietly.

"I have a promise to keep... to an old friend." A singular tear rolls down her cheek, and David uses his left forearm to wipe it away. He embraces her, feeling deep empathy for the loss of her friend.

"He was an amazing person, Sam," he says.

Seeing him using his bum limb to wipe away the tear, Sam inadvertently spits a bit as she begins laughing again. Her eyes follow the stump. David sees his stump and starts laughing as well, until the two are laughing uncontrollably.

"Hey, you gave me this!" he says to her, wincing.

"And I saved your life! You're welcome!" she exclaims, playfully, albeit empathetic to the pain that he's feeling.

"Yeah, yeah. Thank you, Sam." They sit in silence again for a time.

"So, no cigarettes or anything like that... but how about a coffee?" he says, proud of himself.

"I'd like that," she says smugly. "A lot."

David again fights the urge to kiss her, not wanting to seem too eager and wanting to take things slowly. Sam, on the other hand, wishes over and over again that he'd just go for it. She considers going for it herself, but doesn't want to make him feel uncomfortable. They look at each other. He gently brushes her hair back behind her ear. His touch is soothing and puts her at ease. She wraps her arm around his waist, and he wraps his good arm around her. Both of them blush, tripping themselves up mentally with not wanting to seem too eager to the other.

"Tell me something else I don't know," Sam says, smiling.

"I need a vacation!" David says without an ounce of hesitation.

"Me, too," she says.

"Where do you wanna go?" he says, without even filtering his words. Sam blushes intensely.

"Did you just ask me... on a vacation?" she teases him.

"Oh!? Uhhh... I... I mean... I..." David says, ever the anxious person that he is.

"I'm just kidding. I would love to," Sam says.

"R- Really?" he asks. She gives him a smug look.

"I am a woman of my word."

David grins from ear to ear. She does as well, although she is snuggled up in such a way where she can hide the excitement on her face. The sounds of the water of the river brushing up against their vessel are extremely soothing. Their minds are finally at peace, knowing that they'll reach Cameroon's capital, and then home, soon.

After a long silence with both of them grinning, Sam looks at him and jokes, "How 'bout an African Safari?"

Now he shoots *her* a smug look, nearly twisting his neck to do so, as if that was the worst idea in the world.

"Nah!" he says.

After another brief pause, David catches an idea.

He looks at her and asks, "Ever been to Canada?"

EPILOGUE

UNITED STATES OF AMERICA.

Graveyard shift Police Sergeant Barnes and Officer Serrano sit in their police cruiser in the dead of night. There is little traffic along one of the main roads, where they are parked.

Barnes has been grateful for an entirely peaceful night shift. His years of experience on the force have taught him that if nothing happens, then that's a good thing. As the adage goes, "No news is good news." His less experienced partner, on the other hand, is bored. They discuss their spouses, their kids, their problems, and, above all, which women they find attractive. Barnes reminds his younger partner that, although they are both married, there's nothing stopping them from "looking at the menu," as long as they "don't order."

"Damn, dude," Serrano says to him. "Gotta get one of those heat-controlled cups. You know, what's that one brand that's supposed to keep your coffee hot for seven hours? This coffee's already piss warm!"

Barnes laughs.

"Listen, kid," he says to Serrano. "They all say that on the side of the mug when you buy it, but don't actually expect seven hours! Those things only keep your stuff warm for two hours max. Better than nothing, sure, but it sure ain't seven."

Barnes reaches for one of their last two remaining croissants, and makes a mental note to watch his carb intake. His uniform, he noticed as of late, has been a bit tight around the midsection. The croissants are from the restaurant that he and his partner hit up every night, just after waking up, to grab a bite and some caffeine before their shift. Unfortunately, this coffee joint closed hours ago.

"Yeah," Barnes says. "I could use some warmer coffee, too. Is there anything open other than Mickey D's and Jack in the Box? 'Cause I try not to mess with that crap. Gets old after a while."

"Got that right," Serrano says. "Do what Ricky does at the precinct! Comes in every night with the same hundred dollar mug. Hey, did you hear that he *actually*—!"

Serrano is suddenly interrupted by the microphone in their car radio. He and Barnes perk up as they listen to it.

Ending their hours-long streak of not getting a single call all night, the dispatcher informs available units that there's a homeless individual behaving erratically. Almost immediately, Barnes and Serrano suspect the same thing.

Moments later, their suspicions are confirmed. Barnes rolls his eyes and Serrano releases his deep breath with a sigh. There have been many complaints about this individual in the past, and this isn't the first time they're responding to the subject.

"Must be *her* again," says Barnes.

Too many residents of an apartment complex downtown have called to complain about a "crazy" homeless lady shouting and crying and having some kind of mental episode all night that's keeping them, their kids, and their pets awake.

Barnes turns the ignition and the cruiser comes to life. He and Serrano don't even bother throwing their siren on since this isn't what they would consider to be a life or death emergency.

Although the two men don't remember the details, the police department has interacted with her enough times that most graveyard shift officers have a bulletin on who she is.

Barnes drives while Serrano pulls out the "manifest," as he likes to call it, using a fake British accent. He turns on his flashlight to glance it over. He examines a couple new details.

"So check this out," he says to Barnes. "I didn't see this part before. Maybe they updated it. Apparently she was only recently 5150'd for the first time." He looks up at his more experienced partner behind the wheel, confused, before going on.

"That's weird, though, right? Because if it's schizophrenia, usually symptoms for that come up a lot earlier in life, right? And she's definitely past her twenties."

"Hmm," Barnes mumbles.

After a short drive through the city streets, the two officers come upon the apartment building. Two other P.D. cruisers have already arrived on scene, their overhead lights on. As the two pull up, they can see the homeless lady moving erratically as if she's pacing and fidgeting around at the same time. As they're pulling up from the adjacent intersection, where civilian cars are passing by every few seconds, they can hear her screaming and yelling without even having to roll down their windows.

"YOU DON'T UNDERSTAND WHAT'S ABOUT TO HAPPEN!" she yells at Officers Lui and Reyes.

"THEY'RE GOING TO COME FOR US ALL!"

"Ma'am, please, we're trying to help you!" Officer Lui says to her, putting her hand up in an attempt to get her to calm down.

"Miss," Officer Reyes says, pointing to the multi-story apartment building in front of them. Thanks to "the lady," many tenants' yapper dogs are going crazy barking at the woman making a ruckus on the street below.

This isn't the first time that she's been here.

"We just need you to calm down. We have hardworking people in these homes here. They got kids, kids that have school tomorrow! And we just need to keep a lid on things so that..."

"NO!" the homeless lady screams.

She shakes violently, grabbing the blanket that's wrapped around and perched on her head like a Russian babushka.

"You think you know me? I DID WHAT I HAD TO!" she screams to nobody in particular, now facing the third floor row of apartment unit windows. In a window on the eighth floor, Serrano catches a glimpse of a resident, an older woman in her nightgown, angrily shaking her head and slamming her curtains shut. It's the middle of the night, hours before the sun rises again.

Barnes and Serrano step up closer to her. Barnes gestures for Reyes and Lui to take a few steps back, such as not to overwhelm the already mentally unstable subject.

"Miss," Barnes says to her, warmly, taking a new approach.

"I am Sergeant Barnes. You are *not* in trouble. We don't mean you any harm, okay?"

The homeless woman stares at him, trembling violently. He can barely see her face. The only thing he can see well is her eyes. Barnes is, for a second, taken aback. Only once before has he seen such fear behind a human being's eyes. The abyss of fear behind her gaze strikes him to his core.

It's dark and, with the flashing blue and red lights from their squad cars, even he can hardly see her under the blanket wrapped around her head and shoulders, even though he's now the closest officer to her. The woman starts making an eerie whimpering sound like an abused dog in distress. Barnes takes a second before speaking again.

"Miss," he says again, calmly. "We just want to help you. That's all."

The woman starts violently whipping her gaze around, the trembling intensifying so badly it looks like she's going to erupt. The trembling manifests as a god awful, human-like scream that's off-putting for blocks in every direction. The scream reeks of pure terror. True mental illness.

"THEY'RE GOING TO KILL ME!" she yells at the top of her lungs.

"The spiders! The spiders! THEY'RE GOING TO KILL US ALLLLLL!" she screams, bursting into sobs.

"Miss?" Serrano tries to say, in vain.

"NOOO!" she screams right at him, catching him off guard a bit.

"NO! YOU DON'T UNDERSTAND! THEY'RE GOING TO KILL ME! THEY'RE GOING TO KILL US ALL!"

Over and over, the homeless lady shouts manically about "the spiders."

Finally, Sergeant Barnes gives it up. He walks over to his partner and takes the bulletin with a deep sigh.

"Poor crazy woman," Barnes says, making sure that he's far enough away from the unstable homeless lady so that she can't hear their conversation. He sighs again.

"We're gonna need to bring her to the loony hospital. *Clearly* the homeless shelters won't do."

"Who is this person, anyway?" Serrano asks him. The Sergeant looks down at the bulletin and puts on his readers, pushing them up onto his nose.

"Hmmmm," Barnes says, examining it.

Something written in the bulletin catches him off guard, as if there's a detail here that he's never seen before. His eyebrows scrunch up a bit, bewildered.

"Name of 5150 in question ... Dr. Molly Hendricks."

ABOUT THE AUTHOR

ZACH CUTLER-ORREY IS A YOUNG CREATIVE WHO WORKS BY day to support his beautiful family while fitting in his passions wherever he can. He has enjoyed storytelling throughout his life, whether through acting or writing. Zach wasn't the kind of student to hold a 4.0 in school; not even close. He never took AP English or advanced language arts, and he never went to college. Yet, this (formerly) broke teen dad-turned-author wrote a highly original novel which blends sci-fi/horror with the genres of thriller, suspense, mystery, action, drama, adventure and even romance. "Screams of the Jungle", his very first novel, is his breakthrough work. Zach lives in the San Francisco Bay Area with his wife, son and cat (who he loves very much). Zach strives every day to be grateful and to have fun.